Liz Byrski is the author of eight novels and a number of non-fiction books, the latest of which is *Getting On: Some Thoughts on Women and Ageing*.

She has worked as a freelance journalist, a broadcaster with ABC Radio and an advisor to a minister in the West Australian Government.

Liz has a PhD in writing from Curtin University where she teaches professional and creative writing.

www.lizbyrski.com.au

Also by Liz Byrski

Fiction
Gang of Four
Food, Sex & Money
Belly Dancing for Beginners
Trip of a Lifetime
Bad Behaviour
In the Company of Strangers
Family Secrets

Non-fiction
Remember Me
Getting On: Some Thoughts on Women and Ageing

LIZ BYRSKI

Last Chance Café

PAN
Pan Macmillan Australia

For Mark and Neil

First published 2011 in Macmillan by Pan Macmillan Australia Pty Ltd
This Pan edition published 2014 by Pan Macmillan Australia Pty Ltd
1 Market Street, Sydney, New South Wales, Australia, 2000

Cataloguing-in-Publication entry is available
from the National Library of Australia
http://catalogue.nla.gov.au

Typeset in Palatino by Post Pre-press Group
Printed by IVE

The characters in this book are fictitious and any resemblance to real
persons, living or dead, is purely coincidental.

MIX
Paper from
responsible sources
FSC® C018183

ACKNOWLEDGEMENTS

It takes a whole team of people to turn a manuscript into a book and I do know how fortunate I am to work with people who understand and respect my work. My special thanks to my publisher, Cate Paterson, for her wisdom and friendship; to editor Emma Rafferty for her thoughtful and creative contributions which always make me wonder why I haven't thought of them myself; to Jo Jarrah for her forensic but sensitive attention to detail and to Jeannine Fowler, brilliant publicist and queen of the road. Thank you, too, to the whole team at Pan Macmillan for your commitment to design, production, marketing and sales – who get the finished product to people who want to read it.

Special thanks to the fabulous Danielle O'Leary for the inspiration of the raspberry cakes.

The following books were very helpful to me in writing *Last Chance Café*:

Walter, Natasha. *Living Dolls: The Return of Sexism*, Virago, London, 2010.

McRobbie, Angela. *The Aftermath of Feminism*, Sage, London, 2009.

ONE

The mall is seething with Saturday morning shoppers, couples joined at the hip, families with screaming toddlers and grumpy adolescents, noisy groups of teenage girls, and elderly people doggedly doing circuits in the centre's motorised carts. Margot hates it; not just this mall, which is inappropriately named Central Park, but all shopping centres. The harsh lighting, the crowds, the noise and the air devoid of negative ions suck the life out of her. This morning she is searching, with mounting irritation and a touch of desperation, for something to wear to her sister's golden wedding anniversary. A dress, or perhaps a loose top matched with a well-cut skirt which will need to have an elasticised waistband; either way it must be designed for comfort and concealment. But although there is adequate evidence that many women her own size and larger shop here, the mall has little to offer. Margot longs to abandon the search, get a coffee or just go home, but she has to find something because the party is tomorrow and she can't get into her only decent dress.

It is as she is making her way out of yet another boutique that caters for stick insects that she notices a small crowd gathered around the escalator that leads exclusively to the beauty salon and day spa on the gallery level. Some of the salon staff, fetchingly dressed in matching shell pink uniforms, are leaning over the balustrade, watching the drama unfolding on the ground floor. Invisible at the centre of the crowd someone, a woman, is shouting something unintelligible, and heading towards the knot of people are two burly security guards, one talking into a radio handset, the other carrying a pair of bolt cutters. An accident perhaps? Margot wonders. Someone trapped on the escalator? Somewhere a camera flashes. Edging her way into the crowd Margot stretches up on tiptoe. A woman, a tiny elderly woman with bright burgundy hair, has chained herself to the stainless steel railings on either side of the escalator, effectively barricading it.

'Dot?' Margot gasps. 'Oh my god!'

Dot it is; striking as ever, entirely in black except for a large square of cream canvas stitched inexpertly to the front of her sweater. On the canvas is a message written in red felt pen: 'Want to be Beautiful? Be Your Age!' And Dot is shouting something now about the ugliness of the beauty business, about makeovers and consumerism.

Margot can barely believe her eyes. Dot! It's ages since she's seen her – almost three years since she took off ostensibly for a longish holiday, and since then just a few postcards from India – no explanations, nothing. Even Laurence hadn't had a clue what she was up to. The crowd shifts slightly, making space for the security guards, and Margot pushes through to the front.

One of the guards is speaking to Dot now; his tone is low and apparently conciliatory but Dot is not in the mood for conciliation.

'Don't you patronise me,' she shouts, glaring up at him. 'I'm not some silly old woman who's lost her marbles.'

Unfortunately for Dot this is exactly how she appears both to the guards and the crowd. But then, Margot thinks, they don't know Dot.

'Come on, love,' the man says, loud enough now for others to hear. 'You can't stay here, you know. People can't get up and down the escalator. Just give me the key to the padlock or we'll have to use the bolt cutters.'

'Don't you *dare* cut that chain,' Dot cries, 'don't even think about it. It's *my* chain.'

'Then give me the key to the padlock.'

'I've swallowed it!' Dot retorts, with a gleeful cackle.

There is a murmur among the crowd, a mix of amusement and amazement. The security man rolls his eyes and nods to his partner to start cutting.

'That's damage to my personal property, and in front of witnesses,' Dot yells. 'I shall sue!'

'Now look here, love –'

'And don't call me love!'

He takes a deep breath. 'Very well then, *madam*,' he says, unravelling the now-severed chain and taking her by the arm. 'Now, I'd like you to come quietly to the centre manager's office, if not . . .'

Margot knows that the chances of Dot going anywhere quietly are as remote as a snowball's chance in hell. Next thing she'll be lying on the ground, forcing them to drag or carry her.

'Excuse me,' she says, elbowing aside a teenager with a video phone and tapping the guard on the arm. 'This lady's with me.'

'Margot?' Dot says, twisting around at the sound of her voice. 'Good lord, what are you doing here?'

'Shopping,' Margot says, turning a fierce gaze on Dot in the hope of silencing her. 'We're shopping, remember? And now I'm taking you home.' She turns to the security guard with a smile that she hopes is kind but firm. 'I'll look after her now, so sorry she's caused all this trouble.'

'Don't you apologise for *me*, Margot,' Dot says. 'I won't have it.'

The man hesitates. 'I'm not sure . . .'

'She won't do it again,' Margot says, with an assurance she doesn't feel. 'She'll be fine when she's had a nice cup of tea.'

'Well, if you're sure, we don't want to come on too strong, not with . . . well, an elderly lady who's a bit . . .' He falters and exchanges a nod with the other guard.

'I *might* do it again, in fact I probably *will*,' Dot says. 'I have plenty more chain.'

'Come along, Dot!' Margot insists, smiling at the guards. 'Thank you so much.' She grabs Dot's arm and drags her, protesting, away from the scene of the crime, to the accompaniment of laughter and some mild applause from a few of the rapidly dispersing crowd.

'Whatever were you *doing*, Dot?' Margot demands once they are out of sight of the security men. 'You could have been arrested.'

'I probably would've been if you hadn't shown up,' Dot says, swapping an obviously heavy green shopping bag to her other shoulder. 'That's what I was aiming for.'

Margot steers her to the safety of a café and nudges her into a booth with upholstered benches. 'Don't you dare move from there,' she says. 'If you cause any more trouble they'll cart you off to the manager's office and call the police. You didn't really swallow the key, did you?'

'Of course not,' Dot grins, reaching down inside the neck of her sweater. 'It's here on this very nice lanyard sent to me by Amnesty International. If you're getting the coffee I'll have a long black, please.'

'I've done it before, many times,' Dot says when Margot returns with the coffee. 'But then, you know that.'

Margot does indeed know that; she has seen her do it on at least four occasions, from one of which she was dragged off shouting and thrown into the back of a police wagon. 'I remember,' she says, 'particularly the first time I saw you do it – the Save Our Sons campaign. A lot of very respectable-looking women in hats and gloves marching with banners, and the lunatic fringe chained up outside Parliament House.'

'I remember that,' Dot says. 'We were all there. You had Lexie with you, and Emma in a pusher, and Laurence was there too.'

Margot nods. 'That's right, Emma was still quite small.'

'How *is* Laurence?' Dot asks. 'It's ages since I saw you and even longer since I saw him.'

'He's okay,' Margot says. 'He's away, doing that horrendous walk to Santiago de Compostela. It's madness, of course, I don't think he'll last the distance. You know Laurence, exercise is not his thing, but he's been a bit out of sorts lately. He was seventy-four last month.'

'Everyone's younger than me,' Dot says, grimacing. 'Just turned seventy-five.' She sips the hot coffee cautiously. 'No, it doesn't sound at all like Laurence. I'd love to catch up with him when he gets back. But it's great to see you, Margot, and amazing because you hate shopping centres.'

'Desperation really,' Margot says, and explains about the party.

'She's pretty fearsome as I remember her, not my kind of woman, Philippa.'

'Phyllida.'

'Of course, Phyllida – unusual name, I always mix it up. I think I once called her Falada after that talking horse in the fairytale . . . er, yes, *The Goose Girl* . Unkind of me, but she *was* a bit of a bossy mare, wasn't she?' And they both dissolve into laughter.

'Ah! Dot, it's so good to see you,' Margot says. 'I got so used to having you around, I really missed you, and you're a hopeless correspondent. So, tell me about India. What were you doing? What made you stay so long?'

Dot rolls her eyes. 'I know, I know. Went off on holiday and didn't come back, didn't let anyone know, totally unreliable, don't deserve to have any friends. Like I said when I left, Margot, I planned to go for several weeks, maybe even two or three months, but India . . .' she pauses, 'well, it hung onto me I suppose. It's such a culture shock. You'll laugh but I got that *finding myself* bug, and ended up at a retreat centre in a decaying old palace in the mountains; amazing place, glorious scenery, lovely people. I did it all: meditation, fasting, being silent, writing down every thought, every memory.'

Try as she might Margot couldn't imagine Dot meditating on an Indian mountain, or anywhere else for that matter. She can't see her in a white robe, ohm-ing peacefully, eating chick peas and dhal, and especially not being silent. It sounds too still, too regimented, too passive. Was she allowed to smoke? Did she attempt to reorganise the place? Did she have to let her burgundy hair grow out? Were there any protests to organise? It is so entirely un-Dot. 'Sounds a bit confronting,' she says. 'So *did* you find yourself?'

'Unfortunately I did. You know, Margot, I was absolutely sick of myself when I went there. Sick of being that Dot Grainger person; you know – curmudgeonly columnist, broadcaster, chain smoker, activist ratbag. I needed to see who I was underneath all that.'

'And what did you find?'

'Well, sadly, I discovered that was it. That *is* who I am. I'd hoped that it was some sort of shell and I might discover a finer, more measured person lurking within, but it seems that's who I am, right down to my bone marrow. Such a disappointment.'

'I think it's a relief,' Margot says. 'I never imagined for a moment that all that passion and commitment came from anywhere but the heart and soul.'

'You're very kind, but I'm so over myself you wouldn't believe it and I couldn't even get away from me at the top of some Indian mountain. I stayed a full year so you can't say I didn't try. And then I thought, well, maybe I need to be *doing* something, rather than, you know, just *being* there contemplating my navel. After all, I am a *doing* sort of person. So I went to Mumbai and worked with an aid organisation that helps slum dwellers. Oh the awfulness of it, Margot, the children, the poverty . . . anyway, I just got stuck in, cooking, washing, dressing wounds, things I never dreamed I'd do.'

'And?'

'Well, that sort of thing *does* change you, but I still didn't find the finer person. I was still a ratbag even in India, but at least I was a useful one. I got back about three weeks ago and I've been finding it hard to settle, and even I haven't had the cheek yet to start calling people to say "I'm back, take notice of me".'

'Well, you should have. I missed you and a couple of postcards didn't stop me worrying about you,' Margot says. 'And this morning? What was all that about?'

'Protesting again, of course, although I made a very bad job of it. That's the thing, you see, I would never have gone at it like that in the past. I'd have planned it with other people, had a strategy. Collective action was always my thing. Good thing you turned up when you did.'

'But what's it *about*?' Margot persists. 'Even *I* couldn't understand what you were on about.'

Dot looks uncharacteristically sheepish. 'I know. That's a sign of my own disorientation, I think, because it's about everything, really, and that's the problem. Coming back here . . . it's a culture shock . . . the consumerism . . . and everything seems to be about appearance . . . I can't really explain it . . .'

'Mmm. Well, you won't change anything doing what you did this morning,' Margot says. 'Work out what your issue is and plan your strategy carefully – that used to be your mantra.'

Dot rolls her eyes. 'Well, I was right. Pity I didn't take my own advice this time. And chains are a bit dated, I suppose. I need to find another way or I'll start to sound like a nutter.'

Margot nods. 'A nutter is exactly how you looked and sounded this morning. Activists these days do it with blogs.'

Dot sighs. 'I suppose so, but you know, Margot, doing stuff alone is hard and no one seems to care about sisterhood anymore.' She leans forward, grasping Margot's hand in her own. 'Remember the women's movement, working together! Remember marching for childcare centres, and equal pay, and breast cancer testing? It's not the same now. It's all about the individual and bugger everyone else. Pole dancing as liberation, what a travesty! Remember how thrilling it was back then?'

Margot does remember; she remembers marching in pouring rain and blazing heat, carrying placards, stuffing envelopes, and worrying if she'd be home in time for the kids. She remembers having to choose between doing the shopping and going to another one of those endless meetings with no agenda because agendas limited the free exchange of ideas. Meetings where everything everyone wanted to say was written on huge sheets of butcher's paper and more time was spent deciding the order of the topics than on the topics themselves. 'I do remember,' she says now, 'although I suspect with not quite as much affection as you do. I was just an exhausted working mother, but you were famous.'

'Famous? I thought we agreed on minor media personality aka MMP.'

'Okay, but you were practically a household name.'

'Mmm, like toilet paper or drain cleaner. Ah well. That's all over now. One day a rooster now an old chook with her feathers falling out. Anyway, I've been rabbiting on about myself far too long. What about *you*, Margot? What are you up to now?'

'Much the same as ever, really. I still help out at the law

centre from time to time, filling in when people are away, covering sick leave, that sort of thing. There's not a lot but I still enjoy it and the money helps; living on the pension is no joke. And I look after Rosie quite often.'

'Rosie, of course. Emma and her husband split up, didn't they?'

Margot searches in her handbag and pulls out a photograph. 'Yes, Rosie's eight now and she lives with Grant and his sister.'

Dot studies the picture; she's never had much interest in individual children, although she has campaigned for their welfare, and for safe and affordable childcare. Socially she finds them irritating and demanding but she *is* interested in custody arrangements. 'So that's working out okay?'

'Really good; Grant's always been terrific with Rosie, even when she was a tiny baby, and Wendy's just lovely, and they're both very steady and responsible. Actually, Dot, I really admire Grant. It's not been easy for him but he's handled it so well, no rancour; he and Wendy seem like extended family.'

'It's an odd sort of set-up though.'

'I know, but it works and that's what matters. Em wasn't coping at all, that's why it all fell apart. She just wanted out and back to work, wanted to get away from anything remotely domestic. She went back to her job at Grangewood; they own this place,' she says, indicating the shopping centre, 'and a couple of other malls. She's the PR manager. Good thing the press didn't spot you out there or she'd be in damage control by now! Motherhood totally freaked her out.'

'A girl after my own heart,' Dot says. 'But fortunately I knew it from a very early age!'

Margot nods. 'Well, it's not for everyone, that's for sure. Anyway, Dot, as I've saved you from ignominy this morning, I think you should help me find something I can wear for Phyl's party. I'd rather be trawling through the op shops but I've left it too late.'

'I'm complaining about consumerism and you want me to go fashion shopping?'

'Balance, Dot,' Margot says, handing her a pair of nail scissors from her handbag. 'You were always good at that. Cut that sign off your sweater or you'll end up in custody in the centre manager's office. Anyway, you're a fine one to talk, you could always shop 'til you dropped.'

Dot snips the stitches on the four corners of the sign and rolls it up. 'I *was* a bit of a shopper, wasn't I? I suppose there's always been a part of me that is deeply politically incorrect.' She stuffs the sign into her canvas bag and lugs it onto her shoulder, sending their empty cups flying across the table.

'What on earth have you got in there?'

'More chain. I was going to start again at the other end of the centre once they moved me on.'

'Ridiculous,' Margot says, grabbing the bag and stuffing it down on the floor in the corner of the booth. 'We're not taking that with us.'

'They might think it's a bomb,' Dot protests. 'We'll never be able to come back here again.'

'Well, it's not a bomb, and there are plenty of other cafés that serve better coffee.' She slips her arm through Dot's. 'Now, we're just two old dames going shopping, and the nice thing is we're invisible. No one gives a damn what we get up to.'

'And that's another issue,' Dot says. 'We're invisible *because* we're *old women*, it's a real –'

'Oh do shut up, Dot,' Margot says, 'or I'll have you forcibly shipped back to that Indian mountain.' And she leads her along the mall and up another escalator to the opposite side of the gallery, and into a shop full of clothes that she really can't afford.

∽

Lexie hasn't shown the letter to Ross. She can't because he's away and he was away when she brought it home with her from work. She wouldn't have shown it to him anyway; Ross would always have been among the last to know. She hasn't shown it to anyone since it was handed to her at four o'clock on Friday afternoon by the practice solicitor. She'd read it, put it back in the envelope, resolved not to look at it again for forty-eight hours and to stay cool in the meantime. Then she'd left the office without a word to anyone. She hasn't shown it to her mother either, because Margot's unwavering support and loving concern would be more than she could bear at the moment. And she hasn't shown it to her younger sister because Emma – well, she never quite knows how Emma will react to things. And now it's four o'clock on Sunday and she's sitting at the kitchen table staring at it again, and in the forty-eight hours since Friday she has not, for a minute, stayed even remotely cool.

Not surprising, really – after all, she's worked there for twenty years, starting as the receptionist when old Dr Faraday was in practice on his own, and on through the expansion when he took on a younger partner. Then a few years later young Dr Faraday had come on board, turned the place into a medical centre and sent Lexie off on a business management course so she could be the practice manager. And now here she is, forty-eight and redundant thanks to a chain of problems that began with a lengthy, expensive and damaging case of medical negligence. On a Saturday night, two days after the court found against the practice, Dr Faraday the younger committed suicide in his consulting room, using a lethal cocktail of drugs, and wasn't found until the Monday morning. After that everything started to fall apart and Lexie began her efforts to patch it back together; meanwhile the doctors negotiated deals to move to other practices, disheartened nurses opted for agency work and anxious patients changed their GPs.

'I'm very sorry,' the solicitor had said as he handed her the letter on Friday. 'I know how hard you've worked to keep going this long, but they can't go on treading water, and frankly the doctors don't have the will for it, they have other plans. I guess you saw it coming.'

Of course she'd seen it coming, she'd have been a lousy business manager if she hadn't, but she had deliberately looked away, hoping that by pouring all her energy and ideas into developing new plans she could somehow reinvigorate everyone. So now she is not only redundant but hurt, disappointed and absolutely exhausted. And while the lump sum that she is owed, plus a generous ex gratia payment for more than two decades of dedicated service, is helpful, it's no compensation for the loss of what was so much more than a job.

Folding the letter again Lexie wonders idly whom she might consider telling. Her father, possibly? He would be affectionate, solicitous, ask if he could help and offer her money and then he would leave her to get on with it. But he is overseas on some walking holiday. She certainly wouldn't tell her Aunt Phyllida because she would immediately tell Uncle Donald, who would froth and bluster and start phoning his contacts in the higher echelons of the medical fraternity to find her another job. The people she might like to tell are her former brother-in-law, Grant, and his sister, Wendy, who have become good friends. But one thing's for sure, she won't be telling Ross. He will be the last to know.

What Lexie feels like doing is running away. She wants to be somewhere completely alone where she doesn't have to talk, where she can step outside the door knowing she won't bump into anyone who might ask her how she is, or what she's going to do next. The job was her; without it she is invisible. Lexie slips the letter back into its envelope, pours herself a very large gin and tonic and drinks it rather quickly. She *never* drinks alone. Then she pours another equally large one and takes it with her to the shower, imagining as she does so that she is not getting ready to go to her aunt's anniversary party, but that she is preparing to leave, to disappear some-where where no one can find her.

'Where would you go, Lex?' she asks her reflection in the bathroom mirror as she turns on the shower. 'Vanuatu, Penang, Fiji . . . or maybe somewhere in Europe? Prague, perhaps, or maybe Venice? Yes, Venice, and don't tell anyone and don't come back 'til you're ready. If ever! Ha!' And she gives a short dry laugh, swigs the last of the gin and steps into the shower.

What a blast that would be, she thinks, and then what would happen? For a few satisfying moments as the water cascades down her body, Lexie allows herself to imagine the domino effect. She visualises the chaos of the remaining staff sorting out the winding up of the practice. She hears them casting her as a deserter, a rat leaving in the last days of the sinking ship, a fallen angel; she sees the nods and winks and the mention of hormones and the onset of menopause. She imagines the family's disbelief, the worry, the arguments in which people would say one thing to one person and something different to the next.

Sighing, she squeezes shampoo into the palm of her hand and begins to massage it into her hair. She could, of course, take a decent holiday but she has to work two more weeks to finalise all the accounts and everyone's pay. And meanwhile she's supposed to turn up at this wretched anniversary party and act as though nothing has happened. She should have been there earlier in the day, she'd promised to help them set up for it, but this morning she'd sent Phyllida a text saying she couldn't make it. Now she's stricken with guilt, but the last thing she feels like doing is putting on some sort of brave face and being part of a celebration.

Lexie has no idea how to get herself to the party, how to smile or talk to people, how to pretend everything is nor-mal . . . it's all just too hard, and that's when she starts to cry. Great big sobs surge through her body, huge tears mix with the shower water, and she heaves and moans until eventually the tears stop. She leans, exhausted, against the shower screen and slides down to sit on the tiles with the water still beating down on her until it starts to run cold and she gets out, wraps herself in a towel, winds a second towel around her head, goes to her bedroom and sends a text to her mother.

TWO

At six o'clock on Sunday evening Dot is preparing to draw the cork from a bottle of wine and is reflecting on the pleasure of that chance meeting with Margot: their conversation, the frock shopping and all the memories it has revived. But her pleasure is tinged with anxiety. What must Margot think of her after that bungled attempt at a protest? How ridiculous she must have looked; a ridiculous old woman making an exhibition of herself. She would never have done that in the old days, it would have been a proper group action. It's a sign, she thinks, that she has been spending too much time alone since she got back. And then she made it worse by talking to the journalist from the Sunday paper who had phoned yesterday afternoon.

'Someone just emailed us a picture from the shopping centre,' he'd said. 'My editor recognised you, but we're not sure what you're protesting about.'

So off she'd gone, ranting on about shopping malls and cosmetic surgery and makeovers, and god knows what else. Margot will have a fit, Dot thinks, but with any luck it'll be tucked away on an inside page and she won't see it. She hasn't been able to bring herself to go out and buy a copy to check. Margot's right, a blog might be the thing, at least it would be a start, but the first thing to do is to nut out what she's going to aim for. Dot picks up her glass, but as she takes her first sip and settles down to watch the news the door-bell rings. She pauses, weighing up the possibilities; almost six-thirty on a Sunday is not a time for door-to-door sales persons, not even those selling religion. She pads softly on socked feet along the passage to peer through the spy-hole in the front door. A man, tall, youngish and wearing a black jacket and jeans, is standing with his back to the front door, facing the street. Dot tilts her head in an attempt to get a glimpse of his profile, and then reels back as he turns suddenly and presses his eye to the spy-hole.

'Don't *do* that,' she shouts, flinging open the door. And now it is his turn to recoil in shock. 'How dare you peer into my spy-hole? Who are you anyway?'

'Whoa! Sorry!' he says, holding up his hands as if to ward off attack. 'I couldn't actually see anything – you can't, you know, not from this side.' He hesitates. 'I rang the bell and you didn't answer but I could hear the television . . .'

Dot looks him up and down; he's not as young as she first thought. He has hair like Hugh Grant, but that's not a crime. 'It's none of your business if the television's on,' she says. 'I might just be choosing not to answer the door. Do I know you?'

He gives her a disarming smile that fails to disarm her. 'Patrick,' he says. 'I emailed you, remember?'

Dot stares at him, frowning.

'Last week. About talking to my students. You said to pop round this evening.'

'Ah . . .' Dot's expression softens, although she's already regretting the invitation. 'Yes, I do remember. Did I really say come on Sunday evening when the news is on?'

'Well, you actually said to come Sunday about six-thirty, which is now, but I could come back another time . . .'

She shakes her head and opens the door wider. 'No, no,

you're quite right. Come in. But you must promise never to peer into my spy-hole again.'

'Never,' he says. 'Scout's honour. Not yours or anyone else's.'

'Come along then. I've just opened a bottle of wine.'

'Well, if you're sure . . .' He hands her a small bunch of perfect, hothouse violets swathed in a cone of glossy white paper, and walks into the hall. 'You should still catch the news,' he says. 'It's only just started.'

'Yes. Thank you for the violets. Old ladies' flowers.'

'Well I . . .'

'They're my favourite.' She leads him down the passage and gestures towards the sofa. 'Make yourself comfortable, I'll get another glass.'

'Castro's announced his resignation,' Patrick says, nodding towards the screen and the archival footage of Castro in the sixties.

'About time,' Dot says, handing him a glass and settling into her own chair as a close-up of Fidel Castro, now looking like an ancient monument, fills the screen. 'Cheers.'

'Cheers. It's really good of you, I hope I haven't disturbed –'

'You haven't,' she says, 'but you will if you don't shut up till the news has finished.'

'Sorry,' he says, and he sips his wine and leans further back into his corner of the sofa.

Dot tries to concentrate on the news, which is vital to her sense of being on top of what's happening at home and abroad – it's a feeling she finds increasingly difficult to maintain these days – but, hard as she tries to concentrate, Patrick's presence distracts her. She sneaks a sideways glance at him; he certainly doesn't look like an axe murderer, but then he wouldn't, would he? She remembers that in his email he'd said he was a lecturer in cultural studies. It conjures up images of dead and largely incomprehensible French philosophers, possibly boring but bearing little similarity to axe murderers, although the two are not mutually exclusive. Anyway, he seems harmless, sitting there relaxed with his wine, watching in silence, and Dot realises her unease is not because Patrick is young, or male, or a stranger, but simply because it's so long since she's sat and watched the news here, or anywhere else, with anyone at all. It is, she supposes, the price she's paying for decades of immersing herself in work and various causes at the expense of relationships and friendships. The pigeons come home to roost as one gets older, Dot thinks, only this particular pigeon is starting to feel more like an albatross. Loneliness is something she has never had to face and now it seems to be thundering along behind her flapping its wings and threatening to roost here in her own house. She looks across at Patrick, and this time flicks the mute button on the remote control.

'I'm going to make a toasted sandwich,' she says, getting up. 'Will you join me?'

'But I thought you wanted to watch the news.'

'I did, but your presence is unexpected and distracting.'

'I could go.'

'Definitely not. Now you're here you have a responsibility to stay and entertain me.'

He smiles and gets to his feet. 'In that case, yes please, cheese if possible, and I should probably tell you more about why I'm here.'

'You want me to talk to your students, although I can't think why. I imagine I'd bore them stiff.'

'I doubt that,' he says, 'but before we talk about that I want to ask you a more personal favour.'

Dot looks at him across the bench. 'You're pushing your luck! Tomato with the cheese?'

'No thanks. And, yes, I know it's a cheek but please just say no if you want to. I wondered if you'd come out to lunch with me and my Aunty Win. It's her birthday soon and it would be a terrific treat for her. A surprise, you know – just turn up at the restaurant? She and my mum were huge fans. They listened to you on the radio and Mum kept scrapbooks of your articles and columns. She used to make me read them too.'

'How flattering for me and how boring for you,' Dot says. 'You could only have been a teenager.'

'It was okay as long as no one at school knew,' he says. 'Actually I plagiarised one in a Year Twelve essay about violence on television. Copied several paragraphs of your column and only changed about five words.'

'Good heavens,' Dot said. 'I hope you got a good mark. Would your mother come to lunch too?'

'My mother . . . no, she's . . . well, she's dead. Ten years ago. My father too, a couple of years earlier.'

Dot puts down the block of cheese she's holding. 'I'm so sorry, how sad for you.'

He shrugs. 'I'm over it now, except that you don't ever get over it. You just learn to live without people, don't you? Anyway, Aunty Win has kept all Mum's scrapbooks – you were their hero.'

'How nice,' Dot says, hoping she doesn't sound fatuous.

'So you see it would mean a lot to her – lunch, I mean.'

Dot rummages in the cupboard for the sandwich toaster, her head buzzing with conflicting reactions: how tedious, just what I don't need . . . how flattering, just like old times . . . it'll be a couple of hours at the most and when did you last do anything for someone else? . . . I'd rather stick pins in my eyes . . . but on the other hand . . .

'Would I have to leap naked out of a birthday cake?' she asks, playing for time.

Patrick laughs. 'No way – although if you fancy it . . . no, just kidding. Seriously, just being there would be great, she'd be over the moon.'

'She might prefer to spend her birthday with you; it could seem like an intrusion.'

'She'd love it, believe me, and so would I.'

Dot makes a hurrumphing noise and pushes the bread towards him with a knife. 'Cut two slices for me and as many as you want for yourself,' she instructs.

'Of course I'll understand if you'd rather not, but I –'

'All right,' she says. 'If you think she'd like it.'

'Wow! Really? That's totally brilliant – oh shit!' Blood drips in dark spots onto a slice of bread. 'Bugger, so sorry, I've cut myself in my excitement.'

She regrets it immediately, regrets it as she dabs the cut finger with tea tree ointment and applies a plaster, as she makes the sandwiches, and as the evening continues, and while she thoroughly enjoys Patrick's company. Aunty Win, she thinks, must be the price she'll pay for such a pleasant evening.

And she regrets this and more, much more, later that evening, when she thinks about what else she has agreed to do. How did he do that, get her talking about the past, dragging out her books of clippings and photographs? She has made a complete fool of herself, behaved like a boring old fart, the sort of old person that young people dread. But Patrick had started it with all his questions, asking how it all began, her career, her activism, and the Push, of course, most of all the Push; people always wanted to know about the Push. Dot blushes at the realisation that she has been name dropping: dead names, names still living, people she'd been with on campaigns, worked with, slept with. Oh lord, did she actually tell him that too? Perhaps not, but she may have implied it with a tone, the twitch of an eyebrow, a particular sort of hesitation that spoke more clearly than words. Well, too late – who cares a stuff these days anyway?

'How important we thought we were, back then,' she remembers saying, 'so entirely up ourselves. We thought we were shaping a new world.'

'In many ways you were,' Patrick had said, 'and it's

fascinating. I'm running a course on subcultures in cities and the Sydney Push is one of them. It would make it so real for my students to meet someone who was a part of it – an activist.'

'Well, we certainly thought of ourselves as *libertarians* and tried to live that way, but I don't think we really *were* activists; we spent a lot of time in the pub talking, setting the world to rights. We analysed everything, came up with ideas and solutions, wrote papers, talked about how things ought to be. I mean, some people in the Push *were* activists, but a lot of them were armchair or bar stool activists.'

'*You* were an activist,' he said. 'The anti-Vietnam protests, weren't you arrested several times? And then later there was Women's Lib – all that would be very interesting.' He'd paused then, grinning. 'And according to today's paper, you're still protesting.'

Dot groans. 'So that shopping centre thing got in the paper?'

'Front page.'

'Oh dear, how embarrassing.' She hesitated. 'Well, I suppose I could . . .' and the words were out of her mouth before she knew it.

'Really? You're sure you don't mind?'

'Not entirely,' she'd said, 'but unusual things seem to be happening this weekend. I think it's a sign I should go with the flow.'

It had been flattering, but now that Patrick has gone Dot feels embarrassed and ridiculous.

'Thanks so much,' he'd said as he left. 'I've had a terrific evening. You're a living archive, Dot. The students will love meeting you.'

She'd paused, looking at him closely in the shadowy light of the porch. He'd seemed genuine.

'Living archive,' she mutters to herself now, 'more like the eternal egoist. You just can't let it all go, can you? Drop out, leave town, leave the country, try to get over yourself, and now at the first opportunity you rake it all up again. Well, this was an error of judgment on both our parts, probably too much wine.'

She drops the empty bottle into the bin and snaps off the kitchen light. Ah well, too late now. She's made this pathetic, ego-driven grasp at the past, a last ditch attempt to reclaim a vestige of what was only ever minor celebrity, and now she's stuck with it. 'You're a boring, selfish old woman,' she tells herself. 'Lunch with Aunty Win, for goodness sake, and talking to students; you'll make a fool of yourself with them no doubt, but Aunty Win is probably a very nice woman and you are going to smash all her illusions.' And she pads up the passage in the dark, wondering if there is a remote possibility that Patrick might call tomorrow and tell her it's all off, and if he does whether she will be relieved or disappointed.

THREE

'You look very nice, Margot,' Phyllida says as they wait for the guests to arrive. 'That colour suits you; you should wear it more often.'

Phyllida herself is looking exceptionally elegant this evening in a three-quarter length black crêpe dress stitched with an intricate pattern of sparkling jet beads. A little age-ing, Margot thinks, but exquisite taste, as always.

'Yes, Mum,' Emma says, looking critically at her mother, taking in the deep purple top that fits around her narrow shoulders and flares out around her waist and hips and the straight, ankle length black skirt. 'It's very nice, different. You don't usually wear things like that, but Aunty Phyl's right, it looks really good.'

Emma and her aunt are two of a kind, clothes horses both of them, a two-woman combat arm of the fashion police, so it's interesting for Margot to be approved of as she is tonight. She is used to being treated as a serial recidivist when it comes to fashion crimes.

'Where did you get it?' Phyllida asks.

'Central Park, yesterday,' Margot says. 'Em, why is it that there is virtually nowhere for bigger women in these shopping centres? Even a size sixteen is hard to find these days, and if you ask for an eighteen they look at you as though you crawled out from under a stone. Anyway, I bumped into an old friend –'

'Speaking of which,' Phyllida cuts in, 'you don't get the *Sunday Telegraph*, do you? That friend of yours who used to write the column in the *Age* was at Central Park yesterday too, she's on the front page.' She looks around for the paper. 'Now, where is it? I put it aside for you. There's a picture – apparently she chained herself to some railings, ranting on about beauty treatments and . . . now what was it I read? Ah! Here it is. Yes – the new sexism.' And she pulls the folded newspaper from a rack near the door and hands it to Margot, who unfolds it and stares at the picture with a sinking heart.

'Shit!' Emma says, leaning over her mother's shoulder. 'This is dreadful. Oh my god, listen to this: *In addition to her controversial views on what she calls the "sexualisation of women and girls in the service of consumerism," Dot Grainger believes that shopping centres should provide more choices and more diverse representations of women in their advertising and promotions. "It's all part of the new sexism that defines women by how they look. Women are made to feel that they are not beautiful enough, young enough or glamorous enough as they are," Ms Grainger says. "The shopping centres capitalise on that with the promise that they offer everything women need to make themselves over and they are caught in the cycle of before and after in which after becomes the next before, always drawing women back in."* How could she do this? And the blasted paper hasn't bothered to get a comment from me or even from the centre manager!'

'Don't start worrying about that now,' Donald says, topping up her glass. 'Party time, time to forget about work and enjoy yourself, isn't that right, Margot?'

Margot nods distractedly, and reads on.

'But we ought to have been asked for a response,' Emma says. 'Bloody journalists; you'd think they'd want a comment from the centre manager. And my mobile's always on, they could have called me.'

'You have delusions of grandeur,' Donald says benignly. 'You PR bods can't shape every message, you know. Now drink up and forget about it.'

'Don't worry, darling, no one will take any notice,' Phyllida says. 'It's just attention seeking. She was always like that, always going on about something. Wasn't she, Margot?'

'She's always been an activist if that's what you mean,' Margot says sharply. 'Have you finished with the paper, Phyl? Can I keep this?'

'Of course. We never actually read it. I don't know why Donald buys it.'

'Cartoons,' Donald says. 'I like the cartoons. Now, where *is* everyone?'

'Grant won't be long,' Emma says. 'He and Wendy were picking Rosie up from a party on the way.' She smooths down the skirt of the cream silk Collette Dinnigan dress that everyone has already admired at length, crosses to the window and tweaks the blind to look out onto the street, clenching and unclenching her fists.

For years Margot has wrestled with herself about where she went wrong with Emma. She was always a restless child and now she is a restless woman, but it's more than that – is it tension, anxiety, anger? Margot is never quite sure but sometimes she aches with concern and with the frustration that however and whenever she attempts to reach out to Emma it never quite works. All that seems to work for her is constant shopping and endless beauty treatments, all the things that Dot was attacking in the newspaper. Margot doesn't understand it. Emma is not stupid; she'd begun as a receptionist at Grangewood and worked her way up to become a publicist and now she's responsible for the publicity for three of the shopping centres. Every time Margot has, as she is having now, a stab of panic about her younger daughter's well-being and state of mind, she reminds herself of the professional Emma, and tries to merge the Emma she knows into the woman who everyone outside her family seems to see. She glances at her watch. Still no Lexie, and she hadn't turned up earlier in the day to help either, which is most unlike her.

'I hate this bit,' Phyllida says, 'waiting for everyone to arrive. It's like being in limbo.'

'Better than purgatory though, old thing,' Donald says, patting her shoulder. 'Limbo leads somewhere splendid, purgatory goes on forever. I'll check on the kitchen. Guests'll be here soon.'

'Don't you go near that kitchen, Donald,' Phyllida says. 'Emma has organised everything down to the last detail, and the caterers can manage perfectly well without your interference.'

Emma has certainly organised everything. The invitations, the caterers, the wine, the string quartet playing softly in a corner of the entrance hall; even the DVD with the continuous slide show of photographs from Phyllida and Donald's fifty years together has been scanned and compiled by Emma. Margot wonders where she gets the time and the energy.

'Lexie's late,' Emma says irritably and seems about to say something less than charitable but is silenced by a ring at the doorbell.

'Oops, here we go,' Phyllida says with a frisson of excitement. 'First guests,' and with a quick glance at herself in the mirror over the fireplace, she hurries out to the door.

Margot loathes the prospect of this party; she is not keen on most of Phyllida and Donald's friends, and cocktail parties are not her thing. But she's happy for her sister tonight, not just because of the anniversary, but because last month Donald announced his retirement and she knows that Phyl has been hanging out for this. He's been promising to retire for the last five years – it's not as though they need the income now – but he'd kept putting it off, reluctant, Margot suspects, to give up the hallowed status of consultant and the ever present band of surgical groupies and nurses hanging on his every word. Well, now it is done and Phyllida is determined to mark the start of what she's been calling her new life, beginning with plenty of midweek golf, and next month a visit to friends in California followed by a cruise to the Bahamas.

There are several people at the door, among them Ross, who, having kissed Phyllida and shaken hands with Donald, makes straight for Margot.

'Where's Lex?' he asks, kissing her cheek and almost choking her with the scent of his aftershave.

Margot leans away in self-defence. 'Crikey, Ross, whatever is that perfume?'

'Ralph Lauren for men,' he says, 'costs a bomb.'

'Well I think Ralph Lauren may have meant it to be used more sparingly,' Margot says, stifling a cough. 'I thought Lexie would be coming with you.'

Ross shakes his head and lifts a glass from the tray of a passing waiter. 'Been on a fishing weekend,' he says. 'Left lunchtime Friday and got home this evening and she's not there, so I thought she'd be here with you.'

It's almost an hour later, when all the guests have arrived, the champagne is flowing, the food circulating, that Margot, worried now by Lexie's non-appearance, decides to call her. In the spare room where she left her coat and bag she switches on her mobile and discovers a text message: *Can't make party. Have to get away for a few days. Love and apologies to P and D. Don't worry. Don't call, will email soon. Love Lex xxx PS Don't tell Ross.*

Margot takes a couple of deep breaths to quell maternal anxiety. She is accustomed to worrying about Emma, but worrying about Lexie is something new; she is almost boringly conscientious and reliable. Even as a child she'd been four going on forty, as though there was a part of her always programmed into restraint and thoughtfulness. Margot is torn between concern at this unpredictable and unexplained absence, and satisfaction that Lexie, for once in her life, has done something totally uncharacteristic. And don't tell Ross what? What is there to tell?

Margot hesitates, decides to ignore her daughter's request, and dials her number. The phone switches to the answering service and she gets ready to leave a message, only to find that Lexie's greeting has changed, and instead of being asked to leave a message she is being told, in Lexie's irritatingly calm voice, that she is not accepting messages. Margot switches off the phone and sits for a moment before getting to her feet. 'Good on you, Lex,' she says aloud, 'about time.' And she glances in the mirror, pats her hair and returns to the party.

'Lex isn't answering her phone,' Ross says after he tracks Margot down. He looks anxious and irritable.

Margot is not devoted to Ross; he and Lexie have been together for almost six years and while Margot has found it hard to warm to him, his worst crime, as far as she knows, is just that of being a waste of space. Laurence had told her recently that he thought Ross might be involved with someone else, but they don't actually *know* that. Lexie hasn't said anything and they still live together, although no one pretends that this is due to anything but inertia on both their parts. 'I got a text, Ross,' she says. 'Lexie seems to be taking time out. She'll be in touch soon.'

'Fuck!' Ross says. 'Time fucking out, what's that supposed to mean? Well, I suppose I know what it means. Where is she?'

'I don't know,' Margot says. 'And if I did I probably wouldn't tell you, because then it wouldn't be time out, would it?'

Phyllida is having a splendid time, the caterers are excellent, the guests have all arrived, Donald is drinking moderately and being a model host, and there is a tantalising pile of gifts on the hall table which she probably won't get to open until tomorrow. What a lovely evening; everyone dressed up in their finery for her and Donald. So gratifying; even Margot has made the effort and is wearing a very smart outfit from a proper boutique rather than something eccentric picked up in an op shop. Phyllida often despairs of her sister; ever since they were girls she has been trying to sort her out, but Margot has always gone her own way. She recalls a ridiculous crocheted bikini, a shaggy student look, all in black with an ugly green beret and lots of smudgy black mascara, and later cheesecloth and, worst of all, floral bell-bottom trousers. So perhaps it's not so surprising that she's ended up in later life haunting the op shops and coming up with weird things she thinks are bargains.

A woman with whom Phyllida plays golf once suggested that although she doesn't have a classic or a fashionable look, Margot has her own style; it was an eccentric style, she'd said, but distinctive and interesting. Phyllida can't see it herself but it's a relief to know that not everyone views Margot quite as she does. And she's so unfortunate with her weight of course, poor Margot, such a shame she inherited their mother's physique, unlike Phyllida herself who has their father's lean and rangy genes. Still, one can't blame one's parents for these things – not that Margot ever does, of course.

'I think I'll do the speech now, old thing,' Donald says, 'that all right with you?'

'Perfect timing,' she says, smiling at him. 'Now just remember, not too long. You're inclined to ramble once you get going.'

'I know,' he says amiably, swallowing the last of his drink. 'Short and sweet. Fifty years, eh, Phylly, and you're still speaking to me.'

'Most days!' Phyllida says. Affectionate conversation is not something either of them do with ease. 'When you're not being a complete pain in the neck. We have done rather well, haven't we?'

'Bloody well, and I'd do it all again, you know. I really would. So let's get this show on the road,' and he picks up a spoon from the table and taps it against his glass.

He's an odd sort of man, Phyllida thinks, watching as Donald calls for silence, as he waits for it and shifts his bulky body around getting comfortable, getting ready to speak. Not the easiest of men to live with, demanding really, self-important, noisy, convinced he's always right, and stubborn of course, absolutely pig-headed and impatient. 'You're not in the operating theatre now,' she often tells him. 'The nurses might tolerate your tantrums but I won't.' But he's got a good heart, and he's generous to a fault. And a brilliant surgeon of course, but still really a bit of a boy, and far too accustomed to having everything done for him, but she knows she's partly to blame for that. He farts a lot too, but apparently men do, or at least that's what the woman had told her when she went for the colonic irrigation. All men fart a lot, she'd said. She was probably right but it's difficult to imagine Hugh Jackman or Daniel Craig farting quite as loudly and as often as Donald does, although Prince Philip might and she's often wondered about Clive James. You get to know a person pretty well when you've shared a life, and particularly a bed, for fifty years. You've seen the best and the worst of them. There is not much left for Phyllida to learn about Donald and that's a relief really, no nasty surprises, not like poor Margot finding out about Laurence all those years ago. What a terrible time that was. No chance of any nasty secrets with Donald, certainly not now, and if there was in the past – well, she'd rather not know. This is their time now, California, the cruise . . . she has waited a long time for this stage of her life to begin.

Donald, having welcomed everyone and thanked them for coming, has now launched into reminiscence. He's talking about their first date all those years ago, when they'd met on the steps of the post office building. He's describing it in detail even down to the blue floral dress with the white belt she was wearing. How come he remembers that when he never notices what she wears these days? He is onto the hat now, shiny straw, he says, with a wide brim and a big white flower on the side, but suddenly he stops. He blinks a few times and rubs his hand across his eyes. Then he shakes his head, as though trying to free it from something, as if he has walked into a cobweb, shakes his head again and continues. Phyllida smiles at him and moves closer and he reaches out to take her hand.

'So here she is,' he says proudly, his glass raised in his other hand. 'My wife, my trouble and strife, the love of my life. Fifty years we're celebrating tonight . . .' and he stops again, and this time he screws up his eyes, tosses his head furiously from side to side like an angry carthorse and the glass drops from his hand like a stone, the champagne spreading in a golden pool on the cream carpet. For a few seconds he stands there, arm still extended, and then, letting go of Phyllida, he puts both hands to his head. 'What?' he cries out. 'What's happening . . .?' And suddenly, like a great tree felled in the forest, he crashes to the floor and Phyllida hears the crunch of glass as the champagne flute is crushed beneath him.

❧

There is blood on Emma's dress; a great scimitar-shaped slash of it fiercely scarlet against the cream silk. She has tried to cover it by keeping her coat on her lap but at the same time she is compelled to look at it, unable to focus on anything except how she must appear sitting here wearing this hideously defaced dress. There is blood on her legs too, her knees are patterned with it from where she knelt on the bloodied carpet to help Donald's colleague move him and stem the flow from the cuts. A jacket might have minimised the cuts but Donald, grumbling about the heat in the room, had taken his off sometime earlier. He is always too hot, largely because he's considerably overweight and drinks vast quantities of alcohol in defiance of his own extensive medical knowledge and constant nagging from friends and family. His only exercise is a leisurely round of golf once a week, quite often riding in the golf buggy. He eats a lot of everything and sweats a lot. It's a family joke that there is always a nurse on stand-by in the operating theatre with a cloth to stop the sweat from running down into his eyes. So when he keeled over at the party everyone thought stroke or heart attack. But they know now that it is a cerebral aneurysm. And, as they sit here in a small private waiting room at the hospital, an unusual privilege for anxious relatives, Donald's colleagues, who have decided on an emergency craniotomy, are right now cutting into his head to surgically clip the artery.

Emma is trying not to think about any of this; the thought of her uncle's large, sweaty and distinctly unhealthy body malfunctioning horrifies her. She has always loathed the ugly and messy aspects of the human body, her own and other people's. It had made pregnancy, childbirth and motherhood unbearable and she had been thankful to hand Rosie over to Grant as soon as possible. She concentrates now on her dress, the blood, and the fact that the harsh white hospital lights make even the unmarked parts of the silk look dull and discoloured. Perhaps cream is not her colour, but she saw it and had to have it despite the enormous price tag. If she could just change her dress everything would be very much better. It horrifies her that she is here at the hospital looking such a mess. She'd wanted to stay behind, wanted to be the one to sort out the caterers, pay the musicians, organise the clean-up.

'I'll stay and sort things out here,' she'd said, as the

ambulance was about to leave and Grant was helping Margot into his car to follow it.

'No, Emma,' Phyllida had wailed from the ambulance, 'come please. We need you.'

'It's okay, Phyl,' Grant said. 'Margot and I are coming with you.'

'I need Emma too,' Phyllida insisted. 'Please, Em.'

'It's okay, Emma, you go,' Wendy had said. 'I'll stay on here and clean up a bit. Rosie's already crashed out upstairs. She'll be fine.'

And so here she is, here they all are, sitting in vinyl, backward tilting armchairs which are too low for comfort and in which they feel as defenceless as upturned turtles each time they attempt to sit upright. They are, Emma thinks, the most disempowering chairs for people already disempowered by fear and confusion. And where is Lexie? How come Lexie escapes while she, Emma, is going to be stuck here all night, and still needs to be at work first thing tomorrow to do something about this crazy old woman chaining herself to railings and badmouthing the shopping centre? Is there no end to it?

Bile rises suddenly in Emma's throat, and she realises that although she's had at least four glasses of wine, she's been so busy she hasn't eaten anything since breakfast. Clapping her hand over her mouth she makes a dash for the toilets which are, thankfully, empty. She dry retches over the basin, splashes cold water on her face and blots it with a paper towel. Her face, greyish white and drawn, looks back at her from the mirror, haggard in the harsh fluorescent light, and she rummages for her makeup purse, only to remember that she has left it in Phyllida's bathroom. She can hardly bear to look at herself like this; the new eyeliner guaranteed to remain faultless for twenty-four hours has disappeared leaving only smudges under her eyes. And her lips! She's always hated them, so thin, and they make her look old. Well that settles it, she's definitely going to get her lips done. The plumping treatment and a permanent colour and lip liner. It's supposed to be hideously painful but she doesn't care. It's better than looking like a gummy old witch. And squeezing her lips together to bring back the colour, she returns to the waiting room.

'Em,' Margot says quietly as she slips back into her chair, 'Phyl's calmer now, and the people here all know her. You must be exhausted what with the preparations and everything. Why don't you go home now, get some sleep? I'll stay on and I'll ring if there's any news.'

'That's right,' Phyllida says, her voice thick from shock and crying. 'You should go, you've been wonderful, the party, everything . . .' The tears begin again.

'I can drive you home if you like, Em, and then come back,' Grant volunteers. 'You look exhausted. This is Donald's stamping ground and he's in good hands. It's not as though there's anything we can do except wait.'

But Emma shakes her head. 'I wouldn't dream of leaving,' she says. 'It'd be different if Lexie were here of course, but goodness knows where *she* is.' But of course if Lexie *were* here she would, by unspoken consensus, have been granted authority. In her quiet, irritating and super competent way she would be interpreting medical information, managing the practicalities, and calming everyone's emotions. But Lexie is not here and this is Emma's chance to make the decisions and organise everyone. Wendy has already usurped her preferred role of looking after everything back at the house and so she's certainly not going to slink off into the night and leave Grant here – they already think he's some sort of saint. And while she's not blind to his many qualities, there is no way she'll let this become another opportunity for the application of more polish to his halo.

FOUR

Suspended from a beam above Laurence's bed an ancient ceiling fan clunks and rattles, stirring up the heat trapped in this windowless loft under the clay tiles, where a couple of skylights allow light but only faint whiffs of fresh air. Laurence lies very still, hoping that this will maximise the work of the fan. How is it possible to be this hot in Spain at this time of year when yesterday morning they were all complaining about not being able to get warm? He has never been so hot in his life. Well, actually he has, but he doesn't believe that as he lies here in this makeshift dormitory in what was once army barracks and now masquerades as an oasis of overnight comfort for exhausted pilgrims.

Laurence doesn't really regard himself as a pilgrim, but he likes the fact that others assume he is on a pilgrimage. A pilgrimage has depth and meaning, a significance that attracts thoughtful questions, whereas saying you're going on an eight hundred kilometre walk to take your mind off the fact that your life is falling apart is an immediate conversation killer. Now, buggered by the end of the third day of walking, he knows he was mad to agree to what's beginning to feel like a very bad joke. For some reason which he can't now recall it had actually sounded like fun. A group of friends enjoying Sunday lunch in a Melbourne garden, plenty of wine, a huge paella, talk of Spain, a bit of foot stamping and miming of the *paso doble* on the verandah, and somehow, by the end of the day, a decision to walk the Camino de Santiago de Compostela.

'Aren't you a bit old for that?' Margot had asked when he'd told her a few weeks later. 'It's an awfully long way.'

'About seven hundred and ninety kilometres,' he'd said, 'but we won't be rushing. There are inns and old monasteries where you can stay along the route. Imagine it, Margot, rustic monastic cells, delicious food and wine, church bells ringing in the crisp dawn, on the road at daybreak. Marvellous.'

'You hate walking,' she'd said in that irritating, down to earth way she always used to deliver unpleasant truths. 'You always have, and you loathe getting up early.'

'This is different,' Laurence had said. 'It's a once in a life-time experience; a pilgrimage. And I'm already in training for it.'

'What about Bernard?' Margot asked.

'Well, he's not coming, if that's what you mean. He's been invited to Vietnam – a Visiting Professor.'

Margot had raised her eyebrows and said nothing, which had simply served to harden Laurence's resolve. It was a pain in the arse having someone who could always see through him, who could dismantle him in a single sentence. He is still very fond of Margot, and in view of everything that has happened they have retained a remarkable friendship, but sometimes she's a bit too all seeing, all knowing, for Laurence's comfort.

His present exhaustion is due not only to the rigorous trek of the first few days, but to the fact that several weeks earlier he'd reneged on the training which everyone had agreed was essential. He'd started off all right, swimming a couple of times a week and doing some work at the gym, but then he'd slacked off, observing his friends' committed efforts with a certain amount of indulgent amusement. It was only walking, after all, you did a bit each day, had a rest and then went on again the next day. How hard could that be? One day at a time, rest longer if needed. And the others – seven of them altogether – were hardly spring chickens; the youngest was fifty-five, Laurence himself and a couple of others the oldest at seventy-four. He'd actually envisaged himself walking with a gnarled wooden pilgrim stick and leather sandals until Griff, the self-appointed leader of the pack, had made the rule that no one could go unless they were properly equipped. That meant super lightweight everything, including high tensile collapsible sticks, and sturdy walking boots with thick socks.

Lying flat out now on their beds further up in this vast dormitory, Sheila, Griff's wife, and Fred, his brother, are also crashed out in the heat, Fred snoring loudly, Sheila twitching restlessly in her sleep, her muscles doubtless reliving the last agonising hill on the route to Villava. Laurence closes his eyes, feeling himself drifting into sleep. No one had mentioned that the wonderfully rustic and atmospheric accommodation along the route could be very short on comfort, nor had they mentioned steep hills that would make the blood drum in his ears. Most of all they hadn't mentioned that walking, something one did every day, could be a killer activity designed to shred your feet, burn muscles you never knew you had, and torture what remained, at this age, of one's hip and knee joints. Laurence would like to blame others for the fact that he's in danger of becoming a millstone around the neck of the group, but he knows that it's his own failure to prepare, or even to think seriously about what he was taking on.

'Fucking arrogant, that's your problem,' Griff had said to him at the end of the first day. 'Train, I told you. Train, train, train, but no, you just gave me that superior fucking smile as though you were secretly running ten kilometres a day and swimming twenty laps. I don't think you're going to make it to the end, Laurence, I really don't. In fact I'd lay a hundred bucks on your not making it halfway.'

So of course Laurence took the bet and now he *has* to make it; not just to Santiago but also that additional leg to Finisterre. And it is his pride, not the money, which makes finishing essential. He'd reneged on the exercise thing because he was so distracted that he hadn't been able to stick to anything. What he had told Margot about Bernard's 'visiting' status in Ho Chi Minh City was simply a cover for the fact that Bernard was leaving him for good. Neither of them had actually said it but the slow deterioration of their life together over the last couple of years, and Bernard's urge to cram more onto his CV before retirement, made it inevitable. The sixteen year age gap between them had not seemed to matter until now. Laurence is not actually sure whether he committed to this trip as a means of coming to terms with this or distracting his attention away from it, but the more he hears stories of what happens to people who walk the Camino, the less likely it seems that it will provide distraction from grief or assuage a fear of the future. Closing his eyes he thinks miserably of the sort of horrors he may have to face on the road ahead. When they had stopped to eat their lunch alongside a group of other, more experienced pilgrims who had walked the route several times, there had been talk of bleeding sores on the feet, sunstroke, muscle spasms, dehydration, slipped discs and heart attacks, and that was before the emotional torment even began to hit.

Laurence feels himself sinking into a gloomy doze. There is a minimal softening in his aching joints and the fire in his feet is starting to ease when a piercing ringtone jolts him back into consciousness. Fred leaps up swearing, and Sheila sits bolt upright, dishevelled and bewildered, and then flops back down again, while further up the dormitory others grunt and toss around on their bunks, irritated by the interruption of their siesta.

'It's mine,' Laurence mumbles, reaching out for his phone. 'Sorry, forgot to turn it off.' It's a lie of course; he'd deliberately left it on, because it made him feel better, less cut off. Even though he'd doubted there would be a signal there was still something reassuring about having it there ready for global roaming to link him to civilisation at the first opportunity.

'It's me, Dad,' Lexie says, her voice breaking up in the weak signal. 'How's it going? Are you enjoying it?'

Laurence flops back onto the bed, his heart rate settling to normal again. 'Fantastic,' he lies, keeping his voice really low, his face turned to the wall. 'Absolutely marvellous – the scenery, the company, magic. Bloody tiring though. I've got a few blisters already.'

'Good. Well not good about the blisters, the rest of it, I mean. I thought maybe you'd heard from Mum so I'm calling to let you know I'm fine.'

'I haven't heard from anyone since I left home.'

'Ah, well that's all right then. It's just that . . . I thought I'd tell you myself.'

'Tell me what?' Laurence asks, rubbing his eyes.

'Well I . . . I've sort of taken a bit of time out. I left on Sunday afternoon, just before the fiftieth anniversary bash.'

'I see,' says Laurence, not at all sure that he does. 'So where are you?' he asks, only slightly unsettled by Lexie's news but spotting an opportunity for dignified withdrawal from the pilgrimage. 'Are you okay? Would you like me to come home or meet you somewhere?'

'Definitely not,' Lexie says, her voice surging through more strongly now. 'I need to be alone, maybe for quite a long time.'

Laurence runs a sweaty hand through his damp hair. 'What about work?'

'Redundant. The practice is being wound up. I suppose I knew it was coming but it's a blow, after all this time – half my life down the drain.'

'No,' Laurence cuts in, 'not at all. You did a terrific job, and look at the experience you've racked up. But it's sad, very sad. Getting away is good, give yourself time to think about what comes next. And what about Ross?'

'Oh well, Ross . . . you know Ross. I've emailed him and told him not to contact me. I need a break – I'm really not in the mood to talk to him right now.'

Laurence's antennae twitch anxiously at the possible onset of parental responsibilities. 'So what are you planning . . .?'

'No idea. Not a clue. Time out; that's it for now, time to sort myself out.'

Laurence hesitates, wondering fleetingly if he will confide the reasons for his own time out, and then deciding against it. 'You okay for money? I can organise it from here.'

'I'm fine for money, thanks,' Lexie says. 'Just wanted you to know I'm okay in case you got another version. Anyway, gotta go now. You take care, Dad, have fun. *Hasta la vista* and all that stuff.'

'Yeah,' Laurence says, 'you too Lex – *adios*. Take care. Ring me again, let me know how . . .' but the line is dead. Lexie has gone, back into her time-out capsule, leaving him with no reason to quit, and an unfamiliar sense of fatherly concern about her well-being. Lexie is the most consistently conscientious and reliable person in the world. Laurence is not one to dwell much on guilt but he's never underestimated the difficulties he created for Margot and the girls by leaving. Lexie, eleven at the time, had responded by standing alongside Margot with fierce, almost protective determination. The stories about how Lexie coped when Margot returned from hospital after a hysterectomy, how she established a herb garden, cleaned all the windows and took the cat to be put down when no one else could face the task, are the stuff of family legend. She is the head prefect who keeps track of everything and everyone, cranks up the support systems when necessary and winds down the arguments. She is not a person who takes time out; she is the one who facilitates it for everyone else. Just like her mother, which is, of course, why Laurence had married Margot all those years ago; he believed she would keep him on track, keep him safe. But of course what he hadn't realised then was that not even Margot could keep him safe from himself. And now, here he is again, hiding the truth from everyone, pretending that this is some great adventure, when it's really about the fact that his own life is on the rocks – again.

∽∽∽

Lexie puts the phone down and stares at it. One thing about her father, she thinks, is that his reactions are entirely predictable, and while that's irritating it's also reassuring. There is no risk of him rushing to her side with bowls of nourishing chicken soup. No risk that he is sitting wringing his hands wondering whether his failure as a parent has driven her to this. No sense that she might not be meeting his expectations, because he has none. He loves her just as she is, there is nothing to live up to, and while she has sometimes resented his inability to make the leap of imagination into her emotional space, right now that detachment is just what she needs. There is too much to think about, too much that she has been putting off for too long. Instead of trying to pretend that she could save the practice Lexie knows now that she should have been looking out for herself, making plans for the future, just as all the other staff had done. A couple of Dr Faraday's friends had sounded her out about working for them, and the CEO of a pharmaceuticals company with which she'd dealt for most of her time at the practice had offered her a management position, but she had convinced herself that there was still a chance to rebuild. So she has no one but herself to blame for not having grasped the moment and made plans. But it's not her professional life that is on Lexie's mind right now.

Liz Byrski

Wandering out onto the balcony she thinks about Ross coming home from his fishing trip to find her gone – his irritation, his confusion, his slight sense of panic that things are not as he expects them to be, the niggle of guilt about what he's been up to. How simple it would be, Lexie thinks, if Ross took this opportunity to gather up his possessions and go. If he just got into his car and drove off to this 'other woman', probably Carole, the estate agent with too much lipstick and a skirt that's not much larger than a belt. Lexie imagines going home, opening the door and finding no trace of him, no odd socks, no computer magazines scattered across the coffee table, no real estate brochures on the bench top, no pile of washing, no stubbies in the fridge, no bland eighties disco music to numb her brain. It's a liberating prospect; bliss in fact. The relationship had fizzled out like a damp squib and for months she's been playing the game of not knowing, not seeing, punctuated by moments when she tells him she does know, and he insists that she's imagining it. But it's different now, she's done with games, done with the caution that has made her hang on at home as she hung on at work. She wants it to be over. Ross is not a bad person, just the wrong person, and he doesn't do decisions, so Lexie knows that if someone is going to call time it will have to be her. What better time than this?

On that Sunday afternoon, three days ago, she had sent a hasty email to the practice listing the tasks that needed to be done and directing them to the location of various files. It was the first time in her life she had ever walked out on her responsibilities and she found it surprisingly easy. She threw a random selection of clothes into a suitcase, packed her laptop and a couple of books into her computer bag, and took a taxi to the airport with no idea of where she was going. The next flight with seats available was to Sydney and she'd handed over her credit card and was airborne in less than an hour. This wasn't a matter of choice about where to go, just a means of escape. Since then she has been suspended in a state of shock, half expecting someone – her mother, perhaps, the practice solicitor or one of the doctors, but definitely not Ross – to arrive at the door of her hotel room and insist she come home immediately. Now her conversation with Laurence has changed something. Telling someone else has shown her the enormity of what she has done. She has run away from home, only in a very minor sort of way – indeed, some people would think it a pathetic effort – but for her it is a big, important step. Lexie knows that she has cracked open something within herself that she doesn't yet understand, something that won't be complete unless she acts now.

Turning back into her room she collects her laptop, carries it out to the balcony and sits at the table looking out at the lights of the city reflected in the waters of the harbour, the curving sails of the Opera House white against the darkening sky. A couple of weeks ago, stuck in traffic, she'd been listening to talkback about whether it was acceptable to dump one's partner by email.

'Can't see the problem myself,' one man had said. 'People have been dumping each other by snail mail for centuries – what's the difference?'

'No, you gotta tell them face to face,' a woman had protested. 'It's only fair. You've gotta give them that respect.'

Lexie remembers laughing at this, thinking that if she were to end it with Ross he'd much prefer email because it would mean he wouldn't have to respond, protest, argue, act hurt. She would be giving him permission to leave. After all, they're not married, the house is hers, they have very few shared possessions, he had moved into her life and now it's time for him to move out. But it's harder to write the email than she anticipated, and she reads it through over and over again, choosing each word to avoid ambiguity, to control how he will read it, trying to acknowledge the good things and not dwell on the rest of it, attempting to convey determination rather than hostility, finality without castration.

Once she's sent it she leans back in her chair and stretches her arms above her head, unwinding the tension from her shoulders, feeling the slackening of her muscles. Relief. Sadness, much more sadness than she imagined for the loss of what might have been, for their failure to make it work. With this final stroke she has slashed the ropes of her own safety net. The ultimate planner has no plan, not for tomorrow, next week, next year. She can choose anything and the choice is terrifying.

FIVE

The trouble with Donald, Margot thinks, is that there is so much of him. His body, his ego, his opinions, the noise he makes, his sense of entitlement and authority, all create a field of energy which, like quicksand, draws the unwary into its depths. Once there you become, willingly or otherwise, subject to his authority. Margot has always clung doggedly to her foothold on firm ground at the outer edge. Sitting now at one side of Donald's bed, she finds she is confused; despite years of dislike, hostility and active resistance, she feels almost fond of him. There is something immensely sad about all that commanding energy, arrogance and authority and, to be fair, all that brilliance, reduced to a huge comatose mound attached to a battery of tubes and wires.

On the other side of the bed Phyllida, body slumped, head thrown back, lips parted, is fast asleep, snoring in gentle unison with Donald's breathing. To Margot this posture, the open mouth, the snoring, the vulnerability of her sister asleep in daytime in a place where she might be seen by strangers or, worse still, by people she knows, is what's really disturbing. For decades Phyllida has exercised meticulous control over the way she is seen by others; firm, upright, controlling, even sometimes intimidating are the words that people use to describe her, and her tall, slim figure always immaculately if unimaginatively dressed confirms it.

Even as a teenager she had had an authoritative, bossy manner, but in those days it went with authority on the sports field along with cups for tennis and running, and captaincy of the school hockey team during which she berated the younger, less enthusiastic players (Margot among them – actually, Margot in particular) for their incompetence. From sports champion to sports mistress to senior mistress of the upper school – extraordinary, really, at a time when teachers had to resign when they married. But the nuns who ran this small Catholic school were proud and fond of Phyllida, one of only a few lay teachers at the convent, and they ignored the regulations of the wider world. Phyllida had stayed on, the small community of the school and her unassailable position within it carrying her through the years of waiting for a pregnancy that never materialised, and then beyond that into a time when it was no longer a possibility. She had retired at fifty but even today Phyllida is still in charge – chairing committees, organising charity collections and fundraisers.

Margot shifts in her seat, leaning forward to look at her sister more closely and wondering, as she does so, how Phyl will cope if Donald dies as it appears to everyone except her that he surely will. Almost three weeks have passed since the aneurysm and the subsequent surgery, and in that time he has also suffered a stroke; nineteen days as an unconscious body in a bed and, Margot muses, commanding as much or possibly more attention than when he was conscious and vertical. If, on the other hand, he does pull through, how will Phyl and everyone else cope? His medical and surgical colleagues cannot predict how much of Donald might emerge from the darkness, only that it will be a very limited edition of his former self. Margot's surprising flash of fondness is mingled with a less admirable sense of relief.

When Phyllida had first brought him home to tea Margot had been a plump and irritatingly brainy teenager with two huge, angry spots erupting on her chin. Donald, then in his twenties with a repertoire of crude jokes and the noisy insensitivity of a rugby playing medical student, had named her as a rare species – 'the greater spotted Margot'. It was a very bad start, although to Margot's annoyance Donald seemed totally unaware of it. Through the intervening decades he continued to treat her with the rough and condescending affection appropriate to inconvenient but harmless younger sisters. In youth she had felt impotent rage; now, in old age, just defensive hostility and boredom. But Phyllida without Donald is a worryingly unknown quantity and more worrying still is the prospect of her devoting every waking moment to his care. Margot, overcome with anxiety at the thought, gets up and thrusts her arms into her coat in a sudden desperate need to escape from the sterile atmosphere of the hospital. But her movement disturbs Phyllida, who jerks awake and sits up blinking, fiercely alert.

'What is it? What's happened? Oh it's you, Margot.' She rubs her eyes and stretches. 'Sorry, I must have fallen asleep. How long have you been here?'

'About half an hour,' Margot says. 'It seemed a shame to wake you. You ought to go home, Phyl, there's nothing you can do. Why don't you come and have lunch with me? Central Park perhaps? A bit of retail therapy always cheers you up.'

Phyllida's eyes light up at the prospect of shopping, but then she looks at the unconscious Donald and shakes her head. 'I really can't. He might wake up. I'll stay until tonight.'

'I don't think day and night mean anything to Donald at the moment. If he's going to wake up it could just as easily be at three in the morning. You've got your mobile and we can be back here very quickly if there's any change.'

Phyllida leans over the side of her chair and retrieves the knitting that has slipped from her knees to the floor. 'I can't,' she says firmly, 'I really can't.' And she inserts the needle into the first stitch.

'But it's ridiculous your sitting here day after day,' Margot begins. 'Donald doesn't know, and you need to look after yourself, conserve your energy for when he does come round or when, well if . . .'

'No!' Phyllida says. 'I shall stay until eight as usual and I shall be back here at nine in the morning.'

Margot shrugs. 'Okay, if that's want you want.' She walks around to her sister's side of the bed. 'I brought you some Turkish Delight.'

Phyllida's face breaks into a smile and she puts down her knitting. 'Bless you,' she says, levering the lid off the plastic box. 'Goodness – it's huge, I'll be as fat as a pig. Any news of Lexie?'

'Not a word. Well, that's not quite true, I did get a text the day before yesterday, assuring me that she's fine. But she can't be reading her messages because I let her know about Donald and if she knew she'd have got in touch or come home.'

'Would she?' Phyllida asks, straightening her shoulders. 'I'm not sure we can assume we know what Lexie would do anymore. She didn't turn up to help with the preparations for the party, nor to the party itself, and she took off to god knows where and doesn't even tell her own mother where she is. I find that all very strange and . . . well, hurtful . . . especially in view of what's happened. I've always considered Lexie to be a very responsible and reliable person, but apparently I was wrong.'

'Oh for goodness sake get off your high horse, Phyl,' Margot says. 'Lexie *is* a very responsible and reliable person and *you* know it – sometimes I think she's too responsible. This is totally out of character, she obviously needed to get away. But I am a bit worried about why, and why now. You know, some time ago Laurence told me he had a feeling Ross was seeing someone else.'

'Well her going off like this won't help to sort that out,' Phyllida says. 'It's giving him carte blanche to do what he wants if you ask me.'

'I didn't ask you,' Margot says. 'And frankly I don't know why they're still together, neither of them has their heart in it anymore. I think Lexie would be a lot happier on her own.'

'Being alone doesn't suit everyone, Margot. Me, for example, it wouldn't suit me.'

She stops suddenly, darts a look at Donald in the bed and takes a deep breath and Margot feels the chill of her sister's fear. It is as though every possible outcome of this situation is flashing through Phyllida's mind on fast forward.

'Well you're not, are you?' she says, clearing her throat. 'You're not alone. Now, is there anything you want me to do? I've cooked some meals and frozen them for you, and I'll put them in your freezer on my way home.'

Phyllida shakes her head. 'No, thanks. The meals will be a godsend though. I sit here all day doing nothing and get home too exhausted to cook.'

Margot nods and leans down to kiss her. 'I'll see you sometime tomorrow. Ring me if you need anything.'

Outside the hospital rain is falling in tanker loads from a gunmetal sky and Margot pauses beneath the canopy at the entrance breathing the damp air with relief. The stifling atmosphere of Donald's room and Phyl's insistence on staying there, hour after hour, day after day, make her want to scream. How long is this to go on, and what is she, Margot, supposed to do about it? It's not that she doesn't want to support her sister, but the responsibility for managing the varying strands of her and Donald's lives seems to have been allocated to her, and she has no idea what she ought to be doing; preparing people and arrangements for death, or for a very different life? Margot wonders whether perhaps the hospital has an advisor one can talk to in these situations, although that person is unlikely to be able to help her manage her resentment about being lumbered with this. She has gathered in the unravelling strands of other people's lives for so long that it's now taken for granted and she doesn't know how to stop it. Now it seems that her own life has been put on hold by Donald's illness and its attendant uncertainty. Margot has always struggled with the idea of uncertainty. When they were younger Laurence often talked about its creative advantages, but Margot craved certainty, preferring to live with its illusion.

The wind is driving torrential rain horizontally under the canopy and Margot is almost as wet as if she were standing out in the open. This sudden spell of unseasonal bad weather has taken the city by surprise. Water gushes down the slope of the hospital driveway and a car sweeps into a puddle, drawing to a halt and drenching her legs in a wave of water. The driver leans across to open the passenger door and a young woman darts out of the building and leaps the puddle into the front seat. As the door slams shut the driver spins the wheels and pulls away, churning up another wave. Margot feels the soaking fabric of her trousers clinging to her legs but she doesn't move. The weather, the car, the girl's swift, youthful flight from kerb to car has galvanised her memory.

A Sydney bus stop almost fifty years ago; she is standing in the rain when a car draws up. The passenger door swings open and he is gesturing her to get in; there is a micro-second of hesitation before she jumps the puddle, and as he reaches across her to close the door she feels the heat of his body and his breath brushes her cheek. How sharp the memory is, how intensely it revives the moment, the thrill of the unknown, the heat of desire. Odd, really, Margot thinks now as she watches rain pounding into surging puddles, how certain moments are etched with clarity while so much else is vague and blurred. Is it just the turning points that remain like the scratch of diamonds on glass; the moments when something profound was happening, when you were making a choice that would determine the future and you didn't even know it? What if she had stayed at the bus stop? What if she had remained out there in the rain until he drove away – what then? Who, what and where would she be now?

It seems to Margot that this need to understand the past is increasing with age, as though by understanding she might have one last chance to remake it. In the sixties and seventies, as she had juggled being a wife and mother and later a sole parent with a full time job and the battle for women's rights, she had envied and admired the older women around her. They seemed wise, confident, sometimes even serene; she had imagined herself becoming like that, an elder in the tribe of women. But there is no longer any tribe. The heat and dust of that movement of women has cooled and settled and those who were part of it have become irrelevant. What are they supposed to do with all that experience, with all that history? She had believed it was leading her somewhere but now it feels as though time is running out and somewhere has become nowhere. She feels, as she has often felt, a crushing resentment that she has spent her life responding to other people's needs, soaking up their problems, dispensing love and care, and all it has done is drain her energy and make her invisible.

Invisible – that's what Dot had said. Is this what Dot feels? Is this the same feeling that drove Dot to the shopping centre with her padlock, her chains and her passionate but muddled protest? Margot is wearied by the servicing of other lives and the promise – always just out of reach – of a time and a place to examine and nourish her own. It is the gap between the potential of that young woman waiting at the bus stop all those years ago, and the reality of what she has become: an old woman who has, over decades, allowed other lives to erode the centrality of her own. Margot sighs, unfurls her umbrella, steps out into the rain and picks her way through the puddles to her car.

⌒⌒⌒

Dot is rehearsing in front of the mirror when the doorbell rings. The date arranged for the talk to Patrick's students is still a few weeks away but the idea of it is both exciting and daunting. Planning it – doing some research to refresh her memory, sorting out some of the pictures and clippings – has saved her from herself. There is so much she wants to say, but so much she has forgotten. The past is a ragged mess of bits and pieces, of events and people captured like tiny disconnected fragments of film. Each morning she wakes wondering where to start searching for shape to the story, worrying about tone, about the mix of history, memory and anecdote. It's exciting but it's also overhung with anxiety because it has become tremendously important to her that she gets it right, that she does well, that she doesn't end up a laughing-stock or sending them all to sleep. Dot knows she's her own fiercest critic and that she will have to live with that critic's judgments for a very long time to come. But she knows too that this is when she can be at her best; she likes the creative tension of preparing something for an audience.

'Let's face it,' she says aloud to the mirror, 'you're a shameless attention seeker, but at least you are doing it with some purpose.'

Once again the doorbell is an annoyance. She wanted to do a bit more work on this before going out for lunch, and so she walks very softly to the front door and peers cautiously through the peephole. On the doorstep, sheltering from the rain, is Margot, and she is looking decidedly glum. Dot throws open the door in delight.

'Am I interrupting anything?' Margot asks, dripping onto the doormat. 'I can go away if you like.'

'No way!' Dot says, drawing her in and down the hall.

'This cold snap is such a shock. It's usually another couple of months at least before I have to light the fire. My blood must be thinning with age because I succumbed this morning. Here, take your coat off and sit in front of the stove, you're soaked.'

Margot hands over her raincoat and, pinching the fabric of her trousers just above the knee, she shakes them gently away from her legs.

'You'd better take them off,' Dot says. 'I'll put them in the dryer.'

Ten minutes later, Margot, minus her coat, trousers and socks, is sitting in front of the open door of the stove looking rather less glum, clutching a cup of tea, a blanket wrapped around her from the waist down, her bare feet resting on the warm bricks of the hearth.

'So no change in Donald then?' Dot says, sipping her own tea. 'Poor sod, but more importantly poor Falada, she's stuffed whether he recovers or not. But how did you get so wet if you've only been to the hospital?'

'Standing outside in the rain thinking,' Margot says sheepishly. 'About the past mainly, about . . .' she hesitates '. . . well, about how things have turned out. Your fault of course, turning up out of the blue again, stirring it all up.'

'Tell me about it,' Dot says. 'I've agreed to talk to some students about it, the past – our past, the Push, the women's movement, all that stuff. I agreed to do one session, and now somehow it's grown into two, assuming that I don't bore them to death the first time.' And she goes on to tell Margot about Patrick. 'My unfailing determination to grab the centre stage whenever possible,' she says ruefully. 'I'm enjoying getting ready for it all, but the events themselves are going to be another matter entirely.'

'And what about the lunch with his aunty?' Margot asks. Dot's energy, the way she charges headlong into everything, has nudged her, as it always did, out of her dark mood. 'Have you done that yet?'

'Today!' Dot says, glancing up at the kitchen clock. 'In one hour's time, in fact, in Carlton. Actually, Margot, you could come with me.'

Margot laughs and splashes tea on the blanket. 'No way! You got yourself into this, Dot, you're on your own.'

'But you owe me,' Dot says with a grin. 'Who helped you find that purple and black outfit for Falada's party?'

Margot snorts with laughter. 'You're outrageous! Absolutely not! You're a guest; you can't just turn up with someone else in tow. And I'd look as though I was trying to bum a free lunch from a stranger.'

'Sometimes, Margot, you are very middle class especially, as I remember it, when it comes to money. I plan to pay anyway. You know, slip the credit card to the waiter before I get to the table. Go on, Margot, it'll be torture for me but fun if there's two of us, and your trousers will be dry in time.'

'Definitely not,' Margot says. 'I'm adamant. Patrick and Aunty Win are all yours and that's my final word on the matter.'

'I was thinking,' Margot says almost an hour later, as they search for a parking space close to the restaurant, 'while I was standing in the rain, about who we were then, you know, in the Push days, and later. I thought I was going somewhere then, I thought we all were. And *you* did. And Laurence did. And there I was flying high, scholarship student, literature prizes, I was supposed to be a writer, everyone said so – a literary star. But something happened, it all went pear-shaped, and I'm not just talking about my body.'

Dot accelerates swiftly into a parking space immediately outside the restaurant and peers out through the rain. 'This is it,' she says, 'at least it looks okay. I'm so glad I conned you into coming with me.' She switches off the engine and turns around to face Margot. 'Of course something happened,' she says. 'Laurence happened. A baby happened. Domesticity and another child happened, and then Laurence buggered off.'

'I never thought it would be that way,' Margot says, and there is a crack in her voice. 'I thought I would do so much, and yet here I am almost seventy and I've done none of it. Nothing at all and now it's too late.'

SIX

Phyllida has a pretty good idea of what is going on in Margot's head, at least she thinks she does. She recognised the expression on her sister's face as she left the ward; it was that bruised, aggrieved expression that Margot first wore as a teenager when she felt she was being overlooked. It had dropped out of service for a few years when she went to university and started hanging around with that tawdry Push mob. And then it appeared again when all the talk of libertarianism turned out to be just a lot of hot air. Phyllida shakes her head, libertarians indeed! All they ever did was hang out at the pub, drinking between parties, and slipping out to place bets on the races. And the women, well, Margot had told her once that women acquired prestige by sleeping with the men who were high up in the Push hierarchy. So much for free love and promiscuity in the sixties – it was still the men calling the tune and disappearing out the back door if the women got pregnant.

Phyllida leans back in her chair, her back aching from sitting so long, and she fidgets around to find a more comfortable position. Margot had been eighteen, away in Sydney at university when she got involved, even though Phyllida, who had heard talk about the Push, had warned her to stay away from them.

'They're nothing but trouble,' she'd told Margot when she came home in the holidays. 'They're anarchists, you know, and there's a lot of . . . well, sex and debauchery. There's another lot like that here – in Carlton. You don't know what you're getting into.'

'But they're cool,' Margot had said, 'and interesting. Better than your stuffy pretentious friends at the tennis club. Besides, it's none of your business,' and she'd flounced off to some party and hadn't come home that night, much to their parents' dismay. The atmosphere at home was uncomfortably chilly and Phyllida had been glad when Margot caught the bus back to Sydney, to university and to the grotty little flat that she shared with a couple of other young women from the Push. Phyllida sighs and stretches her arms above her head; well, it's no good Margot regretting it now, more than forty years later; she has no one to blame but herself.

Phyllida, of course, has no cause for regret. Early in their relationship she had made it very clear to Donald that sex before marriage was not on the agenda, although she did relent once they were officially engaged. It was a reward for his staying power. They were engaged for three years before Donald had qualified and they got married, and even Phyllida would have thought it unreasonable to have held out all that time.

Having finally lost her virginity she had wondered what all the fuss was about. Sex seemed pretty tedious and offered small reward for women, but at least it kept Donald happy. Now, sitting here, watching the steady rise and fall of her husband's chest, Phyllida wonders what she might have missed by only ever having had sex with one man. Not much probably, she thinks, and there's a certain comfort in knowing that your entire sexual history is the property of just one person. Margot had grown somewhat smug in the early days of her sexual freedom, sneaking around with a Cheshire cat smile that implied knowledge of secret pleasures. She seemed to think that being younger and more sexually experienced made her an object of envy. Phyllida assumed that it was a phase from which Margot would eventually emerge. She had never asked her sister at that time, nor any time since, how many men were included in her sexual history, although she had often wished she could; purely out of curiosity, of course, because as far as she was concerned sex was a waste of time and not worth the risk unless it was with someone you were going to marry.

'How are we doing here?' says a voice from the doorway.

A different nurse – an Asian woman, probably in her fifties, Chinese, Phyllida guesses – crosses the room and fiddles with Donald's tubes. Phyllida, who is by now familiar with most of the nursing staff, is disturbed by the arrival of a stranger. Donald has been head of surgery here for more years than she can remember, so she has been comfortably at ease with familiar faces since the panic of their arrival in the ambulance abated.

'We're fine, thank you,' she replies stiffly. 'And you are?'

'Sister May Wong,' the woman says, lifting Donald's chart from its rack and noting something down on it. She looks closely into Donald's face, takes his hand in hers, lifting it and then putting it gently back again on top of the bedspread.

Phyllida, who is used to being treated with a degree of deference by the staff, is now riled by the lack of it. 'I sense that he's making very good progress,' she says in her haughty voice.

Sister Wong looks down at her and then back to the chart. 'Really?' she asks. 'Has there been any change since Dr Phillips saw him at ten o'clock?'

'Not exactly,' Phyllida says, 'but I feel it in my bones. He's definitely on the mend. When you have lived so long with someone you can feel these things, you know.'

The nurse gives her a chilly look and replaces the chart in its rack. 'Mmm. Well I'd rather trust the vital signs than your bones, Mrs Shepperd,' she says. 'And sadly the vital signs show no change.'

Phyllida, who is an expert when it comes to chilly stares, directs one at the woman on the other side of the bed. 'I think I can be trusted to detect things about my husband's condition which might not be apparent to anyone else. The physical signs are not the be-all and end-all, you know, May.' The use of the first name is, she feels, a masterstroke which makes it clear who's in charge here.

'They're a pretty good indicator of the patient's progress towards either recovery or deterioration,' the nurse says. 'And Sister Wong will do nicely, thank you.' And she turns on her heel and heads off out of Donald's room and up the corridor.

'Well really, how rude,' Phyllida says aloud. 'How very rude and uncalled-for. When it comes to bedside manner she'd make a good parking inspector. Don't you think so, Don? Who does she think she is?' She turns to him and pats the arm that is lying heavily on the blanket. 'She won't be talking to me like that once you're awake.' She is trembling with a mixture of anger and anxiety, the stress is getting to her, no doubt about that. Surely there will be a sign of change soon and she feels her anger directed now at Donald, lying there in the bed, sleeping peacefully while she must sit here worrying herself sick about the future.

That's the thing about Margot, of course, she is wearing her injured expression because she is picking up the slack of Phyllida and Donald's life, at present. Phyllida understands that it must be frustrating for Margot that she herself has chosen to opt out of everything except keeping vigil, that she won't engage in conversations designed to plan for a range of different outcomes. She knows Margot thinks that she is just not facing the fact that Donald may die, or may end up in residential care, or that he might need difficult and complicated home nursing. But of course she *knows*, of course she's *thinking* about it. What else would she be thinking about, sitting here knitting, something she hasn't done for years. It's simply that she cannot possibly talk about it, not to Margot, not to anyone. All she can do is sound and appear optimistic in the hope that she might, in the performance of it, manage to convince herself as well as everyone else.

Phyllida picks up her knitting again and begins work on the small sleeve, while outside in the corridor feet pad back and forth, their rubber soled shoes squeaking on the vinyl tiles, and the stop-start progress of the lunch trolley grows slowly closer.

'Hello, Aunty Phyl,' says a voice from the doorway. 'Goodness, you're knitting. I didn't know you could knit.'

Emma, immaculate in a tight fitting crimson suit with a very short skirt, teeters across the room on perilously high heels and plants a kiss on her cheek. 'I suppose it's that crisis thing, back to wartime and knitting socks for soldiers. This brings it all back.'

Phyllida sighs and shakes her head. 'I was four when the war broke out, Emma, and ten when it finished. I have never knitted a sock for a soldier in my life, not that I have anything against socks or soldiers. The trouble with you young people is that you have no sense of history. Anything before nineteen sixty is a backward blur until you get to a Jane Austen adaptation.'

'Sorry,' Emma says, 'silly of me, I wasn't thinking. What exactly is it that you're knitting?'

Phyllida held up her needles. 'A jumper for Rosie.'

Emma stares at the knitting and swallows. 'Lovely, but the colour – it's a bit . . .'

'Olive green and gold are the new school colours,' Phyllida says triumphantly. 'Grant brought her in yesterday afternoon. He said it was magic that I'd got the right colour purely by chance.'

'Really? Oh well . . . yes, well done, you. How's Uncle Donald doing?'

Phyllida, counting stitches, continues to the end of the row. 'No change, so they tell me, but I sense improvement. You do, I think, when you know someone really well. You can sense what's happening to them rather better than strangers can, despite all their medical qualifications. I can tell he's on the mend.'

'That's good then,' Emma says, perching on the edge of a chair. 'Very good, I'm so glad, because I have to go away in a couple of days. It's the annual sales and marketing conference in Sydney, I'm so sorry. Of course if . . . if anything sort of, well,' she takes a deep breath '. . . sort of happened, then just a phone call and I could be back within hours. Otherwise I'll be away about ten days.'

Phyllida sees Emma as the daughter she never had. It's a delight to her that they are so alike in many ways, but she is not blind to her shortcomings. 'Ten days for a sales conference?' Phyllida says now. 'Amazing, I never knew they took so long.' And she looks quizzically at her niece.

Emma blushes. 'It's not just the conference, there's team building too, so I really have to be there.' She is the most transparent of liars.

'Team building? I hope it's not the dangerous orienteering sort, Em. Somehow I can't see you hurling yourself across raging waters on a flying fox, or finding your way back to camp with a compass. But of course you must go. There's nothing you can do here anyway, and he's making progress. By the time you get back he might even be home with me.'

It is at that moment that Donald's arm shoots suddenly upwards in a Nazi-like salute and his body jerks violently in the bed. The monitors which have been calmly measuring his vital signs are now a mass of flashing red lights, and a chilling single tone replaces the previous steady beeps. Within seconds the door is thrown open and Sister Wong and two other nurses burst through the door with a trolley, closely followed by two doctors, white coats flapping open, stethoscopes bouncing against their chests, yelling instructions.

'I can't believe it,' Phyllida says as she and Emma sit out in the corridor, while behind the door of Donald's room the fight for his life goes noisily on. 'Whatever will it be next? I don't think I can take much more of this.' And despite their shared distaste for adults who cry in public, she tips sideways and clings to her niece and her tears make a dark, damp patch on the lapel of Emma's soft cashmere jacket.

SEVEN

Vinka closes the door of her apartment behind her and leans back against it. On the floor her slippers are neatly lined up in front of the hallstand. It seems weird that they can still be there waiting, unmoved, unchanged, just where she left them when she went out. When something extraordinary happens as it has today, she thinks, you expect everything to be changed by it, but of course it's not, everything is just the same, at least on the surface.

She slips off her coat and shakes it lightly over the doormat before hanging it on the hallstand. Then she sits down on the mustard velvet upholstery of the chair in the corner and, using a buttonhook that she keeps here for the purpose, she begins to undo the buttons that run up the sides of her crimson leather boots. Each time she does this she marvels that she is still wearing the boots which are nearly as old as she is and once belonged to her mother. They've been repaired of course, re-soled and heeled many times, and ten years ago she had to have some of the buttons and hooks replaced. It was hard to find a shoemaker able to do the job, but when she did find one, down a narrow laneway in Balaclava, he'd been so delighted to see such a beautiful old pair of boots that he'd also done some expert polishing on the toe leather, and fitted some arch supports. That is the point of quality, she thinks, things last, and if you also buy good design it never goes out of fashion.

She puts the boots down beside the chair, wiggles her toes and rotates both ankles. The downside of the boots is their discomfort, but they make her feel glamorous which is important at her age, especially on her birthday. Leaving the boots in the hall to dry, Vinka slips on the black satin slippers that Patrick brought back for her from a trip to Beijing five years ago, pads through to the lounge and stands for a moment by the French windows looking out across the rooftops to the tall buildings of the city.

It is still raining but not cold, and she opens the narrow wooden framed doors onto the black and white tiles, and leans against the balustrade that encloses the balcony, thinking, just thinking. It is a frustrating sort of thinking because she doesn't really know *what* to think, her mind just keeps churning over what has happened. Suppose Beate had been there – what then? What would she have done, what would she be saying now, what might happen next? But of the four people sitting around the table she, Vinka, had been the only one that had any idea of the true situation. She was the only one of the four of them who had done anything more than have a delicious lunch, in a small Polish restaurant in Carlton, in very pleasant company. But for Vinka everything changed when those two women walked in. Maybe it won't matter, she thinks, maybe this secret knowledge will remain a secret – after all, why shouldn't it, why worry? Perhaps there will be no uncomfortable decisions, no consequences, but on the other hand . . .

In the shocking moment of recognition Vinka had thought she might faint. She remembers staring at that face, so familiar from newspaper photographs, and asking Patrick how he had found her. He'd looked completely taken aback.

'Find her? Dot, d'you mean? I tracked her down online actually.'

'He's very pushy. In the nicest possible way of course,' Dot had added then, reaching out to shake hands. 'We had a wonderful conversation about the things we're both interested in, media, writing, politics, all that sort of thing. And I bored him stiff with stories from the past.'

'And I said please come to lunch and meet my aunty.'

'He said a few other things as well,' Dot had said, sliding into the chair Patrick was holding out for her. 'He asked me to go and give a talk to his students, and since then it's grown to two talks. He's very pushy your nephew. Anyway, Win, I'm delighted to meet you. Happy birthday!' And she had handed her a small parcel wrapped in silver tissue. 'Something for your collection. Patrick says you collect decoupage.'

As Vinka replays the last few hours in her mind it's hard to recall the conversations. Something was said about Dot's friend Margot and why she was there, and then Patrick had poured some very good French champagne, they had drunk to her health and Vinka had opened the parcel. It was an exquisite black lacquered wooden bangle with a decoupage design of gold and orange flowers and unusual symbols.

'But it's beautiful,' she'd said, 'and too much. I mean, I hardly know you . . . well . . . I feel I know you from reading everything you wrote – my sister and I, we followed you always – but a gift like this . . . too much.'

'I'm glad you like it,' Dot said. 'I brought it back from India. A friend there makes them.'

By this time Vinka had more or less recovered, although she was still thinking of Beate – suppose *she* had been here, what would have happened then? What a disaster that could have been. But the two women were so nice, so easy to talk to, and Patrick was so obviously delighted with the result of his birthday secret that she slowly began to relax and enjoy the company and the fuss they were all making of her birthday.

'Eighty!' Margot had said. 'I don't believe it, you look so young. Have you always lived in Melbourne?'

'Since nineteen fifty-one,' Vinka had explained. 'I came here from Poland with my mother and my sister Beate. I was twenty-three and Beate just eighteen, post-war resettlement – many of us came then from Eastern Europe.'

'But your name is English – Win, Winifred . . .' Margot said.

'It is Patrick calls me Win when he is just small,' Vinka said, smiling at him. 'I am Vinka, after my grandmother.'

And then it felt, quite suddenly, as if they knew each other, as if they were old friends, as though it might be okay to relax and just enjoy her birthday after all, enjoy the conversation and the company. Vinka is usually inclined to keep herself to herself; there are a few old friends from the Polish club and a couple of women she worked with in the sixties, but these days they talk only about the price of things, the bad behaviour of young people, and about getting old – aches and pains, and funeral plans. But lunch was different; they talked about music, books and history, the sort of conversation she usually only ever has with Patrick. It had felt a little like the old days, when she and Beate had begun to make friends here, when there was so much to do, so many places to go and a whole new life seemed to stretch in front of them. And now here she is, back in her own little flat in this lovely old building which feels like a little piece of Europe, and she has promised to meet them, Dot and Margot, next week. They will have afternoon tea and go together to the art deco exhibition at the gallery.

Vinka steps back inside from the balcony and takes a black Sobranie from the enamelled box on the table beside her, lights it, inhales deeply and sits down in her favourite chair. They are such an indulgence these cigarettes, so expensive, but she has smoked them for decades and rations herself now to two a day, although today's events seem to merit this extra one. Leaning back, she watches as the smoke from her cigarette curls upwards and is captured by the breeze from the open balcony doors. Perhaps, after all, none of it matters, she thinks, perhaps it is all too long ago, perhaps there really is nothing to worry about. Why not enjoy this?

'And what do *you* think, Beate?' she asks aloud of the framed and faded photograph on the table. 'What would you have me do?' But Beate is gone, ten years gone, leaving her alone with the secret and its awful responsibility. 'Perhaps I am just too old to worry about this,' Vinka says. And she takes another long draw on her cigarette and closes her eyes, savouring the rich fullness of the flavour and the memories it always brings of a time when she was young and beautiful, and anything, absolutely anything, seemed possible.

∞

Emma is engaged in the search for the perfect handbag. It's something she does frequently and she has a cupboard full of bags to prove it. It is, she thinks, a strange fact of life that you never have the right bag; it is either too large or too small, or it would be perfect if it had one handle instead of two, or two instead of one, or a shoulder strap you could clip on, or a cross strap that didn't look weird where it crossed between your boobs, or would be perfect with more bling or less, or without the leather tassels that make it look like a Dolly Parton cast-off. It's not just her, she knows that, there are thousands of women who understand the lure of the bag; it's seduction with the promise that it will change your life. It's the smell of the leather, the strength and softness of the feel, the subtlety or the richness of the colour and, like magic, credit cards self-eject from wallets into the hands of sales assistants.

The bag is wrapped in another bag, a cloth one with a drawstring and a logo, and placed inside a carrier bag made of thick, glossy card with silky cord handles. And Emma knows only too well the next stage: the race to the nearest coffee shop or toilet to transfer the contents of the old bag into the new one, stuffing the cast-off into the carrier bag.

Transformation! It is always *the* bag, the one she has always wanted, always needed, the bag to end all bags. It says something elegant and sophisticated about any woman who carries it, and yet, so soon the love affair is over. The bag doesn't work, it just isn't quite right. Today's quest is the triumph of hope over experience; in fact Emma's belief that she will one day find the perfect bag is stronger than ever today because she is not in Melbourne but in Sydney: different shops, different feeling, different bags and she is here with her credit card and time to spare.

The sales and marketing meeting had not figured largely in Emma's plans until the Monday morning after Donald's collapse. As soon as she had called the journalist at the Sunday paper to deal with the debacle over the mad woman with the chains, Emma had gone straight to the director of marketing and public relations and announced that she would like to take seven days' annual leave and stay on in Sydney when the conference finished. The promise of escape, although still weeks away, had kept her going through the harrowing visits to the hospital, the tedium of watching her aunt's knitting grow (knitting, for god's sake – what was that about?), and then the shock of Donald's heart attack and the subsequent gloom and anxiety. Emma found it all too much; Phyllida was off the planet and Margot was being both noble and resentful at the same time. The whole scene in the hospital room was weird and suffocating and there appeared to be no end in sight.

Emma knows that both her mother and her aunt have rumbled her on the duration of the sales conference, and in consequence the edges of her blessed escape are now singed with guilt and embarrassment. But here she is, a week later, searching for a bag and with no frantic calls for a mercy dash back to Melbourne. Time is still on her side, which is a good thing because right now Emma needs time – time to recover, because she is not looking her best. She is, in fact, looking dreadful: hiding behind an oversized pair of fake Christian Dior sunglasses, much too big for her small face, her lips swollen in a trout pout. She just knows that everyone is staring at her right now, thinking how weird she looks, until fleetingly she glimpses her reflection as she passes a shop window. Do the scarf and sunglasses along with the pout actually make her look like a celebrity in disguise? But no; she just looks . . . well, odd – or as though she is hiding a huge hangover and a bad haircut. Normally Emma wouldn't dream of going anywhere but to her usual beauty therapist in South Yarra, but getting some treatments had seemed like a good way to use her time in Sydney. The concierge had recommended a salon which was a favourite with the hotel's clients and so she'd booked in for a Botox top-up on her frown lines, and a permanent lip liner tattoo and colour.

As she had settled back into the reclining chair to the soothing background music of pan pipes and harp mixed with the sounds of a waterfall, Emma thought she had died and gone to heaven. In a couple of hours, less even, she would be transformed; full, sculpted lips filled with rich colour would make her look so much younger.

'Have you considered the permanent eyeliner?' Rachelle, the beauty technician, asked, drawing on a pair of latex gloves. 'You see, the lip treatments will give your mouth greater definition, terrific definition in fact, but that might make your eyes sort of, well . . . you know, disappear. They *are* rather small.' Rachelle handed her a mirror. 'Imagine your face with full, colourful, well-defined lips, but with these rather small eyes. Is that a look you want? How about I just show you the eyeliner tattoo colours?'

Five minutes later Emma had signed up for the eye treatment as well, and she leaned back again, wishing she'd brought some Valium with her. Lips were supposed to be painful but eyes even worse. She took several very deep breaths and closed her eyes. 'Okay,' she said, swallowing hard, 'ready when you are.'

'Makeover here we come,' Rachelle said, and she sank the first needle into Emma's top lip. The pain was excruciating and Emma flinched and gasped.

'Oops! You must keep very still,' Rachelle warned, her own artificially plumped and flawless face half hidden behind a surgical mask. 'We don't want an irregular line, do we?'

'I don't think the anaesthetic is working,' Emma said, dabbing her streaming eyes with a tissue and settling back again.

'We don't guarantee it to be a painless process,' Rachelle said curtly, and she plunged the needle in again.

Emma gritted her teeth, gripped the arms of the chair and tried to concentrate on the moment when she would walk out of the salon with gorgeous full and glossy lips and huge, seductive eyes.

'No pain without gain,' Rachelle said. Emma resisted the temptation to point out the error; an offended Rachelle with a needle in her hand was not an appealing prospect.

'The swelling does take a few days to go down,' the girl on the desk said later as Emma signed the credit card slip for almost three times what her usual therapist would have charged her. 'You'll love it though.' She leaned forward and looked at Emma's pout. 'Rachelle did a really good job. She only started today, you know, you're her first client.'

Emma would not normally be seen dead in fake designer sunglasses, but as she left the salon, eyes bloodshot and burning, lips swollen and throbbing, the display stand at the corner of the street seemed like the answer to her prayer. For fifteen bucks she got the huge black pair with diamante initials on the wide arms. From there she fled to a dark corner of a small café and ordered a bottle of water and a straw. There was no way she could manoeuvre her lips around the rim of a coffee cup, and the thought of hot liquid anywhere near them made her toes curl. Even her forehead felt unusually stiff and painful from the Botox. She considered going back to the hotel to watch movies on the TV but as she got up to leave she was reminded of her irritation with the bag she had bought last month. The prospect of finding a new bag was like swallowing a Valium, incredibly soothing but rich with promise. Peace, calm and a sense of purpose enveloped her and that's when she finished her water and stepped out across the street to David Jones.

Now, almost an hour later, just as she is about to leave the store having exhausted its handbag possibilities, Emma spots a display of cute dolly bags. 'For Little Big Girls' the sign above them reads, 'gorgeous bags for your gorgeous little girl.' The bags are pink and purple velvet, some with fake ostrich trim, sequins and embroidery. In a sudden and uncharacteristic surge of maternal feeling Emma gets out her iPhone and dials Grant's number. It infuriates her that he won't allow Rosie to have a mobile phone; he has even confiscated the pink and silver Nokia that Emma bought her.

'She's too young, it's unnecessary, Em,' he'd said. 'She's only just eight. Stop trying to make her into a teenager. She's just a little girl.'

It is Wendy's influence of course, Emma is sure of that – Wendy with her PhD in political science, and her endless voluntary work for causes from refugees to Chinese black bears, and her collection of healthy sprouting foods and organic vegies. Wendy who, despite the fact that she seems to spend her life in jeans (admittedly well-fitting designer ones), black boots and a selection of black jumpers and t-shirts just like all the other uncool people in the university, still manages to exude style. Emma reckons Grant takes far too much notice of his sister when it comes to Rosie, and Rosie adores her.

'I'll get her for you, Emma,' Wendy says when she answers the phone. And Emma hears her calling Rosie in from the garden.

'I'm making a funeral for a dead bird,' Rosie announces breathlessly, 'so I can't talk to you for a long time.'

'Okay, honey-bun, but I just saw some lovely little bags with sequins and some with feathers. I thought I'd see which you'd like me to bring back for you – you can have pink or purple.'

'Actually, Mummy,' Rosie says, 'I'd rather have a compass, you can get them in the Australian Geographic shop, I saw one the –'

'A compass?'

'Yes, it's how you find directions.'

'I know what a compass is,' Emma says. 'But if I get you one of these bags it'll go beautifully with the dress Aunty Phyl bought you the other week.'

'But I don't *like* that dress,' Rosie wails. 'It's babyish, it has bows on it. Mum, do you know Daddy and I went to see Uncle Donald again and he's *still* asleep, he's been asleep for ages, and he had water running out of his mouth, like spit and stuff, it kept dribbling onto his pyjamas.'

Emma shivers with revulsion. 'Oh dear . . . well, Rosie, sometimes when people are ill they can't –'

'Yes, I know,' Rosie cuts in. 'Grandma told me all that stuff. So can I have a compass? Grandma and I are going to do like an exploration of the Botanic Gardens and draw a map, so I *really* need it. When are you coming home?'

'Thursday evening,' Emma says, picking up the pink bag. 'So we can do something on Saturday if you like.'

'Why are you talking funny?'

'I've had . . . I've got a bit of a sore lip and it hurts when I talk. It'll be better by the weekend. Anyway, darling, you'd best get back to the bird funeral. I'll pick you up on Saturday.' And she blows a kiss down the phone, hangs up and heads for the pay desk. The bag plus a compass should win her some maternal brownie points.

Catching sight of herself in a long mirror she stops and quickly takes off the sunglasses to look more closely at her face; it is a mess – livid, swollen, horrible. Thank goodness no one she knows will see her like this. The delicate skin surrounding her eyes looks bruised and she is about to lean in closer to the mirror to touch it with her finger when, to her horror, she sees another face behind hers in the mirror.

'Em!' Lexie says, 'I thought it was you but whatever happened to your face?'

~∽~

'It lasts forever . . . well, a few years at least,' Emma explains later as they sit on a bench seat near the fountain in Hyde Park, she with another bottle of water and straw, Lexie with a cheese and tomato sandwich and a takeaway latte.

'Mmm,' says Lexie, peering more closely at her sister's lips. 'And what if you don't like it?'

'I will. Of course I will. Don't be so negative, Lex, and anyway, where the hell have you been all this time? Someone from Faraday's said the practice had been wound up – I knew things were bad there, but not that bad.'

'I was hiding,' Lexie says, biting into her sandwich. 'Time out. Aren't you hungry? I could break little bits off it and feed you if you like. You know, like a baby.'

Emma shakes her head and yelps with pain as she catches the drink straw on a particularly sore area of her lower lip. 'Ow! That really hurt.' She presses the chilled water bottle against her lip. 'I'm sorry about the job, Lex, it must be awful. You'd been there forever.'

Lexie sighs. She hadn't expected that it would be Emma with whom she'd have the first conversation about this. 'Ah well. I saw it coming at me but foolishly I pretended I didn't, and along it came and ran me over. So I . . . well, I lost it really . . . couldn't bring myself to tell anyone and cope with their reaction. Most of all I knew everyone would be asking what I was going to do and I would feel ridiculous because I hadn't a clue. . . so I ran away.'

'Well, you didn't run far.'

'I'd have gone much further but once I got here and started thinking about somewhere lovely to go I realised that in my lightning dash from the house I'd forgotten my passport! Hopeless runaway, aren't I?'

'Oh well, p'raps you weren't meant to go further. But what about Ross? Grant ran into him in the supermarket and he said he was moving out.'

Lexie nods. 'I ended it – by email, actually. Modern, aren't I? Should have done it long ago, it's been over for ages really, but neither of us did anything about it. Well actually, *he* did something about it. He started seeing that woman he works with, Carole, you know, with –'

'Yes, I know her, thunder thighs with very short skirts?'

'That's her. Anyway I emailed Ross and told him it was over. I asked him to move out so he's probably gone by now.'

Emma has turned on the seat to look more closely at her sister. 'So are you okay? I mean, Ross was hardly Captain Excitement, but it's a big step just the same.'

'It is; but it's the right step.' Lexie pauses. Emma's apparently genuine concern for her is a side of her sister that she hasn't seen for a very long time and she wonders briefly if it's because of where they are – away from everyone else in the family.

'The night I sent the email I felt this enormous sense of relief,' she says. 'I even opened half a bottle of champagne that was in the mini-bar. And then when I got into bed I started crying and couldn't stop. I felt like a complete failure. My life so far has been a series of relationships that never really made it and fizzled out. I just never get it right. I don't know what it is because everyone else seems to manage it.'

'Not me,' Emma says. 'I made a complete mess of it.'

They sit for a moment in silence. 'Not at first, though,' Lexie says, turning to her. 'For quite a long time you and Grant were going really well. Or at least that's how it looked.'

'We were, until we decided we could make it perfect by having a baby and . . . well, you know what happened.'

'So do you think you and Grant might still be together if you hadn't got pregnant?'

Emma drains the last of her water through the straw and screws the cap back on the bottle. 'Maybe . . . probably. I can't really see why not. It was motherhood I couldn't cope with, not Grant.'

Lexie struggles for the right thing to say, fails to find it and the silence settles on them again, more heavily this time.

'So,' Emma says eventually, 'are you any closer to knowing what you're going to do?'

Lexie shrugs. 'I haven't worked that out yet, although I've been thinking about going back to uni.'

'What, pick up where you left off?'

'No, start again. Something different, but don't say anything at home. I haven't made up my mind. Anyway, what about you, apart from the face disaster?'

'Can you please not use that word,' Emma says, and she explains about the sales conference. 'And so I thought I'd duck out of hospital duty for a while, it was really freaking me out and –'

'Hospital?' Lexie asks through a mouthful of sandwich. 'Who's in hospital?'

'Well, Uncle Donald of course . . . the aneurysm, at the party . . . you mean you didn't know? Mum emailed you.'

Lexie has gone white with shock. 'An aneurysm?'

Emma nods. 'He collapsed at the party. Went to hospital in an ambulance and they did a craniotomy, and he's still unconscious, and then last week he had a heart attack.'

Lexie stares at her sister. 'And he's *still* unconscious?'

'Yep. Aunty Phyl is sitting by his bedside knitting, twelve hours a day, like those women sitting by the guillotine. And Mum's . . . well, you know what she's like, being noble, taking responsibility for everything and looking martyred, cancelling their holiday, trying to organise Phyl into some sort of plan for if he dies, or if he doesn't. But she emailed you with all this.'

'I stopped reading email,' Lexie says quietly, rolling her sandwich wrapping into a ball and tossing it into a nearby bin. 'Come on, we'd better get a taxi.'

'Where are we going?'

'Your hotel and then mine. I'll call the airport while you pack, then we'll pick up my stuff and get the next available flight home.'

'No, Lex!' Emma protests. 'No, please. I can't cope with all that stuff. It freaks me out all that illness and mess and everything.'

'Emma,' Lexie says firmly, gripping her sister's arm and dragging her down the steps to the pavement. 'We are going and we are going *now*. Both of us.' She steps out to hail a taxi. 'We can't leave Mum to cope with this on her own. Even Dad's away. But we *are* going. You are so bloody selfish –'

'Me!' Emma shrieks. 'Me selfish? You're the one who disappeared for weeks.'

'Shut up and get in,' Lexie says, pushing her into the back seat of the cab. 'There's selfish and selfish, and mine is different from yours.' And she climbs into the taxi behind her sister, switches her phone on and dials Margot's number.

EIGHT

The lecture theatre is small but packed, the tiered seating full, and those who have arrived at the last minute are sitting on the steps. Dot, who had imagined a classroom with perhaps twenty people in it, is gobsmacked. She had planned for a casual, interactive session, but the smart little lecture theatre and the sizeable audience suggest an expectation of something rather more formal. Her stomach does a somersault; it is more years than she can remember since she spoke in public, unless you count shouting slogans while chained up at the shopping centre.

'Did you call rent-a-crowd?' she asks with a nervous laugh.

'I just made up a little poster and put it on a few notice-boards,' Patrick says, glancing around the lecture theatre. 'There's been a lot of interest – staff as well as students. When you're ready just give me the nod and I'll introduce you.'

Dot takes a deep breath and nods, and Patrick switches on the microphone and begins his introduction by telling them that she was seventeen when she quit her first job in a record shop after just a couple of months and ran off to Sydney to get a job as a copy girl on the *Sydney Morning Herald*. He mentions the sixties and the Push, the anti-war protests and then the seventies and the women's movement, and he goes on to talk about her as a journalist, a columnist and a broadcaster who began making feminist programs when so much women's radio was still focused on the domestic.

'Dot Grainger's name may be new to *you*,' he says, 'but tell your mother or your grandmother that you met her here today and they will either be fascinated or horrified. They may tell you how they discovered the women's movement through her, that she is their hero and role model, or they may tell you that she is a ratbag troublemaker and a meddlesome woman who never shut up. But one thing's for sure, they'll know her name and one way or the other they'll have an opinion about her.'

Dot's heart thunders against her ribs, her mouth is dry, her throat closing over. This is infinitely worse than she expected; the rows of faces, the heat of the room, the healthy welcoming applause and now expectant silence. Grasping her notes she steps up to the lectern. Way up at the back she can see Margot and Vinka, who have insisted on coming with her. An hour ago she was more than grateful for the moral support, now she is horrified at the prospect of making a fool of herself not only in front of strangers, but in front of an old friend and someone who seems like an important new one. But there is no escape. She rests her notes on the lectern and goes to take her glasses from the chain around her neck, but neither the chain nor the glasses are there. Frantically she pats her pockets, but both are empty and in a dizzying moment of absolute clarity she sees them sitting on the kitchen bench as she walked out of the door.

Dot grips the corners of the lectern and looks at the expectant faces; her notes are useless and her memory is a blank. From the second row a vaguely familiar face looks up at her – a beautiful face with glowing skin and eyes that seem at first blue and then green. The girl breaks into a smile and gives Dot an almost imperceptible nod, and a thumbs up.

Dot hesitates – who *is* she? But it doesn't matter because the smile and the thumb work their magic. Someone out there is rooting for her. She pushes the notes aside, tilts the microphone slightly so she doesn't have to stand on tiptoe and leans in to it.

'Good morning,' she says. 'It's good to be here – or at least it was until a moment ago when I realised I'd forgotten my glasses, so now it's pretty scary.'

A frisson of amusement moves through the audience like a Mexican wave and the warmth of it seems to dissolve her fear and she is back in her comfort zone, connecting with an audience. And with the ease of a conversation among friends she begins with the day when one of the reporters at the *Herald*, now a distinguished and retired political correspondent, took her for a drink at the Royal George in downtown Sydney, home of the libertarians who called themselves the Push.

'It wasn't the most attractive of places,' she says with a laugh, 'thick with cigarette smoke, dense with people and the smell of tobacco, sweat and beer. It was noisy too, loud voices, mostly male, mostly opinionated – even in the Sydney Push it was still very much a man's world. But it was exciting. Ideas, arguments, fierce conversations bounced off the walls. That night I felt I was standing on the threshold of a great adventure. I had wanted to stay on at school and go to university but there was no money, so I was frustrated by a feeling of missing out. That night I saw an alternative route, an escape from ignorance and exclusion. Back in the fifties and sixties, if you wanted to learn you had to grasp every opportunity and try to hang on to it in case it slipped through your fingers, and there I was in Aladdin's cave . . .'

Leaning back in her seat Margot draws a deep breath of relief and rests her head against the carpeted wall. Her own involvement with the Push had begun later than Dot's and her disillusionment had arrived somewhat sooner, but even she feels a shiver of nostalgia as she listens. It is a part of her life that she looks back on, sometimes with pleasure, but more often with ambivalence and sometimes even with distaste. It had certainly been exciting at the start, and it had formed her social conscience, but much of her present discontent seems to stem from that time and place.

On the other side of the lecture theatre Margot sees Grant's sister, Wendy, and discreetly lifts a hand in greeting. Margot likes Wendy, she thinks she is very good for Rosie. Emma had once accused Margot of thinking that Wendy was a better mother to Rosie than she was. Margot had denied it forcefully, more forcefully than she might have done had it not been true.

Dot is talking now about how things worked in the Push, how people wrote and delivered papers, the discussions that followed and those endless debates that went on day after day. 'Intellectual wankery,' Laurence had called it once, years later, when they had all fallen into various states of disenchantment. At the time it had seemed as though they were at the cutting edge of social change; those conversations in smoky bars, or the coffee house, were the beginning of a new world. But for Margot, whose dreams failed to materialise, the memories are tempered with disappointment. It is easier for her now to remember the seedier side of the sexual life of the Push, the arrogance, the intellectual bullying and the frustration of so much talk and so little action.

'In the early postwar years people were exploring ideas of society and democracy,' Dot is saying now. 'They were moving from passivity and acquiescence to questioning the authenticity of what they were told by institutions like the government and the church, rejecting established ideas that seemed to entrench privilege. This,' she says, 'is the climate that gave birth to the Push.'

'She is very good, yes?' Vinka whispers, leaning closer so that the scent of Russian tobacco tickles Margot's nostrils. 'I am impressed. She is like she is being a lecturer all her life. This I am finding most interesting.'

'Yes, she's *very* good,' Margot whispers back. 'I'd forgotten *how* good, and I think she had too.'

Watching Dot now, Margot knows that she is not watching the Dot of the Push years but of the seventies onward, when her fierce energy and rhetoric found its purpose in the women's movement. The Push had been her training ground; there she had been a sponge, soaking up knowledge and ideas. She remembers Dot as she first saw her, huddled in a smoky corner of the Royal George, deep in conversation with two men whose names she can't now remember. The intensity of her concentration was so obvious that it was intimidating. Later that same evening she saw her again, this time at a party, dancing with Laurence. It was before Margot and Laurence had met but she had seen him several times and felt then a sharp jolt of jealousy to see him so deeply involved with this small eccentric woman with her dyed burgundy hair and fierce expression. They were dancing close, wrapped around each other, and later, sitting on the stairs together, they smoked and argued with the force of intimacy.

It was later, almost ten years later, by which time Margot was having her own intimate arguments with Laurence, that Dot emerged as one of the leaders of the women's movement, writing her column, organising marches and demonstrations, speaking out on women's rights from the steps of Parliament House, and taking on politicians in radio debates. Before that, as the Push was fading, she had disappeared in much the same way as she had recently, first to some unspecified job up near Byron Bay and then apparently travelling, making her way as a freelancer, her stories sometimes popping up in the newspapers from unexpected places. It was in 1970 when Margot met up with her again. Laurence had been offered a lectureship in Melbourne, and they moved from the flat in Sydney to a small terrace house in Richmond. Lexie was almost nine by then and Emma a toddler. There had been another pregnancy before Emma but it had ended in a late and painful miscarriage and now the move back to her home town had made Margot feel that her life was back on track again, but she missed the friends she had made in Sydney, women who were talking politics and wanting action.

'Can you ask around at uni or look on the notice boards?' she'd asked Laurence. 'There must be a women's group I could go to.' A week later he came home one evening with a name and a phone number. A few days later, with Emma in a pusher, Margot walked into a consciousness-raising group in Carlton and found herself face to face with Dot once again.

'You're back!' she'd said in delight. 'And you're here – in Melbourne.'

'The bad penny always turns up,' Dot had said, hugging her. 'I thought you two were still in Sydney. And who's this?' she'd asked, bending over the pusher.

Emma had taken one look at Dot and immediately burst into tears.

'These are very famous people she talks of,' Vinka whispers now. 'I know of them but until now I don't know of this Push club. All these years in Australia and I am still so ignorant.'

Margot shakes her head, leaning closer. 'No, not at all. It was very much a Sydney thing and the people Dot's talking about now – Germaine Greer, Clive James, Robert Hughes – those people made names for themselves later. The Push may have motivated them but their success was individual. That's true of Dot too, it was some years later that she made a name for herself.'

'We were libertarians,' Dot is explaining, 'and anarchists. People assume that the word anarchist describes someone who is not only socially and politically disruptive but also violent, rather like a terrorist, and of course history is full of examples of anarchists who were just like that. But the Push had a code of non-violence. We were intellectual anarchists and that's a very attractive thing to be when you're young. It means you don't have to be responsible for anything. You're a free thinker, you advocate freedom for everyone, and you live your life as freely as possible. In the fifties and sixties this was the only intellectual social life to be found in Sydney. It was diametrically opposed to everything we'd been brought up with; it was vivid colour after the drab greyness of the postwar years. It was intellectual and sexual freedom and it was very seductive.'

A hand was raised in the audience and Dot nodded.

'But what did the Push actually *do*?'

'Well, sadly, not a lot,' Dot says slowly, looking out across the room. 'By the late sixties I had abandoned the Push due to disenchantment. I was tired of talk and wanted action. On reflection I think its value lay in what followed – what individual people did post-Push. We took what we'd learned there to other areas, to academia, government, social reform. I took mine to journalism and the women's movement. It's hard to measure something like that – it was an education and education finds its way into all areas of your life, and to others through you. I like to think that it was valuable, that in this way, at least, we did something worthwhile.'

A young woman sitting at the back of the lecture theatre raises her hand. 'What about the sexual freedom?' she asks. 'I read somewhere that the Push was all about free love. Can you tell us about that?'

There is a rustle of renewed interest in the lecture theatre and Dot laughs.

'Well yes, I can tell you a bit about that. The Push did advocate sexual freedom and that was really radical. Theoretically everyone was equal – the women had the same sexual freedom as the men – but that freedom seemed to be measured by having a *lot* of sex rather than whether it was physically and emotionally satisfying. There was a lot of talk about it, but I don't think anyone talked about what they really wanted or needed sexually. Sexual freedom in the Push, as in the broader sexual revolution of the late sixties, made more women available to men, but it was still the men who called the tune. It made it easier for women to say yes, but harder to say no, because it seemed unfriendly. It was all a bit mundane really. And it was largely the women who took responsibility for contraception and who usually found themselves on their own if they got pregnant.'

'You were brilliant,' Patrick says later as he steers Dot out of the lecture theatre. 'See, I told you they love the personal experience, it brings the history and the theory to life.'

'It did seem to go well,' Dot says, elated but attempting modesty. 'And they seemed to have stayed awake.'

'Awake and attentive,' says a voice behind them, and Dot turns to see the girl from the second row smiling at her again. 'Hi, I'm Alyssa, that was really interesting.'

'Thank *you*,' Dot says. 'Your thumb came up at just the right moment. Have we met before?'

Alyssa shakes her head. 'No, but I feel as though I know you. We live in the same street. I often run past your house in the mornings.'

'Of course,' Dot says, fitting the face to the figure in a tracksuit or shorts waving to her as she passes the gate. 'You wear those headphones. Well it's nice to meet you, Alyssa.'

'I saw that article in the Sunday paper a few weeks ago.'

Dot pulls a face. 'Embarrassing.'

'No, no! It was interesting. I wondered ... there's something I'd like to talk to you about, a campaign we've started ...'

Margot, Vinka and Wendy are bearing down on them now making lunch signs, and Dot waves and nods. 'I'm sorry, I missed that,' she says, turning back to Alyssa. 'You wanted to talk to me?'

'Yes, could I pop in some time? I'd really like the chance to tell you about this.'

Dot, bathed in the glow of success, succumbs to the gratification of generosity even as she suspects she'll regret it later. 'Of course,' she says, grasping Alyssa's hand, 'but not before ten o'clock. I'm not up to much earlier in the day.'

Dot thinks she has never been as tired in all her life as she is this afternoon. Since Margot and Vinka dropped her home after lunch she has sat here in her chair, looking guiltily out over the garden that is dying of neglect. That morning in the lecture theatre, once she'd really got going, she'd felt sharp again, energetic, absolutely on top of her game. It was the adrenaline rush of fear that did it, of course, fear of embarrassment, fear of sounding like a dotty old woman in front of a crowd of younger people.

'I don't know why I'm so tired,' she'd said from the back seat of Margot's car on the way home. 'Not so long ago I'd have been able go back to work after something like that.'

'It *is* actually a long time ago, Dot,' Margot had said. 'And none of us are getting any younger. We're old women.'

'But inside we are the same,' Vinka said. 'The same but different. We are young inside, I think, but we do not want the same things as when we are young. It is nice not to want so much.'

'I don't know about that,' Dot had said. 'Sometimes I just want everything I always wanted, absolutely everything.'

'No!' Vinka had laughed. 'You want a boyfriend, Dot? You want a man in the bed, or waiting for you to make the dinner?'

'Lord no!' Dot shrieked. 'Not that. Thank god I don't have to do all that stuff again.'

'It is a relief really, isn't it?' Margot said, catching Dot's eye in the driving mirror as she pulled up at the traffic lights. 'When you're young you worry so much about losing what you've got – looks, I mean, sexual attractiveness. It feels as though life will stop when all that disappears, and then you get to a point where you couldn't give a shit anymore.'

'And all you can think of is the time – weeks, months, even years of your life you've wasted on trying to hang on to it,' Dot agreed. 'Time you could have spent doing much more interesting things.'

Vinka nodded, half turning in her seat to look at Dot. 'Yes, but it is nice still to dress up, I think, to look good. We are old women, but smart. What do they say? Funky, we are funky old women.'

Dot smiles now, remembering how the three of them had laughed at the idea of being funky. Margot is right of course, it's stupid to expect to be able to do at seventy-five what one was doing in one's thirties or even fifties. The important thing, Dot thinks, is to enjoy what one *can* do, to be totally in the present and not constantly trying to grasp at what used to be. She sits forward in her chair to watch a couple of birds hopping around the birdbath. 'But there are things it would be fun to do again,' she says aloud, and the birds hear something through the glass, cock their heads towards her and take off. Flirting, she thinks, flirting was fun.

She leans back again and closes her eyes, remembering the thrill of a man moving in close to light a cigarette, eyes meeting over the flame, the intoxication of mutual desire. And then the word games, the signals, the gestures, the smouldering eye contact across a crowded room, and the dancing. Oh yes, the dancing! Dot sighs, recalling the intimacy of a hand resting just a little lower than the small of her back, the heat of a body moving against her own, a rough cheek and warm breath on her neck. She wonders vaguely how many men she has danced with in her lifetime and whether she will ever dance with one again. It seems pretty unlikely. And how many has she slept with? More than she'd admit to if asked, but that was all a very long time ago. Slowly she tries to summon them up but there are faces without names, names without faces, and then those she really remembers, with either distaste or pleasure, with shame or affection.

Laurence stands out of course, because the memory is preserved by their ongoing friendship. He and one other left their imprint on her life. It's a good thing, Dot thinks, that she never kept a journal – reputations would have been at stake, her own included. And now Laurence is on a pilgrimage and, according to a card Margot showed her, is suffering from bleeding blisters and diarrhoea. Dot laughs softly: poor Laurence, he had good feet for dancing and she remembers too how it felt to dance with him, to be in his arms, knowing that very soon she would be in his bed. She remembers a party, low lights, Sinatra on the record player and a young woman she didn't know watching them, her and Laurence, with a sort of hunger. In that moment Dot had felt a brief and triumphant sense of ownership; it was fleeting of course, monogamy was not a characteristic of Push men. Margot had got what she had wanted and what a disaster that turned out to be.

NINE

'What a relief to be out of there,' Margot says as she and Lexie stop off for a walk and a coffee at the Boatshed Café on their way back from the hospital. 'I don't know how Phyl can bear it but she won't budge. How long do you think they'll let this go on?'

Lexie shrugs. 'Hard to tell, but not much longer I suspect.'

Margot nods and they walk in silence along the path, disturbing a flock of seagulls that rise in unison heading out over the choppy water. 'I was going to say it feels as though everything has come to a standstill waiting for Donald, but of course it hasn't.' She hesitates, choosing her words carefully. 'Rosie, who has a particularly good nose for news for one so young, tells me you're going back to university.'

'Ah!' Lexie says. 'Sorry about that, I *was* going to tell you myself, this morning actually.'

'She blurted it out while we were doing our survey of the Botanic Gardens,' Margot says. 'Naturally I pumped her shamelessly for details but you know Rosie, she only provides the headlines. Was it a secret?'

'Not really a secret,' Lexie says. 'Rosie must have overheard me talking to Wendy. I wanted to get some advice from her and make up my mind before I told anyone.'

'And have you?'

'I think so. You know, Mum, if the practice hadn't collapsed I would probably have stayed in the same rut, but it happened and now I'm forty-eight and unemployed, and it can either be a disaster or a chance to start again. Do something new.'

'Would you do the same degree?'

Lexie shakes her head. 'No. I know I did well in the sciences at school but it wasn't what I was most interested in. I'm going to do art history.'

'Art history?' Margot stops walking and turns to her. 'Lexie, how wonderful. It's been your passion for so long. Of course that's what you should do.'

'Really? You don't think I should be a bit more responsible, go for something vocational where I can get a job when I graduate? After all, by then I'll be over fifty. I'll get something part-time of course . . . while I'm studying.'

Margot laughs and slips her hand through Lexie's arm as they walk on. 'I'm sure you will, and you've spent more than twenty-five years being hugely responsible in every way. Now it's time to do something you really want to do. I'm delighted, Lex, really I am, and your dad will be too. Will you get any credit for what you did before?'

'Probably not, it's too long ago. But Wendy's arranging for me to talk to a colleague of hers at university to get some advice. Oh look! There's a table free on the deck. You grab it and I'll go and order the coffee. Will you be warm enough out here?'

Margot nods and claims the table, watching as Lexie disappears inside the café. It's such a relief to have her back, and not just back home but more like the old Lexie, the one she was before Ross, before she embarked on the struggle of trying to make that relationship work. Well now she has the chance to start again and no one, in Margot's opinion, deserves it more.

'I'll have to get a part-time job,' Lexie says, bringing the coffee back to the table, 'but I'll be okay. All these years I've been putting my money away and now I feel as though I know what I was saving for. So you really think it's a good idea?'

'The best. And we always said we'd go to Florence together, so now we absolutely have to!'

'We certainly do. But first of all we just have to hope they'll let me in.'

'Of course they'll let you in,' Margot says, scooping the froth from her cappuccino. 'I'm so pleased for you; it's the next best thing to doing it myself. I always wanted to go back and finish my degree.'

'So why didn't you?' Lexie asks. 'I mean, I know you dropped out when you got pregnant with me, but couldn't you have gone back later, when Em and I were at school?'

Margot shrugs. 'It wasn't that easy. Laurence and Bernard were in Europe and I was on my own with you and Emma. It was all a bit of a struggle. I did think about it in the late seventies after Whitlam abolished university fees. There were a lot of women my age who went back then and I actually got accepted.'

'I remember that now,' Lexie says. 'I remember you talking about it and asking me how I'd feel if my mum was a student.'

'That's right.'

'What did I say?'

Margot smiles. 'You were horrified. You said you'd be terribly embarrassed and you wouldn't know what to tell your friends.'

Lexie groans and hides her face in her hands. 'Oh, Mum, I'm so sorry. How awful of me. That wasn't what stopped you though, was it?'

'No,' Margot says, laughing now. 'I thought you'd survive the embarrassment. What stopped me was the money, or rather the lack of it. Laurence was paying maintenance but Emma wasn't far off high school and you were a teenager and planning on going to uni yourself. I think I was just kidding myself when I applied; I needed to keep working. I was working for Derek Matthews at the time, the lawyer, do you remember him? He was a lovely man and it was a good job with decent pay. It was him who pushed me to do that paralegal training in the eighties, a bit like Dr Faraday sending you on the management course, so I just stayed on there and kept working.'

'And you never made it back to finish the degree.'

'No, too late now.'

'You must have felt terrible when I dropped out.'

'Oh well, it was a bit disappointing but I kept hoping you'd go back. And now you are. And what about Ross? You're still sure you did the right thing?'

'Absolutely sure,' Lexie says. 'The right thing for both of us.'

'You've seen him then?'

Lexie nods, and sips her coffee. 'He rang and asked if he could come by and pick up a few things he'd left in the garage. It was really weird, we actually had a proper conversation, something we hadn't done for ages. I think we were both just relieved that we didn't have to pretend anymore.'

'So, no regrets?'

'No. But I do feel quite sad about wasted time, and about the fact that I've got to this age and still can't get the relationship thing right.'

'You've got plenty of time,' Margot says. 'And you know, Lex, some people are actually better on their own. Being single has quite a lot going for it. Anyway, there are other things to think about now – being a student again, what a challenge that'll be.'

Laurence seeks out a flat shelf of rock near the lighthouse and sits on it. It's a relief to get away from the rest of the party. Tempers have been wearing thin over the past weeks and exhaustion, blisters, cuts, torn muscles and aching limbs are only a part of it. It's the sociability. Friendships pushed to the limits by too much time spent together in strange and difficult circumstances, but most of all, he thinks, it's the Camino itself; the very nature of the country, the tracks, the history and the traditions around it do seem, inevitably, to create the sense of a pilgrimage. Even those, like Laurence himself, who began as sceptics seem to surrender to it as though recognising that it really was the emotional and spiritual challenges that brought them here. It's decades since Laurence gave up on religion and started speaking of himself as a humanist, but now he's not so sure. There's something about the places they've passed through, the peaceful villages, the cool and silent interiors of the churches at dawn, the swish of cassocks and rosary beads, the incense curling blue-white above altars, the stillness of the countryside. And there's the obvious, unapologetic faith of the people – the locals and the pilgrims themselves, their commitment, their respect for the journey and what it means, people doing this for the third or fourth or, in a couple of cases, the eighth time – that has made him think again. From the end of the first week, as he struggled with pain, exhaustion and many dark nights of the soul, Laurence has felt himself drawn into the spiritual power of the Camino, and its consolations and challenges have made him question what he does indeed believe.

He leans back again against the rock enjoying the silence and the cold salt wind off the ocean. Finisterre. The edge of the world some guide books call it, the most westerly point of Europe: *finis terre*, the end of the land. Before him the ocean stretches westward to the coast of America. He had thought he might have to give up once they made it to Santiago, the final destination of pilgrims, but once there he knew he wanted this, this strange remote fishing village perched high above the Atlantic on the edge of the continent. Somehow he'd convinced himself that if he made it here it would be a significant marker – an epilogue to his life with Bernard, a sign that it was time to start again. And so, he thinks, he will leave it here, the burden of loss and sadness, and when he turns away from the ocean to the land a new stage begins, the solitary life which he must now learn to live after almost half a century of being a husband and then a partner. Tomorrow a bus will take them back to Santiago and from there a coach trip and the start of the tedious airborne journey home.

'One hundred bucks,' Griff says, appearing alongside him and choosing a slightly lower level of rock. 'I suppose I'll have to pay up. I honestly never thought you'd make it, mate. I thought we'd be shipping you off home by the end of the first week.'

'To be honest so did I,' Laurence admits. 'In fact I was desperate for an excuse to escape in the first few days, but pride got the better of me.'

Griff nods, looking out across the ocean. 'Thought so, but I've got to hand it to you, Laurence, as the least fit, most underprepared person in the group you've made a fist of it. Better than some of the others.'

'Odd, isn't it,' Laurence says, 'the effect it has, the power of it. I feel changed by having done this.'

'I said that to Sheila just this morning,' Griff says. 'And she said "Oh you'll soon forget all about it when you get back home." But I'm not so sure. I've thought about things, felt things these past weeks on the road that I've never thought about or felt before. I don't *want* to forget about it.' He clears his throat and his voice is gruffer when he speaks again. 'I want to use it . . . for the future . . . for as much of it as we have left at this age.'

In all the years he's known Griff, Laurence has heard him talk about almost everything. He could probably recite

Griff's views on foreign policy, the future of China, the need to develop a nuclear power industry and everything that's wrong about soccer and right about Aussie rules, but he's never heard him talk like this before.

'That's just it,' he says. 'And you know what? From the minute I got that sense of what I was really doing, I wished I'd done it years ago. But now that it's over I'm glad I did it now, when I can appreciate it in a way that I think I could only do at this age.'

'Last chance,' Griff nods. 'Know what you mean.'

They sit in silence for a moment and Griff lights up a small cigar. The bluish smoke drifts past Laurence reviving a memory of Bernard, years earlier when he was only in his thirties, reluctantly accepting a cigar pressed on him by a colleague in a Prague café, and almost passing out as he took his first draw.

'Anyway, Laurence,' Griff says, 'a bet's a bet. Will you have it in dollars or euros?'

Laurence hesitates, thinking, and he's about to tell Griff to forget about it and then he changes his mind. 'Euros, please. I'll match it with the same amount and we'll put it in the collection box in the church in Santiago, a parting gift. I think it would be a good way to wind things up.'

∽

'They all look so young!' Lexie says, glancing around at the students wandering the paths with backpacks and spreading themselves across the low stone walls and seats beneath the trees. 'Some of them look as though they should still be in Year Ten.'

'Mmm,' Wendy agrees, 'and frankly that's where some of them belong! But I think it's more a sign that we're getting old.'

They are on their way from Wendy's office to meet her colleague in the café and Lexie is suddenly daunted by the size of the place and the casual confidence of the young people around her. 'Don't remind me!' she says, her own confidence sinking lower by the minute. 'I'm going to stick out like a sore thumb if I do this.'

Wendy stops walking and turns to look at her. 'You won't, I promise.' She glances around, craning her neck to get a better view, and then points towards the library building. 'Look,' she says, putting her hand on Lexie's arm, 'over there, that woman on the steps of the library, the one in the green shirt – see her?'

Lexie looks to where she is pointing and sees a woman with long grey hair and a backpack sitting on the steps talking to a couple of younger women.

'Enid,' Wendy says. 'She's sixty-four and five years ago she was doing just what you're doing now. Her husband had just left her for a thirty-two-year-old nail technician with plastic breasts, so her confidence was at zero and she was very fragile. I really don't know how she got herself here to enrol but she did and she stuck with it; started from scratch like you, and now she's onto her PhD. You won't be on your own, Lex, there's plenty like you. Every class you take you'll find two or three mature-age students and they're most likely to be older than you.'

Lexie watches Enid, talking and laughing now with a couple of young men who have joined her and her companions. It's obvious that she fits easily in this group, seems, in fact, to be at the heart of it. She stretches her arms behind her head, picks up her hair, twists it into a knot and fixes it in place with a chunky clip taken from her bag, then moves off with them up the steps and into the library. Lexie struggles to visualise herself on those steps, with that same confidence, the same air of fitting in, but somehow she can't quite see it. It's not only the predominance of all these smart young things, so much smarter, she is sure, than she is, and with the advantage of recent study experience under their belts, but it's also the numbers and the way they are wandering vaguely around the campus. There is no sense of order.

'And don't think these guys are smarter than you because they're young,' Wendy says, as though reading her mind. 'They're not, and they're often paralysed by shyness, and really worried about looking stupid and uncool. You'll be surprised, Lex. Most of the older people who enrol totally underestimate the value of life experience in a university, but the younger students recognise it and appreciate it. Despite what you see the classroom is where the age barriers really will dissolve – if you let them.'

Lexie nods, not entirely convinced, and they walk on, weaving their way between the students chatting in groups, or strolling alone, their ears glued to mobile phones or plugged into their iPods. It seems chaotic, such a culture shock. She had been telling herself that going to uni would also bring shape and order to her life, the sort of order that she was used to at the Faraday practice. But of course it's not like that at all. At Faraday's she created and maintained the order, she had employed and trained the administration staff, she had run the place like clockwork, and even the nurses and partners did as they were told on things relating to the organisation and running of the place. She was, as they'd constantly told her, an outstanding business manager and manager of people, but she wouldn't be managing anything here except herself, and for a moment Lexie pauses at the edge of the brick path, stunned by her own naivety. At Faraday's the only really unmanageable elements in terms of her responsibilities were the patients, and even they were to some extent manageable, dependent as they were on the goodwill of the admin and nursing staff and anxious to gain access to the doctors. This huge, unruly place, the systems, the timetables, the people who work here, is another world, one in which she will have no control, and the prospect is completely unnerving.

'You okay?' Wendy asks, glancing up at her. 'You've gone a bit pale.'

'It's just . . . well, I'm realising how totally different life will be if I come here. How different I'll have to be.'

'Well that's what you wanted, isn't it?' Wendy says. 'New start, new direction? And stop saying "if". You're coming, and you're going to love it.'

Lexie manages a smile. 'If you say so, *mein führer*.'

Wendy laughs and takes her arm. 'Sorry, I don't mean to bully you, but I really do believe this is right for you. You'll love it and you'll do really well. Anyway, what about the rest of your life – Ross, have you seen him?'

'Only once,' Lexie says, and relates the occasion of his visit as she had done to Margot. 'I think he's as relieved as I am that it's over, and over in a civilised way.'

'Really? Not too civilised, I hope – after all, he *was* cheating on you.'

Lexie shrugs. 'Oh well, that's history now and, like you said, a new start. But what about you? No one gorgeous on the horizon?'

'I wish! Oh there he is,' Wendy says, spotting her quarry at a nearby table. 'No, I swear this must be the only campus in Australia that's full of straight women. Not another dyke in sight, with the exception of the vice chancellor, and she's not my type. Besides, she wouldn't fancy me if I threw myself naked at her feet. Here we are, Patrick, sorry we're late. I got caught up on the phone. Lexie, this is my colleague, Patrick Kelly; and, Patrick, this is my friend Lexie, who's thinking of enrolling. At least she *was* until she set foot on campus, so I need you to reassure her that it's not as intimidating as it looks.'

'It certainly isn't,' Patrick says, getting to his feet and shaking hands with Lexie. 'It's actually much worse, but Wendy and I are experts in the art of pretending we understand it. Great to meet you, Lexie. I've met Grant and the formidable

Rosie a few times, and a couple of weeks ago I met your mother when she was here with Dot Grainger, so I seem to be working my way through the family. Who's next, I wonder?'

⁓

Several days have passed since Margot's conversation with Lexie but the emotional aftermath still haunts her. It niggles at her as she drags a bag of potting mix out onto the back verandah and tips the contents into the waiting pots. It interferes with the pleasure of pressing the moist compost around the roots of the geraniums and finally, unable to concentrate on what she is doing, she straightens up, pushes her hair back from her face streaking it with traces of compost, and stands, hands on hips, looking out at the garden. It's taken decades of hard work for her to end up owning this small weatherboard cottage and it's been worth the struggle, but now that she does own it not a month seems to go by without the need for some sort of repair or maintenance. It is frequently too hot or too cold, new draughts or leaks appear as if by magic, but she loves it, and on days like this, when the sun fills the house with light and the garden seems to sigh with joy after the first autumn rain, the gaps in the skirting, the flaking paint and the clunky noises in the plumbing don't seem to matter. What *does* matter is that she has acquired a space for her old age – it feels like an achievement. Margot drags a chair into the sun and sits down thinking that this is, in fact, her only achievement. What else does she have to show for her life?

'But your lovely daughters,' a friend had once said when, flushed with wine, Margot had disclosed her feelings. 'Beautiful women, *they're* your achievement.'

'They are their *own* achievement,' Margot had said. 'And yes, they bring meaning to all those years and I'm tremendously proud of them. But I was going to do so much more.'

So where did it go, the intellect, the talent, the drive of that young woman who leapt the puddle into Laurence's car all those years ago? Dot has achieved so much and continues to generate the sort of energy that indicates she is about to do a great deal more. Even Phyllida has her time as senior mistress at a prestigious girls' school to look back on, and now, as president of this and chair of that and member of so many things that Margot would actually hate to be involved with, her sister is nonetheless a reminder to her of all that she herself is not. Phyllida, although now, of course, dealing with such terrible worry and uncertainty, still has the satisfaction of a long and largely happy marriage, and the reassurance of financial security, wealth even, to sustain her.

Margot reviews her old dreams of a life as a writer, a successful writer, shortlisted for awards, occasionally winning one and being photographed in the kitchen of a large family home full of children and dogs, or in a sunlit study, its shelves crammed with books, sitting at a desk piled high with papers and copies of her own books. It was not a dream that lacked foundation – a couple of awards for short stories, a university scholarship, a publisher showing an interest in the first few chapters of a novel – but now, at sixty-eight, there is no place for Margot to hide from her own reality; she has even wasted the years since the girls grew up, the time and space that came as they left home, time that she could have filled with writing.

The 'ifs' of Margot's life torment her: if only she hadn't got pregnant, if she had finished her degree, if she had not always had to put food on the table, buy children's shoes, pay the rent. But her true frustration runs deeper; if only she had brought the politics of the women's movement to her own inner journey, rather than simply articulating it to others. If only she'd had the courage to make the political personal and change herself, then perhaps things might now be different.

'What I don't understand, Mum,' Lexie had said that day as they drew up outside the house, 'is why you stopped writing. You were always at it – at night when we'd gone to bed, Sundays in the garden, on holidays. What happened to it all? What happened to all those Moleskine notebooks? You used to take it so seriously.'

The question had felt like a blow to the chest and Margot had caught her breath. 'It was just scribbling,' she said. 'I can't imagine that anyone would be interested in anything I'd write. Anyway, too late now,' and she opened the car door and got out.

'Mary Wesley was seventy when her first novel was published and she wrote dozens more after that,' Lexie had said, looking out at her across the empty seat. 'It's never too late.'

Margot shrugged. 'Mary Wesley is the exception that proves the rule. Thanks for the lift, darling.'

'Everything I've ever read about writing says that most people do their best work beyond middle age,' Lexie called, starting the engine.

'Not this far beyond.'

Reliving the conversation now, Margot hears her own resistance, her stubborn refusal to contemplate the possibility, and she hates herself for it. Why *did* she stop? Getting up she goes back into the house, to the cupboard where her Moleskine notebooks, in neat chronological order, occupy several shelves. She runs her hand over the leather spines, remembering the joy of starting a new one, the strong, silky quality of the pages, the thrilling sense that this notebook might just be the one in which she would discover what it was she was meant to write. Taking the first notebook from its place on the shelf, she slips off the elastic and opens it to see a Christmas sticker which sends her back to the bedroom for her glasses.

To the Greater Spotted Margot, for your writing. Happy Christmas, Love, Donald. Christmas 1958.

This reminder that her first Moleskine had been a gift from Donald fills Margot with guilt. He had introduced her to the literary tradition of the Moleskine, given her the first one.

'Never compromise on the things you need to help you do your best work,' he had said. And for a long time he had continued to supply her with Moleskines and she had greeted them with mixed feelings. They were the notebooks she most wanted, hard to find and never cheap, but rather than gratitude she had chosen to believe that she registered so little on Donald's radar that he couldn't be bothered to come up with a different gift. In fact many of these Moleskines came to her as gifts, from either Donald or Phyllida, and from Laurence, who sent them from Prague when he and Bernard were working there. What strikes Margot now is the recognition that back then they had taken her writing seriously, but she herself has never taken it seriously enough to develop anything substantial or complete. And how long is it since she *stopped* keeping them? How long have the new notebooks, still in their cellophane wrappers, been sitting unopened on the shelf? Margot takes out five more notebooks at random and returns to the verandah where, back in her chair, she opens the first, flicking through, reading extracts, rediscovering long-forgotten ideas and random thoughts, laughing at cruel character sketches, cringing at observations about herself, remembering who she was, and who she had imagined she might become.

It is late afternoon when finally, shivering in the chill, she stops reading, returns the notebooks to the shelf and takes out a new one. And settling herself in a warmer spot she once again begins to write on one of those pristine pages. But after a few minutes she stops, reads what she has written, slaps the notebook closed and throws it aside.

'No!' she says aloud. 'No, not again,' and getting up she goes to the spare room which doubles as a study, switches on the computer and, after staring for several minutes at the blank space of a new document, she begins to type.

TEN

'It's me,' she says when Dot opens the door. 'Alyssa, from down the road, and from the lecture. You said to pop in.'

'So I did,' Dot admits reluctantly, wondering what on earth had prompted her to make the offer, and then remembering Alyssa's encouraging thumb. This is the second time that she has invited strangers to 'pop in' and although Patrick has turned out to be a delightful person, she wonders now if she can really be bothered with someone in her early twenties who lives close enough to become a nuisance. In her days as what Margot calls 'a celebrity' and Dot herself dubbed a minor media personality, she would never have dreamt of telling anyone to pop in; time had been precious and limited, and she'd never tolerated fools, pedants or time wasters gladly but had often attracted more than her fair share.

'I brought cake,' Alyssa says, holding out a plastic container, and Dot, who has a very sweet tooth and is shamelessly greedy when it comes to cake, takes it from her and peers inside. 'Raspberry and white chocolate,' Alyssa says.

'You have spoken the magic words, my child, come into the den of the evil old witch,' Dot says. 'I see you've brought your laptop as well.'

'I wanted to talk to you about something, and I can do it better if I show you stuff on the computer.'

'Well, cake first,' Dot says. 'Would you prefer tea or coffee with it?'

'Coffee, please, strong black if possible,' Alyssa says. 'This is a lovely house.'

'I bought it back in the seventies, for what now seems a ridiculous price but was hard to manage at the time.'

'It's a bit like the one we're renting further down the street. Same layout, I think, but ours hasn't been renovated like yours.' She wanders around, admiring the leadlight windows, the renovated kitchen which is worthy of a far better cook than Dot has ever been, and the sunroom at the back which she had added in the eighties.

'These cakes are divine,' Dot says, having pounced on them immediately they were seated out there. 'Did you actually make them?'

'I did. My mum is big on cakes, this is her recipe.' Alyssa takes one for herself and leans back in her chair. 'But I didn't just come to bring you cake. I'm hoping you might be interested in something we've started.'

'We?' Dot asks through her cake.

'Me and my housemates, Lucy and Karen, and a couple of other friends at uni.' She opens up the laptop and switches it on. 'It's a campaign.'

Dot's heart sinks. The last thing she needs is an amateur campaign thought up by a group of students. Pretending interested attention she starts to formulate a script in which she commends the idea, whatever it is, and graciously points out that she is too busy, too old, too out of date, too anything to get involved.

Alyssa puts the laptop on the coffee table and turns it so that the screen faces in Dot's direction. 'We've called it CASE,' she says. 'Campaign Against Sexual Exploitation. We want to raise awareness about the sexualisation of children, particularly little girls.' She clicks the mouse. 'Not sure if you'll have seen this stuff,' she says as a slide show of images begins to drift across the screen. There are tiny tots dressed up as if for adult beauty pageants, frilly knickers peeping out under their skirts, five-year-olds in satin corsets and fishnet tights, six and seven-year-olds dancing in leotards worn over obviously padded bras, all of them made up, spray tanned, with teased hair, glossy lips and nails. 'We believe that the standards of the sex industry have infiltrated the fashion and beauty industries, and the advertising of all sorts of luxury and everyday things,' Alyssa says. 'Advertising, television, music videos, women's magazines – that whole consumer culture sexualises women and restricts its representations to the young, the beautiful and the sexual. A lot of it is like soft porn. And it influences how women are seen and how they see themselves, how their worth is measured, and now that's reaching into children's lives as well.' She pauses. 'I can tell you more, there is much more . . .'

'You don't need to,' Dot says. 'I'm as appalled as you obviously are. Is this also the subject of your PhD?'

Alyssa nods. 'And as you can probably tell I'm a bit obsessed about it. I, we, believe this sexualisation of little girls is a part of a vicious circle.'

'Go on.'

'Four and five-year olds dressed up as sexy adults are being set up to believe that this is what it means to be beautiful. It's the slippery slope. They compete on how they look, the look is always sexy and the competition is fierce and brutal. The winners are rewarded and the others learn that they are not quite good enough, and it's not quite good enough in a very powerful way because it's about how they look and what they think they're worth. They're learning that this is how their worth is measured. But it's not just the lunatic fringe who are letting this stuff infiltrate their kids' lives, it's right on the doorstep: the cosmetics for toddlers, the branded pencil cases and mini handbags, the padded bras for five-year-olds worn under t-shirts emblazoned with overtly sexy messages. It's all part of what you were saying at the shopping centre, that women are trapped in a culture of youth and beauty, dominated by unrealistic sexualised images, where appearance is what matters and getting old is terrifying.'

Dot reaches for her coffee and leans back in her chair. 'I feared you might want me to help save the whales, and while I love whales and am all for saving them, it's not something I would personally put my time into. But this . . . well . . . tell me how I can help.'

'Well,' Alyssa says, leaning forward, 'it started with something my nan said. I think you know her, she was in some women's lib stuff with you in the seventies – Glenda Dunne?'

Dot nods. 'I remember her well; you're a lot like her.'

'Well, I was over at her place the day that story about you was on the front page of the paper. She showed it to me. She said she'd been waiting for years for you to get back up on the soapbox again, and she said it was a shame you didn't still write the column in the paper because we could ask you to write about this. And that gave me the idea . . .'

Dot grabs another cake, wondering what's coming.

'I wondered if you'd be willing to run a blog, about all the same sorts of things you wrote about in the seventies and eighties, but particularly featuring stuff about how women are portrayed. The things you said in the paper would tie in with our campaign. There are heaps of people who remember you, Dot, and when they find your blog they might follow the link to our site. I'd set it up for you, you could just write whatever you want, and we can get you on Facebook and Twitter. You could pull heaps of people into the campaign, especially mothers and grandmothers.' She hesitates and it's as if she is suddenly losing her nerve, backing down. 'And there's something else too. We need someone to make us look serious, respectable, give us some gravitas. But of course it's only if you . . . well, if you want to, if you're interested . . . Perhaps you need time to –'

'Don't!' Dot cuts in and Alyssa jumps. 'Never back down, and don't ever let anyone see you're losing your nerve even if you are. You've done something terrific, now stand behind it and sell it.' She gulps the remains of her coffee and fixes Alyssa with a gaze that has had many lesser women blinking like rabbits in the headlights. 'This is the first time I've ever been accused of respectability or having gravitas,' she says. 'Perhaps it's another of the many advantages of getting old. How long does it take to build a blog?'

'A couple of hours.'

'Well then, you'd better get started. It's four o'clock already.'

～∽～

Emma spots a space in the hospital car park, reverses into it, switches off the engine and sits there, trying to think herself into a better frame of mind before she goes inside. Around her people are getting in and out of their cars, walking anxiously, armed with flowers, fruit and magazines, to the hospital entrance, while others emerge stricken and tearful, heading silently hand-in-hand in the opposite direction. Emma wishes she had a hand to hold but these days she doesn't seem very good at letting people hold hers. It seems too hard, too dangerous, to get into hand-holding and all that it implies. Safer to stick her hands in her pockets and walk alone.

She takes the key out of the ignition, gets out of the car, walks briskly in through the entrance and presses the button for the lift. Perhaps someone else will be there too, Lexie maybe, or Margot, or one of Donald's friends' wives. Anyone at all would be a relief, a diversion in the awfulness of that room with its tubes and pads, its dials and drips and the overbearing monitors that testify to the workings of Donald's body. Nothing seems natural in there. Even conversations with her aunt – which have always been a pleasure because they have so much in common, like their love of clothes and shopping, the same taste in movies and TV programs, a slight shared disapproval of Margot's liking for op shops and Lexie's preference for art galleries over shopping malls – now seem incredibly awkward, freighted as they are with the knowledge that as each day passes the likelihood of Donald's recovery diminishes.

There is a soft swish as the lift stops and as the doors begin to open Emma steps forward and almost crashes into three people who are coming out.

'Oh whoops, sorry!' she says, stepping back. 'Bit too eager to get in.'

'And we're pretty eager to get out,' the man says. He is carrying a small overnight bag, and the woman beside him is carrying a baby wrapped in a white crocheted shawl. She is staring intently into its face and a nurse with some papers in a plastic folder is escorting them out of the hospital.

'Taking the baby home,' the man says. 'Very exciting.' His pleasant, open face is pink with pride and pleasure, and he reaches over to move the edge of the shawl so that Emma can see its face. 'Isn't she beautiful?'

Emma swallows hard, smiles and leans in closer. 'Absolutely gorgeous,' she says. 'Congratulations. You must be dying to get her home.'

'Can't wait,' the mother says, obviously still spaced out, exhausted by the birth but also mesmerised by the wonder of it all. And she smiles vaguely at Emma as the nurse steers them towards the exit.

Emma steps into the lift, leans against the wall of smoky glass and presses the button as the doors close behind her. Her stomach heaves as the lift jolts upwards and she stares at her own reflection on the opposite wall, remembering the terrifying sense of panic that had gripped her as she and Grant stepped out of that very same lift with a newborn Rosie. In that moment she had wanted to run, run as far as she could and keep running until she reached a safe distance, until she was free of the certain knowledge that had haunted her pregnancy, that she had committed herself to something she really didn't want, and at which she was destined to fail. The indicator light settles on the number four and Emma takes a deep breath and steps out into the passage. She pauses, waiting for the wave of guilt to pass, and then walks slowly in the direction of Donald's room.

∞

Phyllida knits the last stitch, fastens off and spreads her work on the edge of Donald's bed, delighted she chose this particularly soft light wool. Well actually she didn't choose it, she'd given Wendy the pattern and sent her off to the wool shop with instructions, and now that it is done she can forgive Wendy for not getting the exact colour she'd asked for.

'I think this would suit Rosie better,' Wendy had said, handing over the bag, 'but of course if you really would prefer the pink I can take it back tomorrow. They said they'd change it.'

Phyllida, by now reliant on knitting to keep her calm, could not survive another twenty-four hours without it. Perhaps Wendy was right, she had thought grudgingly – after all, she probably knew Rosie better than any of them, with the exception of Grant.

'It's called burnt orange, and Rosie's rather keen on it at the moment, but it's up to you,' Wendy went on.

Now that the poncho is finished Phyllida can see that this colour is far more suitable than pink, and she picks it up and carries it to the window – the hospital's fluorescent lights distort everything.

'Is that a poncho?' Emma asks, appearing in the doorway and moving over to greet her aunt. 'I haven't seen one for years.'

'It is indeed,' Phyllida says, returning her kiss. 'Rosie ordered one. Apparently her new best friend has one, although hers is designer-made in Peruvian yak wool or something equally exotic.'

'I didn't even know you could buy them these days,' Emma says. 'They're very eighties.'

'Earlier than that,' Phyllida says, folding the poncho and putting it into the carrier bag in which Wendy had brought the wool. 'Maybe they're coming back and Rosie and her friend are at the forefront of fashion.'

'Hmm,' Emma says, 'hard to imagine. I suspect she thinks it's like a surplice for conducting bird funerals. But it *is* nice, I like the colour.'

'Well you'll note I'm not offering to knit anything for *you*,' Phyllida says. 'I'm well aware of your distaste for anything without a designer label.'

'Well only for me, not for Rosie,' Emma says, 'and I bet you're not knitting anything for yourself either.'

Phyllida grins. 'Too right. Rosie is bearing the brunt of my current need to knit, poor kid.'

'How is he today?' Emma asks, nodding towards Donald.

'Odd,' Phyllida says. 'Restless, moving about a bit. I've been so frustrated with him lying there day after day just breathing, and then this morning he jerked his arm and knocked a cup out of my hand and I actually shouted at him. Isn't that awful?'

Emma smiles. 'I think it's natural. It's very bad for you, sitting here all the time. We all think you're overdoing it.'

Phyllida knows very well what *they* think, but they are not married to Donald. It is she, not them, whose life will be changed in almost unimaginable ways by what happens next. Being here is the only way to cope with that. And despite her annoyance over the tea, she's convinced herself that this moving is a good thing, a sign of improvement. Until today she has faced every morning in the belief that this would be the day when Donald's oldest friend would sit her down and tell her that they should decide to let him go. She had wondered whether, if Donald were not one of the hospital's own, this would have already happened by now. But movement, she thinks, makes a difference, it must do.

'Don't you think his face is a better colour?' she asks Emma now.

Emma moves closer and looks at Donald's face, which is as ashen as it has been for weeks. 'Well . . .' she hesitates, 'it's hard to tell in this light, isn't it? Anyway, you're probably right, moving is better than nothing. But I do think you need a break. Let's go down to the café, or we could have a little walk outside. You need to get some fresh air.'

Phyllida pauses. 'Well, I don't know really . . .'

'Do you think he'd want you to be cooped up here all the time?'

Phyllida sighs. 'Probably not. If he could speak he'd probably tell me to bugger off and do something useful.'

'Well then . . .'

Reluctantly Phyllida picks up her bag and takes another look, a closer look, at her husband's face. 'I'm going out with Em for a bit, Don,' she says. 'Coffee, fresh air. Back soon. Don't go anywhere.' And she smiles down at him and follows Emma out into the passage.

It's a beautiful autumn afternoon, the sky a brilliant blue streaked with high cloud and a fresh breeze and as they settle on a bench with their cardboard cups, Phyllida closes her eyes, enjoying the sun on her face. Emma was right, she needed this; and she is filled with a sudden and urgent longing for normality, for her life to be back once again as it was, busy, filled with things that need to be done, things she knows how to do and does well. She longs for the structure, the daily rituals, the minor irritations and rewards of her ordinary life, and the certainty that was a part of it. And although she now knows to her cost that certainty was just an illusion, it's one she would very much like to reclaim.

'I want my life back,' she says suddenly, turning to her niece. 'I so want all this to be over, Em.'

Emma smiles and puts a hand over hers. 'Of course,' she says. 'Of course you do.'

Something strange is happening as they step out of the lift. Beyond the woman in the green overalls who is making slow progress along the corridor with the tea trolley, way past the elderly man in a crumpled suit who is grasping the arm of a frail woman in a blue dressing gown, there is panic and a flashing red light, the clatter of a trolley and the streak of white coats disappearing through a door. The old man stops and turns to look; the tea lady, filling a cup from the urn, cranes her neck to see past an inconvenient cupboard, and from somewhere in the opposite direction another, very familiar doctor, white coat flying open, races past them and in that moment Phyllida knows that it is Donald's light that is flashing, Donald's life that is in the balance. Her chest is tight with shock and tugging her arm free from Emma's she runs as fast as she can, the leather soles of her shoes slipping on the tiles, the old man and his wife watching in trepidation as she skids to a halt outside the room and almost falls through the door.

Donald is lying flat on his back, his pyjama jacket open, and alongside him a doctor in charge of the resuscitation trolley is counting backwards from three.

'Clear,' he shouts, and as others pull back he slams the pads onto Donald's chest.

Phyllida gasps in horror, her hand over her mouth, as Donald's body wrenches upwards in a twisting spasm and falls again. The staff watch mesmerised as a line on one of the monitors peaks and drops again.

'Get her out of here!' a doctor yells, spotting Phyllida, and a nurse hurries to her side and takes her arm.

'Get off,' Phyllida shouts, pulling away from her. 'Stop it, you have to stop.'

'Clear,' the doctor cries again, and the current sends another spasm through Donald's body, and the line lifts and jerks and flattens once again.

'Come outside please, Mrs Shepperd,' the nurse insists.

'Leave me alone,' Phyllida shouts, and she strides to the bed, staring down at the great mass of Donald's chest, and above it his strangely distorted, ashen face, and she knows he is no longer there.

'Three, two . . .'

'Stop!' Phyllida shouts, grasping the doctor's arm, and he turns to her in shock.

'Out of here, Mrs Shepperd, I insist,' he says, stepping back. 'You *must* leave now.'

'No,' Phyllida says. 'You must stop – *now*. I know he's your friend, but he's also my husband and he's dead, for god's sake. You know he is, he's been dead for weeks. We have to let him go.'

The man's face is stricken; he has worked with Donald for years. He steps back, and around her Phyllida sees the staff exchange awkward glances. One nurse, hand over her mouth, looks as though she might cry.

'Time of death sixteen-thirteen,' the doctor says, his voice husky in the sudden and awful silence.

'Please leave, all of you,' Phyllida says eventually, surprised by the authority in her own voice and the sense of calm that has overtaken her.

Slowly they get ready to withdraw, the trolley is wheeled away, instruments are collected from the bed and the night table, dials turned, and switches flicked to off, tubes are removed and a nurse begins to close Donald's pyjama jacket, but Phyllida leans across and pushes her hand away.

'I'll do it,' she says firmly. 'Just go away. Please go away.'

The door closes and one by one she fastens each pyjama

button, straightens the top sheet, folds it neatly back just below his top button and smooths it across his chest and under his arms.

'You too, please, Em,' she says, looking at her niece white-faced and stricken on the other side of the bed. And Emma pauses for a moment, appears about to say something but changes her mind, and turns towards the door, squeezing Phyllida's arm as she passes.

Phyllida looks down into Donald's distorted face; she strokes his forehead and gently, with the fingers of both hands, she massages his face back to familiarity.

'I told you not to go anywhere,' she says softly, 'but you had to have it your way, didn't you? Well there it is, all over now.' And taking his hand in hers she sits down beside the bed, still talking, until she has said all she needs to say.

ELEVEN

Nine weeks, almost to the day, since Donald was taken away in an ambulance, Phyllida watches from the front door as the last guests stroll to their cars. It's almost five o'clock; she had hoped they would all have had enough of the wake by four, but some were reluctant to abandon the very good wine and opportunities for reminiscence. The sky is a dull steely grey and a blustery wind is playing havoc with the young Norfolk pines that she ordered on Donald's instructions just a year ago.

A week, Phyllida tells herself, I have been a widow for one week and I still feel nothing, no grief, no anger, no sense of panic. What sort of woman am I to feel so much of nothing? All the emotions that had threatened to smother her during those weeks in the hospital have evaporated; she is disconcertingly calm, thinking clearly, as she had been on that day a week ago when she had banished the medical staff from Donald's room. Even at night, alone on her own side of the king-size bed, she lies still, her thoughts moving between past and present and settling on nothing until she sinks eventually into sleep. It is as though she is standing outside herself observing all this happening to someone else, and while she can remember the hysterical outpouring of fear and grief on the night of Donald's initial collapse, those feelings are now beyond her reach. During those tense weeks at the hospital her whole being had hummed with anxiety and fear; now she is cocooned in exhaustion, quarantined from what should surely be terrible grief, but she has not shed a tear. It's the shock, she tells herself for the hundredth time, just shock, and she closes the door and leans back against it.

From the kitchen she can hear the sounds of Margot, Lexie and Emma loading the dishwasher, putting things in cupboards, talking as they work. Phyllida knows she's not ready for that, she needs some time alone, and she crosses the hall to Donald's study. It's an uncomfortable room in her opinion and as always the awkward juxtaposition of elegant art deco and ugly modern technology offends her eye. The large glass and steel desk and the dazzling white computer with its vast screen seem an insult to the panelled walls and art deco fireplace, the walnut veneer drinks cabinet and the matching radio gramophone. Donald loved technology and gadgets, his boy toys he called them: the CD player, sleek and silver, stands alongside the headphones on the shelf of an exquisite walnut cabinet; the iPod sits in its docking station on a walnut wine table, and in the elegant bay of the full length windows the golf simulator crouches like a monster in the failing light. All of this, Phyllida thinks, all of this stuff, his toys, his books, these files and papers, the CDs, the 78s, and everything else – his clothes, his shoes – everything has to be sorted out and the task is hers alone. Picking up the remote control from Donald's desk she points it at the huge, wall-mounted flat screen TV, sinks into his favourite leather chair and within minutes she is asleep in front of Sky News.

It is Margot who wakes her almost an hour later with a tray of tea, and who settles silently opposite her to pour it, and offers her a plate of toast spread with peanut butter and cut into quarters – their childhood comfort food. It is this unspoken reference to childhood, to sisterhood, that shifts something in Phyllida and a surprising tear slides down her cheek and she smiles at Margot in a way that says much more than a mere thank you. Margot settles back in her chair, cup in hand, and they sit in silence for a while, eating their toast, until Margot moves to pour more tea.

'We've restored everything to normal in the kitchen, and the lounge,' she says. 'Emma's vacuumed and Lexie is just washing the kitchen floor. There's nothing to do but I don't think you should be alone tonight, Phyl. I can stay, so can both the girls if you like. I just don't think you should be alone in an empty house.'

Phyllida shakes her head. 'It's lovely of you,' she says. 'I do appreciate all you've done for me, not just today, ever since this started, but I think an empty house is what I need. I got used to it while Donald was in hospital. I think I'm at peace with it.'

Margot nods. 'Well okay, if you're sure. By the way, that man next door – Trevor, is it? – he was at the wake and then he came back about half an hour ago. You wouldn't believe the cheek of it, he wanted to see you to tell you that when you're ready to sell the house he'll make you an offer.'

'Bloody hell,' Phyllida says, 'he didn't waste any time, did he? What did you say?'

'I said I thought he was insensitive and opportunistic and that if you wanted at some point to sell the house you would put it in the hands of an agent and he could deal with them. Then he started to go on about avoiding agent's fees. In the end I told him to bugger off . . . well, not quite in those words, but you know what I mean. Was Donald friendly with him?'

Phyllida shakes her head. 'Not really. He used to talk to him sometimes, but he didn't like him. Sell the house, indeed, what an idea. As if I would.'

And the two of them sit then in awkward silence, each

knowing that the other is thinking that selling the house is, in fact, the obvious thing to do.

What, Phyllida wonders, will I do here all alone? What does a widow in her early seventies need with four bed-rooms, two and a half bathrooms, a huge lounge and dining room, a study, a sunroom and a kitchen in which you could cater for a small army? It was miles too big even for the two of us, and Donald took up a lot of space. What will I do now he's gone?

❦

Laurence had been among the first to leave the wake; telling lies about dead people while juggling a plate of tiny triangu-lar sandwiches and a glass of semillon was not to his taste, and staying longer would have demanded some spectacular lies. He would, for example, have had to agree with people who told him what a terrific bloke Donald was, what a great surgeon, husband, family man, philanthropist, golfer and drinking mate. He would have had to look interested as Don-ald's medical chums told tedious tales of his escapades as a medical student, or his golfing mates talked about his prow-ess on the green. For Laurence, who has always thought that Donald was an arrogant, bullying piece of shit, the whole thing was too hard. So he had turned up at the funeral and watched as the coffin made its final journey between the red velvet curtains, wondering what Phyllida would do now. Then he had turned up at the wake, made sure that Margot and the girls saw that he was there doing the right thing, said a few reassuring things to Phyllida and then slipped away. He needs to have a serious conversation with Emma, but the wake just wasn't the place for that.

Now, back in his car, Laurence can't bear the thought of going home. He's only been back in the country a few days, having gone from Finisterre back to Santiago and then for a few days' visit to an old friend in Paris. The house feels bleak and neglected, which is exactly how he himself feels. He hadn't wanted to be at the wake but having left he now realises that he needed something that was there: connection, familiarity, affection, love. Will he ever be able to live peacefully in the house now that it lacks the emotional warmth of a home shared with someone he loved? Bernard has gone and gone for good, taking with him not just personal effects but certain 'shared' possessions gathered over decades: a couple of limited edition prints, a small antique leather chair, every Bach and Wagner CD, half the cutlery, bed linen, his desk, his electric wok, and some indigenous art that had hung on the wall of the sitting room. Laurence is still not clear what else has gone and while, to an outsider, the house may appear unchanged, to him these gaps are as obvious and gut-wrenching as the empty space beside him in their bed. And still Laurence is keeping his loss to himself because he hasn't a clue how to share it, any more than he has a clue how to be single again.

As he heads reluctantly home via Lygon Street, he slows down outside the cinema and sees that it is screening a festival of classic films; *Brief Encounter* starts in ten minutes' time. He parks the car, buys a blueberry chocolate bomb and a bottle of water, and fumbles through the darkness to a seat as the opening credits begin to roll.

This original version has always had a special magic for Laurence; Celia Johnson's primly tragic voice mixing with Rachmaninoff's *Second Piano Concerto*, the gloomy station with its café where brittle voices intrude on tender whispered conversations, and all those lingering looks as trains hiss steam and rip through fragile emotions. The first time he'd seen it was with Dot, in the late fifties or maybe a little later. She had hated it, whereas Margot, with whom he'd seen it several years after that, had loved it and cried her eyes out most of the way through. They had always enjoyed the same films, he and Margot, and thinking of her now as he watches the familiar story unfold in black and white on the screen, Laurence is once again reminded not only of his own grief, but of the irony of his own situation and what the break-up might revive for Margot.

Losing Bernard is like bereavement; there is no balm for this grief, no ritual to mark it, just the loneliness, and an overwhelming sense of failure. Is this how Margot felt when, on that day more than thirty years ago, she had woken him in the middle of the night and demanded the truth? The shame, the guilt, returns to him now as he remembers the shock that crossed her face when he admitted what she was accusing him of – an affair with a student. And then the disbelief, the confusion, the hopelessness that claimed her when he explained that the student was a man.

On the screen, in the station café, Trevor Howard is removing a piece of grit from Celia Johnson's eye with the corner of his handkerchief, a moment of intimacy and unfolding sexual tension between strangers. It was a moment Laurence remembers Margot once described as marking the unconscious ignition of passion. They'd enjoyed the same music too, although Margot had never thought much of the Rolling Stones. But not so long ago Lexie had told him that Margot had recently developed a bit of a thing for the ageing Mick Jagger, although he still came second to Rod Stewart in her affections. Laurence had always thought Rod Stewart's voice sounded like a metal plate being dragged across paving stones, but Rod and Mick were probably their only points of difference when it came to music.

Laurence had loved Margot but not, as he had always been aware, in the way that she loved him. All those years ago he had known that when she had told him she was pregnant and he had promptly suggested that they should get married, she grasped it not just as a solution but as a sign of something more profound; an expression of a love as strong as her own. She had not known that for Laurence it had seemed a sort of salvation from what he feared in himself. A wife, a family – safe, respectable, mainstream. He had thought that the haunting attraction to other men that so scared him in its intensity would be laid to rest. He was in his mid-twenties then and it was several more years before he came to understand that what he had thought of since his teens as his dark side was, in fact, his true self. By that time he was a husband and father. Years later, long after the divorce, Margot had told him that the hardest part had been the recognition that she had never really been what he wanted; that every time he had made love to her he would have been acting against his nature and wanting an entirely different person; that she had, for him, always been a substitute for the real thing.

As the cinema empties Laurence swallows the final gulp of water from his bottle and strolls out into the street through the incoming audience for *Casablanca*. Going home is not an option and for a moment he contemplates eating something at Jimmy Watson's, but remembers that Margot told him that Dot was back from India. It's ages since he's seen her and he gets out his phone and dials the number. The call rings out but just the same he thinks he might head off to her place in case she is just not picking up, and if she *is* out then he'll get a meal at the little Italian café on the corner, and by the time he's eaten she might be home.

Ten minutes later Laurence is driving past Dot's house, which is in darkness. He heads on down the street, parks the car and is walking back towards the café when he spots that trademark hair glowing in the café's lights. Dot, looking reassuringly the same, is sitting with a rather exotic elderly woman in a colourful velvet coat, and a younger man, and they are eating pasta and sharing a bottle of wine. Laurence hesitates briefly, considering the wisdom of interrupting, but it's an awfully long time since he last saw Dot and the impulse to surprise her wins the day.

'Laurence! How wonderful!' Dot says, jumping to her feet

with genuine delight, hugging him and standing back to take a good look at him. 'You look a bit off colour – too much pilgrimage. Come and join us, have a glass of wine.'

And she introduces him first to her friend Vinka, and then to the man who is Vinka's nephew. Laurence, desperate for convivial company, accepts the invitation to join them and they shuffle their chairs to make room for him. He orders tagliatelle with pesto, a green salad and a second bottle of wine.

'So,' says Vinka, looking him up and down, 'you are the late husband of Margot?' and she looks around in surprise as they burst into laughter.

'Well not exactly the *late* husband,' Laurence says, sipping the wine Dot has poured for him. 'If I were that, it would mean I was dead. But I *am* Margot's *ex*-husband.'

'Ach!' Vinka says, shaking her head in annoyance. 'This I get wrong again. I always think I will remember it the right way and then I forget.'

'I wondered which member of the family I'd meet next,' Patrick says. 'It was Margot first, then Lexie last week. Wendy and I are helping her sort out her uni enrolment.'

'And you are one of the Push men, I think, Laurence?' Vinka cuts in.

'Really?' Patrick says. 'When you turned up we were actually talking about the Push, particularly the men in the Push, and the parties and the politics too of course.'

'Yes, you must tell us,' Vinka says, 'we must hear your version. Maybe we do not believe all what Dot tells us about you men in the Push.'

Laurence is immediately drawn to Vinka: the aged but still beautiful face, white hair pulled into a soft bun and fastened with a large tortoiseshell comb, and that amazing velvet coat. And Dot, dear Dot, who conjures up so many memories at a glance. He is delighted and thankful to have found them this evening.

'We weren't all sexist bastards, you know,' he says to Vinka, 'but the sexual freedom was pretty seductive and some of us may have been a little opportunistic. But why do you want to know about the Push?'

Patrick tells him about Dot's lecture, and the one still to come. 'I inveigled my way into her home and then bullied her into talking to my students.'

Laurence laughs. 'Anyone who can bully Dot into *anything* has my total respect,' he says.

'It wasn't that hard,' Patrick says. 'I caught her at a weak moment the day after the shopping centre protest.' And he tells Laurence about Dot chaining herself to the railings.

'Good lord, Dot,' Laurence says as his pasta arrives. 'You're not still doing the chaining up stuff, are you? It all sounds a bit weird and random.'

'Too random,' she agrees. 'Anger and frustration got the better of me; it certainly wasn't my finest hour. But tell us about your pilgrimage.'

'Well, I started out thinking it was a walking holiday, but the very nature of the places, the people and the pain of sticking with it did seem to turn it into a bit of a pilgrimage,' he says. 'It was amazing, extraordinary and really quite a humbling experience and physically gruelling. Within the first few days my feet felt as though they'd been shredded and I thought I was heading for a heart attack. I was on the verge of pulling out but then, well, I just seemed to get into the swing of it and to start to enjoy it in a masochistic sort of way. So I made it all the way to Finisterre, which feels like something of an achievement. And I'm very glad I did, but I won't be repeating it.' As he speaks he can feel the warmth of Dot's affection for him and it's what he needs most right now. 'You will have to suffer the photographs, Dot.'

She smiles and pats his arm and it crosses his mind that he might be able to confide in her, tell her about Bernard. But, no, he owes it to Margot to tell her first, and anyway, this is a brief interval in which he can try to push his grief into the background. He is enjoying himself, he wants it not to end, not to have to wind up the evening watching the late news or some mindless reality TV show alone in an empty house.

'We should go on somewhere,' Patrick says as the waiter removes their empty coffee cups. 'A club, maybe, listen to some music.'

'No way!' Dot says. 'It'll be packed with people in their twenties and the music will be head-banging stuff. It's already past my bedtime.'

'But it's only just nine o'clock,' Patrick protests.

'Exactly!'

'I know a place where there are older people and good music,' Vinka says. 'Sometimes I go for catching up with old friends. Many years ago I used to work there. Good Polish vodka, sometimes entertainment, it is a gentle place – it makes a good end to the evening, I think.'

'Brilliant,' Patrick says, 'the Polish Club. It's only five minutes' walk from here. Let's do it! Come on Laurence, Dot.'

'I suppose I could,' Dot says, 'but not for too long.'

'I once had a Polish girlfriend who drank vodka,' Laurence says, and Dot rolls her eyes at the others. 'She had terrible tantrums and cried a lot.'

'That wasn't because she was Polish,' Dot says. 'Maria had tantrums and cried because she was your girlfriend. We all did.'

'Rubbish,' he says. 'We argued a lot but you never had tantrums or wept buckets, and neither did Margot, nor the others.'

'We all did, Laurence,' Dot repeats. 'The only difference was that Maria had her tantrums and shed her tears in front of you, unlike the rest of us, who did it with our girlfriends or in the lonely silence of our bedsits.'

'No? Really?' Laurence says in genuine amazement. 'You're kidding, Dot.'

She shakes her head. 'You blokes were all the same, you had no idea what havoc you were wreaking on us. Until of course you were caught out by circumstances as *you* eventually were. It was a strange time. The more I think about it the stranger it gets.'

'I think,' says Vinka, looking straight at Patrick, 'that we take them to the club and give them plenty of vodka and they tell us much more, no?'

'Absolutely,' Patrick says, urging Dot to her feet. 'Come on, Dot, you wouldn't deny me this research opportunity, would you? If you don't come I'll only get the blokes' version.'

'Oh well, in the interests of balance,' Dot says. 'I can't believe I'm going clubbing at a time when I ought to be in my pyjamas. You're a bad influence on me, Vinka.'

'Yes I think so,' Vinka says. 'This is good.'

'Very good,' Laurence says, taking Dot's arm and drawing it through his own. 'Far better than chaining yourself to railings – and I must say, Dot, it's bloody marvellous to see you again.'

TWELVE

'It was a really silly thing to do, Emma,' Kristy says, peering down at Emma's lips. 'You should've waited until you got back and had it done here. It's a mess. What did the doctor say?'

'He said I shouldn't have had it done at all. I think I might change and go to a woman doctor next time. Anyway, he gave me antibiotics to kill off the infection but it doesn't seem to be working yet. It's ages now. I keep thinking it's clearing up and then it flares up again.'

'Mmm. These are a mess too,' Kristy says, looking now at Emma's eyes and moving an eyelid with a latex covered finger. 'Even when it all settles down, *if it does*, they're still going to be a mess. Look here.' She holds a magnifying mirror in front of Emma's face. 'See – just here the lines aren't even and there are blotches.'

'But you can get rid of them?'

Kristy shakes her head. 'I don't think so. I don't know if there's a process for removing tattoos from eyelids. It's not like a tattoo on someone's arm, you know. And it's the same with the lip lines and colour. Even when you get rid of the infection and the swelling goes down, it's not going to look good.'

'But it must be possible to fix it,' Emma says, her voice rising in panic. 'I can't keep on walking around looking like a freak.'

Kristy shrugs. 'I don't know. I'll talk to Theresa, she's got more experience, but it's her day off. I suppose you might have to end up going to a cosmetic surgeon.'

Emma sighs. 'I can't believe this. And the Botox didn't even work, not like when you do it. My forehead was frozen for a few hours and then it wore off and the lines were still there. Anyway, can you just top it up for me now, at least I won't have wrinkles on my forehead.'

'No way,' Kristy says. 'I'm not touching you until all this has cleared up, or at least until I've talked to Theresa about it.'

'Well I'll just have to find someone who *will* help me,' Emma says, and she swings her legs down from the reclining chair and stands up. 'I might try that place in the arcade, perhaps they'll be a bit more helpful.'

'Don't,' Kristy says, grabbing her arm. 'Seriously, Emma, don't do anything 'til I talk to Theresa. You could end up worse than you are now. Come in tomorrow and I'll get her to take a look, round twelve o'clock, say? And keep taking the antibiotics.'

Outside the salon the sky is darkening with storm clouds but Emma puts on the new and genuine designer sunglasses which she bought to replace the fakes, and makes her way slowly down the street. The last thing she feels like doing now is meeting her father but yesterday, at the funeral, he'd made no attempt to hide his shock when he saw her face, and before he slipped away from the wake he'd asked her to meet him for lunch.

'I'm working, Dad,' she'd said.

'Don't tell me you don't have time for lunch,' he'd replied. 'Twelve-thirty at Christo's. I'll see you there.'

She glances at her watch: twelve-twenty-five. Too late

to cancel, and anyway, if she doesn't turn up he'll track her down in the office or at home. He's like that, hands off for months at a time and then full-on interference. It's as though every now and then he remembers he's a father and turns up to put in a bit of a performance. Anyway, she knows what this lunch is about. He had been horrified when he saw her face yesterday, so if it's going to be an interrogation she might as well submit to it now, when she can legitimately cut it short by going back to work.

The lighting in the restaurant is low but she manages to spot Laurence reading the paper in his favourite booth by the window.

'Are you planning to keep those glasses on all through lunch?' he asks once they've ordered their food.

'I was,' Emma says. 'I managed it yesterday at the funeral; nobody seemed to think it was odd.'

'They assumed you'd been crying,' Laurence says. 'Believe it or not, some people had been crying a lot, not, I noticed, any of the family, not even Phyllida.'

'Aunty Phyl did cry a bit last night,' Emma says.

'Well that's probably a good thing. She was scarily calm all through the service and at the wake.'

'Not that you'd know much about that,' Emma says. 'I saw you skulking off; you were only there about ten minutes.'

'Twenty-five actually,' Laurence says, 'but we're not here to talk about me.'

'I thought you were going to tell me all about your *pilgrimage*,' Emma says, emphasising the word in a way she hoped would distract him into talking about himself.

'That can wait,' Laurence says. 'We have more important things to talk about, namely you. And can you please take off those fucking glasses and look me in the eye, this is serious.'

Reluctantly Emma removes her glasses and lays them on the table.

'Christ!' Laurence says. 'You look like a panda.'

'Thanks, that makes me feel a whole lot better.'

Laurence takes her hand across the table. 'I'm sorry, my darling, but they have made a mess of your beautiful face. Can they sort it out?'

Emma shrugs and relates her conversation with Kristy. 'It's a nightmare, Dad. I guess it'll look better when the infections have cleared up but it's been really badly done, and I think I might just have to wait for it to fade, and that can take years!' Emma puts her hands over her face. 'You can't believe how awful this is. I feel like a freak.'

'Em, look, it's not as bad as you think . . .'

'You just said I look like a panda.'

'Yes, but like you said, it'll be better when the infection clears up. But why did you do it anyway? I mean, pumping lethal poison into your face is bad enough, but this . . .'

'My lips are much too small and they fade into the rest of my face.'

'Not anymore!' Laurence says.

Emma glares at him.

'Sorry, that wasn't funny.'

'No, it wasn't. The woman said my eyes would look piggy once my lips were done.'

'And you believed that?'

Emma shrugs. 'I have to do something. I don't want to get old.'

'No choice about that,' Laurence says, 'and frankly the alternative is not appealing. It's okay, Em, getting older is okay, in fact it's quite nice.'

Emma sighs with irritation at his inability to understand. 'For you maybe,' she says. 'Not for me. I'm a woman. I don't want to look in the mirror and see an old woman.'

Laurence raises his eyebrows. 'Old women can be beautiful,' he says, an edge of frustration in his voice. 'Your mother, for example, she's a good-looking woman, a beautiful woman.'

Emma grimaces. 'I certainly don't want to get like Mum, or Aunty Phyl, thank you – wrinkles, age spots, all that loose skin . . . no way am I ever going to look like that. And right now I don't want to look like a forty-two-year-old has-been.'

'That's ridiculous,' says Laurence, clearly irritated. 'Are you saying that who you are isn't good enough so you have to pretend to be something else? I suppose it'll be surgery next – a new nose, perhaps, or bits of fat cut off your arse and implanted somewhere else? You'd rather go through agony and shell out a small fortune to end up looking younger? It's madness.'

'This didn't cost a fortune,' Emma says, fidgeting uncomfortably. Laurence seems really overbearing today, and he really hasn't a clue what it's like for her, single, past forty, and no man in sight. She just wants to escape back to work.

Laurence raises his eyebrows. 'I know exactly how much it cost, Em,' he says, dropping several envelopes onto the table. 'Here's your mail. As you can see, a lot of it's still coming to me, so can you please get it redirected? It's more than a year since you started using my place as a mailing address.'

'Sorry, I'll do it this week,' Emma says, sweeping the envelopes across the table towards herself, but as she does so she realises that the top one, from the bank, has been opened. She has a horrible sick feeling in her stomach and it begins to rise up into her chest. 'Hey, you opened my mail. You have no right to do that, Dad. How would you feel if I opened yours?'

'Annoyed,' Laurence says. 'But it was a mistake. There was a pile of mail when I got home, and we have the same bank. I assumed it was addressed to me.' He puts down his knife and fork. 'They're cancelling your credit card, Em, and they're threatening to freeze your cheque account. How long is it since you looked at one of these?' He picks up one of the unopened bank statements and waves it at her. 'Or made a payment on the credit card?'

Emma hesitates and glances around the restaurant. 'A while, I suppose. Anyway, you haven't told me about the pilgrimage. How are the blisters?'

'Don't change the subject. You owe them more than twenty thousand dollars. And where's it gone? Beauticians, clothes, handbags, cosmetics, shoes, shoes, shoes – there aren't enough days in a year for you to wear all those shoes.'

'It's okay, I've got another credit card,' Emma says. Her whole body is rigid with embarrassment. She feels like a child again, caught out doing something wrong, knowing she's let her father down. 'Anyway, you had no right to open my mail.'

'No, but I'm glad I did. Have you been paying your share of Rosie's maintenance?'

Emma glances out of the window, longing to escape into the busy street. 'I could have missed a few . . .'

Laurence throws his hands in the air. 'Look, Em, it's not just the money, there's all the shopping and the things you're doing to yourself. I'm worried about you. You need to make a plan, start paying back the money. I'll help you with that, but the main thing is I want you to see someone . . . a psychologist, a counsellor . . . I don't understand why –'

'No,' Emma cuts in, standing up and scooping the mail into her handbag. 'No, you wouldn't, would you, you never have. But don't worry, Dad, you don't have to. It's none of your business anyway, so why don't you just eff off and mind your own – that's what you've always done anyway, isn't it? Okay, I'm a lousy mother, and you think you were such a brilliant father?'

And before Laurence can get to his feet to stop her, Emma jams her sunglasses back onto her face and strides out of the restaurant.

⁂

Phyllida has made herself a rule for coping with her grief and adjusting to the enormity and silence of the house. She has a list of things that have to be done and at the end of each day she must be able to cross off at least one thing that will demonstrate progress; progress to the future, a different sort of future, although so far she has no idea what that might be. It's helping. She has already crossed off many of the smaller things – the letters of thanks, approved the plaque for Donald's portrait at the hospital, organised the headstone – and has put in writing her agreement to the naming of an operating theatre in his honour. She has gone through the tedious process of advising the banks, the health insurance company, the superannuation people, and more. Three significant and burdensome tasks remain. Sorting out and disposing of his clothes, and the contents of his study, and making an appointment to see the solicitor who has already left several messages saying he needs to see her about matters relating to the will. Right now it's the clothes that are occupying Phyllida's attention; the will, she thinks, can wait. She knows she gets everything other than a couple of small bequests each to Emma and Lexie. What's the rush? The solicitor is at the bottom of the list.

On several occasions Phyllida has stood helplessly in Donald's walk-in robe and then walked out, daunted by the prospect of all those suits, shirts and shoes. Now she is undecided about whether to take Margot up on her offer of help, or wait for Emma who, just this morning, called to ask if she might stay for a while as she had to give up her flat.

'How lovely, Em, of course you can stay,' Phyllida had said, 'if that's what you really want, but I'm fine here on my own, you know.'

'Oh I know that,' Emma had said. 'It's . . . well, between you and me, Aunty Phyl, I'm having this teeny financial crisis, and the rent here is pretty hefty. It would help me out while I look around for something a bit cheaper. I'll pay my way, of course, food and things, share the bills . . .'

'You'll do nothing of the sort,' Phyllida had said. 'It'll be an absolute pleasure to have you here and while I am certainly a widow I am not a destitute one. Now, when would you like to come? Soon as you like as far as I'm concerned.'

They made a date for the end of the week.

It is a couple of hours later, when she is upstairs considering whether it should be Margot or Emma who helps her with Donald's clothes, that the bell rings and she opens the door to find her neighbour standing very close to the entrance and about to put his foot inside.

'G'day, Phyl,' Trevor says, edging forwards so that she has to let him in. 'Just came around to check up, see if you need a hand with anything,' and he strides past her to the kitchen. 'Thought we'd have a cuppa and a chat. Got the kettle on?'

'Was there something specific you wanted, Trevor?' Phyllida asks, following him into the kitchen. 'I'm rather busy and don't have time for a chat.'

'Won't take a minute,' Trevor says, settling himself on a stool at the breakfast table. 'And it'll be to your advantage. White, three sugars please.'

Phyllida sighs noisily and switches on the kettle, keeping her back to Trevor. She has always thought him a singularly unattractive man, large but not in Donald's rubbery, cuddly way. Trevor's body is a solid mass in the style of a commercial refrigerator, and he doesn't have the height which had always added some dignity to Donald's enormous girth. Trevor's neck is thick and red, his slightly greying hair shaved close to his head; in a suit he looks like an escapee from a James Bond movie, a Goldfinger acolyte, likely to pull a revolver from his inside pocket at the least sign of trouble. Today, though, he has no inside pocket, no hiding place for a weapon, as he is wearing an unattractively tight pair of jeans and an even tighter black t-shirt that rides up to reveal an area of fat white belly where his waist might once have been. Donald had believed that Trevor was employed by some sort of local mafia chief in the car business as there was no way he could have made the money to buy his enormous house in this extremely expensive suburb, several investment properties on the Gold Coast, a massive yacht and more, just by selling cars. 'Trevor's part of the Melbourne underworld, you can take my word for that,' he'd said on more than one occasion.

Phyllida doesn't care how Trevor makes his money. She has always disliked him and now just wants to get rid of him as soon as possible. She pushes a mug of tea and the sugar bowl towards him and sits facing him across the benchtop.

'So what was it you wanted, Trevor? As I said, I don't have a lot of time.'

'No worries,' Trevor says, piling sugar into his tea and stirring it. 'I had a word with your sister after the funeral, expect she told you.'

Phyllida waits for him to go on.

'Thought I'd leave you to think it over for a while and here I am now, following it up so to speak.'

'Following up what exactly?' Phyllida asks, knowing just what he means but determined to make things as difficult as possible.

'Well,' he clears his throat, 'as I told your sister –'

'What *was* it that you told Margot?' Phyllida says, looking puzzled. 'I can't quite remember.'

'About the house,' Trevor says, obviously struggling with the effort of managing his frustration, and as he launches into his idea of helping her out by taking the house off her hands, Phyllida sees now that he really has assumed that she has been considering his offer, and preparing to do a deal with him.

'Of course,' she says now, standing up and walking over to the sink. 'I *do* remember Margot mentioning that, but I'm not thinking of selling, so I'm afraid you've wasted your time.'

Trevor leans precariously backwards on the stool and clasps his hands behind his head. 'I realise it's not long since the dear old Don departed this earth, Phyllida, but you don't want to leave it too long. You've seen the news, the sub-prime crisis in the US, Fannie Mae and Freddie Mac getting into trouble, Lehman's looking wobbly, Iceland teetering on the edge of bankruptcy, we're on the verge of a financial crisis, and it's global and that means Australia too.'

'I am well aware what global means, thank you, Trevor, and I do follow the news. What does this have to do with my house?'

'Real estate will plummet,' Trevor says. 'House prices will hit the bottom of the shit tank – the value of this place will drop by half. You need to offload it now before the crisis really hits.'

Phyllida tips her almost full cup of tea down the sink and turns to look at him. 'Well thank you for your concern, Trevor, but it's entirely unnecessary as I am not intending to sell now or at any time in the near future.'

Trevor sucks in his breath and shakes his head. 'Not wise,' he says, 'not wise at all. Very big place, expensive to maintain, and you here on your own. Who knows what might happen?'

'No one knows,' Phyllida says, 'least of all you, I suspect, Trevor. And with all this gloom and doom on the horizon I certainly wouldn't want to saddle a neighbour with a property which, from what you're saying, is something of a burden, a white elephant. And you really don't need to worry about me, my niece is moving in here.'

Trevor slams his mug down on the benchtop, splashing the remains of his tea. 'Well don't say I didn't warn you,' he says, shaking his finger at her. 'Don't come moaning to me wanting today's price in six months' time, because right now, Phyllida, it's deal or no deal.'

'No deal! And if you don't mind, Trevor, I have things to do.'

'I had a deal with Don, you know,' he says, heading for

the door, his face now a shiny flushed crimson. 'I suggest you think again. I'll be back.'

'Please don't bother,' Phyllida says, grasping the door handle. 'It's no deal, remember. No further discussion necessary.' And she slams the door and leans back against it, her heart pounding. 'Bastard,' she murmurs under her breath in a most un-Phyllida like way. 'You won't intimidate me.' And she goes straight to Donald's study, pours herself a large whisky and downs it in two gulps. 'A deal with Don indeed! You can stuff your deal up your arse, you greedy, obnoxious little bastard,' she says aloud, and immediately bursts into tears.

❧

Vinka makes her way slowly up the stairs, wondering how much longer she will be able to manage this. In the last year or so she has become uncomfortably aware of her vulnerability as a single woman of eighty living on the top floor of a building with no lift, where the rubberised trim on the staircase is dangerously loose. She has recently taken to holding tightly to the banister and counting the stairs, each one a step closer to safety. Today as she pauses for breath at the third floor, her handbag hooked over her shoulder and a bag of vegetables from the market in her free hand, the door of one of the three flats is flung open and a man steps out and takes the bag from her.

'Vinka, I am waiting for you,' he says. 'Come in, please, and I make you tea. We must talk,' and he ushers her into the gloomy hallway and through into the kitchen where a kettle is whistling on the gas stove. 'Sit down, sit down,' he says, gesturing towards the kitchen table. 'Rest while I make the tea and then we go to sit in comfort.'

Glad of the chance to sit Vinka perches on the upright chair, thinking how fortunate she is to live in a place so reminiscent of what she remembers of old Europe. This building with its twelve small flats, three on each of the four floors, is a community of people of different races. Stanislav, who is currently pouring water into a small silver teapot which once stood on his mother's sideboard in Moscow, has lived here since the seventies, and is just a year younger than Vinka herself. Some of the flats have been empty for a while now. There is a young Greek couple on the ground floor, alongside them a Frenchwoman in her sixties. Opposite Stan is Mal, a former shearer whose daughter and her family live in the adjacent street, and upstairs on one side of Vinka is an alcoholic English poet and, on the other, Mrs Lee, Chinese – a widow since her husband died not long after he'd fallen on the stairs last winter. It is Mr Lee's fall, his broken hip and the subsequent and fatal pneumonia, which has made Vinka so painfully aware of her circumstances.

'Come,' Stan says, placing two glasses of tea on the tray and indicating to Vinka to follow him into the sitting room. 'Sit, please. We must talk.'

The room is crammed with mementoes of Stan's family, his late wife, his parents, aunts, uncles, grandparents, and the living – a son and his wife and family who have returned to the new Russia with all its apparent opportunities, about which Stan is more than a little sceptical.

'O'Connor has been here today while you are out; we are given notice, Vinka.'

'Notice?'

'The building, he is selling the building. It is to be converted into apartments.'

'It is already apartments,' Vinka says, taking the tea from him. 'Apartments is flats, same thing.'

'Luxury apartments,' Stan says. 'One on each floor. Four only, in the whole building. Imagine it, Vinka, where we have three flats there becomes one apartment, a whole floor. Imagine that.'

Vinka doesn't want to imagine it. She wants only to

imagine what she has always imagined – herself living out the rest of her life here in this place where she has lived for more than thirty years, where she has planned to stay until she is carried out feet first.

'No,' she says. 'It is our home, Stanislav. He cannot sell it.'

'But it is done. We have until the end of January, six months, so they give us time.'

'Time!' Vinka says, the hand that holds her cup shaking angrily. 'This is no time, we are old, what are we to do?'

'But he's right, you know,' Stan says, rubbing both hands through his wiry grey hair, leaving it standing up like a wild halo. 'By the law he has only to give us one month's notice.'

Vinka knows this is correct, and she has seen many old buildings in the inner suburbs demolished to make way for offices, or renovated to provide housing for wealthy young professionals. 'He left these,' Stan says, handing her a large brown envelope with her name on it. 'From the department of something or other. It is for aged care accommodation, for us to apply.'

Vinka takes the envelope and slides out some leaflets, some forms and a brochure with pictures of pleasant leafy gardens where elderly people play bowls and croquet, and wave to each other as they wander along the paths that weave between small houses, each one exactly the same as those on either side of it.

'We are entitled, O'Connor says, as Australian citizens, it is our right.' Stan waves a hand, shaking his head. 'Look at it, Vinka, we must go tomorrow, you and I and Mrs Lee, to put our names on a waiting list. The others I don't know. Arthur doesn't answer his door – drunk, I suppose. The Dimitriades are young. Madame Velly says she will move to her sister in Williamstown. Mal is not here.'

'This is my home,' Vinka says.

Stan nods. 'I tell him this, but he says there is world crisis of finances, and everyone is affected. He is losing money, he must offload assets, losing money hand over wrist.'

'Fist,' Vinka says. 'It is hand over fist that he loses money. And we lose our home.'

'When you lose your home you lose who you are.'

'No,' she says, 'we have known worse in the war. We don't lose ourself.' But as she says it Vinka wonders if she believes it. Vulnerability on the stairs is nothing to this. She has become what she has most feared but refused to face: a homeless old person, living on a pension, with only one relative, and she is very, very frightened.

THIRTEEN

Margot tries to ignore the hammering at the door, just as she has ignored other callers and telephone messages in recent days. She stares harder at the computer screen, focusing on the words, but it's no good, whoever it is this time is not giving up and she sighs, pushes her glasses up onto her head and wanders down the hall. She looks a wreck, still in her pyjamas and dressing gown, sleep-mussed hair sticking up in unattractive tufts, socks with a hole in the big toe, and she's totally lost track of time – again.

'At last!' Laurence says when she opens the door. 'Where the hell have you been, Margot, I've been ringing you for days.' He notices the pyjamas. 'Oh lord, you're sick. I'm so sorry, why didn't you call? What can I do to help?'

'I'm fine,' Margot says, opening the door wider to let him in, 'just haven't had time to shower this morning.'

'It's afternoon,' Laurence says, glancing around the kitchen, taking in the washing up piled in the sink, the rubbish that hasn't been taken out. 'Half past two, in fact.'

'Really? How time flies. How's Bernard? Is he back yet?'

Laurence hesitates. He should tell her now, but this is all so weird. 'What's happening here, Margot?' he says instead. 'The place is a mess, you *must* be sick.'

'I'm fine,' Margot says. 'I've just been busy. Do you want tea or coffee?'

'Coffee please.'

'How's he enjoying Ho Chi Minh City?'

'In all the years I've known you, including those when we lived together,' Laurence says, desperate to change the subject, 'I've never known you to leave dishes in the sink or miss a rubbish collection. And I have certainly never seen you in your pyjamas at this time of day except when you're sick, so what's going on?'

'Like I said, I've been busy,' Margot says. 'I still am but I probably do need to have a shower and get dressed. It won't take long. Can you make the coffee? I'll be back in a minute.' And she disappears out through the lounge towards the bathroom.

Laurence, who arrived fearing the worst after his calls had gone unanswered, is not quite sure what's hit him. Carefully he loads the dishes from the sink into Margot's half-size dishwasher, noting as he does so that these are not just the breakfast dishes but those from several meals, all of which appear to have been toast and cereal. When he has cleared the sink and rinsed it, he ties up the garbage, takes it outside and returns to put a new bin bag in place. Then he rinses out the coffee plunger, dries it and makes the coffee. There is no milk in the fridge; in fact there is not much of anything in there – a few sad looking vegetables, a cube of dried-up cheese, three eggs and some sliced bread. It is all totally out of character for Margot.

Laurence catches his breath and hesitates by the fridge door. How long has this been going on? he wonders. Could he have missed the first signs of dementia? He was, after all, away for a longish time, so what other strange things might have happened in his absence? He will have to get her to a doctor; there will be assessments, specialists probably, she will need someone as her advocate. Laurence takes a couple of deep breaths as he braces himself for the task; Margot, he knows, would do the same for him if the situation were reversed.

'Ah! You've cleaned up,' Margot says from the doorway. She is dressed now and obviously showered; her hair is still damp and she looks like her normal self. 'That's nice of you. Where's the coffee? Was there any milk?'

Laurence shakes his head and Margot goes to the pantry and pulls out a carton of long life.

'This okay? Or will you have it black?'

'Milk please,' Laurence says, gesturing towards the carton. 'Margot, do you think perhaps we should sit down and talk about this? I mean, how have you been feeling lately? Your memory, for example – is it okay?'

'My memory's fine,' she says, watching as he pours the coffee from the plunger into two mugs and then struggles with the milk carton. 'Why?'

'Well, well look at you, look at this place . . . the washing up, the pyjamas, and then there's the phone, you haven't been returning calls.'

A flash of understanding crosses Margot's face and she laughs. 'And you think I've lost it! Poor old Margot, she's finally flipped. No, Laurence, I'm fine, it's just that, as I said, I've been busy, totally absorbed and ignoring everything else.'

'Busy with what?'

This tone of disbelief infuriates Margot. It implies that it's unthinkable for her to have something so involving and important that it can keep her from washing up and returning phone calls. But she holds her mug between her two hands, sips the coffee cautiously, and reminds herself that she is behaving somewhat out of character. 'Delicious,' she says. 'Thanks for making it – my first today.'

'Your first? You always said you couldn't start the day without two cups of strong coffee.'

She grins. 'Seems I was wrong about that. I don't think I had any at all yesterday. I'm writing, you see.'

'Writing? I thought you gave up on writing years ago.'

'I did but now I've started again and I can't seem to stop, At least not for trivial stuff like housework and cooking.'

Laurence is not reassured. 'So it's back to the notebooks then?'

'No. I began with them. I actually started a new notebook by writing a sort of catalogue of my failures as a mother and as a writer. Then I realised that all those notebooks were just like that, total self-indulgence. All those Moleskines are about me, Laurence, the fiction, the poetry, the non-fiction – all of it is all about me.'

'Aren't most writers always writing about themselves?' Laurence asks, beginning to relax now.

'Not in this way, not like me. Boring, pathetic self-indulgence. So I tore out those pages.'

'What, all of them? All the notebooks?'

'No, no, the old notebooks are useful. I just tore out the new ones.'

'You can't tear pages from a Moleskine, it's sacrilege. It upsets the stitching.'

'I know, but I did it,' Margot says. 'I had to, you see. When I read what I'd written I saw that it was what I'd been doing all my life. A whingeing journal just written in different genres, designed to convince myself I was doing something worthwhile. So I tore out the pages and sat down at the computer instead. Which reminds me, I must call Grant and get him to help me choose a new computer. Mine is old and slow. I need more of those byte things and more RAM. He'll know what I need.'

'I see,' Laurence says, nodding. 'Well, that's good, I suppose. Is it? Is it good?'

'I hope so. It's good for me, but whether what I'm writing is good I don't know, not yet. I just know I have to do it, from the minute I wake up until I get stuck and then I eat something, and sometimes I get dressed but yesterday I didn't.'

'And what is it that you're writing?' Laurence asks.

'A novel. A novel of contemporary life.'

'Not *your* life, I hope.'

She laughs. 'It's okay, you're not in it, although I guess bits of you may appear in some other guise, but you won't know it. The characters are figments of my imagination, although I guess that everyone I've ever known is in there somewhere. Life is the seed capital for fiction, isn't it? So you're all there but none of you are, if you know what I mean.'

'I know what you mean.'

'But it does seem to have taken me over. I'm compelled to keep at it and I don't have much time or energy for anything else at the moment. So what were you calling for?'

Laurence takes a gulp of his coffee. 'Emma,' he says. 'We need to talk about Emma. This stuff with her face, and she's in financial trouble. That girl has more handbags than Imelda Marcos had shoes. I don't know what the problem is with her, Margot. She's obsessed. I think she's harming herself. She's in debt to the bank, and she's had to give up her flat because she can't pay the rent. She's moving in with Phyl on Friday.'

'Well that's a really good idea,' Margot says. 'They get on well and Phyl can do with the company at present. I totally agree with you about the cosmetic stuff, it's very worrying. Poor Emma.'

'Poor Emma? Is that all you can say? Poor Emma!' Laurence says, raising his voice. 'We have to do something about it, we have to help her. Get her into counselling, fix it; we have to get her out of trouble, Margot, for god's sake.'

Margot sips her coffee slowly, looking at him over the rim of her mug, then she puts it down, adds more coffee to it and drinks again. 'So you've just noticed have you, Laurence? For the past three years Emma has been teetering on a knife edge, and for the past three years I have been talking to her, trying to help her, telling you I'm worried, asking you to speak to her, to help me, and you've just noticed?'

Laurence has the grace to blush. 'Well I knew there was a problem but I thought you . . .'

'You thought I would fix it, like I always do. Well I tried and I can't. I tried everything I know. Emma doesn't listen to me. It makes not a bit of difference whether I scold or cajole or comfort or criticise. I've been pouring my efforts into a black hole and all it's done is make her hostile and angry. She listens to Phyl and she might listen to you, but neither of you listen to me either. So if, after all this time, Laurence, you are really worried about our daughter, I suggest you go and talk to Phyl and the two of you can see if you can do anything together.'

'But you can't just opt out.'

'I'm not. If you and Phyl can succeed where I've failed I'll do whatever you tell me is needed. But I am sick of being the one who's supposed to fix things. I've been doing it far too long, and obviously not particularly well. None of my fixing seems to work so right now I am following Lexie's example and yours, I'm taking time out for myself, for things I want to do. I'm not opting out, just not accepting responsibility. It's different.'

'Well I know you've worked very hard but –'

'There is no but!' Margot cuts in. 'I've not only worked hard, I have been self-sacrificing to a sickening degree and I'm sure you'll agree it's not a very attractive quality. So, no more! I am becoming what I should always have been, a writer. Lexie reminded me that Mary Wesley was seventy when her first novel was published. I intend to beat her so I haven't got long. So now, if you don't mind, I need to get back to my work. Give me a call and let me know how it goes with Phyl and Emma. I'll try to remember to pick up the phone.' And leaving Laurence standing open mouthed,

Margot heads out of the kitchen. 'Take care and don't forget to close the front door when you leave,' she calls over her shoulder, and Laurence, hesitating still in the kitchen, hears the faint sounds of the keyboard as she returns to her work.

∽

As they stand by the lifts in the vast marble foyer, Dot is feigning nonchalance. In fact she is in the grip of the same potentially paralysing grip of nervous anxiety that she has always experienced on entering the corridors of wealth and power.

'They might not give us anything,' Alyssa says as they wait for the lift. 'I suppose they get heaps of people in here looking for sponsorship, and they just walk away empty handed.'

'True,' Dot says. 'But let's not forget that we didn't pursue them, *they* invited *us*.'

The fact that this is a friendly invitation to CASE from the sponsorship department of the bank doesn't make Dot any more at ease than she has been in the past when fronting up to meet government ministers, boards of directors, editors in chief or even a couple of archbishops. She is way out of her comfort zone, and would be much happier on a soapbox in front of a heckling crowd than she is in this intimidating building surrounded by men and women in suits talking into their Bluetooth headsets. She had inherited a reverence for and fear of traditional authority from her hard-up working class parents, and while she has learned to junk the reverence by talking tough, she has never managed to rid herself of the fear. What she has learned, though, is that fear is at its most destructive when it is sensed by others, and she resolved very early in life that she would never let it show, and never allow it to limit what she would do nor whom she would challenge or confront. Even so, it's always there eating away at her, especially in places like this. And it is largely because of Dot that they are here in the first place.

The response to her online debut with the blog and on the social networking sites had amazed not only her but Alyssa and her CASE team. Hits on the campaign website had almost doubled but none of them had been prepared for what happened when a teenager called Katie Romano posted a video clip she'd taken in a Melbourne shopping centre while on holiday with her parents. In the first week that *Aussie Granny's Age Rage* appeared on YouTube it attracted more than five thousand hits. Katie Romano was no cinematographer; the video was speeded up, and the distorted voices and jerky images of a small angry woman chaining herself to railings and declaiming about women being conned by the beauty business and then being tackled by guards with bolt cutters was soon among YouTube's most viewed items. It was Patrick who spotted it first and immediately put up a link to Dot's blog and the CASE site. Immediately the number of people signing up for the campaign surged, and Dot was right up there with kittens falling off windowsills, lions cuddling their keepers and child prodigies playing Mozart violin concertos. *Aussie Granny* was a water cooler topic and was being talked about in the mainstream media.

'But I'm not a granny and I look ridiculous,' Dot had wailed to Patrick, 'demented!'

'Well I wouldn't go that far,' he'd said cautiously, 'but you must admit it's pretty funny and well . . . rather quaint.'

'Quaint! I'm quaint now, am I?'

He'd shrugged. 'It's doing wonders for the campaign, and think of the value to Alyssa's PhD.'

'Don't bother trying to appeal to my better nature,' Dot had said. 'I don't have one. And I'm rather vain. Can't you even slow the thing down?'

But a week later she and Alyssa were guests on Channel 7's *Sunrise* and Nine's *Morning Show*. There were interviews with radio stations and newspapers, the hits on the blog and the website were doubling daily, and there was an invitation from the bank to discuss sponsorship. The video had attracted attention and through it CASE had touched a community nerve. Mothers concerned about their daughters, and older women worried about the younger generation and insulted by the messages about ageing, were quick to register their anger and concern. Even Dot had to admit that *Aussie Granny* had sent the campaign's profile through the roof, and she managed to find sufficient traces of a better nature to laugh at it.

'Imagine what we could do with really big money,' Alyssa says as the lift rises to the ninth floor.

'We'll have to do more than imagine if they decide they're really interested,' Dot says. 'They'll want to see some sort of plan and we'll have to be able to tell them how we'd spend the money down to the last cent. So if we do walk out of here with smiles on our faces we'll also be walking out having made a commitment to get super organised and businesslike.'

As the lift comes to a halt Alyssa is pale with anxiety. 'It's a huge responsibility, big money like that. I don't know anything about that stuff, none of us does –'

'Stop it,' Dot cuts in, detecting a sudden loss of nerve. 'Remember what I told you? Don't let them see you're intimidated. We're going in there to convince them that this is worth doing, because it is, because we believe in it. You started it because you have a passion for it – let them see that passion. And don't worry about the other stuff. We secure their interest first, and we'll worry about the rest of it later.'

But as they step out into the carpeted foyer and are ushered into a meeting room where the walls are hung with portraits of past directors of the bank, Dot's stomach is churning with the old fear, a fear exacerbated by *Aussie Granny*'s success.

Alyssa and the others had come to her for gravitas and to Dot it seems unlikely that she can convey that when what has attracted the bank's attention is a video clip in which she looks entirely ridiculous.

FOURTEEN

Vinka has been shopping and cooking for two days; it's so long since she has given a dinner party she had completely forgotten the amount of work involved – poppy seed cakes, pierogi, barszcz, the dried fruit compote and more. Christmas is still more than three months away but she is breaking with tradition and preparing a scaled down version of *Wigilijna Kolacja*, the traditional Polish dinner served on Christmas Eve. She needs to do this, to cook this special meal for Patrick and her friends, before she begins to pack her life into boxes.

'Maybe it is the last time I can do it,' she says to Stanislav, who has come early to help her move the table to make more space. 'Maybe the place I go doesn't have a kitchen that is good for cooking. Maybe I am dead before next Christmas.'

'You find somewhere nice to live, Vinka,' Stan says. 'I know this, you don't worry about it. There is still plenty of time.'

Vinka snorts in disgust and stalks off to the kitchen. She thinks him a traitor, because the problem of his own future is already solved. He is to share a house with a man whose wife died a couple of years ago. They have been friends for twenty years and Stan seems to have no problem with the

149

prospect of sharing a home. She can just see them, two old men together, walking to the pub, sitting side by side on a park bench putting the world to rights, living in a mess, making beans on toast and forgetting to wash up. 'You probably find a place you like better,' Stan says, following her, watching as she lifts a saucepan from the stove.

'Typical,' Vinka says. 'When it is you who will be homeless it is the big drama. Now it is only me you think everything becomes fine. You are what they call throwback, Stan, a man from the past, who cannot see beyond himself.'

But Vinka knows that it is not just Stan who is affecting her mood tonight. For the first time since his marriage broke up three years ago, Patrick is bringing a woman to meet her.

'Could I bring a friend?' he had asked when Vinka told him about her dinner. 'You'll really like her.'

And she knew from the tone of his voice that this was serious. Vinka believes in love, and although she has never married, she has had long and passionate love affairs, the last of which lasted into her early seventies and ended only with her lover's death. Now, more than anything, she wants love for Patrick. She wants to know that someone else in the world loves him, that there is someone for whom he comes first, someone who will be there when she is gone. But her happiness for him has a darker side of selfish anxiety. This new woman has the power to change things, to draw him away from her. Vinka is not too old to remember what it is like to be in love, nor to understand how intrusive it could be to have a homeless old aunt to consider.

'Dear god,' she says aloud as she stirs the soup and lowers the temperature of the oven. 'Please let her be beautiful and intelligent and loving and let us be friends and let me not get under their feet.'

'Of course you don't get in the feet, Vinka,' Stan says. 'Patrick loves you, he doesn't forget that because he also loves someone else.'

'Who knows?' Vinka says, shrugging. 'Everything is changing – maybe this too.'

❧

As Laurence puffs up the last but one flight of stairs, a double poinsettia in a pot in one hand, a bottle of Polish vodka in the other, the aroma of dinner wafts down to meet him and he stops to savour it. Leaning back against the wall he closes his eyes and recalls struggling up an equally steep flight of stairs for the promise of barszcz, vodka and sex with the volatile Maria, and he wonders fleetingly if Dot was right. Had he really been the cause of all those tears and tantrums? Well, there will be no tears and tantrums tonight, and no sex, but he anticipates a more generous menu, good wine and interesting conversation. He hasn't seen Margot since the day he called in and caught her in her pyjamas, but he's confident the writing will fizzle out as it always has in the past, and very soon she will be back to normal. That will be a relief, because he's really getting nowhere with Emma and needs Margot to get involved. He leans heavily on the doorbell.

'*Dobry wieczór*,' he says when Vinka opens the door, and he thrusts the poinsettia into her hands. 'The dinner smells wonderful.'

'Ha, you speak Polish now?' Vinka smiles and kisses his cheek.

'No! A dozen words only and those were two of them. I'll save the other ten for later.'

'This I look forward to,' Vinka says. 'So *witaj* – welcome. Now you know thirteen words. Come in and Stanislav will pour you a glass of wine.'

❧

'I think the *minor media personality* will really need to be changed to *major*,' Margot says, gasping for breath as they stop for a rest at the third floor landing. 'How the hell does Vinka manage these stairs? She's older than both of us.'

'Frightful, aren't they?' Dot gasps. 'You'd think she might be glad of the move, but it doesn't seem that way. How about *medium* instead of *major*?'

'If you want, but I don't think it'll be for long,' Margot says. 'Besides, it would be better to have my book launched by a major than a medium.'

'How's it going?' Dot asks, setting foot on the bottom step of the final flight.

'Patchy. Some days it swings along and I struggle to keep up, others it's like wading uphill through treacle.'

'That's an occupational hazard,' Dot says. 'I can remember days when words and ideas seemed to spin out of me like magic, and others when absolutely nothing seemed to work and it was just a case of sticking with it until things improved. It's weird and it takes over your life if you let it.'

'A bit like marriage, really,' Margot says, and they both have to stop and lean against the wall as the laughter grasps at their breath.

'Wow, can you smell that?' Dot says. 'It must be our dinner. Woohoo, delicious! Laurence will be in heaven. Maybe we have him to thank for this. The night we went to that Polish club he kept telling Vinka about his favourite Polish dishes.'

'Maria,' Margot says, 'remember her? She started him on Polish food. It's very labour intensive. I once tried to make a poppyseed cake and ended up in tears with all the kneading and trying to make the seeds into a paste. Anyway, how's the campaign going? What did the bank say?'

'They were very encouraging, but we have to get more organised, get a business plan, and offer them some alternatives for the ways we'd use the money. Frankly, despite the wonderful publicity and all the public interest, the whole thing's a bit of a shambles. None of us has a great head for business. I'm hoping Patrick will help.'

'He may be too busy,' Margot says, panting up the last two steps. 'According to Vinka he's in love and the woman in question will make her debut at dinner.'

'Really?' Dot says. 'How interesting. What sort of woman would Patrick go for, I wonder? Intelligent, obviously, serious but sexy without being showy, I think.'

'Probably, but I've only met him a couple of times, so for all I know he might go for one of those blondes with long straight hair and perfect teeth and lots of matching bouncy breasts.'

'I doubt it,' Dot says, pressing Vinka's doorbell. 'I think he's more discerning than that. And I think they only have two breasts each – it's just that it seems like a lot more because they're so sort of in your face.'

Vinka's flat is glowing with flickering candles; the table is covered in a white linen cloth decorated with twists of dark green leaves, and, on the kitchen bench and in the oven, what looks like enough food for an army. And Stan, in a dark suit that has seen rather better days, is filling glasses with champagne.

'I am the man of all work,' he says, handing one to Margot. 'Vinka asks me to help her move the table and now she makes me the wine waiter.'

'Well you're doing a great job,' Margot says indulgently, thinking that the task is hardly onerous. She can't help feeling a little resentful that she's been dragged away from her keyboard.

'Is it a book for girls?' Rosie had asked when Margot explained her reason for not being quite as available as usual. 'Will I be able to read it?'

'Well you'll certainly be *able to*,' Margot had told her. 'But you might not want to. I think you might find it a bit boring.'

'But if you write a boring book *no one* will want to read it,' Rosie said. 'Perhaps you should write a *different* book.'

'I'm afraid I just have to write this one. And of course there may be no one who wants to publish it anyway, in which case no one will get the chance to read it and be bored.'

Rosie had given her a resigned smile. 'Perhaps you're not really a writer, Grandma,' she said. 'You might be too old.'

'Mmm, I've been thinking that myself,' Margot said. 'But I mustn't forget Mary Wesley.'

'Who's she?'

'A writer who was older than me when she started writing,' Margot said.

'Wow, that's *really* old,' Rosie said. 'I'm thinking of writing a book about bird funerals. I'm very good at it, I've written special bird prayers. Selena Murphy has asked me to do one for her canary. She let it out of the cage and it flew round and round and bumped into the window very hard and died. Selena's keeping him in a shoe box, but her mum says he's starting to smell.'

Margot had smothered a smile and agreed that a book on bird funerals would be a very useful thing to have. Indeed, in view of the way she was feeling about her own book that particular afternoon, she thought Rosie's might have a rather better chance of publication.

Vinka, her face flushed from investigating the contents of the oven, joins Margot on the sofa.

'I am so nervous tonight, Margot,' she says. 'It is like I am the mother who waits to meet the person who is perhaps to be a daughter-in-law. I want to like her, and her to like me, or at least that she doesn't hate me.'

Margot nods. 'Remember *we* all know each other but she's walking into a group of complete strangers, so she's probably feeling much worse than you,' she says. But she remembers how it feels to wait in nervous anticipation for first meetings with the men her daughters brought home. Lexie had produced a few safe but dull candidates, of which Ross was perhaps the dullest. As for Emma, there had been various inarticulate youths heavily studded with metal, and then a couple of older men. Margot could hardly believe her luck when Grant not only turned up but demonstrated staying power. Now, Margot feels for Vinka; she grips her hand, recalling the old clench of anxiety, the arrow prayers offered up in case intervention is needed to turn a frog into a prince, or in this case, a princess.

The doorbell rings and Vinka freezes.

'Would you like me to go?' Margot asks.

'No, no,' Vinka says, 'it is not polite for me not to answer the door.' She holds up crossed fingers, pats her hair and hurries to the door.

Margot wanders across the room to where Dot and Laurence are talking by the open window.

'Vinka looks really anxious. Is something worrying her?' Laurence asks.

'Of course it is,' Margot says. 'Don't tell me you've forgotten how daunting it is to have so much invested in someone else's happiness and to be faced with the prospect of a stranger who might change everything?'

'I see – no I haven't forgotten,' Laurence says, looking over her shoulder. 'And if I had I'd be about to receive a timely reminder. Turn around, Margot, Patrick's girlfriend seems to be someone we know rather well.'

And Margot turns and watches as Patrick hugs Vinka and then introduces her to Lexie.

⁓

It was Lexie's decision and she's very happy with it – turning up together at Vinka's dinner was the solution to who should be told about their being together or whether anyone should be told at all.

'I think it went really well,' she says later, as they walk back to the car. 'Mum might have been a bit miffed that she didn't find out before everyone else, but she soon got over it.'

'Yes, and dear old Win, wasn't she thrilled to find I'd found a good woman with first rate connections?'

'Mmm. Well I liked her too, a lot. And I'm relieved they all know now.' She slips her arm through his.

They've been spending quite a lot of time together over the last few weeks and Lexie is slowly discovering a different sort of relationship from those she's had in the past. She had felt at ease with him from the moment they met in the campus café. He'd seemed genuinely interested in her plan to return to study, although there was little more that he could tell her than she had already learned from Wendy.

'I was pacing up and down trying to come up with a convincing reason to call,' he'd said on the phone that same evening. 'You know, some information about enrolment that you don't already have, but I couldn't think of anything even remotely convincing, so I have to opt for honesty. I just wanted to call, to ask if we could meet again.'

And Lexie, who had also been pacing up and down trying to find a reason to call him, responded immediately by telling him so.

'Then dinner tomorrow?' he'd said. 'I could pick you up around seven. And we won't talk about enrolment at all.'

And they didn't. But they did talk about art and politics, about books and music, about a shared lack of interest in football but a liking for cricket, and a secret passion for the manufactured romance of figure skating and an addiction to cooking programs.

'Love 'em,' Patrick had said. 'And I collect cookery books.'

'Me too,' Lexie had said, 'but I never actually cook – well, I mean only when I have to. I only like to look at the pictures or watch other people doing it.'

'No!' Patrick had said with an expression of mock horror. 'What sort of woman doesn't cook?'

'A very happy one with time to spare,' she'd replied, and they'd both laughed longer and harder than it deserved.

'I like your dad,' Patrick says now, reaching into his pocket for his car keys. 'And Margot was lovely to me tonight. She apologised for being a bit distracted, said she's very caught up in the book and it takes her time to readjust to socialising.'

'Book? What book?'

'The one she's writing, the novel.'

Lexie laughs. 'She's *not* a writer, Patrick. She *wanted* to be a writer, she scribbled and jotted away for years and never produced anything. Are you sure you haven't had too much Polish vodka?'

He looks at her in surprise. 'Absolutely not. She may not have written much in the past, but she's certainly writing something now and it's obviously very important to her. She was telling me that when she started it she spent most of that week in her pyjamas eating toast and cereal, glued to the keyboard.'

'No way,' Lexie says. 'Maybe she's the one who had too much vodka.'

Patrick clicks the remote control and the car doors unlock. 'No vodka, no kidding,' he says. 'Your dad knows about it. He said he called in there mid-afternoon and she was still in her PJs typing away like a maniac, talking about Mary Wesley and it not being too late for her.'

Lexie stares at him and now it is she who is miffed, seriously miffed. 'Well she hasn't told *me*. Why *hasn't* she told me?'

Patrick shrugs and opens the car door, ushering her into the passenger seat. 'Perhaps she wanted to keep it to herself until she was ready. I don't think she would have said anything about it tonight except that Laurence started asking her about it while I was with them, so I asked questions too.'

'But I'm her daughter. In fact it was *me* who reminded her about Mary Wesley not so long ago. She could have told me, in confidence.'

'What, just like you told her, *in confidence*, about your astonishing new relationship with a wonderfully dashing younger man?' He slides his arm along the back of the passenger seat and leans over to kiss her, and kiss her again.

'Okay, okay, you're not that much younger,' she says. 'But I *am* too old for necking in the car. Your bed or mine?'

'Mine, I think,' Patrick says with a grin. 'After all, it's king-size.'

'I'm still working out why a single man needs a king-size bed,' Lexie says. 'It seems a bit dodgy.'

'That settles it,' he says, starting the car. 'Definitely my bed – and I'll show you what can be done in much greater comfort than in a measly old queen,' and glancing in the mirror he pulls slowly out from the parking bay and accelerates off in the direction of his own home.

'I do think it's odd though,' Lexie says as they draw up at the traffic lights. 'I don't understand why she didn't tell me.'

Patrick shrugs. 'Margot's a very independent woman, just like you; or rather *you're* just like *her*. And she has her own life that she's entitled to discuss or not as she wishes. She doesn't need your permission to write a book.'

'No,' Lexie says, 'no she doesn't. It's just that . . . well, did she tell you what it's about?'

Patrick laughs. 'Only conceptually,' he says. 'Are you worried that it will contain thinly disguised family portraits?'

'Don't even go there.' Lexie hesitates. 'She wouldn't . . . would she? You don't think that's what she's doing, do you?'

Patrick takes a hand off the wheel and reaches out for one of hers. 'I haven't a clue, Lex, she's *your* mother not mine, and I think you are just going to have to trust her on this. But I doubt that you, your dad and your sister are the sole players in the landscape of Margot's imagination. I suspect she's perfectly capable of writing a novel without putting you in it, and frankly I think you'd be underestimating her if that's what you think.'

FIFTEEN

It is on the fourth day that Emma realises where the dog shit is coming from. She has checked around the perimeter wall of her aunt's garden and nowhere is there space for a dog to squeeze through, but on each of the past three mornings, as she has headed out for her early run, there has been a big stinking pile close to the side wall and each day she has fetched a plastic bag from the shed and removed it. But this morning it dawns on her that dogs are rather more random in their toileting choices, and while this is dog excrement, it was clearly not a dog that dumped it. It began, she realises, on Monday, the day after she'd come home and found Phyllida face to face with Trevor outside the garage. Both the garage doors had been open and Trevor was standing with two pit bulls straining at their leads, and he was saying something about Donald's car, and Phyllida was shaking her head.

'I'm not interested in discussing it,' Emma heard her say. And Trevor had shrugged and started to walk away. He'd turned back at the gate though, and shouted something at Phyllida, but by that time Emma was inside the house and couldn't hear what he said. Phyllida had clicked the remote to close the garage doors and come striding back into the house, slamming the front door behind her.

'What was all that about?' Emma had asked from the top of the stairs.

'I'll tell you later,' Phyllida had said. 'When I've calmed down.' But they had never actually discussed it.

'Bastard!' Emma says aloud now, hurrying to the shed. 'Well I'll show him not to mess with us.' And she grabs the stepladder and a spade, scoops up the offending items and hurls them back over the wall.

'How disgusting,' she says later, standing by the sink with a mug of coffee. 'I can't believe he would do that.'

'Well I certainly can,' Phyllida says. 'It's just the sort of thing he *would* do. I blame Donald, because he hated Trevor but didn't seem able to ignore him. He even bought the Range Rover off him and I wouldn't be in the least surprised to find that he paid way over the odds for it.'

'Uncle Don was so astute, I can't imagine why he didn't tell him to nick off and annoy someone else.'

'Me neither. But Donald *wasn't* actually very astute with people or money. Actually he didn't have a clue. He may have been a brilliant surgeon but he could be quite naive about some things. Thanks for clearing it up, Em. Those dogs are pit bulls, you know, very dodgy. I think it's best not to react. It's probably just what he wants if he's hoping to rattle my cage and get me to move.'

'Well I'm not so sure,' Emma says. 'I've thrown it back over the wall and I hope it landed somewhere really inconvenient. What was the argument about in the drive the other day – not the house again, surely?'

Phyllida sighs. 'Oh look, it was ridiculous. He went past the gate with those bloody dogs and he must have seen me outside the garage, so he came marching in and started going on about the cars. Said he would buy back Donald's Range Rover because I can't need more than one car. And he went on about the slide in prices for second hand vehicles because of the financial crisis, and how his offer wouldn't last. Just like he did about the house.'

'Do you *want* to sell the Range Rover?' Emma asks. 'I mean, you do only need one car and the Forester is much more you, so it might be the easy way to do it. Did he make a reasonable offer?'

'He didn't actually name a figure, and I've no idea what's reasonable anyway,' Phyllida says. 'And yes, obviously I don't need it and I'll get rid of it when I'm ready, but certainly not to him. Over my dead body! That nasty little man thinks he can bully me. He thinks I'm some sort of sitting duck that he can intimidate, so he can make a killing with the house, and now the car. He was really trying to wind me up, kept tapping his nose with his finger and asking whether I'll be disposing of the VW too.'

'What VW?'

'Exactly! We don't own a Volkswagen. I think he's just trying to rattle me. He keeps saying he had some sort of deal with Don. Anyway, I refuse to be harassed by the slimy toad.'

'I can't imagine you being bullied by anyone actually, Aunty Phyl,' Emma says. 'Anyway, I'd better run or I'll be late. I'll be home about seven. Theresa reckons she can fix my face, so I'm going there at five-thirty.'

Phyllida puts on her glasses and looks closely at her niece's face. 'Can't see a thing wrong with it myself. Can't you fix whatever it is with makeup? People don't peer into your face looking for flaws, you know.'

'I'm doing it,' Emma says, tightening her lips. 'And I'm thinking of an eyebrow lift. I've got an appointment with a cosmetic surgeon in a couple of weeks, so I need to get this sorted before then. Okay, I'm off. See you later,' and dropping a kiss on Phyllida's cheek she strides off down the hall and out through the front door.

For Emma, who has already lived at different times with every other member of her family, living with Phyllida is bliss. She has a beautiful room and bathroom to herself, and

Phyllida won't accept rent and only occasionally lets her pay for shopping or lunch when they are out together.

'It might be best if I help you out with that,' she had said when Emma disclosed the extent of her debt. And she'd written a cheque for the full amount. 'Interest free loan,' she'd said as she handed it to her.

Emma was so shocked she could barely speak, but when she got her voice back she had promised to repay it in full.

'We'll talk about that a bit further down the track,' Phyllida had said, and to Emma it sounded as though she was telling her to forget about it.

But it's not just the financial relief. Phyllida, presumably missing the task of looking after Donald, seems to relish the task of looking after her instead. And Rosie's weekend visits are much easier with Phyllida around. Emma alone has never worked out how to be with Rosie, who is so uninterested in all the things little girls are supposed to like – fairy dresses, princesses, magical horses, pretend makeup and dolls – all the things that Emma had loved as a child. She can't quite get a grip on who Rosie is or how they might do things together.

But the best thing about living with Phyllida, Emma thinks, is that her aunt takes her seriously. She makes her feel important. There is something pathetic about being the younger child, especially when the elder sister is so bloody perfect, and so much more like their parents in every way than she is. Emma tends to think of herself as the black sheep, different, awkward, and somewhat embarrassing. Occasionally she likes that and attempts to see it as a strength, but most of the time she resents it and feels trapped by it. A black sheep, she thinks, is only of value if she is either hugely successful or outrageously eccentric, and Emma knows she is neither.

⌒⌒⌒

Each time Phyllida crosses something off her list she feels she is taking a step forward. She has always believed in the value of the list and it has never been more useful to her than now as she endeavours to take life one day at a time in the belief that it will eventually get her where she is supposed to be going, wherever that might be.

With Margot's help, the milestone of sorting and disposing of Donald's clothes has been passed, and the day that she and her sister had packed the boxes and bags into the back of the Range Rover and delivered them to the op shop Phyllida had returned home with a new sense of calm. As she crawled into bed that night she knew that the grief that had wrung her out as she dealt with the contents of his wardrobe had been less for the loss of Donald himself than for the edifice of their life together, its security, its status, all of which had been stripped away by his death. It was a disturbing, unworthy feeling that she didn't plan to share with anyone else and which she tried to push out of her mind. The worst really was over and although the prospect of sorting out the contents of Donald's study still lies ahead, it is a task which, she feels, can be left for another time. Today it is the appointment with the solicitor about the will, and it's long overdue, it's really just a formality, but it's one more job that will be out of the way by the end of today.

Emma's presence is what is keeping Phyllida going right now. Her niece is, she thinks, a blessing, rescuing her from the overbearing emptiness of the house and distracting her from depressing forays into both the past and future. Emma is entirely in the present and although the worrying obsession with her appearance and a serious shopping habit suggest otherwise, she is an intelligent and thoughtful person, and very easy to have around. She is, however, Phyllida thinks, not particularly happy, and a couple of days before she had moved in Laurence had turned up, worried and confused by Emma, and frustrated by Margot's apparent abdication from responsibility.

'I really don't think this is going to get us anywhere,

Laurence,' Phyllida had said, handing him a glass of Donald's best malt whisky. 'Emma's been an unhappy girl for a long time, and Margot's tried everything she knows to reach out to her, so dramatic gestures and raised voices won't help.'

'That's just what Margot said, and I don't understand it, really I don't. What's she got to be unhappy *about*? Margot thinks it could be because we split up but that's donkey's years ago. She seemed okay at the time, and Lexie's okay.'

Phyllida sighed. 'Emma's a different person, and she was only six when you left. She wouldn't have been able to understand that and she may still resent it.'

Laurence gave an irritated sort of snort. 'There would have been other kids at school from broken families though, it wasn't like she was the only one.'

'Maybe it was harder for her because she had to adapt to the fact that you were living with another man.'

'So it's my fault, is it?' Laurence said, waving his glass around. 'All this debt and Botox and shopping is my fault for being gay!'

'You know that's not what I meant,' Phyllida said, refusing to be goaded. Laurence obviously needed some sort of argument to make himself feel better but he wasn't going to get one from her. He was also looking for a quick fix, which she didn't have.

'There are other more obvious causes,' she'd said. 'Margot and I have discussed it. Emma feels she failed Rosie, and I suspect she feels that in doing so she failed her own mother.' She almost added that Emma might feel that Laurence had also failed Margot, but decided to hold back on that. 'It's probably all very complicated. Anyway, now that you've stopped ranting, come and have some soup. I was just going to eat when you turned up, and there's plenty for two. Who knows what's behind all this? Emma may not even know that herself.'

And over pea and ham soup she had suggested a different

approach which involved a few weeks of cosseting Emma in a variety of ways, leading into a slowly tightening regime of financial management, and the introduction of domestic responsibilities. 'And,' Phyllida added, 'maybe some other activities to divert her from shopping.'

'What sort of activities?' Laurence asked.

'Not sure ... maybe something calming and spiritual. Yoga, perhaps. I could do with that myself, or perhaps a hobby of some sort. I might even be able to get her to take up golf. Let's just see what happens when we've spent a bit of time together.'

'Well, you realise you may be stuck with her once she moves in, don't you? Especially if you make her too comfortable.'

'Really, Laurence, that's an appalling thing to say. Have you considered that I might like to be *stuck with her* as you put it?' Phyllida said. 'My own circumstances are rather bleak at present, maybe Emma and I can help each other. And I can promise you that different levels of discomfort will be introduced a little at a time, as and when I think she can handle them. Trust me. You might as well, I seem to be the last resort.'

Now, as she considers Emma's comments about the cosmetic surgeon, Phyllida thinks it might be time for the first little bit of belt-tightening. Emma has been with her for a while now, but it will need to be little by little, kind but firm. Phyllida stacks her breakfast things in the dishwasher, switches it on and glances at the kitchen clock; time to get a move on for the appointment with the solicitor, and when the doorbell rings, she dries her hands on the kitchen towel and hurries to answer it.

The woman on the doorstep seems vaguely familiar; Asian, in her fifties, dark hair greying at the temples, straight faced and serious, wearing a light trench coat over black pants and a black polo neck sweater.

'Yes?' Phyllida says, expectantly.

The woman waits, then sighs. 'You don't recognise me, do you?'

'Should I?'

'May Wong. We met at the hospital.'

'I'm sorry, I . . . oh, of course,' Phyllida says. 'You're one of the nurses. *Sister* Wong, isn't it?' There is some haughty satisfaction in her tone as she recalls this woman's infuriating manner just before Donald's heart attack. 'What was it you wanted?'

'Perhaps I could come in?'

'I'm in a bit of a rush actually, an appointment in town . . .'

But the woman waits, silently, giving no ground until Phyllida, who would not normally succumb to this sort of pressure, opens the door a little wider. 'So,' she says when they are both standing inside the hall. 'What is it?'

'I realise it's been a difficult time for you,' May says, 'but I'm concerned that as you begin to sort through Donald's things, something of mine might get lost or thrown out.'

'I beg your pardon?' Phyllida is irritable now. 'Why do you imagine anything of yours might be here in my house?'

May appears rather more pale than when she first arrived and, looking around her, takes a couple of steps over to a chair and sits down.

'Sorry,' she says, 'I feel a bit dizzy. Tension, I suppose. Look, I'm sure you don't want this any more than I do, so can we just stop playing games and get it over and done with? Donald had a piece of jewellery that's rather precious to me. He took it with him on the day he was taken ill, he'd promised to have it repaired, but of course he wouldn't have had time to take it to the jeweller. It must be somewhere among his things. Perhaps you could find it for me? It's an antique brooch, oval, with garnets and seed pearls in a rose gold setting. Two garnets and a pearl need resetting.

It belonged to my grandmother, so although it's a nice piece the value is largely sentimental. I'd really like to have it back.'

Phyllida stares down at her in silence, her mind racing. The woman must be mad, of course.

'I've no idea what you're talking about. I suppose you want money or something, but you've come to the wrong place,' she says, moving briskly back to the door and opening it. 'Why on earth would Donald offer to get something repaired for you? Please leave now and don't come back.'

'Donald dropped it, that's why,' May says, getting to her feet. 'He dropped it on the bathroom tiles and the stones were dislodged. He said he knew a good jeweller and he'd get it repaired for me.'

'Go,' Phyllida says, 'get out of here now. How dare you come here with this ridiculous story.'

'Phyllida,' May says now in a low voice, 'can we just drop the pretence? There's no one here but us. Just promise me you'll look for the brooch and let me have it back. I'm not asking you for anything that isn't my own.'

There is something about this woman which, in spite of everything, makes her seem plausible. She is quiet, dignified, and appears to be struggling to keep control, and her eyes have the brightness of imminent tears.

'What pretence is it exactly that you would like us to drop?' Phyllida asks.

'You know exactly what this is about,' May says. 'Don't pretend you don't. I've never intruded on you, and all I'm asking for now is the return of something that belongs to me.' She steps through the doorway and turns back at the top step. 'When you find my brooch you can give it to John Hammond, he knows where to find me.' She turns away and goes down the front steps to her car.

In the doorway Phyllida, frozen with shock and confusion, watches her and as the bright yellow Volkswagen Golf pulls out of the drive she feels a tug like quicksand drawing her down to some intolerable unknown depths.

❦

'There are three levels of care here,' the director explains as Dot, Margot and Vinka follow her around the retirement complex. 'Independent living, assisted living and the nursing home. So when a person finds they have increased care needs the transition can be made with the least upheaval. The continuity of care fosters a sense of community and minimises the disorientation that can occur with moving as one gets older.'

She leads them slowly along brick-paved paths lined with bottlebrush to a cluster of units grouped around a paved courtyard. 'These are the independent living units and as you see they face into a central square with seats and gardens, a meeting place, a village square if you like.'

Vinka looks around her, pausing for a moment, and then lowers herself onto one of the long wooden seats that faces a rose bed and beyond it a small gazebo lined with benches. It has, she can see, something of a village atmosphere. But Vinka is not a village person, she thrives in the city. She walks to the corner shop late at night to buy ice cream, or chocolate or a packet of tea. She walks to church and to the doctor's surgery, she walks to buy a newspaper. And she gets on a tram and in less than ten minutes she is in the centre of Melbourne. No chance of doing that here, no chance of walking to civilisation or anywhere else from here.

Close by the director is talking with Dot, telling her how much she used to enjoy her radio program, and that she is now following her blog. Margot joins Vinka on the bench.

'So what do you think of it, Vinka?' Margot asks. 'The gardens are lovely, aren't they?'

'The gardens, yes, fine gardens, very pretty,' Vinka says. 'But it is a long way from town, Margot, almost half an hour on the tram. It feels like – like being put out to . . .' she hesitates, 'to pasture. It is so quiet.'

'It is, and of course a lot of people want that. It's a lovely place but I can understand if it isn't *your* sort of place.'

'Perhaps I have to learn to like it,' Vinka says. 'But that would be hard.'

'If you'd just like to follow me I'll take you into the unit now,' the director calls, and obediently they get to their feet and follow her inside.

The unit is light and modern with pale walls and carpets, a bathroom with gleaming tiles and safety handles in all the right places, a small but well planned kitchen, able to accommodate the demands of a Polish Christmas dinner. Vinka stands in the middle of the living area, which is painted a very pale pink, with a silver grey carpet and full length curtains covered with bouquets of pink roses. Can she learn to live here? Everything she owns fits into a different sort of place. Most of all she herself fits into a different sort of place. But there is not going to be a flat that looks out over the city in an old building of mellow brick and cream plaster. There will not be timber framed French windows with flaking white paint leading to a tiny balcony, just large enough for herself and her chair. That is her past life and she must learn to let go of the idea that she will somehow be able to replicate it elsewhere. Reality is a lead weight on Vinka's chest, it almost stops her breathing. All her life she has taken her own decisions about where she will go and what she will do. Now she sees that her choices are diminishing. She can still choose, but for reasons of age, the threat of infirmity and limited finances, the range of choices is narrow.

'You'll understand that we do have a waiting list,' the director says. 'You do have priority, Miss Renska, as you are required to move from your present home. I know you need to think about this, talk with your family, but I'm sure you'll understand that we will need an answer soon. So, shall we say close of business on Friday? If I don't hear from you by then the unit will go to the next person on the list.'

'I have been lucky,' Vinka says to Margot as they walk out. 'All my life I decide what I want. Now I have to decide from what other people can allow me to have.'

'You *can* turn it down,' Margot says.

Vinka shrugs. 'I must think more. I know I am fortunate to live in a country where there is a good place for me. But to start again, at eighty, this is so hard. Those politicians, they say eighty is the new sixty? They know nothing, I tell you, Margot, nothing at all.'

SIXTEEN

By the time Phyllida announces her arrival to John Hammond's receptionist she has run through various scenarios arising from May Wong's visit. The first, and she feels the most likely, is that there is no brooch and this is the first step in an elaborate con trick to get money out of her. But, if there *is* a brooch, the woman must have been wearing it at some hospital function and Donald perhaps asked to look at it and dropped it. And it's possible too that May was obsessed with Donald, perhaps bothering him at work and, now that he is dead, is attempting to claim some place in his life and death. The final possibility is that Donald did drop the brooch in May Wong's bathroom when he took a shower after having sex with her. The latter is, in Phyllida's opinion, so unlikely as not to merit further consideration. The con trick is the obvious explanation and can probably be dealt with by a stern letter from Hammond telling the woman to stay away and not bother her in future.

But she'd had a moment of doubt just as she was about to leave for her appointment. She remembered that May had referred to Hammond by name. That was certainly odd, but if the wretched woman is a con artist then she would have done her homework first, and that would explain it, although that afterthought had rocked Phyllida's conviction sufficiently to make her question her choice of outfit: by the time she left she had changed her clothes four times. The final choice – an olive green suit with a cream silk shirt and her Broome pearls – says tasteful, confident, dignified and not to be messed with, which is somewhat at odds with the way she feels.

The lawyer's office is flooded with midday sunlight pouring in from the window behind his desk. It settles on Phyllida, making her flush with heat as she sinks into the leather armchair, blinking at Hammond's silhouette behind the desk.

'So sorry,' he says, adjusting the blinds, and the light turns from dazzling white to dappled amber, reflecting the tone of the wood panelling, and he slips back into his swivel chair. 'Thank you for coming in, Phyllida,' he continues, opening a file and shifting some papers. 'I do apologise for chasing you up so many times but there are some things I need to discuss with you – we need to get on with the probate. So, I won't beat about the bush. We need to go through it all together so I can familiarise you with – well, the state of the estate, so to speak.' He hesitates, leaning across the desk, papers in hand. 'Here's a copy of the will so that you can follow it as we go.'

The butterflies in Phyllida's stomach assume the weight of a lead balloon, the print swims before her eyes. 'Just before we do that, John,' she says, 'I must tell you that I had a visit earlier this morning from a woman by the name of May Wong. She's a nurse at the hospital and she claims to know Donald, and possibly you too.'

'Ah!' he says. 'Miss Wong, yes . . . well she is on my list of issues for us to discuss this morning. I'm just sorry that we didn't have a chance to talk about this before the two of you met.'

And in that instant Phyllida knows without a shadow of a

doubt that her world is about to change in ways that she has never previously imagined.

∽∽∽

'Can you believe it, Margot?' Phyllida says, her hand shaking as she takes the cup of tea Margot is holding out to her. 'The treachery of it; *she* will have put him up to it of course. He was always a pushover with women, and this Wong person has just taken advantage of him.'

Margot, to whom the idea of Donald being a pushover with women is frankly ridiculous, takes a deep breath. 'That does seem unlikely,' she says, feeling her way as cautiously as she can. 'After all, you did say that they've been . . . well, that this . . . this relationship . . . started fifteen years ago. So he bought her a car and he left her twenty-five thousand dollars in his will – it's not a great deal for a relationship that lasted so long. She doesn't really seem like a gold-digger.'

'Well, how would we know! He's been drawing large sums in cash for some time and there's no trace of where it's gone, so I think we can assume that some, or all of that, may have gone to her. According to her and to Hammond, Donald told both of them that we had an open marriage and that I had agreed to this continuing relationship as long as I didn't have to know anything about it. It's rubbish, Margot, complete rubbish. You know I would never agree to something like that. I can't believe that Donald would have done a thing like this.'

'Well I can understand that you don't want to believe Miss Wong,' Margot says, 'but I think you have to believe Hammond. He and Donald go way back, they've been friends for years, they played golf every week. If Donald lied to him then it seems likely that he would also have lied to her. I know this is terribly upsetting, Phyl, but it does look as though Donald was deceiving you and lying about it to her. What about your neighbour? Did you say Donald had transferred some money to him?'

'Two payments of five thousand dollars each. I've no idea what this is about – perhaps we'll find something in the files in the study. He bought both the cars from Trevor, but I knew that – although Hammond says in his view the price he paid for them was somewhat inflated. And he bought *her* car from Trevor too.'

Margot shakes her head. 'So he lied about that too. Or lied by not telling you what he was doing.'

'Actually,' Phyllida says, 'Donald was always a fool with money. He couldn't hold on to it. When we got married I took over all the accounting, the banking, everything. It was only when I had the cancer scare and the hysterectomy that he took it over. It was just going to be until I was back on my feet, but somehow I never got around to picking it up again, and I assumed everything was going along as I'd left it. And that was the time when he seems to have started pouring money into a black hole.'

'So let's get this clear,' Margot says, struggling to understand the scope of the problem. 'The things you didn't know about were the bequest to May Wong, the two lump sums to Trevor, and then a lot of big cash withdrawals?'

'Yes. Then there are bequests of twenty-five thousand each to Lexie and Emma, which is what Don and I agreed upon ages ago.'

'Perhaps more of it went to Trevor,' Margot suggests. 'Maybe he got Don to invest in some shonky business. But there are still some investments, and the house and the superannuation are safe and in your name?'

'Yes, of course. I'm not a destitute widow by any means. It's the deception that's so appalling. That woman, it's all her fault. How dare she . . . and turning up at the house this morning, well I . . .'

'Phyl,' Margot says, moving over to sit on the arm of her sister's chair, putting a hand on her shoulder. 'You *have* to stop this. I realise that the shock of Donald's affair is as bad or worse even than the money business. But it was Donald who set all this up, and May Wong has also been taken in by his lies. Blaming her won't help one bit – in fact it just confuses matters and takes your mind off the bigger picture and what you have to do.'

'I suppose you're going to tell me he loved her,' Phyllida says angrily.

Margot sighs. 'I've no idea but it does seem odd that he should have been involved for such a long time, at considerable risk of being caught out, if he didn't care for her pretty deeply. And why would she stick with him under such difficult and limiting circumstances if there wasn't more to it than a VW Golf? It's hardly compensation for having to live out your relationship in hiding. I suppose you haven't gone through his desk and the other stuff in his office yet?'

Phyllida shakes her head. 'Couldn't face it. It wasn't like the clothes, I always looked after his clothes, but the study was his empire, it seemed like such an invasion. Or rather it did seem that way until today.'

'Well when you're feeling a bit better we should sit down and go through everything,' Margot says. 'Who knows whether we'll find things are better or worse than they seem, but either way you'll be clear about where you stand.'

By the time Phyllida leaves, Margot's energy and goodwill is wearing thin. It's not that she doesn't understand how devastating this is for her sister, but understanding and sympathy are diluted with resentment at being drawn once again into someone else's crisis. It's family stuff, after all, she tells herself – who else would Phyllida go to? But her intense involvement with her writing has forced her to create some of the boundaries she has previously lacked, so that now she is less willing, resentful even, that her time and energy are being siphoned off into Phyllida's problems. Phyllida has, after all, been less than helpful in Margot's own times of crisis, and so Margot can't help but think of all the times when her sister has not been there for her.

'You've only got yourself to blame,' Phyllida had said when, at twenty, Margot had confided that she was pregnant. 'Don't think I'm going to help you with this, Margot. You got yourself into this hanging around with that fast crowd from the Push, so you can get yourself out of it. I'm having nothing to do with it.'

And she hadn't. It had been a torturous time; both sets of parents had been shocked and had proved themselves experts in the art of apportioning blame. Margot's memory of her sister at that time was of her in the background tut-tutting and shaking her head with disapproval every time Margot's condition or the forthcoming baby was mentioned.

Some years later, when Margot was pregnant again, Phyllida had learned that she would not be able to have a child of her own and developed instead a passionate interest in her forthcoming niece. And when Emma arrived and turned out to be a particularly enchanting baby, Phyllida took an almost maternal interest in her, often passing judgment on the way that Margot and Laurence were raising their girls. And in that terrible time when Laurence had left to live with Bernard, Phyllida's support had been notably absent.

'You're better off without him,' she'd said. 'Don't waste any more time on Laurence, Margot. It's you and the girls now, that's what you need to focus on.'

Margot has always known that Phyllida loves her and would do anything for her if she asked, but her emotional distance, her air of knowing what's best and her failure to step into her sister's emotional space have always made asking impossible. Phyllida has lived her well-ordered, well-heeled life close by but at a distance, while Margot has trodden water in the financial stress and messy unpredictability of a broken family. In those self-obsessed notebooks she has seen a picture of herself that she doesn't like. It is a picture of a disappointed woman who, while appearing to cope admirably with the loss of her dreams and her husband, has actually been burning with resentment and incapable of being honest about it. Now, writing about characters that are figments of her imagination, she has learned a great deal about herself. If the deck chairs are being shifted in her relationship with her sister, something has to give. She can't do this alone. She's willing to be the sister she has always wanted Phyllida to be to her, but she knows she must find a way of doing that without donating her bone marrow in the process.

SEVENTEEN

'It's not going to work,' Dot says, banging her fist on the table. 'You have to trust me on this, it simply won't work. It'll be a waste of money and effort if we rush into it now.'

Alyssa, who, like Dot, has a sense of the dramatic and enjoys large gestures, sighs noisily and throws her arms in the air in exasperation. 'So you're saying we just put everything on hold, stop the campaign and go off and paint our toenails until after the summer holidays?'

They are gathered around the cluttered table in the house that Alyssa and two of the others share, three blocks down from Dot's own home. As well as Dot, Alyssa and her housemates, Karen and Lucy, there is Sam, an internet studies student who built the original CASE website, Alyssa's mother Jean, and Lexie, who has also enlisted Wendy. There is an awkward silence around the table as everyone watches Dot and Alyssa, two drama queens who both hate to lose an argument. Lexie wonders how long the stand-off will last and whether this is how all the meetings have been so far.

'I'm not suggesting that you paint your toenails, Alyssa,' Dot says. 'I'm not even suggesting that we take time off from the campaign, I'm simply saying we should use the time to plan it properly. Yes, we need to have an attention grabbing event of some sort, but we can't do it in a shopping centre just before Christmas.'

'But if we get in there a couple of weeks before Christmas we'll get the crowds, people will *have* to take notice because we'll make it chaotic.'

'Exactly. We'll be a nuisance.'

'Isn't that how a protest works?' Alyssa says, her voice rising. 'You make a nuisance of yourself so that people have to take notice of you.'

'But there are times when it just won't work,' Dot says. 'Like in those last frantic weeks before Christmas when people are busy and harassed, trying to finish their shopping. They'll just be pissed off – it'll do us more harm than good.'

'I'm with Alyssa,' Sam says. 'We do something asap. Stuff moves fast on the Net and we don't want to lose momentum.'

'Then perhaps you should come up with another way to keep up the online momentum over the holiday period,' Wendy says, 'but I'm with Dot on this.'

'I say do it now,' says Karen, smiling at Alyssa.

'You would,' Dot says crisply. 'You always do what Alyssa tells you.'

Karen flushes. 'I do *not*.'

'You do *so*,' Lucy cuts in. 'I think Dot's right. Christmas is the worst time for it.'

'But it isn't *just* Christmas,' Alyssa says. 'If we don't do it before Christmas then there's the Boxing Day and New Year sales. Next you'll be telling us don't do it in the school holidays. We need to show the bank we can actually do something so they'll give us the money.'

'Have you guys ever actually *organised* a protest?' Dot asks. 'Have you actually taken part in one?'

Alyssa throws her arms in the air again and does some more exasperated sighing. 'Not exactly . . .'

'Dot's right, Alyssa,' Jean says. 'She knows what she's talking about.'

Lexie, whose frustration with the way things are going is obvious from her expression, leans forward. 'Look, I think we're having the wrong conversation,' she says. 'You've done a great job setting this up. Dot's blog and that crazy little video have taken it to another level, and now the bank is interested in sponsoring CASE. But you don't have a plan and without a plan you'll never get the money. I'm not sure you're even clear about what you're trying to achieve.'

'We want to stop it,' Alyssa says angrily 'stop the exploitation, stop the standards of the sex industry wheedling their ways into kids' imaginations, and dictating what it is to be a woman. There's no way kids or teenagers can get away from these images and messages. That's what we're about.'

'Exactly,' Dot says. 'At least we agree on that.'

'And how are you going to do that?'

Alyssa sighs again. 'Raising public awareness, of course.'

'So how will you know when you've done enough of that, and how are you going to direct it? Where are you going to channel all the awareness and support you get?' Lexie asks.

There is silence around the table as people doodle on their pads, shift in their seats and exchange embarrassed glances.

'Look,' Lexie says, 'you asked us here to help decide on a proposal for the bank, but before you can do that you need a business plan and a campaign strategy, you need to know what you're aiming for in practical terms. What are your key performance indicators? How are you going to best spend whatever money you can get? How are you going to use the people who have signed up for the email lists, or those who are volunteering to help? You have nothing other than your energy, the original idea and a vague plan for a protest. None of that will convince the bank that sponsoring CASE would be a good use of its money.'

There is a moment of acute embarrassment and discomfort

around the table, followed by mumblings of agreement. Dot and Alyssa glare at each other but stay silent.

'This has to be fought on several different fronts,' Lexie goes on. 'Governments, the magazine industry, the music industry, entertainment, fashion. It's huge, it takes money, time and organisation. You've got to get serious, demonstrate that you know how to develop it, not just throw together some event to make a splash.'

'She's right,' Wendy says. 'This meeting – these petty arguments – are a waste of time and energy. You can keep this thing ticking along and not really going anywhere and people will drop off and lose interest, but if you want this to fly really high you've got to get serious and get organised now.'

There is a murmur of agreement.

'And there's one more thing,' Lexie says. 'Why a protest in a shopping centre? For lots of women shopping centres are a source of pleasure, even if they can't afford to shop. You're not going to get those women on side by attacking the places they go to escape. Sorry, Dot, I know you tried it with the chains, but I think a shopping centre is a bad move. Keep the stuff going online, and if you want an event you need a good old-fashioned rally. Perhaps in one of the parks. Some rousing speeches and maybe something happening when it's over – invite everyone to bring a picnic and listen to a women's choir, or something like that. Simple but big, and well organised, the way our mothers and grandmothers did it. They knew how to do those things, they kept doing it and it worked. It worked then and it can work now. Back to the future!'

'Sure you won't come in?' Wendy says later as Lexie pulls up outside the house. 'There's some soup I can heat up.'

Lexie shakes her head. 'No thanks, I said I'd go to Patrick's. He's cooking, although the thought of what I've just committed myself to is enough to put me off the idea of food.'

'Mmm, I *was* surprised,' Wendy says, 'but you were terrific, Lex, and it really does need someone to get behind the wheel.'

Behind the wheel is exactly where Lexie knows she has positioned herself by agreeing to write the business plan and more or less manage the campaign. And while it made sense to her, even seemed exciting, during the meeting, she wonders now whether she's taken on too much. She's been enjoying this time without working; it's years since she took a proper holiday, or even had some time at home to relax, and that, plus the freedom of living alone, have made her feel as though she is slowly emerging from a chrysalis. Patrick, she knows, has been a big part of that but, burnt by the past, she still feels the need to proceed with caution. Lexie doesn't like the sort of person she had become with Ross, the one who holds it altogether, who struggles to make it work, who fills the gaps in their emotional and social lives. And who ends up feeling resentful because it is all so one-sided. Being that person sapped her spirit and work became the only thing that could revive her. Never again, she has promised herself, and so far it seems to be working, but she doesn't quite trust it yet, or perhaps it's that she doesn't quite trust herself.

Patrick is making pasta when she arrives, the smell of the sauce is wafting out through the screen door which he has left unlocked for her, and her first thought is that although she's not in the least bit hungry, she's going to have to eat it in order not to hurt his feelings. Unlike Lexie herself, Patrick is an excellent and enthusiastic cook – the food, she knows, will be delicious – but he's a man, and her experience of men cooking is that the meal is served with the expectation that it will be received with a sense of wonder. Considerable creative effort is needed to come up with enough different forms of praise to last throughout the eating of it, and declining a second helping will be seen as criticism, while failure to round it off with a statement liberally scattered with superlatives could cause a stand-off, even an argument. But all that is nothing compared to not wanting to eat at all – that's a declaration of war.

She pauses, hand hovering above the door handle, and the evening ahead just seems like hard work. She's heading into so much that's new and she's too confused about what she's doing and why to have to do all that business of propping up another person's ego. This, she reminds herself, is what it's like to be in a relationship. You don't want this, Lexie, she tells herself, you really don't. Cut and run now, while you still can. She hesitates, then turns quietly away from the door.

'Come on in, it's open,' Patrick calls from the kitchen.

Lexie's heart sinks and, compelled by the habit of a lifetime, she takes a deep breath and opens the door.

'Sorry I'm so late,' she says. 'It all got a bit out of hand.'

Patrick puts down his spoon. 'It's fine,' he says. 'From what Dot and Alyssa have, separately, told me I guessed you might be walking into quicksand. Here,' he pours a glass of wine and hands it to her, 'sit down, tell me what happened. Dinner won't be long.'

Lexie sits at the already laid table and sips her wine, thankful at least that he knows about CASE and the idiosyncrasies of the people involved. 'You won't believe what I've let myself in for,' she says, and begins to describe the tensions of the meeting, and her own intervention. 'So right now I feel like kicking myself. Driving this thing is a whole lot of work that I don't need, and managing Dot and Alyssa is probably going to be a nightmare.'

Patrick pulls the pan from the heat and joins her at the table. 'You'll do a wonderful job, though,' he says, 'and you're just what they need.'

'Maybe, but is it what *I* need? Right now I'm having a terrible attack of cold feet. I'd just talked myself out of the need to be the one who runs things and now I've volunteered for this.'

'Right now you're tired,' Patrick says, 'and you're also thinking you're on your own. You're not, I'm here. I know quite a lot about it already – Alyssa's got me well and truly sucked in. I can help if you want me to, we can do it together.'

'Really?'

He laughs. 'Of course. It'll be fun – or at least some of it will be fun and the rest *will* be a nightmare, but I think we could manage it.'

Lexie hesitates. 'Ross wouldn't even have listened to what I've been saying,' she says. 'His eyes would have glazed over ten minutes ago.'

'So?'

'It was like he tuned out of anything that wasn't one of his things – his job, the music he liked, the footy. He used to claim that he was a good listener but his eyes would begin to drift away and he'd stop listening almost as soon as I started to say something.'

Patrick is silent a moment. 'I'm not Ross, Lexie,' he says in a low voice, 'and I *am* interested in what you're doing. But most of all I'm interested in you, because in case you haven't noticed, I'm in love with you. So how about you start letting go of some of those assumptions and seeing me for who I am instead of who I'm not?'

Lexie stops breathing. It's as though the breath is trapped high in her chest and may choke her. Patrick puts up a hand and strokes her face.

'Now,' he says, getting up and crossing back to the stove. 'Dinner, you must be starving.'

She still can't speak, and he looks back, waiting for a reply, and sees the expression on her face.

'Ah!' he says. 'You're not, are you? The last thing you want is food.' He flicks the switch to off, turns out the light on the range hood, comes back to the table and, taking her hand, pulls her to her feet and wraps his arms around her. And they stand together holding each other for what seems like quite a long time.

'The thing is,' Patrick says eventually, 'I know you're not hungry and that's fine. But I'm starving and could eat enough for both of us. Why don't you pour us some more wine and we can talk this CASE thing through while I pig out.'

~~~

It's quite late when Emma leaves the beauty salon. Theresa's handiwork has lifted her spirits and she stops off to buy some pantyhose and body lotion. There is, she thinks, a luxurious sort of naughtiness about evening shopping, as though it's something that really ought to be forbidden. The temptation to make the most of it is overwhelming and before she knows it she's on her way back to the car with a pair of designer jeans that were on sale and a black t-shirt. The house is almost in darkness when she gets home, but it's clear that Phyllida is in and watching television in the lounge with the light of just one table lamp.

'Bit dark in here,' Emma says, popping her head around the door. 'Sorry I'm so late, but you just have to see what Theresa did. It's such a relief.' And she snaps on another lamp and looks at Phyllida. 'What do you think? I feel like a normal human being again.'

Phyllida looks up, squinting against the sudden light. 'Mmm . . . good,' she says. 'I'm sure it's much better.'

Emma thinks her aunt looks a bit odd, tired probably. 'And look,' she says, tipping out the contents of her bags. 'I got these divine jeans, they fit perfectly, twenty per cent off – don't you love the cut? And this t-shirt, it doesn't look much like this but it's really stunning on, you see it has one bare shoulder, and the other shoulder is covered and it has this long sleeve.' She holds up the t-shirt so Phyllida can see it. 'Theresa says that the cosmetic surgeon does a fantastic eyebrow lift, and I might ask him about my chin – well, at least this sort of thick bit just beneath it. What do you think?'

Phyllida gets up and tosses the remote control onto the coffee table. She's looking different now, not just tired but grumpy or upset perhaps.

'What I think,' she says, crossing to the door, 'is that if you go to a cosmetic surgeon and ask him what he can do to your eyebrows and your chin, he will draw all over you in texta, add in a couple more essential procedures and charge you a couple of hundred dollars to tell you how much more money he can take off you. And it's irrelevant because you can't afford it, Emma, you don't *have* the money. So I suggest you cancel the appointment and pay the two hundred dollars or whatever it would have cost into my account as the first repayment on the money I loaned you.'

'Well, but I . . .'

'Emma, dear,' Phyllida says with chilly calm, 'all those years ago when I bought you your first Barbie doll I didn't intend for you to use it as a role model. It never occurred to me that you would but I see now that I was wrong.'

And with that she stalks out of the room and upstairs to her bedroom, and Emma hears the door slam followed by the sound of the television. She sinks down onto the sofa, her face burning. Phyllida's remarks and the tone in which she made them seemed designed to hurt and they have. Emma feels as she did back in the playground, being jeered at for stuff about her father that she didn't understand, and for some time she just sits there on the sofa gazing at the mute images on the screen, wondering what had happened, what Phyllida had meant and why she had attacked her like that.

She goes to the kitchen, makes some toast, and as she sits down again in front of the television her spirits lift as *Ten Years Younger in Ten Days* is just about to start. For almost an hour she watches two people being criticised and sniggered at by strangers for the way they look, then being patronised by stylists, hairdressers, beauty experts, and finally tweezed, nipped, tucked, drilled and buffed. It's wonderfully reassuring to Emma to see how, in just a few days, a person can be totally transformed. And by the time the victims are fully made over she herself is feeling very much better. She turns off the television, puts her plate in the dishwasher and goes up to bed, but without the distraction of the television the makeover fix begins to wear off. An image of Barbie dangles in Emma's consciousness like an irritating ornament on a driving mirror, and once again she is back in the playground with all the hurt, the confusion and the shame; most of all the shame.

'Phyl not around then?' Grant asks the next morning when he comes to drop Rosie off for the weekend.

'She's still in her room,' Emma says, pouring water into the coffee plunger. 'She seems a bit out of sorts.' She is still feeling wobbly from Phyllida's strange attitude to her the previous evening, and the restless night that followed.

'I could go and cheer her up,' Rosie says, heading out of the kitchen.

'Best not, darling,' Emma says, 'she might still be asleep. You'll see her later, when we get back from shopping with Grandma.'

Rosie heaves a huge sigh. 'Okay,' she says. 'But I'm sure I could make her feel better.' And she opens the door to the garden. 'I'm going to look for dead birds.'

Grant's mouth twitches in a smile and he looks at Emma. 'I guess this obsession with dead birds could be considered a bit sick but I think it's rather cute.'

Emma nods and pushes the plunger and a mug towards him across the bench top. 'I suppose, but then I'm no expert on child development.'

'Ouch! Was that a dig at me or just you being down on yourself?' Grant asks.

Emma shrugs. 'The latter, of course. You are, after all, a saint, as my mother and aunt keep reminding me.' As the words fall from her lips Emma wonders where this is going, why her vulnerability this morning has turned into something bitter without her knowing it.

Grant looks down into his coffee and says nothing. Eventually he lifts his cup, drinks and looks up at her. 'Is this about something specific I've done, or is it general angst?' he asks.

Emma sighs; it's his face that's hurting her. The face she fell in love with – well, not just his face, his whole self, sitting there opposite her now just being himself, being Grant, with whom she had once been happier than at any other time in her life, and with whom she now always feels her sense of inadequacy more acutely than with anyone else, even Rosie. Most of the time she can handle it, but this morning, destabilised and confused by Phyllida's chillingly critical manner, she is on the brink of tears.

'Neither,' she says, looking up at Grant. 'It is specifically about something else, I'm just taking it out on you.'

'Okay,' he says, nodding slowly. 'Okay. Well, would it help if I leave now?'

She shakes her head. 'No. Sorry. I'm pulling my head in right now.'

'Do you want to –'

'No,' she says again, cutting across him. 'I definitely don't want to talk about it.'

'Right, then why don't we take our coffee outside in the sun with Rosie?' he says. And picking up his mug he holds the door open for her. 'You're far too hard on yourself, Em,' he says as she walks past him. 'Why don't you cut yourself a bit of slack.'

And Emma, usually resentful of the accuracy with which

he can still read her moods, now feels an overwhelming urge to confide in him. It's an urge she manages to keep in check.

'It's complicated,' Margot says later, while they're sitting on a seat in the Central Park mall, watching Rosie bouncing up and down on the bumpy castle. 'Phyl's had a few nasty shocks,' and she fills Emma in on the existence of May Wong and the missing money. 'I want you to talk to her, Em, tell her that you know. She needs someone to confide in and she trusts you more than anyone.'

'This is weird,' Emma says. 'Uncle Donald with a mistress! I can't believe it. I can't imagine anyone ever actually wanting to sleep with him, can you?'

Margot allows herself a twitch of a smile. 'Frankly no, I can't. In fact I couldn't even imagine it the first day Phyl brought him home to meet Mum and Dad. But there you go, there's no accounting for taste.'

'But she'll have a fit if she knows you've told me.'

'She'll be mad at me, but she'll get over it. It'll be a relief to have someone on hand to talk to and you really are the best person to listen. She's shocked and hurt, but the worst thing is that she's embarrassed and ashamed.'

'But it's not *her* fault,' Emma says. 'She's got nothing to feel ashamed of.'

'You and I know that,' Margot says, 'but all Phyl can see is that she's been made a fool of by someone she loved and trusted. Everything she believed about her marriage and their life together has been trashed. Donald has made her look ridiculous and no, it's not her fault, but it doesn't stop her feeling hurt and ashamed. You can help her, Em.'

Emma hesitates, this is not a task she relishes. 'Okay,' she says eventually. 'Okay, if you think so I'll give it a go.'

❧

Laurence is packing books – Bernard's books. He is putting them carefully into boxes, sealing them and sticking on the labels with Bernard's address in Ho Chi Minh City. Then he carries them, one at a time, out into the hall and adds them to the pile ready for the courier who will collect them tomorrow morning. It is a painful task; with each box he closes he imagines Bernard opening it, slitting the tape with a knife, folding back the flaps, lifting out each book with that wonderful sense of rediscovering things one so often forgets about when they are on the shelf. Will Bernard think of him as he unpacks the books? Will he imagine Laurence's hands holding them, stroking them lovingly? Will he remember his touch, as Laurence now remembers Bernard's touch? But of course Bernard will not be thinking like this because for him it is over, he has chosen another life. Has Bernard found someone new? Apparently not, but then how would Laurence know? He has no spy network in Ho Chi Minh City.

They had met the year he turned forty and Bernard, just twenty-three, approached him to supervise his PhD, because of his work on Henry James. From the moment Bernard walked into the office Laurence knew that his lifelong struggle to suppress his true nature was about to face its greatest ever challenge. The smart thing, of course, would have been to decline and send Bernard to someone else, but of course he didn't. And in the end it was Bernard who was the first to declare his feelings and Laurence had counselled that for both their sakes these feelings should not be acted on. The Campaign Against Moral Persecution had been established in Sydney in 1970 and its Melbourne branch, Society Five, a year later, but homosexuality was still illegal.

'It's your career and mine,' Laurence remembers saying at the time. 'The risks are enormous, and I have to think of Margot and the girls.'

'But this is who you are,' Bernard had told him, 'who

you've always been. Are you really prepared to spend the rest of your life living a lie?'

The truth of Bernard's challenge that day had freed Laurence from the masquerade and enabled him to grow and work in ways he had never dreamed possible. Before that, however, it had cost him his job. Once he had left Margot and the news filtered out, Laurence knew his card was marked. Sleeping with students, even mature adults, was a disastrous career move especially, as the Dean had pointed out, when it was 'illegal fornication'. Bernard completed his thesis and together they set off for a few years to Prague and later to Paris, and by the time they came home Australia had moved on.

And now Bernard has moved on; he wants the challenge of somewhere new and eventually perhaps *someone* new, while Laurence, almost seventy-five, wants to cling to the present, to preserve what he has or had. He wants the intimacy and tender comforts of familiar love, the cosy irritation of having his sentences finished by someone younger, the peace and the tension of living daily with the rough and the smooth of a partner for whom, until now, he has always come first. For this he left Margot devastated and bewildered with her life in shreds, left his daughters hurt and confused, and now it is over and he's alone.

In hindsight wisdom about the age gap comes easily, Laurence thinks as he adds a box to the stack in the hall. Years ago he had worried that the age difference would be a problem, that they would find they no longer had enough in common to keep them together, or that as he got older Bernard would find him boring, distasteful or just plain dull. But somehow he had assumed that if it was going to happen it would have done so long ago and he had ceased to worry. He had come to inhabit the comforting assumption that they would go peaceably on together forever. And now here he is, an old man alone in an empty house, where half the bookshelves are empty of books, half the wardrobe is empty of clothes and half the bed is still and cold. An old man too sad, too frightened, too shamed by loss to seek comfort by sharing his grief, and who feels he has hurt others too much to expect anyone to care.

Laurence is not normally given to self-pity but it is hard to avoid it in his present situation. He would like something positive to do, something that would force him to focus on reorganising his life, something to distract him into action. He needs to come out about this just as he came out about his sexuality years ago, but so far he hasn't been able to take the first step, and the longer he leaves it the harder it seems.

He tapes up another box, attaches the label and carries it slowly to the hall, leaning back against the front door just as someone rings the bell and follows the ring with the thump of a fist. Briefly Laurence considers not answering, standing stock still, holding his breath, pretending not to be there. Whoever it is rings the bell again, more aggressively this time.

'Come on, Laurence,' a familiar voice calls. 'I know you're there – I saw you walk past the window. Open up.'

Dot, dressed in her trademark black, this time a sleeveless linen dress with an emerald silk scarf, is standing on the doorstep taking a last drag on a cigarette.

'No good hiding from me,' she says with a grin. 'Let me in – oh sorry, I'll put it out.' And she drops the cigarette on the step, grinds it out with her foot and retrieves the stub. 'Where will I dump this?'

Laurence opens the door wider and she steps inside and reaches up to kiss his cheek.

'Haven't you given up that disgusting habit yet?' he says, taking the butt from her and leading her through to the back of the house and out to the terrace, where a few moths are darting around the citronella lamps.

'Not quite,' Dot says. 'I keep trying. I cut it down a lot

when I was in India. I can make a packet last a week now. By the time I get it to zero I'll have died of something else.' She hands him a bottle of red wine and he studies the label.

'Grange!' he says, looking at her over the top of his glasses. 'I'm impressed. What are we celebrating?'

'We're not celebrating,' Dot says, 'we're commiserating. Well, *I* am commiserating with *you*.' She nods towards the mess of books spread on the floor, the boxes in the hall. 'You're packing Bernard's books.'

'Oh well – yes, he needs a few. They want him to stay on a bit longer.'

'Bullshit,' Dot says, sitting down. 'He's gone for good. I bumped into his sister when I was getting petrol. She told me.'

'Ah!'

'Yes, ah! Go and get a corkscrew and some glasses.'

Laurence sighs, puts the bottle on the table, pads back into the kitchen and returns to open the wine. 'How long have you known?'

'Yesterday morning. And I know he left before you went on your pilgrimage. Did all that walking and spiritual self-flagellation help?'

Laurence feels as though his body is resisting a weight greater than he can manage and he sits down abruptly, pushing the bottle and the corkscrew towards Dot. 'You open it,' he says. 'I don't know really; weeks of walking unprepared in the heat was torture, far too much time to think about the past, the wreck of my life, and the way I've wrecked other lives. The most I can say is that there was some satisfaction in actually completing it.'

'And you haven't told anyone?'

'Not a soul.'

'Not even Margot?'

He shakes his head. 'I keep intending to but I always chicken out. I caused her enormous grief and great hardship – coming out, the scandal at the university, the financial problems, the burden of bringing up the girls. And now it ends like this. It almost seems like an insult to her.'

'Bollocks,' Dot says. 'You and Bernard lasted thirty-four years. It's not as though you left Margot for a meaningless fling. And it would have come out some other way; you can't spend your life trying to pass as something you're not. Of course it was bloody dreadful for Margot but you're assuming that she still thinks she could have had a better life if you'd continued to do your straight man act.'

'Well I think she'd have been better off if we hadn't got married.'

Dot pours the wine, pushes a glass towards him.

'You did the honourable thing and that was really important to her at the time. I'd bet that it still is now. Lord knows what would have happened to her if you'd done a disappearing trick or sent her to some sleazy backstreet abortionist. And you have the girls. I don't know how much that means to you, Laurence, but it means the world to Margot. Cheers.'

'Cheers. Yes, it means the world to me too.'

'She's fond of you, Laurence. She loves you – not in the old way, but she knows who you are, she respects that. I probably shouldn't be attempting to read her mind but I don't think she'll see this as an insult. She'll be sad for you, but she does need to hear it from you first, not learn it from someone else.'

He nods. 'You're right,' he says, sipping his wine.

'Good. I know about these things, of course, thanks to my vast experience of satisfying long-term relationships,' and she lets out a hoot of laughter.

Laurence almost chokes on his wine and they both laugh aloud, released now from the emotional tension.

'Don't you ever regret it?'

'What?'

'Well it does seem as though you've spent most of your

life alone or in relationships that you chose for their obvious temporariness.'

She shrugs. 'I was never into the marriage and happy families stuff – missing gene maybe. And anyway, who'd put up with me?'

'So no regrets?'

'You can't get to our age without some regrets, can you? I mean I'd love to be able to say I'm such a free spirit that I regret nothing, but it wouldn't be true.'

Laurence nods. 'Byron Bay nineteen sixty-six? We've never talked about it but I've often wanted to ask you how you feel now, all these years later.'

'Secret women's business,' Dot says.

He picks up the bottle of wine. 'I thought you'd spent a fortune on this very fine wine so we could share our secrets.'

'I didn't buy it, it was a gift, and it's been sitting in the rack for some time. I decided we'd drink it tonight so that you could tell me *your* secrets, not prise mine open.'

She takes a long breath and sits for a moment, unmoving, staring at a moth that comes back time and again in an attempt to reach the light. 'Okay, yes I do think about it. There are times when I've felt haunted by it and, yes, occasionally I regret it. But they're the regrets of age, part of getting old and living in the last chance café, looking back and seeing how I could have done it differently. But I didn't know that then, and I don't dwell on it now – only when, perhaps, I'm a bit maudlin and self-indulgent. It soon passes and present reality seems pretty good. We're still alive, Laurence, vertical, independent, our friends still speak to us, we even have our own teeth – that can't be bad for three-score years and fifteen!' And she pushes her glass towards him. 'More please, and I need something to soak it up. Shall we dial a pizza?'

Laurence refills their glasses and makes the call.

'There's something else,' Dot says, 'another reason I needed to talk to you. You know this campaign that Margot and Lexie and I are involved in?'

'Of course, I'm avidly reading your blog, very reminiscent of the old ratbag Dot, terrific stuff.'

'Good. Well I need you to get involved too.'

'Me? I know nothing about it. I mean, I support you absolutely. If it's money you want I'm happy to make a donation.'

Dot shakes her head. 'I'm not asking for your money, although of course I'll take whatever you want to give. But what I really want is your time, your analytical skills and your advice.'

Laurence raises his eyebrows. 'Really? You have an opening for a grumpy old man with a background in literary criticism?'

'Exactly! Lexie, who turns out to be a brilliant strategic thinker and an absolute stickler for detail, has pointed out that if we are going to take this thing to the next level we need to be really well prepared. She's taking over, preparing a business plan, and working with Alyssa on some projects to take to the bank. But we need to do some research – facts, figures and strong arguments, some idea of what's happening elsewhere – the US, the UK. Margot's on the committee but I don't want to ask her to do this, because after all these years she's finally into her writing. I thought you might be willing to help.'

Laurence stares thoughtfully out across the darkness of the garden, considering his loneliness, his apathy, his unwillingness to do anything other than mope and feel sorry for himself. It's been going on too long, so long it has become a habit, so long that the effort to involve himself in something new seems monumental. He wonders if he is clinically depressed or whether this is just a normal state of grief. Either way, he thinks, the only way to shift himself out of it is to get involved in something that will occupy his time and perhaps jolt him out of gloom.

'Okay,' he says, turning back to Dot. 'I imagine I can get to grips with that and it might stop me wallowing in self-pity. When do you want me to start?'

'How about tonight?' Dot says with a grin. 'I've got a heap of stuff in the car. I can talk you through what we're doing after we've had our pizza.'

EIGHTEEN

The first thing that Phyllida sees when she opens the top right-hand drawer of Donald's desk is a small velvet pouch with a drawstring, and she is shocked that Donald had taken so little care to conceal it. The drawer is not even locked. Clearly he was confident that she wouldn't dream of opening his desk drawers.

'More fool me,' she says aloud, staring at the pouch and wondering if she really does want to open it. It has taken her almost a week to get this far. After that first meeting with John Hammond she had walked blindly back to her car and leaned against it numb with shock, the car keys in her hand. She must have looked upset because a woman pushing a shopping trolley with a toddler in the seat had stopped to talk to her.

'Are you okay?' she'd asked. 'Do you need some help?'

Phyllida shook her head. 'No, no thanks, I'm fine, just a bit shocked.'

The woman took the car keys from her hand and opened the driver's door. 'Why don't you sit inside and I'll get someone . . .'

'You're very kind but I'm all right,' Phyllida said. 'I've had some bad news but I'm not ill. I'll be fine now.' And she slipped into the driving seat and put the key into the ignition.

'Well, if you're sure . . .'

The woman gave her a cautious smile and walked on, looking back a couple of times as Phyllida buckled her seatbelt. Her hands were shaking, not just with the shock but with the sudden realisation that the young woman had seen her in a way that she has never seen herself – an elderly woman, a bit doddery, having a nasty turn in a car park, someone who might suddenly need a wheelchair or an ambulance, someone who might be unsafe to drive. The realisation, coming as it did on top of the news of Donald's betrayals, made her grip the steering wheel in panic; she *was* old, she *was* alone, she *did* feel decidedly shaky and terribly vulnerable and might *not* be safe to drive. So, in an effort to disprove all of this, she started the engine and drove straight to Margot's house where, in giving her sister a full account of the morning's revelations, she was able to mask that vulnerability with outrage, for which May Wong proved a handy focus.

Margot had been her usual sympathetic, supportive self, although in the end she hadn't pulled any punches when it came to where the responsibility and the treachery really lay. But Phyllida had clung to anger – so much more empowering than the shame and vulnerability of a elderly woman deceived by a husband of fifty years. By the time she left Margot's place to head home she was determined that she would go straight to Donald's study and look for the brooch. Dropping her bag and jacket onto the chair where May Wong had sat just that morning, Phyllida strode to the study, flung open the door and then stopped. This was something so raw and final. Searching for and perhaps finding the brooch would mean that they – the Wong woman and Hammond – were telling the truth. She quickly closed the door and hasn't opened it again until today, and the fact that she is here now, sitting at Donald's desk staring down into the drawer, is entirely due to Emma.

'Please, Aunty Phyl,' she'd said this morning, hugging her before she left for work. 'Make today the day you do it. This business of the brooch is like a wall that you're banging your head against. If you can sort that bit out I think you'll be able to start dealing with the rest of Uncle Donald's mess. We can look for it together when I get home tonight if you like, but you can't just stay stuck like this.'

In the last few days Emma has shown remarkable insight and thoughtfulness, and as each day has passed Phyllida has clung to the relief of having someone to talk to – someone who hasn't reminded her that she is saying the same thing for the fiftieth time, someone who hasn't made her feel stupid, incompetent, and shamed for having trusted a man who seems now not to have known the meaning of trust. And so, having promised Emma that today is the day, Phyllida knows that this is something that she needs to do alone.

She picks up the velvet pouch feeling its weight and a distinctive oval shape in her hand first and then she slackens the cord and tips the brooch out onto the desk. It is a very fine piece but there are two small garnets and a pearl missing, and she looks into the pouch and sees that they are still there. How did it happen? What was Donald doing when it happened? A vision of him naked in a strange bathroom having sex with May Wong on a vanity unit flashes before her eyes, and she gasps, pushing it away as rapidly as it had come.

Phyllida runs her finger over the rose gold setting. 'He took it on the day he was taken ill,' May had said, 'he wouldn't have had time to take it to the jeweller.' And it's this which, more than anything, has made it so hard for her to confront the presence of this small piece of jewellery. On that day, their golden wedding anniversary, Donald had spent part of the morning with May, and Phyllida knows exactly how he organised it.

It was mid-morning, Grant had already arrived to help set up for the party, and as they chatted in the kitchen Emma had arrived to do her bit with the photos and music, and to help Phyllida organise the kitchen for the caterers. Phyllida feels a tightening in her chest as she remembers the four of them sitting in the kitchen drinking coffee, Emma saying that the first thing she must do is check that the slide show of photographs on her thumb drive works on the digital television, Grant suggesting a way to organise the furniture to maximise the space, and Donald – Donald getting up and saying, 'Indeed, indeed,' and then his pager ringing.

'Sorry, everyone,' he'd said, 'have to call the hospital.' And a few moments later: 'Going to have to leave you to it, I'm afraid. Patient in a bit of trouble, I need to get over there right away. An hour, maybe, two at the most.' And he had kissed her on the cheek. 'Sorry, Phylly, but Grant and Emma are here, and I'll be back in no time. Plenty of time to get everything ready.'

And he had gone to the hospital, or so she had thought then. Now, of course, she knows different. There *was* no patient. Had he told May to page him? Or did he have a way to activate it himself?

Phyllida's heart is thumping so hard she feels it might burst out of her chest. It makes her giddy and she leans back in the black leather chair and closes her eyes. This woman was so important to Donald that he had been to see her on the very day which should have been Phyllida's alone. Was he unable to stay away? Did he need to reassure her that despite this trifling anniversary party, despite the forthcoming trip to California and the cruise, that it was she, not his wife, who came first?

The image of them both naked in a bathroom returns and she opens her eyes to banish it. Phyllida has never been comfortable with her own body, never sufficiently free or confident to walk around naked, even when she is alone. And she has learned to hide the fact that she has never experienced real pleasure from sex, never actually had an orgasm, although she has learned from movies how to fake one. It had been comforting to discover, in her forties, that there were other women like her, older even, who had never reached orgasm. Did Donald know, she wonders now, did he realise that she was a fake? He was not a romantic or tender man, and certainly not an imaginative lover. Throughout their marriage she had protected both herself and him by pretence. Did he know that their intimate life, minimal as it was, was a lie? Is that why he turned to May Wong?

She feels now like the woman she had been in the car park: an old woman, pathetic, doddery, a woman on whom the world is suddenly closing in. But as she sits there, the brooch lying on its pouch on the desk in front of her, she thinks of Donald that Sunday, lying to them all. She imagines him in a strange bathroom, picking up the brooch, retrieving the lost stones, and watching as May slipped them into the pouch. And then, later, coming back to the house, taking it from his pocket and dropping it into this drawer.

Phyllida gets to her feet and walks across the room to where a framed photograph taken on their wedding day stands on a shelf. She is wearing a full length ivory satin dress with her mother's veil of Chantilly lace, and carrying a bouquet of apricot roses. Her arm is tucked firmly into Donald's, while he, in a grey morning suit and cravat, is holding high a grey top hat in what looks like a gesture of victory. Phyllida sees the hope, the trust, the naivety in her own eyes. She remembers the joy and anticipation of that moment, and the pleasure and satisfaction of those final minutes fifty years later as he spoke about their marriage, when she had felt he made a precious connection between their past, present and future, before he crashed to the floor. But now, sprayed like graffiti across those memories, are images of a naked Donald, in a bathroom with another woman, and of his smiling, self-satisfied return to the party preparations. Phyllida feels something burning deep in her gut; it throbs and roils, rising like a ball of fire up through her chest to her throat.

'You bastard!' she screams. 'You lying, conniving, selfish bastard! I hate you!' And she sweeps her arm along the shelf sending the photograph, a crystal decanter of port and some glasses, along with a heavy glass paperweight, crashing onto the stone hearth of the adjacent fireplace. The strong sweet smell of the port catches in her throat making her cough, and she stamps in fury on the shattered picture, grinding glass and port into the stone and the carpet. 'I will never forgive you,' she says now in a low voice, looking down at Donald's face still smiling through a haze of port and needles of glass, 'and I will *not* let you ruin the rest of my life.'

∽⌒∾

'It's not that I don't like her or admire her,' Dot says. 'I do. Alyssa's a remarkable young woman. I suppose what bugs me is that I can see so much of myself in her, at least myself when young. So I want to save her from making the same mistakes I made, protect her from running headlong at everything. I want her to listen to what I learned and learn from that and . . . well, to be honest, perhaps I'm just a bit jealous of her having it all in front of her.'

'Well you'd better get over it,' Margot says from the kitchen. 'This campaign is not about you.'

'I'm trying, really I am, but it's so hard to sit back and let someone else be the leader when you know there are better ways of doing it.'

Lexie leans back in her chair, listening to them with amusement; for as long as she can remember, her mother and Dot have maintained this no holds barred way of relating to each other, forged, as Lexie knows, in the collective action of the sixties, seventies and eighties when trust was built by working together, not just for themselves but for a cause.

'Try to think of it as different rather than better,' Patrick says. 'After all, Dot, the way you did things in the past is not *necessarily* better.'

'Sometimes it is!' Dot insists. 'Some things you can only learn from experience.'

'Then maybe you need to let Alyssa and the others get the experience and stop trying to take over. Stand back a bit, Dot. Don't try to lead by the nose. Lead from behind – a little subtle nudging is the way to go.'

Dot flashes him a look that has crushed lesser men.

'That'll be the day,' Margot says, putting a lemon tart in the centre of the table. 'You may need to deconstruct that idea a bit for Dot, Patrick. Subtlety and nudging aren't top of her list of people skills.'

'Thanks for that, Margot,' Dot says. 'I will try to control my primal urge to batter the young ones over the head until they do it all my way. That is actually easier since you took charge, Lexie. The business plan is brilliant, as is the plan for the rally. Margot, it feels just like the old days. Don't you want to get the bit between your teeth again?'

'I do,' Margot says. 'And I will – really soon.' She slides a slice of tart onto a plate and hands it to Dot with a small bowl of whipped cream. 'How's Vinka? I did invite her tonight but she said she was going to something special at the Polish club.'

'Still anxious that she won't find a place she actually likes,' Patrick says.

A small and unexpected draft of warm breeze from the window extinguishes one of the candles on the table and Margot reaches for the matches. Lexie watches as her mother leans across the table, holding a lighted match to the wick and waiting for it to ignite. She holds her breath as the flame rises and then blows out the match and turns to speak to Dot.

In that moment, as the two women face each other, Lexie sees something that makes her catch her breath. In the half-light they look so different, so old. Most of the time, she realises, she doesn't look closely at them, they are just there, part of the scenery of her life. Now she sees the stories of their lives etched into their faces and she is transfixed by that elusive iridescence only ever seen in some people old enough to radiate the luminous dignity of a long life. They come, both of them, from a time and place that confined their imagination and their aspirations – their ideas of who and what they might become. Dot has always rattled that cage, crashing through the limits, taking risks. And yet here she is, age and weariness carved into her face, but still fighting, immune to concerns about whether or not she is loved or hated as long as she has something to believe in and to drive her.

But it is Margot whose appearance is more arresting to Lexie tonight. It's as though despite the fact that she sees her almost every week she hasn't really seen her for years. What she sees when she's with her is her mother, and a mother is a person you can meet and talk with, eat lunch and go shopping with, and she is just that, just your mother. They are talking now around the table but Lexie is not listening, she is thinking about what it means, about who a mother is, who *her* mother is. Margot has always been there, constant and consistent, responding to the ways in which everyone else has changed, finding solutions, putting things and people back together, a sounding board, a source of comfort and wisdom, and sometimes of irritation and criticism. Lexie tries to recall a time when, even if only fleetingly, she has moved beyond this to see Margot as others might see her; as a more rounded person, a person of facets and textures, talents and strengths, a person not obscured by the overwhelming effect of being her mother, and she finds she cannot.

As Margot leans over now to speak to Dot, Lexie sees those physical signs of age, the lines and wrinkles, the hollows and the slackening skin, and understands, perhaps for the first time, that she knows her mother well but knows Margot hardly at all. She remembers the day not so long ago when, as Margot got out of the car, she had leaned across the passenger seat and called out that many writers do their best work beyond middle age. Her mother had bent down to look back at her through the open door of the car, her face a mix of emotions. 'Not this far beyond,' she had said. And as she had driven away Lexie had been infuriated by Margot's apparent determination to close off the possibility of doing now what she had failed to do earlier in her life. 'Why not just get on with it, give it a go, for heaven's sake,' Lexie had said aloud to herself as she drove away. 'Just stop making excuses.'

Now, sitting here at the table, Lexie sees something different in Margot. Fleetingly, she feels she is looking at a stranger. Well, Margot took her advice and having done so she is changing. What can it be like, Lexie wonders, what depth of emotional fortitude does it takes to embark, so late in life, with passion and energy, on something that one thought was lost?

'So what do you think, Lexie?' Patrick asks, nudging her. 'Or have you gone to sleep?'

'Huh?' she says. 'Um, no. No, I was looking at Mum and Dot, and thinking.'

The three of them look across at her, waiting for something more.

'Go on then,' Dot says.

'I was thinking,' she says, 'that you are both really rather beautiful, that age is beautiful, and it's so easy to forget that, not to notice it. I think maybe we need to find a way to make use of that.'

Dot throws her head back and the two of them laugh out loud.

'I think you may have had a drop too much wine, Lex,' Margot says. 'Have some lemon tart to soak it up.'

'What are you plotting, Lex?' Patrick asks. 'What do you want to do?'

'I'm not sure yet,' she says. 'Give me time, I'm working on it.'

And as they laugh and tease her again, Lexie watches Margot in the candlelight and she knows with absolute certainty that whatever it is that Margot is writing it will change her, already has changed her, and that it has the potential to change them all.

NINETEEN

Emma is going through a sea change – at least she hopes it's that and not *the* change; the word peri-menopause keeps creeping up on her. She's not sure what it means, what the symptoms are, but probably not this rather elevated mood spiced with occasional glimpses of contentment. So, as she sits here now in Donald's office, working her way through some of his papers, she's opting for sea change.

'You could borrow mine,' Theresa had said when Emma had mentioned this change while getting a facial a few days earlier. 'I've got all three series on DVD. I loved that program. Do you think Sigrid Thornton's had work? I've got a feeling about her lips.'

Emma was only fleetingly confused. 'Not *that* sea change,' she'd said. '*A* sea change, you know – going through a period of transformation. It's from Shakespeare – *The Tempest*, I think.'

'But they didn't have beauty salons then,' Theresa said. 'Mind you, they did all sorts of weird stuff – like, I saw this program where they said actors used pig's blood or beetroot juice to make their lips red. Sea change; I'll remember that. It's good, isn't it, because that's just what we do here – *transform* you. It would make a good name for a salon.'

Emma was about to explain that a sea change was actually an inner transformation but she stopped herself in case Theresa responded with a recommendation for colonic irrigation, which was also available in the salon.

The first stirrings of this change had begun after her conversation with Margot. For the rest of that day, while they were shopping with Rosie, and later as she and Rosie made their way back home, Emma's thoughts kept drifting back to Phyllida. What she could do to help. Just knowing what her aunt was going through had explained everything – well, almost everything. Margot had told her she was the *best* person to help Phyllida right now and as Emma thought more about it she began to feel that she really could be useful. She'd always excelled when she was given more responsibility at work, and this felt similar. It made her feel confident and as though she could be of value.

She felt so positive about it that when they got back to Phyllida's place soon after lunch she'd suggested to Rosie that they could make a cake and take afternoon tea up to Phyllida in her room. It was years since Emma had made a cake, so long that she couldn't remember it, and she certainly wouldn't attempt it without a recipe, so she took down one of Phyllida's cookery books and together she and Rosie searched for a recipe.

'What about this one?' Rosie had said. 'It's called Black Forest Gate U.'

'Gateau,' Emma said. 'It's French for cake. But we don't have any cocoa or chocolate. I think we'll do this one.'

And by four o'clock they had produced a spectacular Victoria sponge filled with jam and cream. Emma looked at the cake in disbelief, wondering if she was dreaming. Baking? Baking with Rosie? Weird! But it had been fun and Rosie was impressed.

'Wendy *never* makes cakes,' she'd said, licking jam and cream off her fingers. 'Even Grandma doesn't make them.'

Emma smiled indulgently, trying to look as though knocking up a perfect Victoria sponge was nothing special. Later they took the cake and a pot of tea to Phyllida's room, where she was slumped in a chair watching a black and white film with Gregory Peck, one of a stack of DVDs on the floor alongside her.

'Anything to stop me having to think about Donald and that bloody woman,' she'd said by way of explanation when she returned with an armful of movies from the video store. But she switched the TV off and her eyes lit up when Rosie stuck her head around the door.

'Oh yes! Tea. Come in, Rosie.'

'And cake,' Rosie said, proudly carrying the cake over to her. 'We made it.'

'Made it? How wonderful, and it looks perfect. How clever of you, Rosie.'

'Mum did a bit of it,' Rosie said, smiling graciously at her mother.

Phyllida took the tea Emma handed her and sampled the cake. 'Delicious,' she said. 'I never knew you could bake, Em. I can never a get a sponge to rise. You'll have to tell me your secret.'

'Oh well . . .' Emma began.

'Me,' Rosie cut in. 'I'm the secret. I did all the measuring nearly by myself and I put the jam on it. Mum just did the beating and stuff.'

As they sat there in Phyllida's room, Emma, enjoying the unusual combination of pleasure and satisfaction, thought that this was probably how mothers were supposed to feel, and she wondered how she might hang on to that feeling.

The following morning as they left to take Rosie home to Grant, Emma slipped two slices of cake into a plastic container.

'You can carry these,' she said to Rosie. 'Hold them carefully in the car, so Daddy and Wendy can see what a lovely cake you made.' Emma's desire to impress seemed less self-serving in the light of Rosie's pride in handing over the cake.

'This is lovely, Rosie,' Grant said. 'Aunty Phyl makes terrific cakes, doesn't she?'

'*I* made it,' Rosie insisted, 'and Mum made some of it too. She's *really* good at cakes.'

'Is she?' Grant said, raising his eyebrows at Emma. 'Well she's obviously been hiding her talents.'

'Fluke,' Emma had said, blushing. 'The last time I made one was probably in high school cookery.' For a few moments she basked in the pleasure of his approval and then hated the fact that it meant so much to her.

Later, as she thought back on the shopping trip and how much she'd enjoyed it, it occurred to her that she and Margot used to do more things together but that seemed to have stopped. When, she wondered, had Margot last confided in her, or asked her for anything? Some of the women at work were always doing things with or for their mothers: shopping, organising family stuff, going places together, to movies or out for meals. As she thought about it now Emma remembered that years ago, especially in the time immediately after she and Grant split up, Margot was in touch much more often. She would call to suggest that they catch up for lunch or go to a movie, or ask if Emma would go with her to buy shoes. And Emma remembers making excuses, wanting to keep her options open for more interesting invitations which never actually turned up, or for work things that always did. Back then it had seemed a bit pathetic to be going places with her mother.

She had been promoted when she went back to work and so had more money to spend and more time to spend it, and she had been determined to make herself over. No more sour smelling trails of baby spit or vomit on her clothes, get her figure back after the birth, get rid of those first telltale signs of age, and look every inch the young, glamorous and sexy but professional woman. And of course she'd done it. So why did she end up feeling just as she had before, lonely, empty, a failure? And why is she now feeling warm, fuzzy and proud because her mother had not only asked her to do something but indicated that she trusted her to do it? Why had this, and making a cake with Rosie, made her feel okay?

That same evening she had sat down with Phyllida and explained that Margot had told her everything. There had been the anticipated drama about Margot having broken a confidence, a lot of anger about May Wong (who Emma thought sounded rather fascinating), a lot of pain and grief, but there was more. She could see now that the protective shell of Phyllida's life with Donald had been ripped away, taking with it her self-esteem, leaving her raw and exposed. And in understanding this Emma knew that Margot had been right in saying that she, Emma, was the best person to help. She, after all, knows all about shame, has lived with its vacillations and inconsistencies, its random attacks followed by brief periods of relief overshadowed by the knowledge that it could attack again at any time. And that night Emma sensed that their conversation might have made a difference.

The following morning, for the first time since her visit to the lawyer, Phyllida had appeared in the kitchen before Emma left for work.

'There's something I want to ask you, Emma,' Phyllida said. 'And you must say if it's too much. Hammond thinks we need to go through Donald's office, the filing cabinet and the computer, to see if there is anything more about those payments to Trevor, and any indication of where the rest of the cash was going. It means going through all the files and the computer too, and feeling as I do right now, I don't think . . .'

'Of course,' Emma said. 'Of course I'll do it. I'll start on it this evening.'

And so tonight she is here in the study making her first

inroads into checking every file and piece of paper. Phyllida has given her *carte blanche* to keep or throw things out or to ask her opinion; she has trusted Emma to rescue her from Donald's mess. And so thanks to a crisis, Emma has, it seems, gained a new level of significance in the life of her family. She has been acknowledged as a person who can sort out business and financial affairs (albeit not her own), and a woman who is really good with cakes (although this probably needs a bit more testing before final confirmation). Most of all, she has been acknowledged as a person who can be relied upon to help someone through a crisis. Perhaps it's not permanent, just a flash in the pan, but she hopes not. It makes Emma feel less restless – in fact she feels quite calm – imagining herself this way, and she savours another sip of the wine Phyllida has poured her and turns her attention back to the paperwork.

A lot of the stuff is easy to deal with. There are more catalogues of golfing equipment, fishing equipment and state of the art digital equipment for the home than any one person could possibly need. There is nostalgia – clippings and photographs of Donald's triumphs on the rugby field, the golf course, and in the operating theatre; photographs taken at formal functions, cards and letters from grateful patients or their families, old birthday cards, and pictures of his parents. There are no letters or cards from May Wong.

Emma packs everything into a plastic box file and labels it, ready to take it out to the storage racks in the garage. As she closes the box file and puts it near the door she realises that the framed wedding photograph that stood on the nearby shelf has gone, and maybe some other things as well, the shelf is bare. There are dark stains on the stone hearth and the carpet. She bends down to investigate a sliver of something bright and finds a tiny shard of glass buried in the pile. For a moment she stands, holding it, conjuring explanations, all of which seem to indicate that Phyllida is getting something out of her system.

For a moment Emma considers stopping work – *Grey's Anatomy* will be starting in ten minutes, and last week's episode was a cliffhanger. She finishes her wine, stretches her arms above her head and then bends down to pick up the unlabelled box file which she plans to start on tomorrow. Quickly she flips it open. There are several loose pages of lined paper covered with dates, and sums of money and notes, all in Donald's spidery hand which she has been trying to decipher most of the evening. Underneath the pages is a manila folder and she is about to close the lid when she notices that on the cover of the folder there is a name, a number and 'DECEASED' is stamped in red across the front above the warning: 'HOSPITAL PROPERTY – DO NOT REMOVE'. Lifting the clip of the box file she takes out the folder and sits down again, turning over the first couple of pages. Why has Donald brought this file home? How long has he had it? Emma feels a horrible sense of unease creeping from her stomach to her chest.

'*Grey's Anatomy* in two minutes,' Phyllida says, putting her head around the door, 'but of course it never starts on time. Are you coming?'

Emma's heart is thumping so hard she believes her aunt might hear it. 'I am,' she says with a deceptively calm smile. 'Just got to pop upstairs and I'll be there. Don't let it start without me.'

And as Phyllida turns away and heads back to the television, Emma tucks the box file under her arm, puts out the lights in the study, closes the door, and runs quietly up the stairs to her own room, where she slides it under some jumpers on a shelf in the wardrobe. Then, glancing at her reflection in the mirror, she closes the door behind her and goes back down the stairs.

'Lies, infidelity and heartbreak in the operating theatre,' Phyllida says as Emma joins her on the sofa. 'Not that there's anything we don't know about that, of course, it's just that it's so much more exciting and glamorous on the box than it is in real life, don't you think? Any amazing finds this evening?'

Emma shakes her head. 'None,' she says, keeping her eyes firmly on the wide opening shot of a Seattle hospital. 'That man had enough golf and fishing magazines to account for the destruction of a small forest.'

⁓

Emma pulls into the parking area of the salvage warehouse and switches off the engine.

'I thought we were just getting party stuff,' Lexie says irritably. 'We won't find anything useful here.'

'Are you kidding,' Emma says. 'Have you ever been to one of these places? Come on, you'll like it, it's like Aladdin's cave,' and she gets out, slams the door behind her, and strides quickly off into the warehouse.

Lexie sighs. It's a really hot day and the last thing she feels like doing is trekking through a warehouse looking for bargains. She thinks she may be getting like Margot and developing a hatred of shopping. Picking up her bag she follows her sister inside. Margot is throwing a party, a small party, for some women friends; at least it started as a small party but now it seems to be getting bigger by the hour. There will be women from the time when she and Dot were involved with the women's movement, other friends from the law centre, the young women from the CASE campaign and of course the family: Lexie herself and Emma, and Vinka, who seems to have become part of the family, and Wendy; surprisingly, because she has always despised what she calls 'girls together' occasions, Phyllida has also agreed to come and is organising the food.

'Come with me to get some things for Mum, Lex,' Emma had said on the phone. 'She needs more glasses and other stuff. I'll come and pick you up.'

Liz Byrski

And so here they are on a hot Saturday morning, the weekend before the party, and Lexie is confused. Emma and a salvage warehouse seem an unlikely match, but it's even more weird that she's asked Lexie to go with her. They rarely do things together, or at least they haven't since Emma and Grant split up; that whole period seemed to fracture their relationship, although Lexie doesn't really know why. Perhaps, she wonders now, she hadn't been supportive enough at the time.

The place is swarming with people, and there are a lot of small children with noisy plastic toys. Two small boys, hiding behind a litter bin holding plastic machine guns, are lining Lexie up in their sights and fire a cascade of imaginary bullets at her as she reaches the entrance. By the time she catches up with her Emma has already loaded the trolley with two boxes of plain wineglasses, two boxes of tumblers, a packet of plastic plates, some paper towels, and now she's checking out the price of paper tablecloths and napkins.

'Wow, these are a bargain,' Lexie says, picking up the wineglasses. 'I might get some for myself.'

'Told you so,' Emma says triumphantly. 'What do you think of these?' She points to a shelf of black metal lanterns. 'We can put citronella tea-lights in them, they'll keep the mozzies away.'

They pile a dozen lanterns and a box of tea-lights into the trolley.

'There's a coffee cart out the back,' Emma says. 'Let's get some before we go.'

They push the trolley out through the back doors of the warehouse to a yard with tables where a young man is dispensing excellent smelling coffee from a mobile unit.

'I didn't really bring you here to shop,' Emma says as they carry their cardboard cups to a table. 'There's a problem, and I need your advice.'

And as Lexie sips her coffee from the spout in the cup,

Emma fills her in on Donald's affair with May Wong, and the extraordinary file she has found in his study.

'So what do you think I should do?' she asks. 'I could show her now, but I thought maybe I should try and find out more first, try to fill in the gaps.'

'Absolutely,' Lexie says. 'Don't tell her yet, she'll freak out completely. Give her time, maybe after Christmas. I'll help you, Em, if I can, just tell me what to do.'

'I'm not sure what to do really,' Emma says, 'where to go next. I think it might be worth talking to May Wong, but she's an unknown quantity. I mean, why should she want to help? It sounds as though Phyl was pretty unpleasant to her.'

A small child on a plastic tricycle rides around their table in circles making motorbike noises as they speculate on what might result from a conversation with May.

'More material for Mum's book,' Emma jokes as they walk back to the car park. 'She can turn it into a mystery.'

'I actually wanted to talk to you about Mum,' Lexie says. 'Not just Mum, her and Dot. You know about this campaign we're working on?'

'Vaguely. Wendy said something about it.'

'Well I need to find a photographer, someone who does good portrait work, particularly portraits of women. I thought you might know someone.'

Emma puts the box of lanterns into the boot and straightens up. 'I know a couple – it depends what sort of thing you want. You'd have to talk to them, but probably Andrea Charlton would be good. She's done a couple of exhibitions. I think one was about country women – yes, "Women on the Land". What's it for?'

Lexie pushes the trolley away from the car. 'An exhibition,' she says, 'so this Andrea sounds good. I want portraits of older women, it needs to be a photographer who can capture something I saw when I was with Mum and Dot, a sort of beauty and an inner light that old women get. I want an exhibition that celebrates age.'

'Well I guess Andrea'll know what you mean. I'll give you her number. But I thought Wendy said the campaign was about girls – you know, Rosie's age.'

'It is, but you can't really separate the sexualisation of little girls from the sexualisation of all women – it's a continuum, isn't it?'

Emma shrugs. 'I suppose, but I can't say I've ever really thought about it.'

'So, if I can get this together, will you see if you can get it mounted in the shopping centres?'

Emma looks puzzled. 'What for? I mean, I don't really understand why you want to do it anyway, but why would Grangewood be interested in having it in the centres, because I suspect you're going to want it for free?'

Lexie looks at her, waiting until she's sure she has Emma's full attention. 'What sort of women are in all the shopping centre ads and promotions now?'

Emma shrugs. 'Well . . . young singles, young professionals, mums with young babies.'

'And?'

'Well – attractive, fashionable, happy, sexy, airbrushed . . . you know.'

'Exactly, and what about the fact that a large percentage of women shopping in the centres are well past middle age or old, and a lot of those women have money to spend?'

'Hmm . . .' Emma says, looking vaguely puzzled. 'Yeah, I see what you mean. Well I could try, I suppose. If they looked good that is, really good.' She tilts the mirror and peers at her face.

Lexie watches her. 'Your face looks a lot better.'

'Yes. Theresa did a good job. I was going to get a brow lift and have my chin done too.'

'Really?'

'Mmm, but I don't know . . . I mean, it doesn't seem to have done me much good.'

'What do you mean?'

'Well here I am doing everything I'm supposed to do to look young and attractive and sexy, but you're older than me, you do nothing to yourself, and you get the man.'

Lexie laughs. 'Last I heard you didn't *want* a man.'

'That was just bravado,' Emma says. 'I'm not desperate, but it would be nice.'

'You don't need to do anything, Em, just relax a bit, stop working so hard and get –'

'Yeah, I know, get a life.'

'Exactly.'

Emma pulls the seatbelt out and snaps it into place. 'Aunty Phyl said I'd modelled myself on a Barbie doll.'

Lexie takes a deep breath, hoping her guilt at having once said something similar about her sister doesn't show. 'I expect she was upset at the time. She wouldn't have wanted to hurt you.'

'I know that,' Emma says, 'but actually it *did* hurt, it made me feel ashamed. It was the *way* she said it. I think she was trying to tell me something and I didn't quite get it.'

'Did you ask her what she meant?'

'No, no I didn't. I can't because it's like I *should* know and I think I do but it's really bugging me. So I thought I'd ask you instead.'

TWENTY

Margot is preparing for the party, unpacking the glasses and plates that Lexie and Emma bought last weekend, counting cutlery, worrying if she has enough chairs. It had started out small but the numbers kept growing as women called to ask if they could bring their now adult daughters who, back in the seventies had sat around with Lexie and Emma during those interminable meetings, bored stiff and asking when it would be time to go home. It will be so good, she thinks, to see those women together, the past, the present and Alyssa and her friends who seem to represent the future. Most of all Margot is pleased that Phyllida has agreed to come.

'She needs to get to know other women,' Margot had said to Emma, 'she doesn't have friends of her own.'

'What about the women at the golf club? They're her friends,' Emma had said. 'And the people they were always having to dinner?'

'They're just golf acquaintances, and the dinner mob are Donald's mates and their wives. Phyl's never really had any friends of her own, she's always rather looked down on women getting together. Does she ever go out for coffee with a friend? Think about it, Em, has anyone popped around to the house to see how she's going? Brought soup? Asked her over for a meal?'

'Well . . . no,' Emma had said. 'You're right. There's no one . . .'

'Exactly. Make sure she comes, don't let her wriggle out of it.'

And although Margot has gratefully accepted her sister's condition that she'll come if she can organise the food, she knows what this is about. There is safety and focus in the kitchen, the work can expand to occupy the duration of the party, and to reduce social interaction to an absolute minimum. But getting Phyllida here is the main thing, Margot thinks, getting her out of the kitchen can be dealt with later.

And so, with no food to prepare, Margot has plenty of time to set up everything else, at her own leisurely pace. At first she thinks she'll ignore the door when she hears a knock – it's becoming a habit these days, and it makes her feel she has control over who and what intrudes on her time. But the person knocks again, insistently this time, and she surrenders.

'I knew you were in,' Laurence says, 'I can always tell. Is this a bad time?'

'No, I was just going to make some tea and have a little break. I'm having a party this evening.'

'And I'm not invited?'

'Nope. Women only. Reviving the seventies and introducing them to the nineties and naughties.'

'Nice,' Laurence says. 'Well I won't hang about but I'll have that tea.'

They take a tray outside and sit on the end of the verandah alongside a huge old wisteria heavy with purple blossom.

'No writing today then?' Laurence asks, taking the mug Margot hands him.

She shakes her head. 'Preparations for tonight, but anyway I'm a bit stuck at the moment. I think I might have hit a wall.'

Laurence tilts his head, watching, listening, waiting for more.

'The characters are infuriating. They're all at crucial points in the story where they need to change but every time I try to move them on it doesn't work.'

'Just like real life?'

Margot shrugs. 'I suppose. Certainly just as frustrating. What's the good of inventing these people and breathing life into them if they don't do as they're told?' She sips her tea and picks up a biscuit. 'Anyway, how are you? I guess you've come to tell me that you and Bernard have split up.'

'You know?'

'Melbourne is a small world, and the circles we move in are smaller still. I'm only guessing but I think you knew you were breaking up before you went to Spain?'

Laurence nods. 'Even before I'd decided to go.'

'That's months ago,' Margot says, frowning. 'Well I'm sorry, Laurence, really, it's very sad.' She leans across to squeeze the arm closest to her and Laurence puts his hand over hers and grips it.

'I should have told you before but I couldn't make myself do it. I kept chickening out.'

'Why? I don't understand why you left it so long.'

'Embarrassed,' Laurence says, looking out across the garden to where Margot has set up some folding tables and chairs that Grant has brought over for her from his house. 'It seemed awfully difficult and sort of delicate.'

'Delicate?'

'Well, I left you and the girls to be with Bernard. I turned your lives upside down. So it seemed important that it was all for something worthwhile, something that would last. Anything else seemed like an insult to you and them.'

'But it *did* last,' Margot says. 'It lasted more than thirty years, of course it was worthwhile.'

Laurence shrugs. 'Maybe.'

'No, not *maybe*. Of *course* it was worthwhile. Bernard is a fine person, I've grown very fond of him. It was the age thing in the end, I suppose?'

'Age and ambition. Bernard is determined not to go gently into that good night. He's fighting it – ageing isn't part of his plan. Whereas I am rather enjoying it. I do understand his drive to wring every drop from the remaining years of his professional life. It's commendable, and I suppose I did that myself, but I'm over it now. He's revving up for the home straight and I'm cruising in the slow lane. I'm sick of conferences and vice chancellors' drinks parties, and ethics committees and reading the latest scholarly articles. I'm even sick of Henry James and I'm a bit sad about that but I'm hoping it'll wear off.'

Margot is silent, looking across at him, searching his face for what is hidden and discovering it finally in the way his eyes flick away from hers, unable to hold her gaze.

'You don't have to make light of it with me,' she says. 'You don't have to pretend you're okay just because you still feel guilty about leaving me for him. I'm capable of compassion, Laurence, I am capable of respecting your grief just as I was capable of respecting your love. Give me credit for that.'

She watches him struggling now, his hand shaking as he puts the mug down on the table and buries his face in his hands. She gets up and goes to the kitchen, returning with a large glass of water and a box of tissues which she puts on the table beside him. Then she moves her chair alongside his and slides her hand through the crook of his arm and down the inside of his forearm to hold his hand. They sit like this for a while; Darby and Joan, Margot thinks, although Darby and Joan would hardly have been discussing the sort of love and loss that once tore her and Laurence apart and which now seems to link them again.

'I think,' Margot says after a while, when Laurence is calmer, 'that you might be assuming that if you hadn't fallen in love with Bernard everything might have gone on as before and you and I would still be together. I actually doubt that.'

'Do you?'

'Of course. You couldn't have gone on trying to pretend you were a straight man. It would have destroyed you. The tragedy is that you felt you had to do that in the first place. No one tried harder than you, Laurence, to prove you were straight – my god, all those girlfriends.' She smiles and squeezes his hand. 'You must have been exhausted.'

Laurence manages a rueful laugh. 'I did make an effort, but coming out in those days just seemed impossibly hard. Perhaps I thought I could convince myself as well as everyone else.'

'Well I'm glad you found the courage to be who you really are, even though it was awful at the time.' She hesitates. 'But there's another thing,' she says, turning in her chair to face him now. 'I think you assume that I've been unhappy ever since you left.'

'Well I . . .'

'I haven't. At first of course, yes, I was very unhappy, but as time went on, no. More, well . . . discontent, and that's not your fault, although for a time it was easier to believe that it was. Easier to blame you for the fact that I abandoned my writing, didn't go back to university, was always struggling financially . . .'

'Well that at least was my fault,' Laurence says.

'Partly, but no more so than for any couple who split up, and you were more generous than most. It's me – I was the cause of my own discontent. All through that roller coaster of the women's movement I could talk the talk, get out and fight for it, but there was so much that I didn't internalise. I never stopped feeling and acting as though being all things to all people was my role as a woman. I've kept on doing it and resenting it and using it as an excuse to avoid risking what I really wanted to do, right up until recently. *And* I let all those other pressures about how women should look and behave exploit my anxiety and take up my time, when I could have been just me, warts and all, getting on with my own life.'

'Like you're doing now?' Laurence says, his face almost restored to normality; the normality of a person adjusting to grief rather than fighting it.

'Yes, and it's taken me until I'm this age – must be a slow learner.'

'I doubt I would forgive with such wisdom and generosity were the situation reversed, Margot,' Laurence says. 'I doubt I deserve it.'

Margot laughs, getting up from her chair. 'Well, if you still have vestiges of guilt you can help me sort out some lanterns and chairs. It's going to be a glorious evening.'

'Perhaps you need to let go of them,' Laurence suggests later when the bulk of the preparations are complete.

'Let go of what, whom?'

'Your characters,' he says. 'Perhaps you have to let them decide what's right, let them find their own direction. Just sit back and wait and maybe they'll tell you where they want to go.'

'Like people?' she says with a sigh.

'Yes, just like people.'

'But what if I made them up just so that for once in my life I get to call the shots?'

He shrugs. 'Then you find another way to call the shots, I suppose. But characters have to be true to themselves, don't they? Just like people. Isn't that what you were telling me earlier?'

'Do come outside, Phyl,' Margot says from the kitchen doorway. 'Everyone's enjoying the food so much and they want to tell you that and to nick your recipes.'

'In a minute,' Phyllida says. 'I'm waiting for a batch of spinach and ricotta puffs. I'll bring them into the garden when they're ready.' She is way out of her comfort zone; all those women talking, laughing, hugging each other, introducing their daughters, sitting on the wall, on the steps, on the grass, at the tables, eating, drinking champagne. Margot has always done this warm fuzzy stuff about friendship, but Phyllida, older and – she has always believed – wiser, never trusted it. Their parents hadn't trusted it either, all that getting involved with other people. Family was what was important and you never knew what might happen when you opened yourself up like this to others.

'Ridiculous,' their mother had said one day when Margot, then in her fifties and divorced, had gone away to a women's retreat in the Blue Mountains. 'I can't imagine what she thinks she's doing.'

And Phyllida, who had always found it hard to make friends, felt entirely justified in agreeing with her. She had been aloof as a child, and had become an aloof teacher distancing herself from the breathy crushes of teenage girls and cautious of the various alliances between nuns and lay teachers in the staffroom. But whatever else she was doing, it was always as Donald's wife. By grounding herself in that identity and the social status it provided, Phyllida had established a solid foundation in a role in which she excelled. She was the perfect hostess, making Donald's friends and colleagues feel at home, getting the men to talk about themselves, making them feel important and interesting, she'd always been good at that. And her voluntary work was part of it too. Looking back now it seems strange, outdated, almost embarrassing, like some Edwardian gentlewoman, keeping to herself but performing wifely and social duties appropriate to her position. Watching these women, the pleasure they take in each other's company, the ease with which they mix across the generations, their openness to each other, Phyllida's own life now seems like a performance.

And what if she does go out there? Nudges perhaps, whispers? Perhaps they are talking about her right now, sly remarks under their breath. Have Margot's friends heard about May Wong? Phyllida honestly believes that she could have dealt with the financial shocks had it not been for the revelation of Donald's infidelity. Was she the only one who never suspected anything? Had everyone at those endless dinner parties been pitying her? Did everyone at the hospital know? A part of her is determined that she will not allow Donald to define her future as he defined their life together, but she has no idea how to change things. And the shame she feels at having been deceived for so long is crippling her. How, she wonders, is she expected to leap this huge gap between her and the women out there? The mere thought of it makes her nauseous and weak.

'Hello, Mrs Shepperd,' says a voice behind her. 'Those little quiches were to die for – in fact all the food is divine. I'm Alyssa Dunne, by the way. You know my mum, Jean Dunne – she plays golf with you.'

Phyllida dries her hands on a tea towel and takes Alyssa's outstretched hand. 'Oh! Yes, I do know Jean,' she says. 'She's a terrific golfer, far better than me.'

'Better than most I think,' Alyssa says, then, dropping her voice, 'but between you and me she can't make a quiche to save her life. Anyway she sent me in to get you – she's over there by the lantana, with my gran, Glenda. She knows your sister from years ago. And I know Margot too because she and Lexie and I are in the CASE campaign together.'

Phyllida looks confused. 'The what?'

'CASE,' Alyssa says. 'Oh, you don't know about it. Wow, well, we have heaps to tell you then. Come on over and join us and we can tell you about it. Time to get out of the kitchen.'

'But there are spinach and ricotta puffs in the –'

'Lexie and Wendy are going to look after them,' Alyssa says. 'Change of shift – look, they're on their way.' And she slips an arm through Phyllida's and leads her out of the kitchen and into the intimidating company of the women in the garden.

❦

Perched on a low wall and partially concealed by an overgrown lantana, Margot watches as Alyssa comes out of the house arm-in-arm with Phyllida. They pause at the top of the verandah steps, talking for a moment, and as Emma joins them, they head for the table where Alyssa's mother and grandmother are sitting with Dot. Margot's toes curl and her stomach clenches with tension as Dot turns to her sister and stands up to greet her. She can't actually hear what's being said, and she's praying that Dot will not revive the Falada disaster. She watches as Dot offers Phyllida her own seat, next to Jean Dunne, and others shuffle their chairs to make room for her. Phyllida looks awkward, nervous and rather vulnerable, and while she understands that her sister is totally out of her element, Margot is also irritated by her unease. 'For goodness sake, get over it, Phyl,' she whispers, 'they're just a group of women.'

Watching them Margot wonders how it must feel to be so ill at ease. Why, she wonders, does her sister not feel that thread of connection and understanding that works when women – well, at least some women – get together? She wants to shake Phyllida out of the prison she has built for herself, force her to see what she has missed, and what is there for her now if only she will grasp it. But Laurence was right, she can no more control these women than she can her fictional characters – she's created a situation, and all she can do is hope that Phyllida recognises that it has something transformative to offer her. In the same way, Margot supposes, that starting to write again is transforming her: 'Better than a makeover,' she had said to Dot a couple of days ago.

'But it *is* a makeover in a way,' Dot had said, 'because you're transforming your inner life – it shows, Margot. And it's a far better look than you'd get from cosmetic surgery and a whole lot cheaper!'

It is as though she can only find her way now through the writing. Rather than chasing that old need for certainty, the heart of the adventure of writing lies in its uncertainty, the way it moves with its own momentum. Almost daily she asks herself if this is what other writers feel, the desperate grasping at the threads, the terror of returning each day to the keyboard wondering will it work again or will it evaporate? She sees everything now through a writer's eyes; it makes her a ruthless carpetbagger poised to cull what she can, store it, taste it, experiment with it; fragments of other lives, shards of strange light, flashes of insight and moments of confusion, a phrase, a sentence, a sigh, a gesture – nothing will be wasted. Everything has possibilities.

'All my characters are parts of myself, I'm all of them and none of them,' she had heard one of her favourite writers say once in an interview. 'Whatever I am writing it's always about me, although of course, it's not me. "Madame Bovary c'est moi!" as Flaubert said. Writing is my way of learning to know parts of myself.'

At the time Margot had thought him pretentious. How, she wondered, could everything be about him, what arrogance, and he even had the hubris to admit it in public. She had almost decided to boycott his next book but had finally succumbed and buried herself in it, searching for that man – the author – at its heart, but all she could detect was an occasional faint whisper of him like a distant sound carried on a breeze.

The book still delighted her and she read on, ceasing to think of its creator. And now she understands what he meant. It is lonely, incredibly lonely, because if she could speak about this to anyone here in this garden a furrow would appear between their eyebrows, there would be a tilted head, a questioning look and a cautious, guarded response. They might well be thinking she was losing touch with reality, but maybe that is just what she needs – less reality, more creative fantasy. Perhaps this is what her resentment has been about all these years, too much reality, or just too much attention paid to it. Margot sighs, gets up and walks over to talk to her guests. Writing, she thinks, is like a benign virus; it infects everything with possibilities, one just needs to learn how to harvest them.

❧

Dot is feeling her age, or possibly more than her age, she has never been good at late nights. Margot's party was a mix of nostalgia, pleasure and subtle attempts to recruit people to the campaign. Now, as she sits here on her bed, almost too tired to bend down and take off her shoes, she thinks again about Phyllida, who had appeared beside her and took her place at the table, silent, nervous and ill at ease. Dot would almost rather have been sitting with the old, superior and distant Phyllida than this wraith who seemed to want to disappear. It was only when the conversation turned to the campaign that she began to take an interest. She had read an article, she said, about teenage girls who wanted to be glamour models.

'They go along to these revolting sessions run by men's magazines, strip off to those awful thong things and crawl all over a bed while a load of boorish drunken men vote for the one who looks the most sexy. And guess what the prize is? The chance to model naked. Free of charge, for the magazine. Can't they see they're being exploited?' she'd said. 'Glamour modelling, I ask you! What a misnomer that is.'

'It's sickening, isn't it?' Dot had said. 'At one time I believed we'd never have to fight these same battles all over again, but it's worse now, because the tentacles of this new sexism are everywhere, even reaching out for little girls. What's so worrying is that so many people just don't see how dangerous it is.'

'I'm going through a difficult time at the moment,' Phyllida had said later when Dot gave her a flier and suggested she join them. 'But I'll think about it. I do need to find something new and useful to do.'

To her own surprise Dot had rather admired Phyllida tonight, had even thought she'd like to get to know her a bit better.

'Why are you so keen to sign her up?' Alyssa had asked later.

'Well, originally I wanted her as a route to Emma,' Dot had said. 'The two of them are really close. Emma's a PR person so she could be really useful. But tonight I was thinking more about Phyllida in her own right. There's lots of energy simmering there and I suspect she's a great organiser.'

'I am so manipulative I almost disgust myself,' Dot says aloud now, finally relieving herself of the shoes by kicking them off. They fly across the room and land by the door and she topples backwards onto the bed. 'But the ends do justify the means, or will do, I hope.' Lying there, spread-eagled on her back in the darkness, the business of getting ready for bed just seems too hard and she hauls herself further up the bed and crawls under the quilt with relief.

Back in the days of sex and drugs and rock'n'roll when overindulgence of various types had sometimes blurred the boundaries of night and day, Dot had occasionally woken up in the clothes she'd been wearing the night before, and in places she'd rather not have been. But since then, apart from a few nights spent in police cells after being forcibly removed from demonstrations, she has maintained a strict bedtime routine. For a person who delights in breaking rules, she is surprisingly disciplined about sticking to her own. They are rules which she has devised for a single woman of uncertain habits living alone. She knows that her weaknesses and her obsessions can lead her to neglect both herself and her living conditions, so hers are rules about looking after herself properly, not letting standards slip, removing makeup, cleaning her teeth, tidying the kitchen before going to bed or out to work in the morning. A few extras have been added over the years in deference to increasing age: extra attention to security, slowing her walking pace to guard against falls, and keeping her mobile with her at night in case of emergencies. But tonight, lying there in her clothes without the scent of toothpaste in her mouth, she has already ignored two of them. The curtains are open still and the bedroom, lit only by moonlight, is deliciously peaceful.

'A quiet day tomorrow,' Dot murmurs. 'I might actually do nothing except read the paper and doze in the garden.' She yawns, stretches and turns on her side, and as she does so remembers that her phone is in her bag which is where she dumped it on the kitchen bench.

'Bugger!' she says aloud. 'Oh well, one night won't matter. I'm not planning on having a stroke or a heart attack tonight.' She turns onto her other side and looks through the open door of the bedroom along the darkened passage to the kitchen. 'Bugger!'

For a person to whom the rules matter, one broken rule disturbs the peace, two are a serious offence and three is an impossibility. 'Okay, I give in,' Dot says, and she throws back the quilt and stands up quickly. The shadow patterns of the trees against the moonlit wall blur and spin and she pauses briefly, steadying herself with a hand on the bedside table. As she sets out across the treacherous polished boards the forgotten shoes lie in wait, and as her foot encounters one she jumps back in surprise, sways, slips, and crashes to the floor. It happens so fast that she makes no attempt to break her fall and there is just a micro-second of shock before her head cracks against the doorjamb. Beyond the bedroom window a cloud drifts across the face of the moon and the darkness deepens, and clears again, and Dot, unconscious and with blood trickling from her head, knows nothing of the changing light.

TWENTY-ONE

Phyllida wakes early and despite rather a lot of champagne at Margot's party, she feels energised, as though this is a day that shouldn't be wasted, a day to do something important. Something strange happened last night as she sat outside with the other women – she actually began to relax and to enjoy their conversation. And so this morning, in a break from her usual habits, she splashes water on her face, pulls on some tracksuit pants and a t-shirt, lets herself out of the house and walks towards the river.

It is almost seven o'clock and the air is clear and mild. A few lycra-clad cyclists whiz irritatingly past her, two and three abreast on the path, ringing their bells for her to get out of their way and ignoring the signs that say pedestrians have right of way. For years this has been one of Phyllida's greatest bugbears. She frequently writes to the council and the local papers about the cyclists, has even on occasion shouted abuse as they whipped past so close and at such speed it was a miracle they missed her, but this morning she strides on confidently, immune to such hazards and irritations. She will walk as far as the Boatshed, her favourite café, have a coffee and then walk back. She needs it – it is too long since she did any exercise.

As Jean Dunne had pointed out last night, it's months since she had a game of golf. The last, in fact, was just a couple of days before Donald's collapse. But normal life came to a dramatic end that day and now, for the first time since then, Phyllida realises that something has changed. She feels hopeful, enthusiastic – not about anything specific but just about life generally, life after Donald, the good bits and the painful revelations. She's almost seventy-four – she could have another ten or fifteen years to look forward to, years of pleasing herself.

This morning, as she walks briskly along the foreshore, she thinks she'd like to do something that would really piss Donald off, but there is little point to that as he isn't around to *be* pissed off. It seems profoundly unfair that he behaved so badly but death saved him from rough justice and spousal revenge. Emma is still working her way through the various files in his office, although as far as Phyllida knows she hasn't yet discovered any indication of where the money went. She seems to be working consistently hard and methodically though, and Phyllida is impressed. This businesslike commitment is a side of Emma that her family rarely sees but which obviously accounts in part for her professional success. If only, Phyllida thinks, this could be expanded into her personal life, Emma might be able to sort out some of her own problems. Probate will soon go through on the will and when it does John Hammond's office will draw down the funds for the girls' bequests.

'Don't tell them just yet,' Phyllida had asked Margot. 'It would be so nice to do it when I can actually hand over the money.' But this was only part of the reason for delaying the news. The money is not a lot in Phyllida's view. A few years earlier she had told Donald that she thought they should bump those bequests up a bit – in fact she had suggested doubling them – but could only get him to agree to an additional ten thousand each. She remembers now how twitchy he was about it at the time, but he had eventually promised to make an appointment with Hammond to amend the will.

'I'll give him a call,' she'd said, 'and when it's ready you can pop over and sign it.'

He'd seemed rattled by this, she remembers now, and had immediately said he'd prefer to do it himself. 'I'll call John today,' he'd said, 'no need for you to bother with it.' But of course he hadn't and now it makes sense – he was far too concerned with whatever it was that was leaching money from the capital to start making changes to his will. When everything is finalised, she thinks, especially when she sells the house, which is what she has now decided to do, she might just give them the extra herself. It will help Lexie with her uni expenses, but Emma's bequest is more complicated. Phyllida knows that the responsible thing to do is to tell her niece she must use the money to pay back what she had loaned her. But she really wants Emma to have this, she wants to amortise that debt and give her niece a real chance to get her life on track.

Phyllida wonders if she could strike a deal with Emma, using the money as an inducement to get some help – sorting out the shopping obsession, getting to the bottom of whatever is about to entice her under the cosmetic surgeon's knife. But somehow it doesn't feel quite right. A bequest is a bequest, so would bargaining with Emma in this way be unethical? Would it amount to bribery? But on this glorious, mild, sunlit morning, Phyllida's mind begins drifting more towards knocking her *own* life into some new sort of shape.

This morning, for the first time, she feels as though she has turned a corner, that this has been coming for a while but it finally happened last night, when Jean Dunne's daughter coaxed her out of the kitchen. As they reached the top of Margot's verandah steps and Emma turned up and took her other arm, Phyllida had felt like a prisoner walking between jailers and she was sure that Margot had organised it. When she saw that Jean was sitting with Dot she'd felt like turning on her heel and running screaming back to the safety of the kitchen. It was years since she'd seen that woman and she'd have been very happy never to see her again. Dot was and had always been, in Phyllida's opinion, irresponsible and a troublemaker. Right from the early days when Margot had met her in the Push and then through all that demonstrating and marching and making trouble in the seventies, it was Dot who had been pulling the strings. Admittedly those women had made a big difference, and Dot in particular had taken a highly principled and courageous stand on many occasions, but that didn't mean that Phyllida had to like her, and she was pretty sure that Dot felt the same about her. So she had been surprised when Dot greeted her warmly and appeared genuine when she offered her condolences. She had expected hostility or cool indifference, so courtesy and sensitivity had taken her by surprise. And it had been nice to see Jean Dunne again.

'It's so long since you've been down to the club,' Jean had said, taking her hand and holding on to it. 'I hope you haven't given up on us. When are you coming back?'

'Well, I'm a bit out of practice,' Phyllida had said. 'It's a few months now, I think I'd slow you down.'

'I don't suppose you would and it wouldn't matter if you did,' Jean said. 'Nobody would mind. We've all been wondering when you'll be back. Tell you what, I'll give you a call next week, come and play a nice leisurely game and see how you feel.'

And then Dot had started talking about a campaign; it sounded interesting, possibly even quite important, and Phyllida, who had thought she would sit there for a few moments just to be polite and then escape back to the kitchen, found she wanted to be a part of the conversation. It was clear that no one was whispering about her, no one seemed to think it odd that she was there. Perhaps they didn't know anything of her circumstances, but Phyllida sensed that it wouldn't have mattered if they did.

The Boatshed is busy as usual this morning, but there is still a spare table outside and Phyllida grabs it and orders coffee and an almond croissant and sits facing the water, watching a couple of shags standing, wings spread out to dry, on one of the old stumps of the jetty.

'It *is* you, Phyllida!' says the woman who brings her order. 'Where've you been? It's ages since we saw you,' and she pulls out a chair and sits down. She's a big woman with reddish-blonde hair and an engaging smile, one of the owners of the Boatshed, and a well-known food writer.

Phyllida hesitates. 'I've been busy, Fran . . .' she begins and then stops. 'Well actually, my husband died recently and I haven't felt –'

'Of course,' Fran cuts in. 'I'm so sorry, Phyllida, how very sad.'

'In fact,' Phyllida says, surprising herself, 'this is the first morning that I've felt any sense of getting back into the world again. I think I've been in hiding.'

'Of course, why wouldn't you? You feel so vulnerable when you lose someone,' Fran says. 'It's such a challenge to reclaim your own reality out of the grief, and work out who you are now that they're gone. Well that's how I felt when my mother died. She was such a character and she'd raised me on her own. It was a terrible loss and it took a long time to learn who I was without her.'

'I remember your mother,' Phyllida says now. 'On the day you opened here, she was telling everyone how proud she was of you.'

Fran laughs. 'That's right, that was her – no false modesty with Lila, and no sense of restraint. Anyway, I'm sure you've got family and friends around you right now.'

'I'm rather inclined to keep to myself,' Phyllida says, 'but I was thinking this morning that it might be time to be getting out more.'

'Good on you,' Fran says, standing up. 'Well, we're always here and happy to see you, and of course we still have our book club. I'm sure you'd know some of the women who come. We're not meeting this month because of Christmas but, look – why don't I give you a flier about the books for next year?' And she hurries inside the café and returns with a list of meeting dates and book titles.

Phyllida scans the list and spots something she recognises. *'Instances of the Number 3,'* she says. 'I've got that book. Someone gave it to me a couple of years ago but I never got around to reading it.'

'Well there you are then,' Fran says, 'serendipity. You're obviously meant to read it now, so do think about coming along then, if not sooner.'

Phyllida walks home more slowly, contemplating the idea of the book club. She could go along once, she muses, just to see what it's like. And in the half-hour it takes her to get back to the house she changes her mind about it at least a dozen times. I'll read the book, she thinks, and see how I feel after that. Back home she has things to do; in the changed state of consciousness which began as she had started to enjoy herself at last night's party, she had invited Margot and Lexie for Christmas dinner, so she needs to get organised.

'Emma and I will cook for you,' she'd said and, noticing the look of amazement on Emma's face, added, 'We're a great team in the kitchen, aren't we, Em? And you must bring your Patrick, Lexie, and his wonderful aunt, whom I've just met.'

And then, in a moment of complete aberration, she had also invited Dot. She was, after all, like Margot and Phyllida herself, a woman on her own. 'Sisterhood!' she had said triumphantly to herself, and then flinched, remembering how much she had hated that word when Margot used it years ago. And later there is something else she has to do, something that must be dealt with before she can finally put the mess of grief, hurt and anger behind her, and she knows without hesitation that today is the day to do it. First, though, she goes to the bookshelf, trying to remember what the spine of *Instances of the Number 3* looks like. She scans three shelves before spotting it and pulls it out. It is a small paperback with an interesting cover of a detail of Da Vinci's *Virgin and Child with St Anne*. The typeface of the cover blurb is too small to read so she takes it to the kitchen where her glasses are sitting on the benchtop. It is, she reads, about a man who dies, leaving behind a wife and mistress who both discover new meanings in their lives. The blurb is cagey, but it implies forgiveness, even friendship.

'What utter rubbish!' Phyllida shouts aloud to the otherwise empty kitchen. 'What total crap.' And she hurls it across the room where it bounces off a cupboard door and lands in the sink.

∽

'I don't know *where* she is,' Margot says into the phone. 'She was supposed to meet us here at the retirement centre an hour ago and there's no sign of her. Are you at her house now?'

'I'm in the front garden,' Alyssa says. 'We'd arranged to do some work together this morning. Dot said ten o'clock, but she wasn't around, and she's not answering the phone or the mobile. So I came back about eleven-thirty, and she wasn't here and now it's two o'clock and there's still no sign of her.'

'What about the car?' Margot asks.

'It's in the garage. And you know, Margot, it just feels odd. At first I thought she'd forgotten and gone off somewhere. Now – well I just get the feeling something's happened, I think she's in there. Do you think I should break in?'

'I think *we* probably should,' Margot says. 'Hang on,

Alyssa, I'll leave now. I can be there in less than ten minutes.' She closes her phone and stands for a moment, heart beating furiously, wondering whether she should call the police or an ambulance, or wait until she gets there.

'What's happened?' Lexie asks, coming out of the office where she and Vinka have been talking with the manager.

'It's Dot,' Margot explains, 'she seems to have gone AWOL and Alyssa's worried that something might have happened – in the house. I have to go, Lexie. Explain to Vinka, will you?'

Lexie nods. 'Of course. Ring us, we can come when we finish here. And, Mum, take care.'

Margot, waiting at the third set of traffic lights, sees her own hands shaking on the steering wheel. The lights change and she accelerates sharply, hoping to get through the next set and manages it, flying across on amber and turning off the main road into Dot's street, past the Italian café, and pulling up outside the house where Alyssa is pacing back and forth in the garden.

'Thank god,' she says as Margot appears at the gate. 'I really think we should break in. I've got a very bad feeling about this.'

'Me too,' says Margot. 'But where? She's got those shark wire security screens. Let's have a look around the back. Can we get through the garage?'

Alyssa shakes her head. 'I tried that, it's locked. She'd have driven in and then gone in through the back door. I could probably climb over the side gate and unlock it from the inside, if I could find something to stand on.'

'Plastic crates,' Margot says, 'in the boot of my car. I was taking them to Vinka to put some of her stuff in.'

They fetch the crates and pile them one on top of the other against the fence, and Alyssa climbs up, grasping the top of the gate to steady herself as the crates shift and threaten to topple her. Finally she gets both arms over the top of the gate and, with Margot pushing from behind, she hauls herself up and rolls over, landing with a thud on the other side.

'Shit!' she says. 'That's higher than I thought.'

'Are you okay?'

'Just about,' Alyssa says, and she opens the gate. 'Come on; let's see where we can get in.'

Dot is security conscious. In the past she's been a target; once for a rabid men's group who had thrown rocks at her windows, and a couple of times when right to life campaigners had spray-painted her front door, and a small group of neo fascists carved abuse into the paintwork of her car. There is only one window which doesn't have shark wire and it's a small one in the laundry, just large enough for Alyssa to crawl through.

'If she's just gone out shopping or something she'll be really pissed off,' Alyssa says.

'Hard luck,' Margot says, picking up a brick from the edging of a flower bed. 'She'll get over it.' And she slams the brick into the window. 'Are you sure you can get through here? Look, there are some towels on the line, we can put them around the frame so you don't cut yourself.'

Alyssa puts two crates in place and wriggles through the window with the help of the thickly folded towels to protect her. 'Thank god for jeans,' she says, sliding one leg through. 'They're really tough. Ow! Not tough enough, that really hurt.'

'Mind your hands. Oh my god, you're bleeding already,' Margot says.

'It's okay, only a little cut,' Alyssa says, wriggling the rest of her way through and ending up in the laundry trough. She jumps down and promptly unlocks the kitchen door.

Margot steps into the kitchen and looks around, waiting for her eyes to adjust to the low light. She peers through into the bathroom and finds it empty, but as she turns to the passage she sees a huddled shape by the bedroom door.

'Quick, Alyssa,' she cries, 'call an ambulance, tell them to hurry!' Blood has seeped from a cut on Dot's head to form a sticky puddle, and one leg is twisted underneath her. Her face is icy cold and Margot feels for a pulse. 'Dot,' she says. 'Dot, can you hear me? It's Margot. Can you open your eyes? Can you say something?' And she sinks to the floor beside her, rubbing one of Dot's deathly cold hands between her own.

TWENTY-TWO

Phyllida chooses her clothes carefully and as she does so she feels the urge to discard several things, not just because they are wrong for today's task, but because they seem so very much part of the old Phyllida and quite unsuited to the woman she thinks she may possibly become. Pulling them from the wardrobe she drops them on the bed and settles on a pair of loose trousers in tan linen and a cream linen shirt. The linen is French, soft and best unironed; she likes the feel of it and she adds a long string of amber beads as a finishing touch. She wants to look good – strong, firm, in control, and ideally a little intimidating. And she certainly doesn't want to look as though she has dressed up for the occasion. Through the open door of the wardrobe she sees the glint of black jet beading. It is the dress she bought for the fiftieth anniversary party; that one certainly has to go, and she slips it off the hanger, adds it to the pile, scoops the lot into her arms and dumps it on the spare room bed.

The apartment is in a small but nicely restored art deco building not far from the hospital and Phyllida parks her car in a visitors' bay, admiring the tasteful choice of colours and the high quality of the restoration. Number five is on

the third floor and as she steps into the lift, where bevel-
led mirrors and walnut veneer have been used to recreate
the original character. What, she wonders, is it like to live
in a place like this, small, elegant, intimate almost? There
are two apartments on each floor and she steps out of the
lift into a carpeted corridor not unlike the foyer of a small
hotel. Phyllida has always wondered how people manage to
live peaceably in such close proximity to their neighbours,
always at the mercy of mutual good will. What did Donald
think of it? What was he thinking when he rode up here in
this lift? Did he greet the neighbours? Did he ever worry that
he might be recognised, his deception discovered?

Just as she is about to press the bell of apartment number
five panic strikes her like a bolt of lightning and she pulls
back, heart pounding. She doesn't *have* to do this – she could
do it through the lawyer – but curiosity compels her; there
are things she needs to know. She wants to see this woman
again, to see the place where Donald came to visit his mistress. She wants to make a small but hopefully uncomfortable
intrusion into May Wong's space, as May had done to her
when she appeared at her front door.

May is clearly shocked to see her and struggles to compose
herself. She is wearing narrow black pants and a loose white
top and Phyllida is astounded to see that in one hand she has
a lighted cigarette. She had often noticed the vague smell of
tobacco on Donald's clothes, a smell he used to attribute to
having stopped off at a bar for a drink with colleagues on
the way home. So was he smoking too? Did he come here
to smoke as well as to do . . . well, whatever all those things
were that men are said to do with their mistresses but not
their wives? Years ago he'd promised her that he'd given
up, but perhaps this had been just another part of his deception. The idea of Donald smoking, of him and May smoking
together, is just as shocking to Phyllida as the idea of bodies
tangled in robust copulation.

'I wasn't expecting you,' May says. 'You could have called to let me know you were coming.'

Phyllida draws breath and focuses on the task at hand. 'You didn't call *me* before arriving on my doorstep,' she says. 'I need to talk to you, but if it's not convenient I can come back another time.'

May hesitates briefly and then steps back, opening the door wider. 'Now is as good a time as any, I suppose.' And she turns and walks away leaving Phyllida to close the door and follow her into the apartment, past the open door to the bedroom into which she desperately wants to look but doesn't. The room into which May leads her is modestly furnished with carefully chosen pieces that match the style and period of the building. From the long window there is a view across rooftops to the city and, close by, the red brick bulk of the hospital. How convenient for Donald, Phyllida thinks, a stopping off place for a smoke and a . . . well, whatever else, before heading home.

'Please sit down,' May says, gesturing to the sofa and sitting down in a chair where she must have been seated when the bell rang, reading the weekend paper, discarded sections of which are scattered on the floor.

Phyllida sits, still taking in the feel of the room, trying to see it through Donald's eyes, to experience it as he might have done. May is silent, watching her. It makes Phyllida nervous – why doesn't the wretched woman say something? – but then she herself is the visitor, it is up to her to explain her visit.

'I have come to return your brooch,' Phyllida says, attempting to revive her imperious tone, the one she had used in the hospital, but she fails and her voice wavers dangerously. She opens her bag, takes out the velvet pouch and puts it on the coffee table. 'It's a very nice piece but not, of course, repaired.'

'Thank you,' May says. 'Does this bother you?' she asks, holding up her cigarette.

'Well I don't smoke myself, but this is *your* home.'

'I'll put it out,' May says, crushing it into the nearby ash-tray. 'I forgot that you don't smoke.'

'Did Donald smoke when he . . . when he was here?'

'Sometimes.'

Phyllida nods. There is so much she wants to ask, and yet she wastes a question on smoking. How much more will she be able to ask before she is shown the door? She sits up a little straighter. 'There are some questions I need to ask you,' she says.

May gestures for her to go on.

'When you came to my house you implied that I was aware of your . . . your involvement with my husband. Is that correct?'

May nods. 'Donald told me that you accepted our relationship on condition that it did not intrude in any way on your life.'

'And you believed him?'

'Of course.'

'You didn't think it strange that I knew this and tolerated it?'

May shrugs. 'I thought you were an unusual woman. I rather admired you, and anyway it wasn't my business. It was between you and Donald. He said you had always had an open marriage, and that in the past he'd had several women – "dalliances", he called them. He said that as you both grew older it had become a marriage of convenience.'

Phyllida's mouth tightens. 'Dalliances – I see. And your . . . your relationship was serious?'

'Yes. When it became serious I told him we should end it, that was when he said you knew about it.'

Phyllida is transfixed by the fleeting expressions of grief and defensiveness on May's face, the proud flash of her eyes, the way her perfectly shaped lips form the words. 'And you,' she asks, 'how could you accept this life, a life in hiding? Didn't you want him to divorce me?'

May shakes her head. 'I am a solitary person, I did not want to live with him. I was happy with things as they were once I believed there was no deception.'

'Did he come here often?'

'Once a week, perhaps, sometimes more, sometimes less.'

'So it was sex then,' Phyllida says. It is a statement rather than a question and she thinks it provides a rather satisfactory summing up of the situation.

'At first,' May says, looking her straight in the eye, 'but as time went on much less sex, more conversation, companionship, someone to talk to. That was the most important thing for both of us.'

'He told me nothing about his "dalliances", as you call them –'

'As *he* called them.'

'Well – yes. He told me nothing. The first I knew of his involvement with you was when you turned up at my door. We did *not* have an open marriage, it's a ridiculous suggestion. I was faithful to Donald throughout our marriage and for a rather long engagement.'

A look of genuine surprise crosses May's face and it is clear that she is both shocked and embarrassed by Phyllida's revelation. 'He told this to his lawyer too,' she says. 'He made me go with him so that I would know someone to speak to if I needed help. It was when he made the bequest to me in his will. John Hammond knows. He believed, as I did, that you knew.'

Phyllida looks away from her towards the window, attempting to hold on to her emotions. 'I realise that now,' she says. 'Do you . . .' the effort of asking is almost more than she can bear '. . . can you tell me . . . did anyone else know? At the hospital, his colleagues, the nurses . . . ?'

'No, I am sure they didn't. If one person knew they would soon all have known, it's that sort of place. Donald and I didn't work together, I'm not a theatre nurse, and we never took risks at work.'

'And you didn't come to the funeral.'

May shakes her head. 'No. That was hard. But I owed it to him not to embarrass you by my presence.'

'And yet you came to the house.'

'When I knew you were alone. I waited for the young woman who lives with you to leave that morning. I asked John Hammond about my brooch, and he said he would mention it to you, but the weeks went by and there was no news. I was afraid it could be lost or thrown out.'

Phyllida nods slowly and takes a deep breath. 'I see.'

May leans forward. 'Can I . . . would you like some tea? This is difficult, for both of us, a shock. Unless you want to leave . . .'

'No, no, not yet. Some tea, thank you, that would be kind.' The heat of her hostility has cooled.

'He lied to both of us,' May says, 'but to you most of all.'

'He lied *to* me and *about* me,' Phyllida says, 'and I think the latter is the hardest to take. He implied that I had a choice and that I chose to collude with him in this. I am not a person who would ever agree to something like that. How dare he.'

'I should have known, should have realised . . .' May begins.

Phyllida shakes her head. 'It's Donald's betrayal that is at the heart of this,' she says. 'It began before you, and he drew you into it. I tried hard to blame you because it would have been easier that way, and of course you aren't without responsibility in this, but the truth is that it is Donald who did this, and he has made fools of us both.'

They sit for a moment in the silence.

'Chinese or Indian?' May asks, getting up.

'Indian, please,' Phyllida says. 'So no one else knows, you're sure about that?'

'I believe not . . .' She hesitates. 'Except . . . yes, I remember now, someone found out. It was around the time he bought me the car, some years ago now. And this man – Terence?'

'Trevor?'

'Yes, that's it, Trevor the car dealer, he found out somehow. Donald was worried at the time but then he stopped mentioning it. I forgot about it – I suppose he must have found a way of getting him to keep the confidence.'

❦

With a black and purple eye and her burgundy hair poking out in spikes above her bandaged forehead, Dot looks rather rakish, and to everyone's relief, two days after her accident she is comfortably propped against the pillows beside the window in one corner of a four bed ward, surrounded by flowers and cards.

'I wasn't drunk, you know,' she tells Laurence when he arrives with a large quantity of chocolate. 'Don't believe the rumours. I only had two glasses of champagne all evening.'

The fall, and the fact that she lay drifting in and out of consciousness on the bedroom floor for hours, has shocked everyone. Apart from the cut on her head and some broken bones in her foot, she has got off lightly, but the hospital is insisting on keeping her in for observation.

'They think I could have had a stroke,' she says, 'but I know what happened – it was the shoes. I haven't had a stroke and I want to go home.'

'You're being ridiculous, Dot. You're seventy-five, of course they have to keep an eye on you for a few days. Stop complaining and be thankful that you're being well looked after. And I don't think you should be living alone – not that you'll consider anything different, but I've brought you these,' and he puts a bundle of leaflets on the bed with the chocolate.

'Oh good, you bought big slabs,' Dot says gleefully,

opening the bag of chocolate and tearing the wrapper off a family size bar of rum and raisin. 'Did you bring coffee?'

'No one said coffee,' Laurence says, and then hesitates. 'Hang on, maybe I got it wrong. Lex said large, strong and dark. I thought she meant chocolate.'

'This is excellent,' Dot says, 'but I could do with some strong black coffee as well.'

'I can get you some from the café downstairs.'

Dot shakes her head. 'No, you need to smuggle it in from outside. The stuff from the café tastes of disinfectant.'

'I'll remember next time. But as I said, Dot, you shouldn't be living alone. It's obviously not safe.'

'In that case you shouldn't be living alone either,' Dot says. 'You're only six months younger than me.'

'That's different,' Laurence says, munching on the chocolate.

'Why? Because you're a bloke, I suppose. What utter sexist rot.'

Laurence has the grace to blush, and in fact he's not as confident as he sounds. In the last few days he's started watching himself very carefully, checking loose rugs and uneven paving stones, wondering how he would cope if something like this happened to him. 'Well at least have a look at these,' he says, picking up the leaflets again and waving them at her. 'You should get one. You just sign up and you get this thing you hang around your neck and wear all the time, then if you fall you press it and it sets off an alarm at the control centre and someone comes out to help you.'

Dot glances at a leaflet and tosses it aside. 'Not much help if you're unconscious,' she says. 'It would have been useless the other night. I was in bed. I'm hardly likely to remember to put it on to get up and go for a pee.'

'I think you're supposed to wear it all the time, even in bed.'

'Probably strangle myself,' Dot says, rummaging in the

plastic bag to check out the other types of chocolate. 'And if I fall in the shower? Don't tell me I'm supposed to wear it there.'

'Well, what about this then?' Laurence says, holding out another leaflet. 'You register with them and every morning you call them at a prearranged time. If you don't call they wait ten minutes and call you, and if you don't answer they send someone around to check on you.'

'And meanwhile I've forgotten and gone shopping,' Dot says. 'Forget it, Laurence, it's not me you're worried about, it's yourself. This orange chocolate is divine.'

Laurence interests himself in the chocolate to hide his embarrassment; he breaks a piece off and samples it. 'Mmm, it is rather good. But the thing is, Dot, you're a woman and old women are more likely to suffer from osteoporosis than old men. You could break a hip.'

'I have the bone density of a much younger woman,' Dot says. 'I had a test a few years ago, Laurence, what about you?' She bundles the leaflets together and hands them back to him. 'Don't think I'm not grateful for your concern,' she says, 'and you excelled yourself with the chocolate. Maybe I'll think about all this sometime in the future, but I'm not ready for it yet. You know, Laurence, last night, when I couldn't get to sleep in this horrible hard hospital bed, I was thinking about you and me, and Margot, the past, the Push – all that stuff. I was thinking about dancing with you, and actually about fucking you . . .'

Laurence chokes on his chocolate and has to fumble for his handkerchief. 'For heaven's sake, Dot, keep your voice down, the whole ward can hear you.'

Dot lowers her voice. 'Okay, but do you ever think about it now?'

Laurence is sure his face has flushed a fiery red, and he glances around for eavesdroppers. 'Well, I . . . er . . . well, yes, sometimes I do.'

'In what sort of way?'

Laurence swallows. 'Well, it was pretty wild –'

'No,' Dot interrupts, 'that's not what I mean. Don't you think it's quite bizarre that here we are, old lovers, old friends, eating chocolate and waiting for the medication and bedpans to take over our lives. But we *are* still friends. I think that's rather splendid.' She laughs loudly and the heads turn again. 'Back then, if someone had shown us what we'd be doing today we'd never have believed them. We never thought about getting old. You don't, do you? You just assume you'll always be young because that's how you feel inside, it's how we *still* feel.'

She is right of course, Laurence thinks later as he makes his way down in the lift and out into the hospital car park, walking along behind a couple, hands in the back pockets of each other's jeans, kissing – almost eating each other – as they walk; eighteen or nineteen, perhaps. A generation who, like every generation before them, think they invented sex. We were all like that once, Laurence thinks, all testosterone and bodily fluids and that incredible flush of power and confidence that came with knowing you could have it whenever you wanted it. Now it's personal alarms and incontinence pads to look forward to. How long will he be able to drive, he wonders, clicking the remote to open the car door; how long will he be able to live independently? As if the loss of Bernard isn't hard enough to cope with, he's aware now of all the risk factors, and the bleak reality of the future. Women, he thinks, are far more capable than men of coping not only with getting old, but with living alone. He'd thought he liked getting old, there was a dignity to it, the pleasure of indulging oneself and feeling you'd earned it. But that was when Bernard was around, when the future was filled with Bernard; it's all different now.

⁓⁓⁓

Even Margot, who is five years younger than Dot, finds herself suddenly sensitised to the challenges of being old and living alone. Should she get rid of loose rugs in case she trips? Dot had slipped on polished boards like these: maybe she should wear rubber soled shoes indoors. And what about the bathroom: wet tiles, getting in and out of the bath? And then there are the steps from the kitchen down into the living room, and at the back and front doors. Life seems suddenly fraught with potential hazards.

'Perhaps we should all be planning for these situations,' she says to Phyllida on the phone. 'Dot's going to have to go home in a wheelchair. She can use crutches to get into the shower and the toilet, and in a week or so start using them to walk. But *her* place is all on the same level. Imagine how I'd cope here if I had crutches or a wheelchair. I might have to go and stay with her.'

'I *am* planning for the future,' Phyllida says. 'Not exactly for the things you mentioned, but I'll bear it in mind.'

Margot thinks her sister sounds different; stronger, perhaps, and rather more relaxed. 'What do you mean?'

'I've decided to sell the house,' Phyllida says. 'I've got a couple of agents coming to value it today and I'll put it on the market straight after Christmas.'

'Good lord,' Margot says, 'this is a turnaround. Are you sure it's the right thing to do?'

'Positive. Somewhere much smaller, cosy. Somewhere that's all mine and has never been Donald's. It's very important to have something that is mine alone, no history, no overtones of the past.'

'But you were so sure about staying there . . .'

'Yes, and I was wrong,' Phyllida says abruptly, 'you know I was. It's a ridiculous idea. What would I do in this great big place anyway? Emma won't be here forever, then what?'

'Well, well that's good . . . have you thought about where you'll go?'

'I'm doing that right now,' Phyllida says. 'And when you see Dot, tell her that when they release her she can come here if she likes. She'd be fine in that ground floor visitor's room with the ensuite. It's all on one level and there's a fridge, kettle, microwave and so on, or she can eat with Em and me. You need to get on with your writing and you won't do it if you're looking after Dot.'

Margot is shocked into silence.

'Are you still there, Margot?'

'Yes. It's . . . it's very kind, Phyl, but Dot's not exactly your favourite person.'

'I was wrong about the house, and I may have been wrong about people too; women in particular. Dot is, quite possibly, one of those people. She's been a friend of yours for long enough, that's a good recommendation. We single women must stick together. And it'll be the last Christmas I'll spend here so I'd like to have a proper celebration to make it special.'

'Right,' Margot says, wondering if she really is hearing this. 'That sounds lovely. And I'll tell Dot when I go in to the hospital tomorrow.' And as she replaces the receiver she sits down on the stool by the benchtop, wondering whether the conversation actually took place or whether she dreamt it.

∽∾∽

While Dot's fall has others evaluating the risks to their own safety, Vinka is more preoccupied with what might have happened if Dot had died. The anxiety she had felt at that birthday lunch has returned to haunt her, but this time its possible solutions seem darker, more complicated. There is more hanging now on her silence than ever before – should she speak or stay silent? How is she to know? If Dot had died, what then? Too late, then, for truth. And what if she herself dies? Vinka paces her beloved fourth floor apartment, back and forth, in, out and around the boxes that are half packed with her possessions and which, like her, will soon be gone from this place. On the dresser a few of her favourite things remain ready for packing at the time when the boxes must finally be sealed and removed. Vinka picks up the framed photograph of her sister and carries it to the light of the window.

'And you, Beate,' she says aloud, 'what about you? You decide. Do I speak or stay silent? Tell me what you would do.' And holding the photograph she sinks down into her chair, sets the photograph on the table alongside it, reaches for a cigarette and stares long and hard at her sister's picture. But she needs something that no amount of looking can give her, and eventually she lowers the frame into her lap, draws deeply on her cigarette, leans back and closes her eyes. Why, she wonders, does it always seem that the hardest, most risky course is also the right one?

'You didn't have to struggle all the way up here, Vinka,' Dot says later that afternoon. 'I'll be back home in a day or two.'

'I do not struggle, and I come because I want to see you, Dot.' Vinka fishes in a large bag and brings out a thermos flask. 'I have good Turkish coffee, and here, some poppyseed cake.' She pours the coffee into the mug by Dot's bed, and a small one for herself in the thermos cap.

'Lifesaver!' Dot says, gulping it so fast that she burns her mouth. 'Vinka, you are a saint, this is *so* good.' She reaches out to take Vinka's hand. 'You look tired; thank goodness the move will soon be over and done with. Do you really like the new place?'

'It is small, but the light is good, and there are no stairs,' Vinka says with a smile. 'There is a feeling, you know, like I can make it seem like home. We saw many didn't we, Dot, and I couldn't feel right with them – this one is different.'

'And you have a garden?'

'Patrick says it is a courtyard more than a garden, but

there are many plants all around, the sun shines through the green leaves and into the house. And this lady is very kind.'

'The manager?'

'Yes, her name is Julie, she laughs a lot. And still I can walk to the places I walk to now. I am very fortunate.'

Dot squeezes her hand. 'I'm dying to see it. When will you move?'

'Two weeks after Christmas,' Vinka says. 'They will decorate it first, new paint. I choose it to be off-white, for the light and the space.'

'Excellent! Well now you must take care of yourself and rest up, get your strength up for the move.'

'You are a fine one for talking,' Vinka says. 'You do not take care and you are in the hospital.'

Dot nods. 'I know,' she says. 'I wouldn't say this to anyone else, Vinka, but something like this makes you realise how easily it could have turned out different. Everyone's telling me, take care, do this with your house, get this support service, but in the end it is the things you can't plan for or foresee that get you. Life is always full of risks but we don't even think about them, and at our age every day is a bonus. So – we must make the most we can of it, even if it increases the risk.'

'I have to take a risk,' Vinka ventures cautiously. 'It is not a risk with safety – not the sort of safety you talk about. It will be the breaking of a trust with my sister, and telling the truth to people whom I love. Perhaps it makes them very sad or angry, perhaps it hurts, but then perhaps also it makes them happy and brings love. What am I to do?'

'You know why I am single and live alone?' Dot says, leaning forward to take her hand. 'Because I've spent my life being too scared of taking emotional risks. Oh, I can spend a night in jail, or bouncing around in the police van. I'll stand on a soapbox and rave on about something that puts me at risk of having rocks thrown at me. But I am, always have been, just too scared of letting anyone in really close.' She looks up at Vinka, who is nodding. 'You're not so foolish as me. Don't leave it too long, Vinka, take the risk and bet on the love, on the happiness. At our age we have no time left for caution.'

TWENTY-THREE

Margot sees it as a scene. A table groaning with food on a warm December afternoon; the characters seated around it, paper hats at odd angles, faces flushed from one too many glasses of champagne. The family Christmas: the parents who are also grandparents, the adult children – the elder daughter with her lover, the younger with her own daughter and, at the other end of the table, her ex-husband and his sister. And then there are the ageing aunts – one recently bereaved, the other alongside her beloved nephew – and the family friend in a wheelchair. A family group; snap goes the camera and captures the image, and somewhere, sometime in the future, someone looks at it, reads into it their own story, speculates on what they were to each other, and what happened next. But the truth is subtle, complex and constantly shifting. This simple scene is a map of intersecting stories, of old loves and old deceptions, of new loves and new beginnings, of broken hearts and broken promises, of new discoveries and passionate inner journeys. She can make something of this, she thinks, and in the same moment that her skin prickles with the birth of an idea, a stab of guilt brings her back into the moment.

Lexie leans gently against Patrick, who slips his arm around her shoulders, and Emma buries her face in Rosie's hair as she sucks melted ice cream through a fat straw. Christmas, Margot thinks, how strange and wonderful that they are all here and each one of them has changed in some remarkable way since this time last year. Dot in an orange paper hat is twisting a chocolate wrapper into the shape of a wineglass for Rosie. Vinka, listening to Wendy, laughs and claps her hands together and Laurence, watching quietly, his arm stretched along the back of Emma's chair – what is he thinking? Is he regretting those lost Christmases without his daughters, and those he will never have with Bernard? And Phyllida, her cheeks flushed, her eyes bright with the effect of the wine, doing Christmas in her own way for perhaps the first time ever.

From the other side of the table Laurence catches her eye and smiles. It's a conspiratorial smile, the sort that speaks volumes, the sort of smile exchanged by people who have their own private language born in intimacy and going back years. And for a moment Margot feels she might dissolve once more into the past, into the longing that for decades she has fought so valiantly to suppress.

'Merry Christmas,' Laurence says, and she half hears and half reads his lips. And she wonders if he has any idea at all how much she still loves him and how hopeless and helpless it sometimes makes her feel.

❦

Lexie looks up at Patrick and he slips his arm around her shoulders. She still can't quite believe that for the first time in her life she has fallen in love with someone who loves her for who she is rather than for what she might be able to do for him.

'Nothing would change if we moved in together, Lex,' he whispers now, as though reading her mind. 'I'm not going to turn into a hopeless couch potato and expect you to start running around after me.'

'Can you put that in a signed, sworn and witnessed affidavit,' she says. It is the second time he has suggested it.

He leans back a little to see her better. 'If that's what you need, no problem. Or I could just write a statement on this paper napkin and get your parents and Vinka to witness it.'

But it's not a lack of trust in Patrick that is holding Lexie back, but in herself. She likes the version of herself that she has become in this relationship and she's not ready to risk losing it in her own confusing responses to domesticity.

'Just think of it,' Patrick says. 'It would dramatically reduce your living expenses, and when you start uni you could be the only student with a live-in academic supervisor.'

'And that would be good for me?' she asks.

'Of course.'

'Mightn't it mean I would rely on you too much, make you a safety net when I'm struggling?'

'You might still do that from separate houses,' Patrick says. 'But if we lived together I would make you coffee in bed in the morning. I would pour wine and cook dinner while you study.'

'*You* might still do that in separate houses,' Lexie says. 'Can I get a rain check?'

'If you must.'

'Ask me again at Easter.'

'Why Easter?'

'By then I'll have survived some weeks as a student, and I'll be weak, defenceless and desperate for someone to look after me.'

'Sounds good to me,' Patrick says, holding out a Christmas cracker. 'Easter it is, I'm putting it in my diary.'

༚༚༚

Dot is sitting alongside Phyllida, and Emma watches as she puts a hand on her arm.

'Thank you,' she hears Dot say. 'I usually hate Christmas but I'm having a wonderful time.'

'Me too,' Phyllida says. 'Strange, isn't it, you and me here like this, dismantling the barbed wire fence.'

'Strange but good. One of the delights of growing old is that you learn it's never too late to mend the fences.'

Phyllida nods and pours them both some more champagne. 'And it's never too late to get drunk together.' She raises her glass.

Emma has been surprised to discover that she too is developing a cautious liking for Dot. As a child she had been scared of her, and had resented her for diverting Margot's attention away from her to all those meetings, campaigns and protests. But Dot aged seventy-five and confined to a wheelchair seems harmless by comparison, and now all Emma feels, like grit in her shoe, is that Dot's presence takes Phyllida's attention away from her, just as it had diverted Margot's attention all those years ago. Emma wonders if she has never quite grown up. Is this like the Barbie factor, as Lexie had called it when Emma had told her what Phyllida had said.

'It's just a bandaid solution, Em,' Lexie had said, 'constantly fixing the way you look. Real change comes from within, just like the real beauty. The problem is that everything around us tells us that the answer lies in cosmetics or clothes or treatments; instant gratification – quicker and so much more fun than learning to be different.'

Rosie slides off her chair and goes walkabout, examining everyone's loot from the crackers, and Grant moves along to sit beside Emma. 'She's an absolute carpetbagger, our daughter,' he says fondly, watching as Rosie slowly acquires one useless plastic trinket after another. 'She may grow up to be a con woman.'

Emma looks at him steadily. 'I doubt it,' she says. 'You and Wendy are raising her far too well for that.'

Grant takes a deep breath. 'Thanks for that, but you do your bit too. I thought maybe it was getting better for you.'

Emma hesitates, twisting the stem of her wine glass, staring down at the tablecloth. Not so long ago she was furious with him, furious for months, years in fact. His apparent ease in parenting Rosie had been a constant painful reminder of her own failure to master even the basic rudiments of motherhood. But somehow it doesn't haunt her in quite the way it once did, and although her guilt over her own shortcomings does flare up as anger and resentment against him from time to time, it soon fades away. Since the day they made their first cake together, Emma has felt more confident and has actually enjoyed spending time with Rosie. She has, she realises, discovered the ability to connect with her daughter. It's an ability Wendy has in spades, but which Emma thought had been omitted from her own makeup. Mothering comes easily to Wendy, Emma thinks; she may not have wanted to take on the shared parenting of her brother's child, but there's no doubt she's doing it well and while she knows how valuable this is for Rosie, for them all, Emma can't quite forgive Wendy for that.

'It *is* getting a bit better,' she says to Grant now. 'I used to be so frightened of the responsibility. Now Rosie's a real little person – I think we're getting to know each other better.' She looks up, surprised that she's actually told him this, although of course he already knew it. It must be the champagne that's loosening her tongue and her emotions.

'She loves you to bits, you know,' Grant says. 'Her mum is the bee's knees, you really must remember that.'

Emma swallows hard, struggling to hold back tears. 'Then I'm a very lucky woman,' she says, getting to her feet. 'Back in a minute,' and she walks away from the table and once inside the house runs quickly up the stairs into her bathroom and locks the door. Grabbing a towel from the railing she buries her face in it and sinks down onto the lid of the toilet.

Crying alone in the bathroom on Christmas Day. She remembers reading about this in a magazine – a couple of pages of stories from women of all ages and in all sorts of situations, hiding from the festivities and from the people they loved, and weeping with frustration or despair, sobbing from loneliness or the need to be alone, drenching bundles of tissues with tears for disappointed love, absent children or the bleakness in their hearts, yearning for something they can't quite define. Emma had found traces of herself in those pages and now, as she stands up and crosses to the basin, she imagines them – the women in bathrooms all over the country, splashing water on their faces, repairing their makeup, smoothing down their hair in an attempt to return to the party and be once again the wives and mothers, the daughters, aunts, nieces, grandmothers and friends they are supposed to be. Perhaps, she thinks now, she is not so different after all. Perhaps the world is full of women dancing as fast as they can to simply keep their heads above water and a smile on their faces, attempting to mask the chaos within. And as she studies her reflection Emma knows that she doesn't want to do this again. She doesn't want to be crying in the bathroom next Christmas, something has to change. Somehow she just has to take the little nugget of wonder she found that day with Rosie and learn to make it grow, and maybe, just maybe, she needs to sort some other stuff out in order to do that, and for that she might need some help.

It's clear, when she returns to her seat at the table, that no one has noticed anything unusual about Emma's absence, and fortunately no one is peering closely at her trying to determine whether or not she might have been crying.

'Look at these, Mum,' Rosie says, dumping her pile of plastic cracker charms on the table beside her. 'Everyone gave me their things.' She pushes the pile towards Emma and then turns, squeezing in between the chairs to crawl onto Laurence's knee.

'Can you make this work, Grandad?' she asks, handing him a small plastic comb from a cracker, sealed in a tiny plastic bag.

Laurence tears the plastic, extracts the sections of the comb and slots them together. 'There,' he says, removing Rosie's paper hat and sliding the comb through her silky hair. 'It works now.'

Rosie takes the comb from him and drags it roughly through his beard. 'Ouch, you're so rough, Rosie,' he says, grasping her hand and kissing it. 'Go gently, I'm an old man.'

'Sorry, Grandad,' Rosie says, flinging her arms around his neck and kissing him several times. 'Sorry, I love you.'

Emma, still struggling with the lump in her throat, sees that Laurence is deeply touched by this. He hugs Rosie and with her arms still around his neck she combs the back of his hair. Laurence looks across at Emma – it's a look she knows from her childhood, a look of enormous sadness. That look is engraved on her memory from the day he turned back at the door before walking out of their house and into another life. If he was so sad, she had wondered then, why would he go? Was it her fault? Back then she had believed it was and now, all these years later when she knows, understands and accepts the truth, when she knows she had no part in it, she still hasn't quite forgiven him for going, nor forgiven herself for not being good enough to make him want to stay.

Laurence smiles and strokes the back of her hand and Emma wishes she could make that final step and have the words fall from her lips as they had from Rosie's. But the words still won't come, and she smiles and grips his hand, and hopes it is enough.

TWENTY-FOUR

Late in January, as the city heaves and sighs under a suffocating blanket of heat, Margot gathers together the typed pages and taps them vertically, then horizontally, on the desk to align the edges. For a moment she holds the stack of paper in both hands, willing herself to remember how this moment feels, to register the relief and the satisfaction of finishing it. It is done and the question of whether she will be able to return to the keyboard each morning, move the characters along and eventually find an ending, are answered. She did, she has. Now someone, probably several people, will shuffle its pages, pencil their comments and questions into its margins and so decide its fate. It has its own life now, apart from her; just like a child on their first day at school, others will nourish or reject it, will trim it or ask her to expand it. They will read into it their own meanings according to their prejudices, their loves and hates, their real pasts and imagined futures. It is no longer hers in the way that it was in the writing. The moment is full of promise: of acceptance and admiration, of rejection and criticism, and of the emptiness of waiting for what lies beyond this hiatus of its passing into the hands of others. And what will she do now, without it, without its demanding presence calling her back day after day?

'It's beautifully written,' the agent to whom she sent a couple of chapters had said on the phone. 'I like the idea and what I've seen so far. So, if you could send me a complete manuscript I'll read it and get back to you as soon as possible.'

How long is that? Margot wonders as she puts the manuscript into a padded envelope and seals it. Weeks? Months? Picking up the package she gets in the car and drives to the post office, still caught in the enormity of this moment. All her life she has dreamed of this, of holding it in her hands, a work entirely of her own creation, and now this has all happened so quickly. Can she really have done anything worthwhile in such a short time? 'Perhaps,' she murmurs to herself as she locks the car and crosses the street, running the last few steps into the post office just as it is about to close, 'perhaps I *have* been at it for years. Maybe I've been writing it for years and all I had to do was get it out of my head and onto the page. Maybe I just had to be this age, at this time and in this place, before I knew what to do with it.' And she hands the Express Delivery package over the counter and watches as her hopes and dreams are tossed into a sack. Then, unwilling to return to the strange empty stillness of a house where there is no work in progress, she goes back to the car, does an illegal U-turn, and heads for Phyllida's place.

The drive is full of cars and the front door is ajar. Margot pushes it open and follows the sound of voices to the back of the house and out onto the verandah where, once again, a crowd of people sits around the table.

'Margot!' Phyllida cries, getting to her feet. 'How lovely, we were just talking about you, come and join us,' and she pours her a glass of wine.

'Another party? You didn't invite me,' she says, sitting down.

'It's a campaign meeting,' Dot says. 'We *would* have invited you but we didn't want to take you away from your writing.'

From the end of the table Alyssa pushes a plate of raspberry friands towards her. 'You should help us eat these, quickly, before Dot wolfs the lot.'

Margot takes one and samples it. 'Delicious. How's it going? Are you planning the march?'

'We are,' Dot says, 'and I'd forgotten what a monumental task it is.'

'We're trying to work out a plan to distribute the fliers and get some advance publicity,' Wendy says. 'Dot's using some of her old contacts, but we need someone to coordinate the volunteers to get the fliers into libraries and cafés and so on.'

'I could do that,' Margot says, through her cake. 'I've done it before, years ago, remember?'

Dot nods but then shakes her head. 'I do, but you shouldn't do anything right now that stops you from finishing what you're writing.'

'It's finished,' Margot says, looking around the table. 'I've just sent it off.' And there is a pause followed by cheers and toasts. 'So I really do need something to do.'

～～～

'I am definitely going home,' Dot says. 'You've been wonderful, I'm so grateful, but I've already outstayed my welcome.'

'Not at all,' Phyllida says from the doorway of the bedroom where Dot is zipping up her bag. 'You're the last person I ever thought I'd say this to, Dot, but I'm really going to miss you.'

'Likewise,' Dot says. 'I misjudged you, Phyl. I thought you were a very different sort of person.'

'You didn't misjudge me, I *was* a different sort of person.'

'Well I like this one better than the old one,' Dot says. '*Much* better.'

'So do I.' Phyllida takes the case from her and hands her the stick she is still using. 'Come on then, let's get this bag in the car and I'll drive you home.'

It is odd in the car; silent, awkward, as though neither of them knows what to say. The ease of the past few weeks seems to have deserted them since they left the house. Dot wonders if this is her fault, if, in her anxiety about going home, she has said or done something stupid without realising it. Phyllida's invitation had come when she was panicking about how she would manage at home alone. She had brushed off all offers of help. The only one acceptable to Dot had been Margot's offer to stay with her. It was the ideal solution but Dot, accustomed to the sight of Margot propping up other people at considerable cost to herself, was not going to consider anything that might disrupt her friend's writing.

'I'll be fine,' she'd said to anyone who asked. 'I'll be able to whiz down to the shops in my wheelchair and whiz around the house. I'll have the crutches for getting in and out of bed, and I can put a stool in the shower so I don't have to stand.'

But that was before she'd done a test run in the chair along the hospital corridor. All that whizzing around turned out to be rather more difficult and hazardous than she'd imagined. It hurt her arms; she got her hand caught in the side of the chair, crashed into a trolley, and ran over a doctor's foot. It was pretty unnerving but Phyllida's invitation had come at just the right time; it offered privacy, comfort, convenience and the safety net of both Phyllida and Emma being in the same house. She had never expected to enjoy it, and she had certainly never expected to feel this fear and sadness at leaving.

'You know, Phyllida,' Dot says now, shifting slightly in her seat, wanting to break the silence. 'I'd forgotten what it was like to sit around with women friends, with a bottle of wine, and talk. I started thinking about it after Margot's party. We used to do it a lot, Margot and I and those other women, but I haven't been good at keeping in touch. I suppose I was arrogant enough to think I didn't need it.'

Phyllida changes gear and looks across at her. 'I've *never* done it before,' she says. 'I've done dinner parties with Donald's friends and their wives, playing golf but not getting involved in the social life of the club . . .' She hesitates. 'When you and Margot were doing it all those years ago I was actively trying to avoid it.'

'Really?'

'Yes . . . I never really knew how to be with other women, and it was partly about putting everything into my marriage and resisting anything that might challenge it.'

'And you thought friendships and the women's movement might do that?'

'Well, what do you think?'

'Ha! Well yes, I guess *so*. It certainly spelled the end of a lot of marriages.'

'I put all my energy and attention into being Donald's wife and built walls to keep myself in and others out. My mother always insisted that it was family that mattered and it was best to keep everyone else at a distance. I never understood how Margot could be so open to people.'

'So what now? What's next?'

Phyllida shrugs. 'Not sure yet. A move definitely, and working out what I really want to do in my old age.' She swings the car slowly into Dot's driveway. 'I suppose you wouldn't fancy trying out a book club?'

Dot's instinctive caution about commitment cuts in. 'What sort of book club? Where is it?'

'The Boatshed, down by the water just –'

'Yes, I know it, I know the women who run it, but I didn't know they had a book club.'

'Been going a couple of years apparently. I've just finished the book for the next meeting. It's called *Instances of the Number 3*.'

'Salley Vickers,' Dot says. 'I've read some of hers, but not that one.' She turns sideways in her seat. 'Okay, I'll give it a go. But I don't promise to keep going if I don't enjoy the first time.'

'Me neither,' Phyllida says. 'I'll drop the book off for you in the next couple of days. Even if you change your mind and decide not to go I'd still like to know what you think of it.'

The house has a staleness about it as Phyllida carries Dot's suitcase through to the bedroom and goes back to the car for the shopping she had picked up for her this morning.

'It feels so strange,' Dot says, hobbling around on her one crutch, opening windows and shuffling through the mail while Phyllida unpacks the shopping and puts it away.

'It does,' Phyllida says, looking around. 'But it's a lovely place, Dot, and you'll soon get back the old feeling.'

They stand facing each other, silence bearing down on them.

'Well then,' Phyllida says, 'I'd best be off. You know you can call any time . . . if there's anything . . .' She stops, swallows and takes a deep breath. 'Well then . . .' and awkwardly she steps forward, hesitates, takes another step as Dot moves towards her. For a moment they cling to each other in a sort of desperation until Dot's stick clatters to the floor. They step awkwardly back from each other and Phyllida laughs, brushes something from her eyes and bends towards the stick.

'No!' Dot says. 'I need to know I can do this alone.' And cautiously, steadying herself with one hand against the wall, she bends and retrieves it. 'Success!' she says, straightening up. 'And independence.'

'Good,' Phyllida says. 'That's very good. Well, you don't need me anymore so I'll be off.' And she turns away and walks briskly along the passage to the front door.

'Phyllida.'

She stops and turns, and Dot hobbles towards her.

'I'm sorry.'

'What for?'

'All that time ago – calling you Falada.'

'Don't be,' Phyllida says. 'I always rather liked it. In fact it was the one thing I did like about you, Dot. Until now, that is.'

TWENTY-FIVE

Melbourne aches under the burden of the heat and the acrid smoke from fires that continue to burn beyond the city boundaries. Fire has consumed lives, homes, businesses, even small towns, and it dulls the spirit and the imagination of those in comparative safety beyond its reach. It hangs like a pall not only across the state but across the nation as people watch its progress on news bulletins and online, as they pledge money, clothes, toys, household goods and effort to help those whose lives have been devastated.

At a table outside the Boatshed Emma waits nervously, shifting her position slightly as the fleeting promise of a breeze falters and is lost. Perhaps this is a bad time, she thinks. Everyone is so preoccupied, even she finds it hard to think beyond the image of the fires. At this time it seems almost trivial to be pursuing questions about something that happened years ago, but Phyllida keeps asking whether there is anything in the files they should be concerned about, and Emma feels duplicitous each time she reassures her. She glances nervously at the other tables where couples and families sit waiting for their food or eating it, pushing away half-eaten lunches, pouring iced water, mopping sweat and trying to distract uncomfortable, fractious children. And then she sees her, walking across the grass between the car park and the footpath, just as she imagined: medium height, in her fifties perhaps, black hair greying at the temples, cut in a jagged modern style, dressed in a white linen skirt and a lime green shirt, with big black sunglasses. Emma has never seen her before but she just knows it's May, and as she crosses the path and comes up the Boatshed steps, she stands up to greet her.

'Hi,' she says. 'I'm Emma. Thanks for coming to meet me.'

May removes her glasses, smiles and takes a seat at the table. 'Donald was very fond of you, he often talked about you. But really I can't image how I can help.'

Emma orders tea and they talk awkwardly about the heat, the horror of the fires, and the women who have turned the Boatshed into a café and craft gallery. The tea arrives and when Emma has poured it May leans towards her across the table.

'Perhaps we should talk about whatever it is that's bothering you?'

Emma nods. 'Yes, yes of course – and I do appreciate . . .' She hesitates, fascinated by this woman who is so centred, so quietly elegant. Why Donald? Emma longs to ask her, along with so many other intrusive questions she will never get to ask. 'Well . . . it's about Donald of course.'

'Of course.'

'I wonder if you know anything about the death of a patient called Tony Stiles, about seven years ago.'

May puts down her cup and looks away, out across the liquid glass of the water as the river curves into the distance. 'Not much,' she says. 'I was away in Hong Kong when it happened, so I only know what Donald told me, and murmurings on the hospital grapevine. Why?'

Emma reaches down into the bag which is occupying the third seat at the table, her heart pounding. Even showing it to May seems risky, but she takes out the file and lays it on the table.

May tilts back in shock. 'You have the file? It was missing. How did you get it?'

'I found it in a box file in his study along with some other papers.'

'You mean he . . . Donald . . . you think he . . . ?'

'Stole it? I think he may have done.'

May shakes her head. 'More deception,' she says. 'He told me that it had gone missing.'

'And when it wasn't ever found?'

'I don't know. When I asked later, he said there was no problem. I should forget about it.'

'So, what did he tell you?'

'A patient died on the operating table. A young man – a street kid, I think. There was a big football match that night under floodlights, and just as the crowd started to leave the grounds a storm broke, thunder and lightning, torrential rain, and there were a lot of people on the streets, there were accidents, and some fighting. Emergency was in chaos. Donald was about to go home, but he stayed on to help. This man . . . boy, Tony Stiles, was brought in, badly injured. I don't know if it was a fight or perhaps he was hit by a car, but he had a head wound, and some internal damage – his kidneys, I think, but I'm not sure.'

'And something went wrong.'

'Yes, but I can't remember what. They were very short of staff and Donald was operating with just the theatre nurse and the anaesthetist. I really can't remember the details, but he died. Donald said it was unavoidable, but he had some sort of argument with the nurse – she blamed him. She was quite experienced but he said she was wrong, unprofessional, and he'd always found her difficult to work with. May I?' She reaches out for the file and draws it towards her.

Emma leans back in her chair, watching, waiting as May reads, sighs, shakes her head, reads on, and finally closes it and looks up, her hand clasped over her mouth.

'So it *was* his fault,' she says finally, shaking her head.

'Well I guess we'll never know now for sure,' Emma says. 'The nurse's statement is pretty clear but Donald denies it completely and the anaesthetist didn't see what happened.'

'But the anaesthetist also mentions that Donald appeared to have been drinking, possibly heavily. And the very fact that Donald has hidden the file . . . well, it seems like a sign of guilt. But then he was a very senior person, they would believe him before the nurse, but he also had much more to lose.'

'That's what I thought,' Emma says. 'But I don't understand why there wasn't an enquiry.'

May shrugs. 'Again, I wasn't there and I'm sorry to be so vague about it, but by the time I got back it was weeks later. There were a few whisperings in the hospital corridors but by then that nurse had resigned and gone.'

Emma leans forward across the table. 'I'm sorry to ask you this, but do you think that he, that Donald could have . . .' She hesitates, unsure how May will take it. 'Could he have covered it up?'

May looks at her long and hard, and then leans back in her chair. 'Once I would have said no,' she says, 'but now I know he lied to me for years. Our whole relationship was based on a lie about your aunt. So yes, I think he could. I wonder if perhaps he and Ron Jamieson, the director, decided together to hush it up. They were old friends.'

Emma nods. 'They were at medical school together. May, did Donald seem worried about it at any time after that? Sometime later maybe?'

May takes a deep breath and shakes her head. 'No, I don't think – oh wait, yes, I remember. Some time, quite a long time later, he came in one evening. He seemed agitated. He said that he'd had a call from someone representing the nurse.

He seemed concerned that it might all blow up again, but he never mentioned it after that. I suppose I thought he would have told me if anything else happened.'

'Something else did happen,' Emma says, 'and it was happening up until the time he died. And the amazing thing is that Uncle Donald kept a detailed record of it, and he kept it along with the hospital file in a box in his study. And it cost him an awful lot of money.'

∞∞∞

Dot crumples yet another sheet of paper and throws it across the room. Nothing is going right; here she is, a journalist who has spent her life writing, and now she can't write to save her life. It's the speech that's driving her insane. While she languished in hospital and at Phyllida's house, the campaign team had been working their butts off getting together a campaign plan and organising the march. Now it seems to have crept up on her. Alyssa will speak first, then a retired former premier, and then it will be her turn. Dot remembers all too clearly how it feels to stand behind a microphone on the steps of Parliament House; to see that mass of expectant faces, the banners and placards, and the police on the lookout for troublemakers. She did it because she could, and because it mattered not just to her but to that mass of women who had turned up to protest. Fear of failure was a luxury she couldn't afford; what she needed was the adrenaline rush that could make her stand and deliver. But that was then, Dot thinks now, as she bundles the fruits of her first attempts into the bin and more crumpled paper spills out across the floor. What about now?

'I don't think it has to be something *new*,' Patrick says when he turns up to see how she's getting on. 'I think what you need to do is to find new ways of saying some of the things you've already said on the website and the blog. Just as long as it's relevant.'

'I don't know what's relevant anymore,' Dot says. 'I'm totally out of touch.'

'You said that when I asked you to talk to the students, but you were terrific. You were relevant then. You're relevant on the blog. If you weren't we wouldn't be doing this now.'

'*You're* not doing it!' Dot says fiercely, rounding on him. '*I'm* doing it. *I'm* the one who has to stand up there and make a fool of myself in front of several hundred people. *Me*! This doddery old shell of a person who should have put up or shut up years ago.' And in that moment, standing there in her study, waving a couple of sheets of notes and swaying perilously without her stick, she does something she hasn't done in front of anyone else for years. She begins to sob.

'Whoa!' Patrick says. 'Careful, Dot, come and sit down.' And he takes her arm and steers her towards her chair. 'I'm so sorry,' he says, putting an arm around her shoulders, but she shakes him off. 'Really, I didn't mean it like it must have sounded. What I meant was that we're all working on this protest, the legal requirements, the communications, the banners, the t-shirts, heaps of us. We're doing that and we're putting you up there because we believe in you, believe in what you can do, the way you can challenge and inspire people. It's a vote of confidence from a whole lot of other people, Dot. That's what I meant.' He grabs a box of tissues off her desk and passes them to her. 'Would you like me to get you a drink or a cup of tea or something?'

Dot shakes her head, and blows her nose. 'No,' she says. 'No, it's okay. Sorry, I shouldn't have flown off the handle like that. I'm so self-centred and childish. It's just that although I've done it many times before, right now it seems such a huge thing . . .' She hesitates as her eyes fill with tears again. 'Look, don't say this to anyone else, I don't even know why I'm telling you – just because you're here, I suppose. But since that fall I've been feeling incredibly nervous about everything. Even going to the shop seems risky and dangerous.

A couple of days ago, when they said I could start driving again, I went over to see Vinka's new place, and you know, Patrick, I was scared; scared of the traffic, scared of getting lost, scared every time I had to make a decision on the road.' She stops, pats her eyes with more tissues and leans back with a sigh. 'I've lost my confidence. All I can think of now is that I've always taken all sorts of risks without any thought for my own safety. And then I fell, and lay here for hours and came to in the ambulance on the way to hospital, and everything changed. Now I see danger everywhere, even in the things I do every day.'

She holds up her left hand which has a large sticking plaster across the base of her thumb. 'I was cutting up some pumpkin and my knife was blunt so I got out the sharpener, and all the time I was sharpening it I kept thinking, "Better not make it too sharp, Dot, or you'll cut yourself, and you could get an infection, or you could faint and bleed, lose a lot of blood and be unconscious on the floor for days." And sure enough, what did I do? I went back to cutting the pumpkin and I cut myself.'

Patrick smiles at her. 'And did you faint?'

'No. I went to the bathroom and put my hand in cold water and wrapped it in a towel until it stopped bleeding. Then I dried it, put antiseptic on it and then a plaster.'

'And it's not infected?'

'No.'

'So you dealt with it just the same way you would have done before the accident?'

'Yes, but that's not the point. The point is the fear, the anxiety, it's there all the time, stalking me, looking over my shoulder. I'm never going to be free of it now.'

Patrick sits still, watching her as she bundles the tissues and tosses them into the bin. 'Look, I don't want to tell you how to suck eggs, Dot; I don't know what it's like to be your age and to suddenly feel vulnerable in all sorts of ways. But

I do know that most people feel vulnerable when something major disrupts their lives. Physically you got off lightly and recovered quickly but it was hugely disrupting to the way you feel about yourself. But you're tough, incredibly tough, and determined, and you *will* get through this.'

Dot leans forward, arms on her knees, shaking her head. 'I don't know,' she says. 'Really I don't. I think I may not be tough anymore. Maybe I just used up the allocation of tough that was given to me at birth. Maybe it just ran out.'

'Maybe you're tired, shaken and under pressure to perform.'

'That too.'

'Do you want us to cancel? It's not too late, we could find another speaker, you know.'

The prospect of someone else taking her place was like a knife to Dot's ego. 'No! Certainly not! This is *my* gig. Don't you dare get someone else; you don't cancel anything for me until I'm dead.'

Patrick claps his hands, laughing. 'Ah, Dot! You are *such* a woman of contradictions and I love you for it.'

Dot smiles and has the grace to blush. 'You mean I am so egotistical. You won't tell anyone about . . . well, about this, will you, Patrick, especially not about the crying bit?'

He hesitates. 'Not even Lexie?'

'Especially not Lexie, or Margot. They'll worry and be watching out for me all the time, and I'll get annoyed. God I'm difficult, I don't deserve such wonderful friends. But if I am going to beat this fear I'll have to do it alone.'

'Okay,' Patrick says, standing up. 'I won't tell anyone, but only if you promise you'll call me if you're in any trouble or need anything, even just to talk about it, even if it's the middle of the night. Is that a deal?'

'Deal,' she says, holding out her hand to him. 'Now let's go and make a cup of tea – that, after all, is what old women do when the going gets tough.'

'Really,' he said. 'I thought they went straight for the gin bottle, or bought a new hat.'

'Don't be so cheeky.' Dot grins. 'Put the kettle on while I go and put cold water on my face.'

TWENTY-SIX

'Wait a minute,' Phyllida says. 'Are you telling me that Donald then covered up this death by stealing the file?'

Emma shakes her head. 'I'm not sure. I think he and Ron Jamieson covered it up together at the time. Whether they decided to lose the file at the same time or later, I don't know.'

'Yes,' Phyllida says, nodding, 'that makes sense. I can just imagine the two of them putting their heads together and deciding to make it all disappear. I wonder how they managed to shut the nurse up. The old boys' club at work again!'

'My guess is that they intimidated her, attacked her professionalism. She saw she couldn't win and went of her own accord,' Emma says.

They are sitting outside at the big table where they all ate Christmas lunch, a table now littered with the contents of the file and pages of Donald's notes, and Phyllida feels as though she has walked into the script of some unfolding crime series. What Emma has just told her seems incredible, and yet she finds it unpleasantly believable.

'It would have been easy enough,' Emma goes on. 'Tony Stiles appeared to have no relatives, no one was asking about him, and no one responded to the police or the Salvation Army, who were looking for people who knew him.'

'So what could have happened to make Donald take the file later? And how much later?'

'Ah,' says Emma. 'This is where it gets very interesting.'

'Stop trying to be enigmatic, Em,' Phyllida says, impatient for answers. 'Just give me the facts.'

'Well, a couple of years later the nurse shows up again. Only not in person, mind you, but in the shape of someone we both know and love – one Trevor Pargeter.'

'Trevor? You can't mean it.'

Emma nods. 'Curiouser and curiouser, as Alice said when she fell down the rabbit hole.'

'Actually I think that bit comes later in the book,' Phyllida said, 'but I could be wrong. Go on.'

'From this messy pile of notes that Donald left, it seems that Trevor turned up one day and told him that the nurse was going to sell her story to the media. It seems that she was going out with a mate of Trevor's. Donald's notes indicate that he thought the woman must have visited Trevor's place with her boyfriend, and realised who lived next door. Maybe she caught sight of Donald, or she could have known where he lived, and she seems to have told Trevor about what happened in the operating theatre.'

'So Trevor demanded money to keep her quiet and I suppose Donald coughed up?' Phyllida sighs, closes her eyes briefly and imagines Donald pacing nervously back and forth behind the door of his study, weighing up the costs of acquiescence or refusal.

'Yes, and more fool him, because then they kept on demanding more,' Emma says, shuffling through Donald's notes. 'Although I'm not sure that it was 'they' or whether it was just Trevor. Those two first payments of five thousand dollars were transferred into an account that Trevor probably set up for the purpose. Did he take his share and give the rest to the nurse, or did she even know he was doing it? I guess we're never going to know the answer to that. But Donald says that sometime later Trevor came back for more, and he wanted cash, and so he paid up and he kept paying, mostly in cash, once by cheque and a couple of times online. It's all recorded here, although it's really hard to read, his writing is awful. I suppose he must have been terrified he'd wake up one Sunday morning and find he was front page news. The scandal would have finished him.'

Phyllida takes a long breath and leans back in her chair, glass in hand, wondering how he could have let it go on so long. How or when did he imagine it might end? Did he really believe that the truth would never come out if he just kept paying? 'What a debacle,' she says. 'I can't help feeling a bit sorry for him, although it does sound as though he was responsible. He told me once – oh, a couple of years after all this must have happened – that he'd had a very close shave some time earlier. He'd thought he might have to resign, but he wouldn't give me any details. Pride, I suppose. But why did he write it all down?'

'Perhaps he did it just so he'd have a record of the blackmail,' Emma says. 'Or he may have done it for you, in case a time came when you needed to know.'

'Maybe, who knows? And I suppose it doesn't really matter. Does he actually say he was responsible?'

Emma shuffles pages again. 'Not exactly, but he does say somewhere . . . ah, here it is: "Bloody unfortunate business, fortunate for me there were no relatives asking questions and demanding enquiries".'

'Heaps of concern for the patient, I see!' Phyllida says dryly. 'In fact a total lack of concern or respect for that young man on everyone's part. This whole thing would look very different if Tony Stiles had come from Donald's side of the tracks.'

'Could he have been drunk?'

'Possibly. Quite often when he came home it was obvious he'd had a few drinks. I thought he was stopping off on the way home, but of course he could have been drinking in his office at the hospital. I thought I knew everything about him, Em – his strengths, his weaknesses, what motivated him, what he wanted from life, what he was scared of. And I did, I knew all that, and yet I knew nothing. I lived with him for fifty years, but I didn't know him at all.' She stops, thinking for a moment, swallows hard and goes on. 'And I don't think I ever let him know me either. What a waste, what a terrible waste.'

'Trevor also knew about May,' Emma says, looking up cautiously. 'Donald brought the VW from him and put it in her name. That seems a really stupid thing to have done but who knows what was going on between him and Trevor at the time.'

Phyllida nods. 'May told me Trevor had found out. But how did *you* know that?'

'May told me too. I met her. I was trying to find out if she knew anything more about this.'

'And did she?'

'Only a little, but it helped me to put it all together.'

'And what did you think of her?'

Emma hesitates. 'Well actually I liked her – in fact I liked her quite a lot.'

Phyllida nods and says nothing, holding the stem of her empty glass and tilting it gently from side to side. 'Mmm,' she says thoughtfully, 'so now we just have to decide how to handle the weasel next door.'

～～～

Emma is exhausted. She had been dreading the day when she would have to lay out the facts about Donald to Phyllida and she had used a lot of time and energy trying to work out how best to do it. At first she had decided, it would be best to have someone there with her to share the awfulness – Margot, probably, or possibly Lexie. But she had eventually come to the conclusion that while that would be best for *her* it was probably not what was best for Phyllida. It was hard to know how her aunt would respond to the news but the possibility of her being overtaken once more by that paralysing sense of shame, or an outburst of emotion, would be doubly painful if witnessed by someone else. Emma knew she had gained Phyllida's trust and her respect and she had finally come to the conclusion that this was something she must deal with alone. Now, as she climbs into bed, the relief is enormous and her fears of a painful emotional reaction have been put to rest. There is no doubt that Phyllida was deeply distressed by what she had learned this evening, but there was no outburst, just sadness, some disgust, and a really practical conversation about what to do next. It is, Emma thinks, the very best she could have hoped for and with any luck Phyllida will get a good night's sleep and won't slide into the grip of shame or depression.

Emma sinks down into her pillows and closes her eyes, enjoying the feeling of unwinding, letting go of the tension, being entirely in the present. It's something she's been practising recently, as a way of dealing with some of her own problems, and so far it seems to be working. She is drifting comfortably towards sleep when a tap at the door jerks her awake. She knew Phyllida was still up from the faint murmur of the television in her room, and then the sound of running water, and now she is outside the door. Emma freezes, stares at the door and wonders if she dares to feign sleep. The prospect of going back over the Donald stuff yet again is not something she relishes.

'Em,' Phyllida says, tapping again. 'Em, are you awake? There's something I need to tell you.'

She sounds calm, Emma thinks, but it's hard to tell. Emma takes a deep breath. 'No,' she calls, 'I'm still awake, Phyl, come on in.'

Phyllida, in her dressing gown, opens the door and tiptoes across the carpet as though fearful of waking someone else.

'So sorry to disturb you,' she whispers, and then laughs. 'Silly me, what am I whispering for? No risk of waking anyone else,' and she sits down on the edge of Emma's bed.

It's a warm night but Emma's exhaustion and the effect of being pulled back from the warmth and comfort of approaching sleep make her shiver, and she pulls the quilt up to shoulder height. There is something oddly secretive or perhaps embarrassed about her aunt's manner that, despite the calm exterior, leads Emma to expect the worst.

'There's something I have to tell you, dear,' Phyllida begins. 'I haven't been entirely honest.'

Emma's stomach churns. More secrets, this time Phyllida's, or is it perhaps a change of heart in the plan for dealing with Trevor? She nods to her aunt to go on.

'I have something to give you,' Phyllida says, drawing a sealed manila envelope from the pocket of her dressing gown. 'Something I should have given you a while ago.' She turns the envelope in her hands, looking down at it. 'I had no right to keep it so long.'

Emma takes the envelope; it is addressed to her but not stamped, and bears the logo and name of Hammond & Partners, Solicitors. 'Hammond?' she says in surprise. 'Why is John Hammond writing to me?'

'Open it and see.'

Emma rips open the envelope and takes out the contents – it's a letter and attached to it is a cheque for $25,000 made out to her.

'It's a bequest,' Phyllida says, 'from Donald's will. It did take a while to get the probate sorted but it took me time to hand it on to you. You see, Em –'

'Oh my god,' Emma says in amazement, her mind buzzing suddenly with what this means. She can feel her face flushing with pleasure. 'That's so kind of him, and of you . . .'

'Well it was supposed to be a bit more than that,' Phyllida says, 'but he hadn't actually got around to changing it, so when I've sold the house there'll be some extra to come. But the thing is, Em, the reason I didn't give it to you earlier –'

'But what about Lexie?' Emma cuts in.

'She gets the same,' Phyllida says. 'I shall give it to her next time I see her, so please don't tell her – I'd like it to be a surprise. But the reason –'

'Of course,' Emma says, 'I won't say a word. It'll really help her with uni.' It will, she knows, be a big help to Lexie, almost as big as it will be to her in helping her along with this new thing she's exploring, and in her excitement she nearly blurts it out, but then reality hits her.

'That's what I thought,' Phyllida says. 'But about you, Em . . .' she hesitates. 'I thought perhaps . . . well I was hoping you might use it to . . . well –'

'I can't take it,' Emma interrupts. 'It's lovely of him, and of you, Phyl, but I can't take it. I owe you it anyway, let alone the fact that I've been living here rent-free for months.' She folds the letter and the cheque back into the envelope and holds it out to Phyllida. 'Can you ask Hammond to cancel the cheque and pay the money to you, then I will at least have paid back what you lent me.'

Phyllida is taken aback. 'No,' she says, moving a little further back down the bed. 'No, Em, Donald wanted you to have this and I want it too. The reason . . .' She pauses and then sighs. 'No,' she says again, 'I was going to ask you to do something with it, but that wouldn't be fair . . . no, forget it. I want you to have it. Donald wanted it, and although in view of what's happened doing what he wanted is not my priority, this is important. I want you to take it, and I am cancelling your debt to me, Em. Having you here has been a real joy, but much more than that. I don't know how I would have got through these months without you. I know I haven't been the easiest of companions. This year is a big new start for me and if it weren't for you I don't think I'd be looking forward to it in the way that I am. So please, take it, use it wisely, and enjoy it.'

By the time Phyllida leaves, sleep is far from Emma's mind. Use it wisely, her aunt had said, and in that moment Emma had almost blurted out that she knew exactly how she would use it and how much help it would be, but she held back. She was sure that what she intended was indeed wise, and in fact it was already proving its value, but she just wasn't sure how Phyllida would view it and the last thing Emma needs now is a critical or dismissive reaction. As she slides further down in the bed Emma can barely believe her good fortune. Whatever it was that Phyllida had planned to ask her to do with it couldn't, she believes, be more valuable than this and one day, hopefully not too far away, she *will* tell her, and by then Phyllida will be in no doubt that it was worth it.

~~~

Laurence stares at the emergency alarm in his hand; the act of slipping it on over his neck seems like an act of surrender but if it's going to be any use then he ought to be wearing it. He won't of course, he's already decided that. He'll keep it somewhere out of sight but easy to get to if he needs it. He's certainly not going to answer the door with an alarm hanging on a lanyard around his neck, but having it does seem like a good idea, as long as no one knows. No one must ever know.

His back is a worsening problem and what concerns him most is that his shower is above the bath. Some years ago when they renovated the bathroom Bernard had insisted that they retain the period character of the house. He wanted a claw-footed bath and had trawled the city and its suburbs and found a magnificent one, and then he'd found a modern shower fitting designed to work perfectly with a character bath. The challenge of climbing in and out of the bath to take a shower as one gets older was something neither of them had considered at the time, but now Laurence curses it every day and fears that his back might just 'go', lord knows how, and then he'll be in deep shit. It happens, he knows that, he's often heard people say 'my back just *went* and there I was – stuck'; it's usually followed by descriptions of excruciating pain and various humiliating medical interventions.

'Where did your back go when it went?' he had once asked, and the person of whom he'd asked it had said: 'Don't be fucking facetious with me, mate, you won't be laughing when it happens to you.'

And now of course it so easily could. It gives Laurence a gloomy sense of satisfaction to know that all this is Bernard's fault and that if his back does go and he dies of neglect while trapped in the bath, Bernard will have to live with that knowledge for the rest of his life. Meanwhile he'll have to take care in the bathroom. Perhaps, he thinks, he should keep the alarm in the bathroom, somewhere he can reach from the bath. As he's pondering this he hears the sound of Emma's car pulling into the drive and quickly drops it into the central cardboard tube of the spare toilet roll that is standing on top of the cistern.

'Hi,' he says, opening the door. 'Where's our Rosie?'

'We're picking her up from a party on the way,' Emma says, kissing him on the cheek. 'Can I use your loo?'

'Sure.' He steps back to make way for her and spends a few anxious minutes hoping that Emma will not need to use the new toilet roll.

'I thought we'd go for a walk along the river and have something to eat at the Boatshed. They've started doing light suppers,' Emma says, emerging from the bathroom.

'Sounds good,' Laurence says, relieved that his secret has not been discovered. 'You look terrific, Em. Where's the party?'

'South Yarra. Rosie has a new friend, Jacinta, she's very taken with her. She's much more of a girly sort of girl so I think she'll be good for Rosie.'

Laurence, who has spent the last few weeks researching material on the branding and sexualisation of children, resists the urge to tell Emma that she should be thankful that Rosie is happy conducting bird funerals and using her compass to draw maps of the park. But they've been getting on well the last few weeks and so he decides not to rock any boats. Collecting his keys and sunglasses from the kitchen, he locks the door and follows her out to the car.

'Wendy, of course, doesn't have a good word to say for them,' Emma says, buckling her seatbelt.

'Who?'

'Jacinta's parents. She says they have more money than sense or taste, the house looks like the Pope's summer palace, and Jacinta's going to turn into a pretentious airhead. But you know Wendy; she does have a rather narrow viewpoint.' She hands him the street directory and a piece of paper with the address. 'Can you navigate when we get a bit closer? I don't know that area.'

Laurence takes the directory and gets his glasses out of his top pocket. It gives him time to consider his reply, and then he decides to risk it. 'I like Wendy,' he says. 'And I think she and Grant are doing a good job with Rosie.'

'They are,' Emma says. 'I quite like Wendy too, now, but you must admit she's a bit lentils and Birkenstocks, and she's tediously super green.'

'I see nothing wrong with any of that,' Laurence says gamely.

'No, I don't suppose you do,' Emma says, but she says it affectionately and turns briefly to smile at him. 'I just hope Jacinta will get Rosie dressing up a bit, like the other girls. Anyway, before we pick her up I need to update you on the secret life of Donald.'

Laurence listens with growing interest as Emma relates the saga of events following the death of Tony Stiles.

'I never liked him and I never trusted him,' he says now. 'Most of all I never understood what Phyllida saw in him or why she couldn't see through him. He was an arrogant, self-serving, duplicitous bastard.'

'None of us saw through him,' Emma says, 'not even May Wong, who's actually really nice. I can't imagine what she ever saw in him.'

Laurence shrugs. 'So what's Phyl going to do about Trevor?'

'She wants to talk it through with us, you and me. So can you come back home with me and Rosie after the Boatshed?'

'You need to take the next turn left,' Laurence says, 'and it should be right on the corner. Yes of course I'll come. Bloody hell, is that it?'

The house is enormous and sports more clashes of architectural styles than seems possible in one building. There are ornate white wrought iron balustrades, fake Doric columns, porthole windows, and what look like remnants of the Parthenon frieze randomly set into the walls. At the top of the steps, which run the full width of its façade, an archway more suited to a small palace leads to the front door which is decorated with a huge pink bow. Pink bows also adorn the manicured miniature trees that stand in pots on either side of the arch.

'Perhaps Wendy was right,' Emma says. 'It really is hideous. Come on then.'

'I think I'll just stay here,' Laurence says. Now that Emma has switched off the engine he can hear music pumping, and it's not his sort of music.

'Please,' Emma says, sounding surprisingly plaintive. 'Don't make me go into this place on my own. Besides, there's that sign on the gate.'

'What sign?' Laurence asks.

'Look there – "Parents and grandparents! Come inside to pick up your gorgeous girl and have a glass of champagne with us. Mick and Sue".'

'Shit!' Laurence says.

'Please, Dad.'

'If I wasn't here you'd *have* to go in alone.'

'But you *are* here, and you're my father. I need you to come with me.'

Just a few months ago Emma had been ready to disown him; now she needs him. Laurence reluctantly gets out of the car and follows her along the path, up the steps and into a huge marble floored foyer with a fountain in the centre.

'Crikey,' Emma says, 'this is pretty gross. I'm beginning to worry about the dress-up bit now. Jacinta's mum was supposed to be hiring heaps of stuff for them to choose from. Look, there's another sign.'

The sign is made of bright pink cardboard scattered with crimson sequins. In one corner there is a large silver Playboy Bunny logo, and beneath it an arrow above the words *To Jacinta's Party*. Beneath it is a white basket of large pink and white bunny ears on headbands, standing on top of a table. *Come in if you're wearing ears*, the sign on the basket says.

'I think you should give the ears a miss,' Laurence says. 'I'm going back to the car.'

Emma grabs his sleeve. 'Don't go, Dad, please, we'll just get Rosie and leave.'

Shrugging, he follows her along the corridor to where the music is blasting out of the open door to a dance studio lit with flashing lights and a mirrored disco ball. At the far end there is a small stage on which a dozen little girls are strutting their stuff in time to the music. Dressed in pink and black Bunny costumes with pompom tails, long ears and fishnet tights, they walk, one hand on hip, the other holding a pink card with a number on it. The tight-fitting satin costumes are cut and padded to create eerily mature curves, and

as they walk they sing. Laurence can't quite hear the constantly repeated phrase but each time they finish it there is a
pause, a double drumbeat and they swing around to face the
front, thrust their hips suggestively forwards, then turn their
backs to the audience and bend over to wiggle their bums,
and start walking again. Behind them a pink satin banner
announces *Jacinta's Birthday Bunny Beauty Pageant*. Watching
in open-mouthed delight, a group of parents, clap and shriek
at every thrust and wiggle. Off to the side a woman in a pink
leotard and tights is sliding up and down one of two pink
poles, watched by four even younger girls, dressed like her
in pink leotards over obviously padded bras. They take it
in turn to copy her moves, wrapping their legs suggestively
around the other pole, pumping, twisting and thrusting in
time to the music.

'Pole dancing?' Laurence gasps in shock. 'Christ, they're
only four or five. And what is that thing they're singing? It
sounds like "is your girlfriend hot like me?"'

'That's exactly what it is,' Emma says, tight-lipped. 'This
is really gross. And where's Rosie? Poor darling, she's probably hiding somewhere. Can you see her?'

'Number eleven,' Laurence says, pointing to the stage.
'Black satin, pink ears and fake tan. I think you'll have to
wait for them to finish before you take her home.'

The colour drains from Emma's face and she stares at
the stage as if unable to believe what she's seeing. Laurence
reaches out to her but before he can grasp her hand she has
leapt up the steps two at a time and strides across the stage
to where Rosie is wiggling her satin clad bum. Emma grabs
Rosie's arm and, ignoring the squeals of resistance, pulls
her daughter to the edge of the stage. 'Stop the music,' she
shouts, 'turn that music off now.'

A man wearing jeans, a pink shirt and pair of bunny ears
turns off the music and marches across to confront her.

'What the hell do you think you're doing?' he demands,

and one of his pink and white ears gets an attack of vertigo and flops down over his forehead. 'You can't just walk in here like this and ruin my daughter's party.'

'What *am I doing*?' Emma asks, looking down at him from the stage, fury burning in her face. 'What am *I* doing? I'm removing my daughter from this disgusting spectacle. How dare you abuse my child like this, turning her into some sort of sex object. What is the *matter* with you?' She looks away from him to the group of dumbstruck parents. 'What's the matter with *all* of you, can't you see what you're doing? That song, these costumes, the pole dancing – *pole dancing*? They're practically toddlers. You're either evil or insane – I just hope it's the latter.' And dragging the protesting Rosie behind her she heads for a rack where the children's own clothes are hanging. 'Pick up your shoes, Rosie,' she orders as she grabs Rosie's clothes and heads for the door, Laurence turning to follow her.

'The costume,' Jacinta's mother calls, running after Emma. 'You can't just take that with you, it has to be returned – you can't just keep it.'

Emma, who has now reached the huge entrance foyer, stops so suddenly that Laurence and Rosie almost crash into her. She turns and draws herself up to her full height, looking stonily into the woman's face. 'I have no intention of keeping it,' she says, and her tone is icy. 'I wouldn't have that thing in my home if you paid me, but I am not allowing my daughter to undress in something akin to a nightclub. You'll have to wait for it.'

And turning away she continues across the foyer, out through the front door and down the path to the car.

'It was sooooooooo embarrassing,' Rosie wails, perched on the lid of Laurence's toilet while Emma attacks the makeup with a face cloth. 'Jacinta will hate me now. *And* you were horrible to Mrs Fletcher, and now I'll never get invited again.'

'You're never going there again anyway,' Emma says. 'Those people must be mad – all of you dressed up –'

'I *told* you it was a dress-up party, and I told Wendy too. So it's not my fault. You're *so* mean. Jacinta's mum got all those bunny things just for us. She had two ladies to do our makeup, and a hairdresser. She used to be a glamour model and she taught us how to walk and wiggle and stuff. I hate you.' The tears begin again, coursing down her cheeks leaving more pale streaks in her foundation. 'You could've let me show Aunty Phyl how I looked.'

'Aunty Phyl would have had a fit,' Emma says, standing up straight and inspecting what other bits of Rosie need to be washed.

'*And* you said we were going for a walk and out for tea.'

'Well there's no way we're going anywhere until we've got you cleaned up,' Emma says. 'This orange stuff is everywhere.'

'It's called Magic Tan, and Jacinta says you can wash it off but I like it. Jacinta says I can go with her and her mum to get a proper spray-tan next week.'

'You are going nowhere with Jacinta ever again –' Emma is shouting now – 'and you are certainly not getting a spray-tan.'

'But *you* did, you got one.'

'Rosie, once and for all –'

'Go easy on her, Em,' Laurence says from the doorway. 'It's really not her fault.'

The bathroom is silent. Rosie, tearful and tan-streaked, kicks her legs back and forth against the lavatory bowl and Emma, her hands now orange, stops scrubbing, pushes her hair back from her own tear-stained face and stares at him.

'No,' she says eventually. 'No it's not,' and she drops to her knees on the tiled floor by Rosie's side. 'Grandad's right,

Rosie, it's not your fault and I shouldn't be blaming you. I'm so sorry, darling.' And she pulls Rosie into her arms. 'I think I'd best get her into the shower, Dad, if that's okay.'

Laurence leaves them to it, goes to the kitchen, switches the kettle on and stands with his hands on the bench top, his back to the door, while silent tears slide down his cheeks and into his beard. His tears are not for Rosie, for her humiliation or disappointment; she is young, she'll bounce back. They are for his daughter, for the confusion, the realisation and the anguish he saw in her eyes. For she always knew it was not Rosie's fault but now Laurence can see that she thinks she's to blame.

He hears the shower being turned on and they are talking now, low voices masked by the sound of the water. Laurence takes a deep breath, rubs his eyes, gets out mugs and milk and opens a packet of Tim-Tams.

'Can I get a clean towel for her please, Dad,' Emma says from the doorway. Her face is pinched and streaked with Rosie's tan, her eyes are red, and she is twisting her hands as she did as a child when she thought she was in trouble.

Laurence puts down the biscuits and clears his throat. 'Of course,' he says, walking over to her, and he takes her hands in his and holds them still.

'It's my fault,' Emma says, 'all my fault.'

Laurence releases her hands and gently grasps her upper arms, looking straight into her face. 'It's *not* your fault,' he says. 'It's far more complicated than that and nothing terrible has happened. This is just one unfortunate afternoon, in the home of people who almost certainly don't see anything wrong in what they're doing.'

'Well they should, they should . . .'

'This will soon be forgotten, Em. Rosie will be back to burying dead birds, and while she may well turn out to favour lentils and Birkenstocks, today is not going to scar her psyche, or turn her into a bunny or teenage beauty pageant obsessive.'

'Mum, Mum, I need a towel,' Rosie calls from the bathroom.

'But *you*, Emma,' Laurence continues, 'you were wonderful – passionate, strong, articulate. I was . . . I *am* tremendously proud of you.' He pulls her back to him, kisses her forehead, and then puts his arm around her shoulders. 'Come on, let's go and find madam a towel, and then we'll have a nice supper at the Boatshed.'

And he leads her out to the linen press, pulls out a couple of towels and gives her a gentle push towards the bathroom.

The sun is setting, hanging in a crimson haze on the horizon as they wait for their food on the deck at the Boatshed.

'Relax,' Laurence says, pouring the wine. 'Look, she's fine, happy as a flea,' and he nods towards Rosie, who has discovered a friend nearby and is leaning on the edge of her friend's table.

Emma, tight-lipped, shakes her head. She still seems to be on the verge of tears. 'I've been a terrible example for her,' she says, her voice quavering. 'I've been so obsessed with myself I didn't think . . . I just didn't think.' A large tear rolls down her cheek and she dabs it with the napkin.

'Darling girl,' Laurence says, 'this really is the proverbial storm in a teacup. Don't blame yourself for this, please. You've had some hard things to deal with and you just tried to find a way to feel better. And you're a wonderful example, you're a smart, intelligent and very successful businesswoman –'

'So why do I still feel like a child, and a hopeless failure who can't get anything right?' Emma snaps back.

Laurence, whose heart has been sadly battered by the events of recent months, now feels it might finally break. 'I don't really know,' he says, trying to keep his voice steady and reassuring. 'I can't answer that, but . . . well, you're not going to like this, but maybe you could get some help working it out. It doesn't mean –'

'You mean see a counsellor.'

'Yes, but not . . .'

'I have,' Emma says. 'I am.'

'Really?' Laurence is stuck for more words, amazed and relieved. He hesitates, desperate for the right response. 'Well, that's good, Em. Great in fact. Good for you. How is it going?'

Emma shrugs. 'Weird, difficult, it's hard to say. I seem to spend most of the time in tears and then go home and cry some more.'

'Well, it's early days – you'll keep going?'

She nods. 'Oh yes, I've hardly got my feet wet yet. It feels a bit like going for a swim on a hot day,' she says. 'You're far too hot so you walk out into the water and it's freezing and it creeps up over your feet and your ankles, and it's agony and you know it'll be worse when it gets past your knees, and truly awful when it gets to your crotch. But once you're in you have to keep going, don't you?'

'You do,' Laurence says, smiling at her. 'You really do. I'm so proud of you.'

A waiter appears with cutlery, bread plates and napkins heralding the arrival of their food, and Rosie comes bounding back to the table.

'Did you get wedges, Grandad? And those fish things?'

'I did, darling,' Laurence says, straightening her chair. 'Wedges for all of us and the Thai fish cakes for you.'

'Cool,' Rosie says. She leans over to him, lowering her voice. 'Louise can't have the fish cakes because she's allergic to something, so she's having some stuff made of beans and it has goat's cheese in it. Yuk! I'm glad I'm not allergic or anything.' She wriggles into the chair and unfolds her serviette. 'And Grandad,' she says, thrusting her hand into the pocket of her jeans and struggling to pull out a lanyard, 'what's this?'

'Wherever did you get that?' Emma asks. 'It looks like a

personal alarm. Someone must have dropped it.' She looks around for likely owners.

Laurence clears his throat. 'It's . . . er . . . well, it's mine actually,' he says, feeling his face flush.

'It was in the toilet paper,' Rosie says. 'I thought you might have hid it but I expect you just dropped it.'

'It's yours?' Emma says. 'You think you need it?'

'Oh of course not, not yet,' Laurence says. 'Not for ages, probably never.'

Emma seems to be struggling now to suppress a smile. 'But you got one anyway?'

'Well, yes . . .' Laurence busies himself with his pasta, which has now arrived. 'Just in case, you know, after what happened to Dot. It . . . well it focuses the mind, rather.'

'And you hid it in the toilet roll?'

'When you turned up, yes, well I thought it might . . . and I live alone now, there's that to think of . . . but I thought it might make me look . . .'

'You don't,' Emma says quickly. 'You don't look like that, not at all.'

'You won't . . . well, you won't tell anyone . . . your mother . . . Phyl . . . ?'

She shakes her head. 'Not a soul.'

There's something different in the way she's looking at him, Laurence thinks, and it's a bit unnerving.

'You look terrific, Dad,' she says, leaning towards him across the table, 'not in any way any of the things you're worrying about.' She pauses. 'And . . . I should have told you this before. I'm sorry about Bernard, really sorry. This must be so hard for you, the sadness, him not being there . . . everything.'

Laurence looks up and meets her gaze and it makes him catch his breath. He sees what it is now, that look in her eyes – she can see right through him into the great aching void inside him, and in that moment he is totally vulnerable, stripped naked of his defences, and he has to look away.

'Can I have *all* the wedges?' Rosie asks, piling them onto her plate.

'Definitely not,' Emma says. 'Grandad needs some.'

And she picks up the bowl and passes it to Laurence and as he takes it from her their eyes meet and her hand lingers on his.

TWENTY-SEVEN

Vinka paces back and forth between the lounge and the courtyard, stopping first in one place and then another. She picks up a cigarette, lights it and as she inhales her stomach heaves; it's hours since she ate anything, not since breakfast, in fact, and now it's nearly six. In the kitchen she hacks a large slice from a dark rye loaf and takes it with a chunk of cheese and a shot of vodka out to her chair in the courtyard. Patrick will be here any minute now, she must try to stay calm, at least as calm as it is possible to feel under the circumstances. She's still not sure that she is doing the right thing; she thinks it is probably right in many ways, but is it the *ethical* thing, the *compassionate* thing? She cannot, after all, predict the result – hurt, anger, embarrassment, shame; all sorts of things are possible. But she has made up her mind that it has to be done, and now her own inner dialogue is exhausting her. She will sit here with her bread, her cheese and her vodka and Patrick will be here before she is finished.

She checks her watch again and starts on the bread, chewing slowly in the hope that it will steady her mind. She makes herself look around at the plants in the courtyard, one at a time, letting her gaze rest on them, measuring their health and strength, using each one to calm her before moving on to the next. She loves this time of the evening before it's dark, when the air is soft and still in the heat. It's so quiet here and yet there are plenty of people nearby, and the city is just outside the gates – it is ideal, really. It is so much better than she had imagined. Beate would have liked it here, Vinka thinks; if Beate were alive they might have finished their days here, together.

She looks again at the time; he is late now, how much longer? And she swallows the last of the cheese and the remains of her drink, and carries the plate and glass in to the kitchen, just as Patrick appears at the screen door.

'So what is it that is so serious?' he says when they are sitting outside, with more vodka. 'It all sounds very mysterious.'

Vinka's heart pounds in her chest, her head spins and she has to close her eyes to stop the giddiness. 'Are you okay?' Patrick asks. 'You look really pale. Can I get you some water? Do you need to lie down?'

She shakes her head. 'No, no, I am all right,' she says. 'Just worried about what I have to tell you . . .'

'You're not ill, are you?'

She sees the concern, even fear, in his eyes and grips his hand. 'I am not ill. Please, Patrick, I must tell you something. If Beate were here . . . but then if Beate *were* here this would not be my decision to make. It is not so easy, let me take my time, let me tell it all before you say anything.'

'Sure,' he says, obviously puzzled. 'Take your time, I'm sure it can't be anything really bad.'

∽≈∾

Margot hasn't told anyone about the phone call, and no one has enquired about the fate of her manuscript. But they are relieved, they have said in various ways, to have her back, for themselves, for the campaign, for each other. What they don't know, what they haven't yet seen, is that she is not quite 'back'; part of her is somewhere else and she suspects that from now on that's how it will always be.

'I'd be delighted to represent you,' the agent had said on the phone this morning. 'It's a terrific novel. In fact it's hard to believe it's your first.'

And so another period of waiting has begun, this time while the agent tries to persuade a publisher to read it. Writing, Margot realises, is not an occupation for the faint-hearted. The waiting is agony, and always in the back of her mind is the knowledge that she may wait for months and then have to start waiting all over again.

'Not long now,' Alyssa says from the head of the table, forcing Margot's attention back to the meeting. 'Let's do a quick round-up to see where everyone's at.' It's her turn to chair the meeting and it's clear from the energy she brings to the table that she's already pumped with adrenaline.

Watching her Margot is reminded of Dot as a young woman; Alyssa loves to be the chair, she has the same compulsion to lead, the same fire in her belly. Dot still has it, Margot thinks, but she's finally developed some sort of inner thermostat which allows her to run hot when necessary, but also to keep something in reserve. Without that the inner fire might by now have consumed her. Years ago Margot had doubted that Dot – the heavy smoker, the stress junkie, the compulsive sampler of any new and risky experience – would make it to sixty, but now, in her seventies, she looks as though she could go on forever, although it's clear that Dot is not quite as convinced of that as she once was.

'What are you wearing around your neck?' Margot had asked when she'd arrived at the house a couple of days ago.

'It's an emergency call system,' Dot had said, leading her through to the back verandah. 'Sit down, have some iced tea. I've made this big jug of it.'

'So when did you get the alarm thing?'

'Last week. Laurence organised it. It's temporary of course, just until I can get rid of the walking stick. It makes me feel like an accident waiting to happen.'

'It's very sensible. You should keep it. Laurence should've got one for himself at the same time,' Margot said.

'He's convinced that being a bloke he's never going to need one! Obviously men do not fall over in the house – or at least not in Laurence's world.'

'Well don't tell him I told you this, but he told Lexie that he's having a lot of trouble with his back since he did the pilgrimage. He's a bit worried about it – not that he'll say that to you or me of course. This is delicious iced tea, it tastes like Phyllida's.'

'It's made to Phyllida's recipe,' Dot had said. 'You know, putting it in the sun and so on. I don't think I'll ever drink the bottled stuff again, this is so much nicer.'

Margot is bewildered by this new friendship between Dot and Phyllida. She looks at them now, sitting side-by-side at the meeting as though they have been great mates all their lives, and she feels a shameful stab of jealousy, as though little bits of each of them which had been hers have now been stolen. Ridiculous, she thinks; not so long ago she was worrying because Phyllida had no friends, now she wants to keep her all to herself – or is it perhaps Dot who she wants to keep to herself?

Alyssa has finished her checklist of the preparations and Lexie leads them through the timetable and the route for the march. Everyone is here tonight, all except Patrick who, according to Lexie, has gone to see Vinka, who sounded on the phone as though she might have a cold or a virus.

'You've all done a terrific job,' she says. 'It's going to be amazing and it'll take us to another level.'

'How many do you think we'll get?' Alyssa asks. 'Hundreds?'

'Let's hope so,' Lexie says, holding up her crossed fingers.

'Margot,' Phyllida says as the meeting breaks up and Emma and Alyssa bring tea and scones from the kitchen. 'Did you have time to read that book?'

'The one about the two women – the wife and the lover of the man who died?'

Phyllida nods. 'Did you find it interesting?'

Margot shrugs. 'It was okay but I think I'm more interested in why you asked me to read it.'

'I'm interested in that too,' Phyllida says. 'Dot and Em and I are going to the Boatshed book club tomorrow, they're discussing it. Why don't you come too?'

'Well I –'

'Do come, Margot,' Dot cuts in. 'Remember that book group when we read *The Women's Room*?'

Margot nods. 'I remember.' And she looks across at Phyllida. 'Okay,' she says, 'I'll meet you at the Boatshed.'

∽∾∽

Emma has stayed in the office for as long as she can. She has watched her colleagues leave to go home to their partners and children, to meet friends for a drink, or evening shopping, for a new date, or simply a quiet evening in front of the television. And she has hung on as long as she can, waiting for the moment when it will be safe for her to leave and make her way to the station. From the moment she woke this morning Emma recognised the signs and has known how her day will be and how it could end, and she has ricocheted back and forth between her old chaotic self and the person she is trying to become. As she has tracked back through her own history of compulsive attempts to make herself over by shopping for new looks, or fixing bits of her face or body, she has realised it always begins in the early morning. She wakes with a terrible sense of her own emptiness – a black hole of self-hatred that threatens to swallow her if she doesn't do something to make herself feel better. As the day progresses it builds to an obsession that drives rational thought straight out of the window.

Christmas had been a turning point for Emma; surrounded by her family she felt suddenly besieged by pinprick insights into her own behaviour. Determined that she wouldn't be crying in the bathroom next Christmas, she had made some enquiries, got some recommendations and on the first day back at work after the holidays had managed to get an appointment with a therapist, only half believing that it might be the answer. But things have started to change. Recognising and acknowledging the warning signs has helped, and several times she has controlled the old compulsions and managed herself through the day by starting out as the therapist suggested.

'From what you've told me,' Mara had said, 'you've built up a good routine since you moved in with your aunt, so make it work for you. When you get those feelings that warn you that you might go off the rails it's *really* important to stick to your routine. So – deep breathing before you get up, then everything slowly, thoughtfully, entirely in the present, thinking just about what you are doing in the moment. Don't skip anything; let the routine keep you grounded.'

But for some reason this morning it began to fall apart. Was it something in the light coming through the bedroom window, that high white cloud combined with oppressive airless heat that she finds infinitely depressing, or perhaps the after-effect of a dream that she can't now recall? Whatever it was, the danger signals were all there and she had lain in bed for a while, grasping desperately at the routine: breathing deeply, reminding herself to stay cool, focusing on the feel of her body against the mattress, the safe and comforting surroundings of the room. She was almost on top of it then, suddenly, everything fell apart. She had thrown back the sheet and moved instantly into the day, her mind reeling and whizzing, and the whole framework slipped and crashed and she couldn't get it back again. She skipped her morning run and went straight to the shower, ignoring the many tiny rituals that had been working so well: making herself feel the water on her body, the feel of the shampoo as she massaged it into her hair, the comfort of Phyllida's huge white bath towel wrapped around her body. But today she dressed with the old edgy tension, the tightness in her chest and the same compulsion to be doing rather than just being that had always preceded disaster. She was revving so fast this morning that she was out of the house and on the train before Phyllida was up.

As the train rattled along its tracks towards the city, Emma did make a serious attempt to get herself back onto her own tracks. She forced herself to think about her sessions with Mara; she recalled the way she had begun by rambling on about everything, from being taunted in the playground to the sheer terror of being faced with the responsibility of the survival of a tiny human being. She remembered talking about the compulsion to spend whatever money she had – and a lot that she hadn't – feeding her craving for something new to wear, to carry, to fix her face, her hair or her body, to make herself new, different, better, happy, whole. And she tried hard to focus on one particular session when, after resisting Mara's questions about how these impulses, once fulfilled, made her feel, she had finally admitted to a sudden and brief rush of relief followed rapidly by an attack of guilt and self-hatred. And she forced herself to remember the crying, the really heavy duty crying that she did in those sessions from which she emerged with wrecked makeup, red eyes, blotchy face, damp strands of hair stuck to her forehead, and feeling as though she'd done three rounds in the ring with the Terminator.

She even thought, as the train pulled into a station and more passengers piled into the carriage, of getting out and going home. Perhaps Phyllida would help her, talk her down a bit and help her get through the rest of the day. After her first few therapy sessions Emma had avoided going straight home so that she wouldn't have to face her aunt or anyone else looking how she felt. On one occasion however she thought that Phyllida was planning to meet Jean Dunne. But when Emma let herself into the kitchen through the back door Phyllida was sitting at the bench top reading a book and eating cheese on toast.

'Good lord!' she'd said, looking up from her book. 'Whatever happened to you? You look as though you've been dragged through a hedge backwards.'

And Emma had promptly burst into tears once again and told Phyllida about the therapist, and owned up to the fact that since the first few weeks she'd been using the money from Donald's will to pay for it. To her surprise, rather than scoffing and telling her she ought to be able to sort herself out on her own, Phyllida had responded with a hug and told her she was proud of her.

So, there she was, apparently making progress, feeling different and hopeful, out of debt and with money in the bank, and yet this morning she was right back where she started – a prickling, twitching bundle of self-doubt and aching need. The only thing that had kept her on track during the day was the sheer pressure of dealing with the barrage of media calls relating to an overnight raid on Central Park by four men in a four-wheel drive who crashed through the glass doors and ransacked the various mobile phone outlets. Now, however, with the evening closing in, the pressure off and the shop windows alight with the promise of retail therapy, Emma is still in the grip of the beast. She is alone in dangerous territory, with no one to call to suggest getting a meal, or seeing a movie – Phyllida, Margot and Lexie are all at a meeting, and Laurence . . . well, despite the recent improvement in relations with her father she certainly isn't going to turn up on his doorstep.

Emma turns out the light in her office, makes her way to the ground floor, steps out into the street and turns right in the direction of Bourke Street. The mall is alive with people hurrying and strolling, avoiding the trams or climbing onto them, heading home or into the department stores. In the narrow arcades leading through to Little Collins Street, women just like Emma are out shopping with their girlfriends, pointing to window displays, laughing, encouraging each other into the shops and emerging with carrier bags made of thick glossy paper and silk ribbon handles, handles that Emma's hands itch to hold. The tantalising smell of leather draws her into a handbag shop but, with a huge effort of will, she backs out into the arcade and follows the scent of sandalwood to the shop that sells saris and silver jewellery. For a few moments she stands by the window drinking in the gorgeous colours of the silks and the sequins and then, in a move that she knows to be dangerous, she straightens up and steps swiftly next door to the lingerie shop, hesitating in the doorway where satin and lace in sexy designs and luscious colours promise to make a difference that will last, that will actually change how she feels.

Once inside it's too late, she is in a different space now, a zone in which rational thought is suspended and there is nothing but that promise. She walks quickly between the racks, plucking out the answers to her problems on their small plastic hangers: bras in purple, red and black, matching lacy knickers, a satin teddy in shell pink trimmed with grey lace, and another in coffee satin trimmed with cream. There is no pain now, just relief, huge relief, she'll only have these, it's not like it was before, one little hiatus, that's all it is, but it doesn't mean anything, and she puts them down on the counter.

'All these?' the sales assistant says, drawing them towards her, and Emma nods.

The woman begins to key the prices into the register. It's

a slow task due to the curve and length of her gleaming, crimson-polished false nails.

'Is that the lot?' she asks eventually, and Emma nods again, reaches into her bag for her purse and takes out her credit card. It is in that moment, as she stands there at the counter, about to hand her card into the clutches of those deep red talons, that something freezes inside her. She stops and steps back slightly from the counter, folding her own fingers protectively around the plastic card.

'Did you want to pay cash instead?'

Emma stares at her for a long moment and the woman exchanges a wary look with her colleague.

'Is it cash or credit then?' she asks again.

'No,' Emma says in a small voice. 'I think . . . no . . . changed my mind . . .' And she turns away from the counter and plunges out into the arcade, head spinning, looking around for the exit. She knows this place like the back of her hand and yet now she's lost. All she wants is to get away, get out before she suffocates, and as people push past her, laughing and talking, she spins around looking for the way out, bumping into a low seat and then steadying herself against it. And then she sees him. Walking towards her, waving, his initial smile fading rapidly to a frown of concern, is Grant, dark suit, white shirt, blue and silver tie, briefcase in hand, cutting through the arcade as he does every night on his way from the office to the station.

'Em . . . Em?' he says, looking into her face and gripping her arm. 'What's wrong? Are you okay?'

Emma shakes her head. The place seems to be closing in on her, more and more people streaming in, the noise and the lights unbearable. 'I must get out,' she says, grasping the sleeve of his jacket. 'Home, I must go home.'

'Okay,' Grant says cautiously, and he takes her hand and draws it through the crook of his arm. 'Okay, home it is. But this way, this is the way to the station, or we can get a cab, just hang on to my arm.' And he steers her gently back out of the arcade and through the darkening streets towards Flinders Street Station.

❦

Dot drives home from the meeting in high spirits. Since her accident so much of the campaign has come together that she had lost sight of the scope of it, but the picture Lexie and Alyssa presented tonight has reignited her enthusiasm. And that fall, she thinks now, was perhaps a gift as well as a robbery. It has certainly robbed her of the torment of wanting to grab the reigns and show the young ones how it should be done; that has been driven out by concern about her ability to manage her own life. But it has also slowed her down, and perhaps that's not a bad thing. Dot has often deliberately talked about herself as an 'old woman'; she has wanted to acknowledge ageing, experience it fully, enjoy whatever it has to offer. But while she spoke of herself as an old woman she never really felt it or believed it. Despite the evidence of the calendar, the mirror and the creaking of her joints, within herself she felt suspended at a point of midlife, when the energy of youth fuses with the growing of wisdom. But that fall changed everything; now, after weeks of struggling with ideas of vulnerability and decline, she sees that she has been accustoming herself to fully experiencing what it means to be old and that this, in itself, is a gift worth exploring.

She drives into the garage, locks the door and walks through to the back of the house, just as there is a ring at the front door.

'Can I come in?' Patrick says.

'No!' Dot says. 'You might have got that virus from Vinka and that's not what I need just before I get my last chance to stand outside Parliament and stir a few passions.'

'It's not a virus,' he says. 'Vinka doesn't have a virus and neither do I. We're both . . .' He pauses and takes a deep breath. 'Well, it's emotional not physical.'

'And not contagious?' Dot says with a smile. 'Well then come on in, although I'm not the world's best person when it comes to advice on emotional problems.'

'I suppose it *is* contagious really,' Patrick says, stepping into the hall and removing his sunglasses. 'Contagious for you at any rate.'

He looks tired and anxious, exhausted, Dot thinks, probably due to the huge amount of work he has put into organising the rally.

'I've never caught anyone's emotional state before – perhaps I have a natural immunity. If you've come to see how the speech is going, it's okay, I'm sure it'll come –'

'It's nothing to do with that,' he says.

There is something about his appearance and the tone of his voice that ignites a spark of anxiety in Dot.

'Right,' she says. 'Tea? We drank a lot of it at the meeting, but I can make you some or would you prefer a drink?'

He shakes his head and drops into a chair, flopping back at first then, seeming to pull himself together, leaning forward, hands clasped between his knees. 'I don't know how to tell you this,' he says. 'It's not like there is an easy way, so please just believe I'm doing the best I can, and with the best will in the world.'

'Okay,' she says cautiously, 'I believe you.'

He hesitates and she waits in silence, her anxiety growing as she feels a sense of dread coming from him.

'It was my birthday last month,' he says.

'I could have guessed you were an Aries,' Dot says in an effort to ease the tension. 'You have many fine –'

'Don't,' he says, 'please don't.'

He seems almost paralysed by some sort of internal struggle and perhaps it is contagious because she feels herself being drawn into its grip.

'March the twenty-sixth. Does that date mean anything to you?'

'Why? Should it?' she asks, with a horrible sense of foreboding.

'Just tell me, please, does it mean anything?'

Dot looks at him long and hard and then she shrugs. 'Well yes it does actually, but you needn't bother asking me why because I'm not going to tell you.'

'You don't need to tell me.'

She turns back to him, gripping the arms of her chair.

Patrick reaches into his inside pocket, takes out a folded sheet of paper and holds it out to her with a shaking hand. Dot pulls back from it, blood pumping in her temples.

'I don't want it,' she says.

'No,' Patrick says. 'Of course you don't, you don't need to see it because you know what it says. It was left in Vinka's care by my . . . my adoptive mother. I doubt this would have stood up in any sort of court,' he says, unfolding the yellowing paper, turning it over in his hands. 'After all, it's an arrangement that was made outside the law, but I believe it's genuine. It's an agreement in which you waive all rights to your child, a son, born at eight in the morning of the twenty-sixth of March, nineteen sixty-six.'

Dot looks away, fixing her gaze on the window but seeing nothing. The silence in the room is almost unbearable and she can't bring herself to look at him. What is she supposed to say? It is the secret that was never supposed to come out. She turns her head now, looking at him. How can she not have known this, how can she not have recognised her own child?

'Do you remember the first time you came here?' she asks; her voice breaks slightly and she pauses to clear her throat. 'As we were talking then I had a feeling we'd met somewhere before, that I should remember you. You told me that your mother, Beate, used to show you my writing, kept clippings for you ... do you remember telling me that?'

Patrick nods. 'I do. And I told you I'd plagiarised something for an essay.'

'Yes. Why? Why did Beate do that?'

'I used to think it was because you were some sort of hero to her. Now I know, because I asked Vinka the same question. She did it because she thought I should have some sort of understanding of you, in case I ever learned the truth.'

Dot nods slowly, watching his face, anticipating the questions and knowing the painful answers she will have to give him. 'She must have been a remarkable woman,' she says. 'And she was clearly a far better mother than I would ever have been.'

Silence again.

'But you *are* my mother.'

Is it a statement or a question? Dot is not sure, but even through her fear and the longing that is now like a physical pain inside her, she knows that he actually needs to hear her say it. 'Yes,' she says, in a voice that sounds old and shaky and unlike her own. 'Yes, Patrick. I am your mother.'

He sighs and closes his eyes briefly. 'Thank you,' he says. 'And my father?'

Dot looks down at her own hands, twisting in her lap. They are old hands, an old woman's hands, the hands of a woman too old and alone to cope with the agony of this and what it may mean.

'I can't tell you that,' she says, getting abruptly to her feet. 'I never expected ... truly I had no idea about you. I need you to go now. Give me some time please, later we can talk, after the rally – let me do this first.'

He shakes his head. 'I can't, you must know that I can't,' he says. 'My mother ... Beate ... gave this adoption agreement to Aunty Win to look after for me. It was in a sealed envelope.

Win knew what was in it and she kept it for me – unopened, so she never saw the name of the person who was with you at the time and who witnessed your signature. But when I opened it I saw it straightaway. The name of the witness is Laurence Attwood. You must tell me, Dot, is Laurence my father?'

TWENTY-EIGHT

'I don't know *why* she's not coming, she just isn't,' Phyllida says as they stand at the foot of the Boatshed steps. She and Emma have walked here, arriving at the same time as Margot appeared from the car park. 'She just sent a text saying she was sorry she couldn't make it.'

'A text?' Margot says. 'Dot hates text messages.'

Phyllida shrugs. 'Well I don't know about that, but that's what the message said.'

'Maybe she got that virus that Patrick and Vinka have,' Emma says.

'She seemed fine yesterday at the meeting,' Phyllida says. 'I'm disappointed; I was looking forward to hearing what she thought of the book.'

'Maybe she just changed her mind,' Margot says. 'She's never been much of a joiner, unless it was something political.'

They walk up the steps, along the boardwalk and in through a side door to a room with a sign for the book club.

'Dad and I came here with Rosie after that awful Bunny party,' Emma says.

Margot smiles, patting her arm. 'Laurence told me. He said you were spectacular.'

'And don't you dare say a word about it being your fault, Em,' Phyllida says. 'We've been through all that, so you can just bottle it.'

Emma and Margot look at her in surprise and then look at each other and burst into laughter.

'Well,' says Phyllida, slightly embarrassed, 'we have, we really have. In a way it's a good thing it happened. It made you more aware of what was going on and it made me see that this campaign is not just about other people's daughters and granddaughters; it's on our own doorstep. Did you bring the fliers for the rally, Em?'

'Phyllida, you came,' Fran says, walking over to greet them. 'And Margot too. Do come and sit down. Can I get you all a glass of wine or some juice?'

Phyllida takes a glass of wine, hoping it will bolster her confidence, although she has come not to talk but to listen. She has read the book twice, avidly, fascinated by the subversion of the expected, going back several times to the ways in which the two women, the widow and the former lover, who ought to be at loggerheads, end up in a strangely intimate and sometimes ambivalent friendship. She can't make up her mind what she thinks about this, but what she does know is that she can't let go of it, that she can't stop wondering about the ways in which they negotiate the slippery edges of privacy and sharing, of intimacy and distance. 'There's a lot of people here,' she says. 'I didn't expect so many.'

'We usually get a good crowd,' Fran says.

Phyllida takes a gulp of her wine and joins Emma and Margot on a low couch. A couple of women from the golf club wave to her from across the room, and someone else waves to Margot. Meanwhile, Emma is chatting to the woman sitting beside her, urging her to take a flier about the march. Phyllida tries to sink lower into the couch.

Tapping gently with a knife on the side of her glass, Fran eventually commands their attention. She hands out a list of books for the next six meetings, with the dates beside them, asks for recommendations for the rest of the year and passes around another list for names and email addresses of people who are here for the first time. She glances down at her notes.

'Well that's enough from me,' she says. 'Let's get on to the discussion of Salley Vickers's book *Instances of the Number 3*. This was May Wong's choice, so where are you, May? Ah, way over there, well maybe you could move forward a bit so we can see you? Excellent; over to you then to introduce the book.'

It's after nine when the women of the book club spill out onto the boardwalk. Their voices and laughter float out on the night air and a flock of seagulls gathered in a pool of light from the Boatshed take off as one, heading out across the inlet.

'You go ahead,' Phyllida says, 'I won't be long. Wait for me in the car.'

Emma and Margot exchange a glance. 'Are you sure?' Emma asks. 'Wouldn't you rather we stayed?'

Phyllida shakes her head. 'I want to talk to her. Please, I'm fine, just give me a few minutes.'

'We'll be over there by the car then,' Margot says. 'I'll drive you both home.'

Phyllida watches them walking away, side-by-side, heads together, talking about her, she thinks, and she knows she's right when they stop, turn back to look at her, wave, and then stand talking, obviously positioning themselves to keep an eye on her.

'We can leave now if you like,' Margot had whispered when Fran introduced May. 'We're right near the door, it's easy.'

And on Margot's far side Phyllida could see Emma's anxious face; she too was obviously ready to whisk her out of there in an instant. Part of Phyllida had wanted to flee, to disappear quietly out of the door onto the boardwalk and then into Margot's car, putting as much distance as possible between herself and that room full of people. But she was also curious. If she stayed she could hear what May had to say about these two characters – the widow and the former lover – and their tentative moves to dissipate the hurt and resentment, and find common ground.

'No. Thanks, but I'm okay,' she'd whispered to Margot, 'I want to stay.' And she had dug herself down a little further into the corner of the settee and waited for May to begin.

Now, as she stands at the bottom of the Boatshed steps, most of the women have left, strolling off along the footpath or, like Margot and Emma, across the grass to the car park. Phyllida wonders if she has missed May. Could she possibly have left through a different exit? But these steps are the only way out. She turns back towards the entrance and there she is. May is standing alone in the doorway, looking around. She seems cautious, nervous even, about stepping out, but finally she seems to decide that the coast is clear and she walks briskly out and along the boardwalk. It is only when she reaches the top of the steps that she sees Phyllida standing at the bottom and she hesitates, and then continues on quickly down the steps.

'I saw you leave,' she says. 'I waited until I thought you'd be gone. I had no idea you'd be here. I've been coming since it started but I never saw you here before.'

'No. My first time. I was as surprised as you. You know, May,' she says as they start to walk towards the car park, 'I liked what you said, about the women in the book.'

'But *you* said nothing. I felt you had come because you *wanted* to say something.'

'I came to test out my feelings against what *other* people said. I'm not used to talking about books, or even being with other women who talk about books or ideas. What I *would* have said though, if I'd been brave enough to speak, is that life is too short to hang on to misplaced pride. The women in the book recognised something in each other that they both needed at the time. I felt . . . that's what happened that day at your flat; it seems to me to be something of value.'

～～～

For the last two nights Vinka has barely slept. She had done what she thought was right – that, surely, was all she could do – and her greatest fear had been that Patrick would be devastated by what he learned. She had feared his anger and hurt and had prepared herself for isolation while he came to terms with the news. He had been stunned at first and then, she thought, intrigued. He had listened to everything she had told him. He had always known he was adopted but had never felt the need to search for his biological parents. She had poured him a drink and they had sat talking for a while and then he had looked again at the adoption agreement and this time he saw something that he had missed the first time.

'What is it?' Vinka had asked, watching as the colour drained from his face. 'Tell me what you have found.'

'Nothing,' he'd said, standing up, and there was a wildness, a look of panic in his eyes. He slipped the paper back into its envelope and tucked it into the inside pocket of his jacket. 'But I have to go now, right now. I need to talk to Dot tonight.' He looked around distractedly. 'My keys . . . where are my keys?'

The shape of his body had changed. He was hunched now, and tense, his face set in a rigid white mask.

'Tell me,' Vinka had insisted, reaching her hand down the side of the chair and retrieving the keys. She held them up so he could see them, at the same time moving them away from his grasp. 'No,' she says. 'You tell me what you have seen. You tell me now.'

He stood facing her, his expression a mix of panic and despair. 'There was someone with Dot when I was born,' he said. 'Someone witnessed her signature.'

Vinka nodded. 'Who? I don't understand.'

He shakes his head and takes a deep breath. 'It was Laurence, he was there – Laurence was the witness.'

Vinka stared at him in disbelief, steadying herself against the table.

Patrick ran his hand through his hair. 'So I must ask Dot . . .'

'You think that means that he . . . that Laurence . . . ?' Vinka stops. 'No,' she said. 'No, he is a *witness* only.'

'Then why was he with her? Why was he up there with her in Byron Bay when I was born? By that time he and Margot were married and Lexie was five. Why would he be there with Dot unless the baby she was having was his? It would mean that Lexie and I . . .'

'No!' Vinka said. 'No, it can't be, and if it is . . .' She'd stopped herself. She had been about to say that it didn't matter, that nothing mattered except that he could cling to his new-found happiness – the love she had wanted for him for so long. She wanted to tell him that no one need ever know; destroy the paper, she wanted to say, burn it, forget you ever saw it. But he couldn't of course, he would never be able to live with that and nor, she knew, would she.

'I'm going there now,' he'd said. 'I have to know.'

And he had hugged her, holding on to her as though his life depended on it. 'I'll come straight back when I've talked to her, however late, I'll come back.'

And of course, when he did get back, there was the relief about Laurence, but also the frustration of Dot's refusal to identify his father. She'd been shocked, he'd said, at least he thought it was shock. It was hard to tell what was happening for her – she said very little other than to reassure him about Laurence.

'I thought we were doing okay until I asked about my father,' Patrick had told her. 'But then it was as though she didn't expect me to ask that question, as though knowing that it *wasn't* Laurence ought to be enough. She asked me to leave; she was almost pushing me out of the door by then. I told her that I felt I had a right to know. Nothing. She just kept shaking her head. Then she said, "I can't talk about this now. You have to let me get through the weekend, then we can talk." By then I was outside the door and she just went back inside and closed the door behind her.' He sat quietly for a few minutes, clasping and unclasping his hands in his lap. 'You know, Aunty Win, I really thought it was going to be okay until I asked about my father and then she just flipped. I suppose I can only wait now, and be thankful that I didn't turn out to be Laurence's son.'

Now, two days later, Vinka is not only exhausted, she is angry and frustrated. Why won't Dot simply tell Patrick the truth about his father? Is it that she had so many lovers that there are several possibilities? Or does she feel she must tell the father about Patrick before she tells Patrick about him? The questions plague Vinka all through the morning and now it's midday. It's all too much. Dot has no right to do this, she tells herself, and what if she keeps it up, keeps avoiding Patrick's questions?

'So,' she says, grinding out her cigarette. 'Enough.' And she picks up the telephone and calls a cab.

❦

Lexie emerges from her lecture blinking in the sunlight, and heads for a seat in the shade of some trees where she has arranged to meet Patrick. Her first weeks as a student haven't been easy. The campus is huge, confusing and not very well signposted, and she feels entirely out of place surrounded by people in their late teens and early twenties. Wendy was right, there *are* two older people in one of her classes, and one in another, but she hasn't managed to connect with them yet, and the younger ones seem so much faster and smarter that it is hard to feel that she will ever be able to keep pace with them. But it's not only uni that is hard to handle right now. The final weeks leading up to the march this coming weekend have been hectic, volunteers are less biddable than staff and some are proving unreliable. And then there is Patrick, wonderful, stable, calm and supportive Patrick, whose life has suddenly been thrown into chaos.

On the night of the campaign meeting she hadn't expected to see him, but as she was letting herself in to the house his car drew up outside.

'This is a nice surprise,' she said as he came up the steps. 'How was Vinka?'

He didn't answer at first, just shook his head, and in the light of the hallway she could see that his face was tense and pale.

'What's the matter? What's happened?' she asked.

But he simply let out a huge sigh and, shaking his head again, put his arms around her and stood there holding her for what seemed a very long time, apparently unable to speak.

Later, much later that night, when they had talked for hours and finally fallen exhausted into bed, Patrick had sunk quickly into what seemed like troubled sleep. As he twisted himself in the sheet, mumbling and thrashing his arms, Lexie had got up and gone downstairs to make herself some tea. While Patrick had related his conversations with Vinka and Dot, telling her of his shock and confusion and the horror of discovering Laurence's name on the adoption agreement, all of Lexie's attention had been focused on him and on her desire to help him through this, to step into his emotional space and be there with him. At the time she had been aware that she did so willingly, because she wanted to, unlike those many occasions in past relationships where she had stepped into the other's space with resentment, knowing she would be sucked dry. While they talked, while he wept, and they talked again, through the questions they asked and failed to answer, and alongside Patrick's hurt and frustration over Dot's refusal to talk about his father, Lexie had known she wanted to be there with him, to be there until the end. She had known that in the worst possible scenario what had become the precious part of her life would have been ripped away from her. Being alone, being single, was okay, good even, satisfying in its freedom, but that was only *before* she had met Patrick. Now it held no attraction at all.

It was only then, as she sat alone looking out at the moon-lit garden while Patrick slept upstairs, that Lexie started to think about Laurence, and inevitably about Margot and Dot. Why was he there with Dot in Byron Bay? Why not Margot? Did Dot and Laurence have some history together that made him the person she called upon to help? Did Margot know? In the same way that Lexie had felt her eyes opened to Margot and Dot the night at the candlelit dinner table, she now saw other dimensions to these three people who had been part of her life for so long. It wasn't so unusual, she supposed, it was easy to take one's parents and their past for granted. You grew up with them, they shaped how you knew them and the past was simply there, possibly inter-esting but not interesting enough to delve into. Only now it was; now it seemed vital and fascinating.

A couple of years ago Lexie had gone with Emma and Margot to Grant and Wendy's mother's funeral.

'The saddest thing,' Wendy had told her tearfully at the wake, 'is that it's only when it's too late that you realise how little you know about them. All these questions come rush-ing into your head when it's too late to ask.'

Sitting here now under the trees, watching with relief as Patrick emerges from his lecture chatting with a couple of students before he turns to walk towards her, Lexie knows that whatever his quest to know Dot and to learn the truth of his father may bring, she too has a part in that. She too needs to strip away the layers of time to discover what lies beneath.

'How was it this morning?' Patrick asks, dropping down onto the seat beside her. 'Good lecture?'

'Yes,' she nods, handing him the sandwiches she has bought from the café. 'Yes, really interesting. Once the weekend is over I think things are going to get a whole lot easier.'

'You're not kidding,' he says, biting into a tuna sandwich. 'Easier in more ways than one.'

'Was *your* lecture okay? Were you wonderful and inspiring?'

'Naturally!' he says, smiling at her, but she can see the signs of strain in his face. 'Yeah, it went okay despite the usual performance anxiety, but it was a bit hard to concentrate. I kept thinking about how easily we are separated from the past, and how extraordinary it feels when we bump into it. And in all my present frustration and confusion about Dot and the mystery father, the thing I need to tell you, Lex, and I'll probably be telling you this for the rest of my life, is that I'm awfully glad you're not my sister.'

⁓

Dot, sitting in her study, hears the sound of the gate and sees Vinka making her way up the path. She sits absolutely still, fearing that even the smallest movement may create a flicker of shadow against the window and reveal her presence. Even stooped a little with age, Vinka is an impressive figure, taller than Dot and solidly built, but it's not this physical superiority that Dot fears. What she senses in Vinka's step is what she saw the first time they met: a strength and determination, a steeliness of character. On that first day, as she and Margot had walked into the restaurant, Dot had seen shock, and confusion. 'How did you find her?' Vinka had demanded of Patrick, and Dot had assumed that it was just the awkwardness of Vinka's English. Surely she had meant 'How did you two meet?'

There had been a moment of awkwardness, and then Vinka's expression had changed to relief and cautious pleasure. Right now, that glimpse of steel is apparent on Vinka's face.

Dot holds her breath, waiting for the knock, but there is silence. Has Vinka changed her mind, gone away? Dot leans cautiously forward, trying to see if she is on the step, and is greeted with a sudden sharp rap on the window that makes her almost leap out of her skin. Vinka is looking straight at her through the glass.

'You want that I knock when I know you see me coming?' she demands. 'You want that I sit on the doorstep to shame you to letting me in?'

Dot sighs and runs her hands through her hair. In the course of her life she has played all sorts of power games, but she's always known that in Vinka she has more than met her match – she'd just never thought there would be a time when it would matter. Taking a deep breath she goes out to the hall and opens the door.

'So,' says Vinka, once installed in an armchair, waiting as Dot pours her a glass of Polish vodka. 'This is the last time I am asking advice from *you*, Dot.'

'Advice?'

Vinka nods. 'In the hospital I am asking you. Dot, I have to take a risk and you tell me, take the risk, Vinka, you say, at our age we have so little chance to change things, you must risk love. But now you don't like it. Now you sulk and stamp your feet.'

'You were asking me about this?'

'Of course, who else would I ask? And you turn on, like they say, the green light.'

'But you would have told him anyway, wouldn't you?'

'Perhaps, perhaps not,' she shrugs. 'I am thinking about it a long time and more since the day we met. Then I think of it many times every day. It is a very big responsibility, a legacy from my sister, one I do not want.'

'I'm not sulking,' Dot says, sitting down opposite her. 'Do you see me stamping my feet?'

Vinka hesitates. 'You speak to no one. You lock doors, you behave like the naughty child. You think of no one but yourself.'

'And why not? This is *about* me. I have been alone all my life, Vinka. Who else am I to think about?'

'Ha!' Vinka slams down her glass. 'And so this is enough, to think about yourself? Don't you want something for your son, for Patrick? This is more important than just one selfish bloody-minded old woman who is frightened to be hurt.'

'But I –'

'No!' Vinka says, silencing her with a look. 'Listen to me, Dot, I am not so clever like you, but I know some things about you. You are alone because it suits you, because it keeps you always at the safe distance. You think you can replace love with fighting some battle for strangers, for people you don't know? The battle is good, it is important, but you do it for the wrong reason. You think I don't know, Dot? Even your friends you keep just so close, no closer. Well now the responsibility is right into your face. *Now* you feel it, and whatever you do now you will live with it every day until you die. So! You want to be the miserable spider spinning yourself into your own web? Or you want to risk that he might care about you, or maybe risk that you care about him?'

Dot is transfixed, bottle in one hand, glass in the other; her throat is dry, her chest tight enough to burst. All her life she has lived with questions about her child, his safety, his happiness, his whereabouts. Who might he have become? What would he think of her? Could he ever understand and forgive? And on the worst of those many dark and lonely nights of the soul, she has returned always to the hardest questions of all – is it possible for me to love and be loved? When, two nights ago, Patrick sat here in the chair where Vinka now sits, he rewrote those abstract questions in a profoundly personal way. She was cornered, unable to respond, unable to imagine the effect of revealing yet another level of the deception that surrounded his birth all those years ago.

'I'm frightened,' she says to Vinka now, 'I'm just frightened.' She pours vodka into her glass and sets the bottle down on the side table. Vinka says nothing, she simply sits, watching and waiting. 'I'm frightened of him,' Dot continues, 'of Patrick. He was my friend, he understood me, and now he is so much more and I will lose him. And you have become my friend too and I will lose you. What does he want from me? I'm not capable of being a mother, Vinka, I don't know how.'

'You are an old fool, Dot,' Vinka says. 'You want that the crowd will love you or hate you even. But you run from the love that reaches inside to who you really are. Tell him, Dot, tell him about his father – if you are sure you know who it was then tell him.'

'I know who it was. And I *will* tell him, but tomorrow, because tomorrow I need him to be strong for me, to get me through what I have to do. If I tell him the truth now it may be too hard for both of us.'

Vinka shakes her head in frustration. 'Tomorrow then,' Vinka says. 'Or I come again and I do not leave until you talk to him.' She gets to her feet.

'You and your sister,' Dot says, 'you made him read what I wrote, he told me that. You let him think I was something special.'

'Beate thinks that it is fair that he knows you through this,' Vinka says. 'She thinks he has a right, because maybe one day he finds out, or maybe we tell him, and then it is good that his mother is not a stranger, he is proud.'

'Proud?' Dot laughs. 'How could he be proud? I gave him away, Vinka, and he was very lucky I did because I would have been a lousy, selfish mother. Instead he got a mother who loved and raised him to be a fine, wise and responsible man. I expect nothing more than his anger and contempt, and that's what is so unbearable.'

Vinka laughs loudly, tossing her head back as she does so. 'Dot, my friend, you know so little about what really matters. Sometimes I wonder how is it that you can be so naive? You know what I think, Dot? I think you are afraid of love. And now you have a chance, your last chance. You want to take it or throw it away?'

oes

'Patrick was afraid it was you,' Margot says, leaning against the bench top in Laurence's kitchen. 'He saw your signature and was nearly out of his mind about it apparently.'

Laurence looks up, concerned. 'Well naturally, he and Lexie . . . what a disaster that would have been.'

'So you knew? All these years you've known that Dot had a baby and adopted it out? I suppose it was that time she just took off without saying anything and then showed up here in Melbourne a couple of years later. I always wondered why she didn't tell anyone she was going or where she was, but now it seems she did tell someone.'

Laurence, who had been making an onion tart when Margot turned up at the door, stirs some cream into the beaten eggs. 'Yes,' he says. 'She told me. She told me because she needed someone to know. It was a sort of anchor for her, I suppose.' He pours the eggs and cream over the soft browned onions on their pastry base.

'You didn't tell me. We were married, we had Lexie. You never said a word.'

'Dot didn't want anyone to know she was pregnant. She wanted to disappear, have the baby adopted, and to feel that if or when she came back no one would know. She asked me not to tell anyone – ever.'

'And that included me?'

'It did. Are you staying for lunch?'

'I need to know, Laurence, I need you to be honest with me.'

'About what?'

Margot sighs. 'I always wondered about you and Dot. You'd had this full-on super hot relationship and then I came along, and I think for a time you were sleeping with both of us. And then I got pregnant and we got married . . .' She stops, looks away and picks up the pepper mill which he has returned to the bench top.

Laurence turns to put the tart in the oven. 'What are you asking me, Margot? Did I sleep with Dot after you and I were together? A few times, yes. After we got married? No, never. And anyway, does it really matter after all this time, after everything else that happened?'

She takes another enormous breath, pushes the pepper mill aside and leans forward, crossed arms resting on the bench top.

'It sort of does matter, because the time we were married was special, it stayed special for me even after you'd left. And when I got used to the fact that you'd gone because you had to, because it had always been wrong for you, it was important for me to remember it as a time when we were happy, when we were good for each other. I don't want that tarnished in my memory, particularly not tarnished by Dot, who is my friend. It seems odd that she told *you* she was pregnant – why didn't she tell *me*? It's the sort of thing women tell their women friends, not their cast-off lovers.'

'You'd just had a miscarriage, remember? Dot couldn't face your knowing that she was going to give her baby up for adoption.'

Margot nods and she's silent for a moment, running her finger through the scattering of crushed pepper that has escaped from the mill. 'Yes, I see, I can understand that.'

'She told me for practical reasons and because she trusted me. She took off and I didn't hear anything for months, and then she phoned me the week the baby was due. She was living in a dingy little bedsit in a decaying old house in Byron Bay and she was scared witless and very lonely. She'd somehow arranged this private adoption, lord knows how, but you know Dot, she excelled at living on the edge in those days. I suppose she did it through the midwife, just sidelined the authorities. I thought it seemed a bit dodgy but she was adamant about it. So she had the baby at home and the midwife called the adopting father, who came to collect him a couple of days later.'

'And you were there?'

Laurence nods slowly, noticing the tightness around Margot's mouth. 'She needed someone with her. She said I was the only person she really trusted apart from you and she couldn't ask you. I told you I had to replace someone at a conference at the last minute and I went up there for a week. I lied about that, I'm sorry, Margot, but at the time it seemed the right thing to do. I couldn't tell you about Dot and I didn't want to leave her on her own.'

'So you were there when he was born?'

'Yes. Not in the room of course, hiding in the kitchen. Then she asked me to leave when the man who was adopting the baby was due. She said she'd be embarrassed if I was there. So I witnessed her signature and went off into town. I phoned you and killed a couple of hours in the pub reading a newspaper, then I went back.'

'How was Dot?'

'Devastated. She almost changed her mind but then she kept saying, "No, it's no good, I'd be a terrible mother." Later she was saying "it's better this way", but I could see that wasn't really what she felt.'

'It's weird, isn't it, them? Dot and Patrick, knowing each other for over a year now, and yet not knowing. So who *is* Patrick's father? Is it someone we know?'

Laurence shakes his head. 'I don't know. All she told me

at the time was that she'd known him for a while, met him in the Push, so I suppose it's possible that we might know him.'

'Did she tell him about the baby?'

He shrugs. 'Well, he was married, she told me that much, so I guess not.'

They stand looking at each other across the bench top.

'I'll stay for lunch,' Margot says.

'Good.'

'If Lexie and Patrick decide to get married, Dot will be part of our family.'

'But she always has been, really, hasn't she,' Laurence says, 'in her own uniquely disconnected, non-familial way? She's a bit like one of those eccentric aunts that turn up in early twentieth century novels, create chaos and then disappear again. She'll have gone to ground now, I suppose.'

'I think so. I've tried calling her several times, so has Patrick, but she's not answering.'

Laurence peers through the glass door of the oven and checks the tart. 'She hasn't mentioned it for years, you know, but we were sitting here one evening recently and I actually asked her if she had any regrets about it. She never gives much away of course, but she did say . . .' He hesitates. 'What was it now? Something about living in the last chance café, looking back and realising she could have done things differently. Stuff about how you see things another way when you're getting old. Anyway, this really is a last chance when she least expected it. Let's hope she sees it as an opportunity rather than a disaster.'

TWENTY-NINE

Phyllida stands a little way back from the window of Donald's study from where she can see anyone coming in through the front gate – not that there is anyone to see just yet. He's late of course, but she'd known he would be. Emma had delivered the message. 'Aunty Phyl has decided to sell the house and she'd like to talk to you,' she'd said. And of course he'd agreed like a shot and said he'd pop over about two. But now he's making her wait because he thinks she'll be tense and anxious and so he'll be able to bully her. Well she *is* tense and anxious, but not in the way he wants. She's just concerned about getting it right, making sure she takes him through everything in the way they've planned. She's rehearsed it dozens of times, and although at this moment she can't recall a word of it, something tells her that when he arrives she'll know what to do.

'Are you okay?' Emma whispers, popping her head around the door. 'Dad says not to worry, he thinks Trevor's just playing power games.'

'I think so too,' Phyllida says. 'I'll be fine, Em.'

Yes I will, she thinks, turning back to the window, and she knows too that she'll be fine beyond today, beyond finding a new home, beyond the fallout from this tawdry situation of

Donald's creation. She remembers standing here often while Donald lay unconscious in the hospital, wondering what would happen if he died and, of course, if he lived. Was she going to spend the rest of her life caring for a demanding invalid or a man diminished beyond recognition? He was clearly never going to be the Donald she knew, and whichever way it went her life had been about to change quite dramatically and not for the better. His death had left her with no sense of a life beyond that moment. And yet here she is, surveying a range of possibilities about how to live; she's thrown herself into the campaign, she's joined a book club, she feels she really has been some help to Emma and, perhaps most surprising of all, she has made a friend of Dot.

There is a movement by the gate; a hand reaches over and slides the bolt and Trevor steps inside and closes the gate behind him. He stands for a moment, hands in his pockets, studying the front of the house, doubtless revising his offer downwards, Phyllida thinks. Then he straightens his shoulders and walks purposefully towards the front door. She lets him wait for a while before opening the door, and once inside he barely glances at her, casting instead an appraising glance around the spacious hallway.

'Best if we talk in Donald's study,' Phyllida says, leading the way. Everything about Trevor is cocky and confident, the strut and the swagger, the barely concealed smugness of his expression, the way his eyes roam across the landscape of what he already assumes will soon be his.

'I was expecting to hear from you, I knew you'd see sense. Mind you, Phyl, I did warn you that property prices would fall, and now they're right down there in the dunny. You should've taken my offer then.'

Phyllida indicates a chair alongside the desk and walks behind it to sit in Donald's chair. Trevor's neck, she notices, is fiery red, and the collar of his shirt is too tight, making his face look fatter, more pink and shiny than ever. He runs a finger between his neck and the collar and she hopes this is a sign of nerves, although it seems unlikely.

'You didn't actually make an offer,' she says. 'You simply offered an opinion on the state of the market and what I should do. You said you'd be helping me out by taking the place off my hands.'

'And as I remember, you were a little bit uppity at the time. Grief, I suppose. A woman alone is very vulnerable and you ladies don't like to admit it, do you?'

'Indeed we don't,' she says, struggling to keep her anger under control. 'And you know, Trevor, I have to admit that the fact that for weeks you were throwing spadefuls of dog shit over my wall didn't help.'

The shock on his face is genuine and Phyllida sees that he has completely forgotten about his efforts to intimidate her. 'Don't know what you're talking about,' he says, colour flushing up from his bulging neck to his face.

'Really? Well you do have a short memory,' she says, more confident now that she senses his discomfort. 'Have you also forgotten that my niece and I were throwing it back?'

Trevor fidgets awkwardly around in his chair and fails to respond.

'Well,' Phyllida says, 'you obviously do remember the conversation about the house and, as you said, time moves on, so what do you think about it now?'

'Irrelevant now. Things aren't what they were and who knows when the market will recover?'

'Of course you're right. But you know us ladies, Trevor. We don't know a lot about the property market, so can you tell me what you think it might be worth to you now?'

Trevor inhales deeply and then exhales noisily, puffing out his cheeks. It's obvious that his brief moment of lost composure has passed, and he stands up, looks up at the ceiling, out through the door into the hall, and through the front and side windows. Pursing his lips he screws up his eyes and tilts his head from side to side. 'Well, I'd need to have a proper look around of course, only been in a few times, haven't seen all the rooms, and I'd need a building inspection –'

'Naturally,' Phyllida interrupts, 'but if all is as you think it is?'

Trevor squints again and names a price which is two hundred thousand dollars lower than the lowest of the three valuations she had obtained from real estate agents.

'I see,' she says, 'that's interesting, very interesting.'

'I knew you'd see sense. You don't want to be saddled with this great place all on your own, do you?'

'No indeed I don't, Trevor, and that's why I've sold it. Very easily in fact, only the second day after I placed it on the market, sold it for several hundred thousand more than the sum you mentioned. No, Trevor, it wasn't the house I wanted to talk to you about. Not at all.'

Trevor's colour begins to rise. 'Sold it? But your niece said you wanted to talk to me about selling the house.'

'I think you'll find she said that I had decided to sell it and that I'd like to talk to you. Not that I wanted to talk to you *about* the house.' Trevor's face is now a worrying shade of purple, and Phyllida wonders fleetingly what she will do if he has a heart attack. 'No, it wasn't about the house at all. I've been going through Donald's things, you see, and I found this.' She picks up Tony Stiles's hospital file. 'You're familiar with the case of course?'

'Never heard of him.'

'Really? That's odd, because Donald kept a sort of journal, certainly a lot of notes about how you and that nurse – Miss Burstall, wasn't it? – or perhaps I mean *you on behalf* of Miss Burstall, threatened to take the matter to the newspapers and expose him unless he paid you rather a lot of money. And yes, look, here's an email from you to Donald, telling him to make up his mind or he'll find himself on the front page of the Sunday paper.'

She waves the email printout at him and there is a fraction of a second in which it is clear that Trevor is considering his options before going on the attack. He stands up and leans forward now across the desk, his face uncomfortably close to her own, and it is all Phyllida can do to hold her position and not recoil from him.

'He deserved to pay, he was responsible.'

'You may be right about that,' Phyllida says, 'but unfortunately there was no enquiry and Miss Burstall resigned.'

'She knew she'd be screwed, that's why. Screwed by Donald and his mate. It ruined her career having to leave like that. Someone needed to take care of her. It was Donald's fault. I wanted to get some sort of justice for her.'

'Rather expensive justice,' Phyllida says. 'And I understand that far from having her career ruined, Miss Burstall is now a senior theatre nurse in a hospital in South Australia, and amazingly, Trevor, after all your efforts on her behalf, the money doesn't seem to have made its way to her.'

'Now you look here –'

Phyllida gets to her feet now. 'No, Trevor, *you* look here. You not only got money out of Donald, ostensibly for Miss Burstall, but you kept *on* extracting money from him and putting it into your own pocket. Why Donald ever thought you'd give up after he paid you off the first time I can't imagine, but in some ways he could be quite naive. If he hadn't been naive he might have realised that Miss Burstall never saw a penny of it. You just kept bleeding him, didn't you, Trevor? He kept records, you see, every time you demanded money he made a note of it, and linked it to withdrawals on the bank statements.'

Trevor is quiet now but Phyllida can feel his fury crashing towards her in great waves, but he holds back, clearly determined not to let her see how rattled he is. 'Donald was an arrogant blustering fool with delusions of grandeur. He got what was coming to him. He knew he'd be finished if the media got hold of it.'

'So you blackmailed him?' Phyllida says, tense now. 'You admit it?'

Trevor leans back in his chair, legs stretched out in front of him. 'He was a pushover. And yes, I took him to the cleaners. I don't like that word *blackmail* – I simply told him pay up, Don, or you're gonna find yourself in deep shit. And every time I tapped him on the shoulder he paid up like a lamb.' He gets to his feet. 'Desperate to protect his reputation, and you wouldn't want to see that reputation sullied on the front pages either, would you, Phyl? So I think we can come to an arrangement . . .'

'Frankly, Trevor,' Phyllida says, 'I don't give a stuff about that reputation now. You can tell whomever you like – I certainly have.'

The door to the study opens now and two men walk in.

'That's fine, Mrs Shepperd, thank you,' says the older of the two. 'We have all we need, we'll take it from here,' and he nods across to his colleague, who walks over to the astonished Trevor and begins to caution him.

'You did a great job there,' he says as Phyllida peels away the tape from her chest and extracts a tiny microphone from inside her shirt. 'We'll get you a job as an undercover agent.'

'Once is enough, thank you, Inspector,' Phyllida says, handing over the equipment. 'But it was extremely satisfying. And it's nice to know that my years as a dedicated fan of *The Bill* were not wasted. That poor young man, beaten up on the street and taken to hospital and then he dies, perhaps because my husband had been drinking.'

'We don't know that yet,' the man says, 'not for sure. We might never know.'

'No,' Phyllida says, 'but I think we can make an educated guess. And it's the cover-up that I can't stand. Donald showed nothing but contempt and disrespect for that boy. This has been a very difficult time, Inspector, and I have been trying to practice forgiveness, but this is one thing that exceeds the boundaries of forgiveness and I think it always will.'

⌘

Emma finds a parking space across the street and sits for a moment in the car, looking at the house and trying to gather the courage to get herself to the door. It's always been hard for her to come here, but today is harder than ever.

'No, it wouldn't be a disaster if you asked someone else to pick your daughter up this weekend,' her therapist had said, 'but it *would* be a big step forward if you could do it yourself. At some point soon you're bound to see Grant again, and I think you'll feel better if you can face up to this.'

Emma lowers the car window and studies the front door. He might not be there, it could just be Wendy and Rosie, and that would be easier, although of course Wendy will know. She'll know all about Emma's freak-out in the arcade, about how Grant rescued her. How he took her home, made tea and toast and talked to her, waited with her until Phyllida got home. Saint Grant again, Emma thinks, but she knows she was lucky that he'd picked that moment to cut through the arcade. He'd just listened and nodded when she told him what had happened, and then – and Emma can't believe she did this – she was so grateful to him that she'd actually told him about the therapist. So Wendy will know about that too, in fact they probably spent the whole evening discussing how totally fucked up she is.

Emma sighs, winds up the window, gets out of the car and walks across the road and rings the bell.

'Hi, Em,' Lexie says, opening it. 'Wendy said it'd be you. Come on in, she's on the phone. Grant and Rosie went shopping and they're not back yet.'

Emma steps inside, heart sinking; so now Lexie knows everything too, and she and Wendy will have been discussing it as well. 'What are you doing here, Lex?' she asks, trying to stay cool, behave normally.

'Stuff for tomorrow – the march. Thanks for volunteering; I can give you your marshal's badge and visibility jacket now, and the list of instructions. Come through to the kitchen, Wendy's got some coffee on the go.'

The house is in its usual state of disarray, thanks largely to Rosie, but it's easy to see that the mess is superficial. Wendy is super organised but she's also relaxed about it and Emma, who needs everything to be in its place all the time, finds this ability to tolerate a level of untidiness unnerving. She moves a couple of Rosie's books off a stool and sits at the bench.

'Hi, Em,' Wendy says, hanging up the phone. 'Thanks for coming to fetch her. They'll be back in a minute. And look, I'm so sorry about that debacle the other day. Coffee?' She pours some into a mug and pushes it across to Emma.

Emma takes a deep breath. Here it comes, she thinks, the interrogation with two inquisitors. Maybe the best thing to do is just meet it head on. 'About the other day . . .' she begins.

'Yes,' Wendy cuts in. 'It's my fault. I should have checked out what Jacinta's parents had in mind. They did say dress-ups and dancing, but I had no idea about the Bunny thing. I'm so sorry. Laurence said you gave them a good serve.'

'He said you were terrific,' Lexie agrees. 'I just hope it made them think about what they were doing.'

Emma opens her mouth, shuts it again and adds milk to her coffee.

'What really surprised me,' Lexie goes on, 'is that Rosie obviously went for it in a big way. It's so unlike her.'

Emma's sense of guilt is still raw but Phyllida's words have resonated with her. 'This is not about you, Em,' she'd said. 'It's much bigger than that, so if you want to do something about it then stop whingeing about it being your fault and get stuck into the campaign. We need as much help as we can get.'

She takes a few sips of coffee. 'Well I guess it's as easy for Rosie to get sucked into something as it is for the rest of us,' she says. 'Especially as I have a horrible feeling she may have thought I'd approve of it. I've been pretty naive about all this. I don't mean the stuff about the little kids, I've always thought that was horrific. But when I've been planning promotions I've picked the images on the basis of how sexy those girls look; the younger, the sexier the better – glossy pouting lips, smouldering stares, pumped-up boobs. It's all sex, isn't it? It's all part of the same thing.'

Wendy nods. 'Sure is, all designed to persuade women and girls that they're making choices, when really it's about pressuring them to believe that the measure of being a woman is how she looks. And that look must be young and sexy. I'm so sick of it being thrust in front of my face every time I turn on the TV or pick up a magazine.'

They are silent for a moment, Lexie checking her lists for the march, Wendy slipping a tray of scones into the oven. Emma watches them; they are so much at ease, so confident, so mature, and quite suddenly she yearns for that, for what she sees in them, yearns for something they share, that is shared too by Margot and Dot, by some of the women in her own office. Is this, she wonders now, why Margot had talked to her about Phyllida needing friends? Could her mother see then what Emma now sees for herself, that she and Phyllida have more in common than she had ever realised? Is this sort of unspoken understanding, this connection, something that she could have, could be a part of? She has always thought that Lexie and Wendy, and practically every other woman she met, was judging her and probably finding her wanting. Now, quite suddenly, she is not so sure.

'I think I got very caught up in it for a while,' she says now. 'I mean, it *is* nice to look good, to *feel* you look good, but it doesn't fix anything, does it? I was like a mouse on a treadmill going round and round in circles, wearing myself out, going nowhere, solving nothing.'

'Well you *are* going somewhere now,' Lexie says firmly, slapping a list of instructions and a map in front of her. 'At least tomorrow morning, and the place you are going is this corner here across from the park. Please take your mobile with you, and the girls down at the starting point will call you when the marchers start moving. But bear in mind there will also be people waiting on the side streets to join the march as it reaches them.'

Wendy looks across at Emma and grins. 'She's incredibly bossy, isn't she?' she says, nodding towards Lexie. 'Was she like this as a kid?'

'Worse actually,' Emma says. 'Had to be in charge of everything.'

'Yes, well I'm getting my comeuppance now,' Lexie says. 'If I learn nothing else from all this I will certainly have learnt never to volunteer to organise anything ever again.'

'We're back,' Grant says, sticking his head around the kitchen door. 'Sorry we're late, Em, but your sister, the leader of the pack over there, said I had to drop off some fliers on the way. Rosie's just gone upstairs to get her bag. She won't be long.'

'It's okay,' Emma says, sliding off her stool, 'but we'll get going as soon as she's ready,' and she swallows the remains of her coffee and begins to gather up the paperwork for the march without looking at him.

'I'll give you a hand,' Grant says, picking up the visibility jacket. 'Come on, Rosie, your mum's ready to go.'

It was what Emma had hoped to avoid, being alone with Grant – well, alone except for Rosie – but a few minutes later he is carrying her things and Rosie's bag across the street and then strapping Rosie into the car seat.

'There you go,' he says, planting a kiss on Rosie's cheek. 'Be good. I'll see you tomorrow at the march.' And he backs out and straightens up. 'Got everything?'

Emma nods. 'Yes, thanks. And . . . well thanks for the other night.'

He shrugs. 'No worries. You okay now?'

She nods. 'Yes,' she says. 'One day at a time, you know how it is. You . . . er . . . well, Wendy didn't say anything.'

'About what?'

'The other night.'

'Well no, she wouldn't. How would she know?'

'You mean you didn't tell her?'

'Of course not. Was I supposed to?'

'No, no, I just thought you would, that's all. You didn't even tell her about the therapist?'

'I assumed you told me that in confidence.'

'I did, of course I did, but I just thought . . .' She hesitates. 'You must think I'm –'

'I think what you're doing now takes courage,' he cuts in. 'I really admire you for it and I actually think you're terrific, always have, always will.' And he kisses her lightly on the cheek, waves to Rosie through the window, and turns away to cross the street back to the house.

◦◦◦

Sunday morning and Dot is restless and ready to go. She's been ready for ages, having woken early and spent the next few hours wandering around in her pyjamas, trying to focus on her speech and being constantly derailed by waves of nausea-inducing anxiety. Time and again her thoughts return to Patrick, to the shock of his identity and to what she must tell him. Vinka's brutally accurate assessment of her may have been well meant but it had increased Dot's fear. She had needed to talk to someone and it was, in a way, refreshing to be beaten around the head by Vinka's forensic dissection of her psyche. But it made her more aware of the anger and distress that might be in store for Vinka when she learns the whole truth, and she dreads the moment when that anger will be directed at her.

'You must tell him about his father,' Vinka had insisted again, just as she left. 'He has a right to know. If it is too hard then you tell it to me and I tell him for you.'

Dot had shaken her head then. 'No, I have to do it myself, and I will. Tomorrow. I promise I'll tell him then.'

In a few hours' time she will have to deliver on that promise and even Vinka, with her great insight, has no inkling of what there is to tell. It would never have been easy for Dot to face the child she relinquished all those years ago. When, over the years, she had considered the unlikely possibility of their meeting, she'd assumed that it would be a slow and cautious dance, each of them feeling out the territory, getting to know each other, and always with an open back door through which she could scuttle to safety, slamming it closed behind her. Never once had she considered that her son might be someone she already knew, someone she admired, someone linked to other friends, particularly to her oldest friends. Who knows who and what will be unravelled by this?

She would like to sit somewhere still and quiet now, some place from where she could watch Patrick as he lives his life: watch as he works, as he talks to Lexie and to his students, to Laurence and to Vinka. She wants to sit in silence as he reads or walks or gives a lecture, to watch every move and every gesture, because in the time that she has known him she has not taken sufficient notice of all these things. She has learned him casually, as one learns a new friend, without consideration of what weight may hang on the connection. She has squandered chances to know him better and now, perhaps, she will never have the opportunity to begin again. After decades of not knowing him, Dot aches for the intensity of connection. Her head throbs with questions, her heart aches with something so new and strange that it seems unbearable.

She stops pacing and sits again, her hands knotted together

in her lap. They are like a stranger's hands, old and knobbly, the backs of them crossed with raised veins and speckled with age spots, the palms soft and pale, with a maze of those fine lines that apparently tell the story and predict the future of one's life. Is Patrick here in one of these lines – his birth, his return to her life, their connection and their future?

This is not the state of mind in which Dot had imagined delivering her speech. She had imagined waking from a good night's sleep with a clear head, ready for a final run through. But this morning she is exhausted with lack of sleep, strung out with anxiety, her head spinning as conflicting demands and emotions intersect. But there is no choice and so, with time to spare, she locks the door behind her and sits down on the long wooden seat on the front verandah, to wait for whoever has been appointed to collect her. It won't be Alyssa, that's for sure; she too has a speech to make and someone will get her to the right place at the right time, ply her with water and encouraging words, just as they will for Dot. It won't be Lexie who comes for her because she, along with Patrick, is directing operations. And it won't be Phyllida, who's in charge of ensuring that the soft drinks and hot dog stands are set up and for getting the women's choir in place. Dot leans back on the seat, resting her head against the tuck-pointed brickwork, the morning sun on her face, eyes closed. She hopes it will be one of those wonderful sparky young women whom she's grown to admire so much; Karen, perhaps, or Lucy, or one of the volunteers. She wants someone energetic, enthusiastic, who knows absolutely nothing about her personal life and who will not call her to account on any of this. So when a car hoots out in the street and she opens her eyes and recognises the blue Barina, she is less than delighted to see that her chauffeur is one who is far too emotionally close for comfort.

'Shit!' she murmurs. 'More explaining, I suppose. God, if you're up there, you really haven't been paying attention.' And picking up her bag, she walks out to the car.

'You're early,' she says, buckling herself into the passenger seat. 'Very efficient.'

'You always like to arrive in good time,' Margot says. 'Are you okay? You look rough.'

'Thanks, that's reassuring,' Dot says. 'Let's just get going, shall we?'

Margot had switched on the engine but now switches it off again as she swivels around in her seat to face her. 'Look here, Dot, you can cut that out. I'm your friend, remember? I'm not criticising you, I'm not making any judgments, I'm just your friend, and this morning I called Karen and told her I'd pick you up because I thought you might need some moral support. But if you're going to behave like a sulky child you can damn well get out of my car and call a cab.'

Dot, who has been staring straight ahead through the windscreen, turns now to look at her. 'Sorry,' she says. 'Sorry, you're quite right. I'm . . . well, a bit defensive this morning. I suppose you've heard the news from Lexie?'

'Of course, and Laurence filled in the blanks.'

Dot nods. 'I'm sorry about that – I couldn't tell you at the time and Laurence, well, he was really good. I don't know how I'd have coped without him.'

'You *could* have told me,' Margot says, 'but I can see how it wouldn't have seemed that way at the time. But I *would* have come myself, I would have understood.'

'Mmm . . . Well I guess I know that now, but at the time it all seemed impossible.'

They sit briefly in the silence.

'Patrick's a wonderful man,' Margot says, 'you should be very proud of him.'

'I can't take any credit for that,' Dot says. 'I feel I can only do him damage.'

'Stop it,' Margot says, thumping her hand on the steering wheel. 'Can't you just accept this, see it as a gift? Laurence says you never wanted anyone to know, but it's too late now, we all know. No one's judging you, and Patrick needs to talk to you.'

Dot takes a bundle of tissues from her bag and blows her nose noisily. 'I *can* see it as a gift, I *do* see it that way,' she says. 'Every instinct, every part of me wants to grasp this chance to know him, to let him know me. You're right, he *is* a wonderful man, more than I could ever have hoped for. But it's complicated, Margot, and I need to discuss that with Patrick before I tell anyone else. The awful thing is that when I *do* talk to him I believe he will hate me, that he will never forgive me, and so there may be no chance to know him as . . . well . . . as my son. No chance at all.'

THIRTY

'I could of gone with Dad or Wendy, you know,' Rosie says as she and Emma stand together at the corner of Collins and Spring Streets. 'Dad said I could go with him to the station, or with Wendy, or to the gardens with Aunty Phyl. He let me choose so I could of gone with any of them.'

'Could *have*, not could *of*,' Emma says. 'Well I'm glad you chose me. It's much nicer than being here on my own. But there might be a lot of people around so don't get lost, and don't wander off.' For Emma, coming so late to the campaign and largely unaware of the number of volunteers and the work that has gone into organising the rally, the fear is that no one will turn up. It's only in the last week, as the lists of volunteers and their responsibilities have been distributed together with the running sheets for the rally, that she's come to realise that it's been planned like a military operation and, according to Alyssa, Lexie has been the driving force behind that. Now she's dreading the possibility of a few straggling protesters standing in a great empty space, making the whole thing look ridiculous.

Rosie heaves a huge sigh. 'I *know*, Mum,' she says. 'But I picked to come with you 'cos Dad said I'd get to wear one of these things . . . what's it called?'

'It's a visibility vest, so people can see you clearly. That's why it's this lime green colour.'

'I like this colour,' Rosie says, 'it sort of makes my teeth hurt. Does it make your teeth hurt?'

Emma runs her tongue thoughtfully across her teeth. 'No, no I don't think it does.'

'Well anyway, it's pretty boring here, so now I've got my invisible vest can I go and stay with Aunty Phyl and help with the hot dogs?'

'Would you rather do that?'

'Yes I would, if I still get to keep the vest.'

Emma laughs. 'You can keep the vest. But if you want to go we'd best go now before it gets too crowded.'

They cross the street into the park and walk down the path towards the place where Phyllida is organising refreshments.

'Aunty Phyl,' Rosie calls, letting go of Emma's hand and running ahead. 'Can I stay with you?'

'Of course you can,' Phyllida says, looking up at Emma as she arrives alongside her. 'If Mummy says it's all right. And if you're going to help me. I need someone to unpack the paper napkins and fold them up for the hot dogs.'

'I can do that,' Rosie says, 'it's boring over there.'

'She's probably better here anyway,' Emma says. 'I'm concerned about losing her if a crowd builds up. I'll meet you both back here later.'

She watches as Phyllida and Rosie open the carton of napkins and then with a final wave she turns away and starts to walk back, past the other stalls: coffee and soft drinks, the campaign t-shirts and leaflets, and the petitions, and largest of all – the display stand with its backboards covered with coloured photographs. Emma slows down and walks closer to look at the photographs: chorus lines of little girls with teased hair and spray-tans, dressed and made up like miniature sex goddesses for beauty pageants, satin corsets and padded sequinned bras, frilly knickers peeking out below short frilly skirts above fishnet stockings. And more little girls in coloured leotards over obviously padded bras, winding their legs and bodies around poles. Tiny tots in can-can dresses bent double with their backs to the camera, gazing upside down at the viewer through their open legs. And Bunnies – Bunnies everywhere, in body hugging satin costumes, the beauty and innocence of their faces heartbreaking in comparison with the distortion of their appearance. Emma stares now at the pictures, sickened by the memory of Rosie dressed like this, doing pelvic thrusts to the beat of a drum. Rage rises in her belly and she turns quickly away and heads back to her marshalling point.

'Just checking you're okay,' Laurence says, catching up with her as she crosses the street. 'They'll be moving off soon. According to Karen and Lucy there's a big crowd at the starting point.' He takes his mobile from his pocket and shows it to her. 'Karen just took this picture and sent it to me.'

Emma takes the phone and peers at the image of a mass of people armed with placards and banners. 'That's amazing,' Emma says. 'There must be, what, a hundred? Hundred and fifty?'

Laurence smiles and closes his phone. 'Four, perhaps five hundred,' he says, 'and there are people waiting in the side streets. Anyway, my darling, I have to go back and talk Alyssa out of her nerves, but I just wanted to see that you're okay.'

'I'm okay,' Emma says, 'and I'm so glad I'm here.' She leans closer and kisses him on the cheek.

Laurence looks at her. He smiles, squeezes her hand and returns the kiss, but for a moment he seems incapable of speech. 'Better get on then,' he says, clearing his throat as he turns to walk away.

Emma watches as he stops at the kerb and looks both ways, although the street is closed to traffic. She smiles; he is so familiar and yet she feels she is only just beginning to know him. 'Take care,' she calls. And Laurence turns and waves and walks on across the street and up the steps.

❧

'She's here, Patrick, over there with Dad and Alyssa,' Lexie says. 'Stop worrying. She'll be fine.'

'Lexie's right,' Margot says. 'Whatever's happening for Dot she's the consummate professional. No one out there will ever know that she has any thought in her head other than what she's saying.' She can feel the tension emanating from him; his need to talk to Dot is palpable.

Patrick nods, although his expression indicates that he's not convinced. 'If she stuffs it up it'll be my fault,' he says. 'I should've waited but I had to ask her about Laurence, I had to know. Imagine what it would have meant for us if he'd been . . .'

'But he *wasn't*,' Lexie says, putting a reassuring hand on his shoulder. 'He *isn't* your father. We've been through all this, Patrick. You had a perfect right and good cause to tell her when you did. God knows why she's being so cagey about your father, but you're not responsible for her if she stuffs up – not that I think for one minute that she will. Now can you go and fix that thing on the stage she's supposed to stand on, it's not high enough. Alyssa's one is fine but Dot's so short they won't be able to see her behind the lectern.'

'I'll come with you,' Margot says. She knows Lexie's really caught up in what's happening but she thinks Patrick needs more in the way of reassurance. 'This stuff is in Dot's blood,' she tells him as he crouches over Dot's stand. 'And once she's out there in front of the crowd she'll fly. It's Alyssa I'm worried about, she's freaking out about facing so many people. But you don't need to worry about Dot. She'll make you proud, I know she will.'

'I *know* she'll make me feel proud,' Patrick says picking

up his tool bag. 'But will she let me *be* proud of her, of her being my mother, do you think she'll ever let me do that?'

Behind the temporary stage Alyssa is vomiting with nerves.

'I'll be fine, now. I promise I will,' she says, straightening up. 'I won't let everyone down.'

Up on the stage a local women's band and people who have skipped the march but come straight to the park are singing along, swaying to the music. And further off, the first of the marchers have already made their way through the gate.

'I know,' Margot says, 'you'll be brilliant.' She hands her a bottle of water and Alyssa gulps at it and wipes her face on a paper towel. 'You need to get close to the stage now, Alyssa, with Dot, so you're both ready to go when the rest of the crowd is in place.' And she steers her back towards the stage.

The park seems to be filling at speed now and there is still a long line of marchers stretching back down the street. Margot, standing on the steps at the side of the stage, looks out across the growing crowd. There are people everywhere, hundreds of people, shifting and swaying. Women of all ages, some with homemade banners, some with small children in pushers, men carrying toddlers on their shoulders, a contingent of people in wheelchairs and elderly couples with posters mounted on card and fixed to poles. Near the front of the crowd she spots a former Premier who is signing someone's banner, and further along a couple of members of Parliament, a senator, and a couple of young women – actors from a soap opera, surrounded by delighted fans. The music, the sight of people surging in, the voices – talking, laughing, singing – bring a lump to her throat. She remembers other times – thirty, forty years ago – other battles that were won and some that were lost and the spirit of the past mingles with this moment and fires her blood. She looks across to the side of the stage where Dot stands, their eyes meet and the past flows like a sine wave between them, and Margot knows she's right – Dot will be fine – she will light the flame as she has done so many times before. And when that is done she will be ready to face Patrick, his questions and the challenge he represents to everything she believes about herself.

◦⌒◦⌒◦

It's better now that she's here, Dot thinks, now that the adrenaline is coursing through her blood. When Alyssa had seen the size of the crowd she had vomited with fear and Dot remembered what that was like, the feeling that you might faint with sheer terror, the parched throat, the spinning head.

'Remember what I told you,' she'd said, gripping Alyssa's hand when Margot had brought her back to the stage. 'Let them see the passion not the terror. Let them see the woman who started all this, let them see *you*, Alyssa. They're here because of what you've done, don't forget it for a minute.'

And Alyssa, white and shaking, had hugged her so hard that Dot thought her ribs were going to crack. The good thing about the need to perform, she thinks now, is that it drives out everything else. It takes over and there is no space for fear or sadness, guilt or shame, or any of the other emotions she has battled with through the night. She is here to do a job and for a while at least there is this and only this. Dot takes a deep breath and as she steps up to the lectern there is a cheer and she waves to the crowd and gazes out across the vast landscape of faces and banners, of waving arms and placards, and close by the television cameras have started to roll.

'Thanks for coming,' she says. 'Thanks for taking the time and making the effort to come here this morning to say something about what's happening to our daughters and granddaughters; to little girls, and teenagers, to young women, to all women. What we're talking about here today is the monstrous virus of sexual exploitation that is invading the lives of innocent children, infecting the way they are seen and valued, and infecting the way they see and value themselves. It's about dressing little girls as sexually enhanced women and encouraging them to compete with each other for approval and attention. It's about smothering childhood and corrupting innocence, in the service of consumerism. It's about grooming girls in ways that set them up to become victims of sexual abuse, and to be trivialised, and then dismissed when they pass their use-by date. We need your support, we need you to channel your anger and your energy, and if you stay with us this morning, we'll tell you just what you can do and how you can do it.'

There are shouts of encouragement from a small group in the middle and it spreads now, building into a roar of support, of cheers, of waves and whistles and pumping fists, and she knows she is on her way. And as she looks around waiting for the cheers to stop so she can continue, she sees him standing by the sound system, arms folded, watching her, intent, straight faced, and as he catches her eye he gives her an almost imperceptible nod, and Dot knows that it has never been more important to get it right and make it work than it is today.

THIRTY-ONE

'It *was* amazing,' Alyssa says. 'All those people, and the TV cameras, and all those signatures on the petition. I can't believe it, we're getting features in three magazines.'

'Well three we know about,' Lexie says, 'but have you looked at the list of media calls that have to be returned. You've created a monster, Alyssa. It's just going to get bigger and bigger from now on.' The number of people who had turned out today had taken her by surprise, and now that it's over, the anxiety has lifted and once again she has the bit between her teeth. They can do more with this, she knows they can, and she's ready to get right back into it all again.

'We'd never have done it without you, Dot,' Alyssa says, perched on the arm of Dot's chair. 'You and your blog and that manic video with the chains. And, Lexie, we'd still be sitting around the table arguing if you hadn't taken charge.'

'The whole thing started with you.'

'Lexie's right,' Dot cuts in, holding on to Alyssa's hand. 'Own it, Alyssa, this is down to you and to Karen and Lucy. Because you made it happen. And this is just the beginning.'

They are back at Phyllida's place, gathered again around

the large table cluttered now with empty pizza boxes, crumpled fliers, some leftover hot dogs, paper serviettes, beer and soft drink cans. In the middle of the table is Patrick's laptop, on which they have watched, over and over again, the downloaded news coverage of the march. And fast asleep on the big wicker chair which is normally Phyllida's domain is Rosie, exhausted and oblivious, still in her fluorescent vest. The girls are ready to go; they're off to a party and Lexie watches them, their energy and exuberance. Their ability to party on after an exhausting day is impressive, but one of the joys of middle age, she realises, is to accept that it's okay to stop.

'A party *now*?' Laurence says. 'It's nearly ten o'clock. Aren't you exhausted?'

'Nah! Come with us, Laurence,' Alyssa says. 'You can last a bit longer.'

He shakes his head. 'No way. Cocoa and slippers for me, or perhaps just a bit more champagne.'

'We're dinosaurs, Laurence,' Dot says. 'Don't you remember how it felt to know you could keep going all night, staggering down the street to the next party, ending up sleeping on someone's floor?'

'I do,' he says, 'and I'm very happy it's over.'

It is quieter once they've left, the fizz of youthful energy dissipates and floats away on the mild night air and the pace changes.

'The best part,' Emma says to Dot, 'was when you talked about how the language of feminism had been hijacked by market forces. How stuff about having choices and power and being *worth it* has been used to make us buy things, specially things to make us look younger and sexy – that, and the stuff about how little girls are growing up thinking that how they look is more important than who they are.'

'That was great,' Phyllida says, passing Laurence another bottle of champagne to open. 'But the bit I liked best was when you said that girls were persuaded to look older than they are until they get into their twenties and see how important it is to look young, and then they start trying to look younger again and they're still doing it when they're ready to claim the pension.'

'Yep,' Emma pipes up, 'you said that thing about . . . what was it now? You said "when is the time" . . . no that's not right –'

'What she said,' Patrick cuts in, 'was "from childhood to our dotage is there ever a time in a woman's life when it's okay for her to look the age she is?" That's what you said, isn't it, Dot?'

She looks at him across the table and nods slowly. 'I think you have it word for word,' she says.

Lexie, sitting alongside him, feels his tension – he needs to be alone with Dot, to hold her to her promise. 'It's late,' she says, getting to her feet, 'we should start clearing up. There's all that stuff in the kitchen, let's get going on it now, it won't take long.'

Slowly they gather up plates, glasses and rubbish and disappear inside the house, and Dot watches them with a sinking heart. She knows what's happening and why she and Patrick are left sitting there alone, and in silence.

'Can we talk now, Dot? Over there perhaps,' he says, indicating the far corner of the garden where a long low seat stands between two frangipani trees. And he gets to his feet.

It is the moment she has been dreading, the moment she had thought might be postponed as the day unfolded into an evening of celebration, but now she takes his proffered arm and together they walk across the grass to the secluded seat that looks back at the house. In the kitchen there is washing and drying and things are being put away or thrown away and tidied, and life is being returned to normal.

'You were splendid today,' Patrick says. 'To use a much overused description, you were awesome. I felt so proud –'

'Stop,' she says, putting her other hand on his arm. 'Not yet. There are things I must tell you. After that you can, and I am sure you *will*, say whatever you want, whatever you feel.'

'Okay,' he says as they reach the seat. 'But I want you to know that I do understand how difficult, how frightening it must have been to be a single woman and pregnant back then, and how happy I am to have found you.'

Dot nods, settling herself on the seat. 'You're a wise and generous man, Patrick. And I must tell you now, while I have the chance, that you're everything I could ever want my son to be. I can't begin to tell you what your friendship and Vinka's has meant to me, which is why what I have to tell you is so hard, because it means that you may both now be lost to me.'

'I'm sure there's nothing you . . .'

She stops him. 'Just listen first,' she says, 'then you'll know how you really feel. You asked about your father, so I'll tell you.' She pauses and then leans a little further back on the seat. 'I met him in the early sixties, when I fell in with the Push. He was different from many of them, in fact he wasn't really a part of it, he was a loner – came and went when it suited him. But he had an imposing presence, he was good looking, a great talker. He would stand in a corner of one of those smoky rooms or bars where we met and hold forth on some issue or another and you had to listen. I threw myself at him shamelessly and we were together for a few months, but I convinced myself that it would last forever. I worked hard at trying to be the sort of woman he wanted. It wasn't easy because at heart he wasn't really a libertarian and he was deeply conservative about women. He enjoyed the sexual freedom of the Push but he resented it when women wanted to exercise that freedom. I had to practise the art of not being myself, of toning myself down. You might find it hard to believe that I was willing to do that, I do too now, but at the time I would have done anything.

'But then one day he just disappeared and I discovered he'd left Sydney and gone to Melbourne. He never even said goodbye. That was that and I heard nothing for months – well, years actually – and then one day I walked into the coffee shop where the Push often met and there he was, sitting at a table in the corner. He told me he was married now and his wife was in Melbourne. I can't remember now why he was back in Sydney but there was a party that evening and we went together. He began to tell me more about his life but I stopped him. I didn't want to know anything about his wife, their house, their plans, nothing. I wanted to pretend that I still had a chance, still mattered to him. I was unbelievably naive. It's amazing how utterly one can convince oneself, so we spent the night together. But for him, of course, it was just a fling; he had *never* been in love with me, not then, not in the past. He had never even tried to pretend that he was, and the following morning he left just as he had left before.'

They sit for a moment in the silence.

Patrick takes a deep breath. 'So, later, you . . . you . . .'

'Yes, I discovered I was pregnant.'

'Did you tell him?'

Dot's head is spinning and she closes her eyes. The sweet scent of the frangipani makes her nauseous and her heart thumps furiously; fleetingly she wonders if she might be going to faint.

'Are you okay, Dot?'

'Yes,' she says eventually, opening her eyes. 'Yes, I'm okay. Yes, I told him. I found out where he worked and I called him. I thought he had a right to know. I told him I'd decided to have the baby . . . well . . . have *you*, and that I would arrange an adoption. He was shocked and frantic about his wife finding out. But I promised that she'd never find out from me.' Dot shifts her position. 'I really didn't expect to hear from him again, I was resigned to that. And then, a few days later he turned up at my flat. He'd driven up from Melbourne overnight. And I fell into that madness again – I thought he'd left his wife to be with me and his child. Talk about the triumph of hope over experience. But he hadn't come back for me, Patrick; he'd come back for you.'

'For me?' Patrick says. 'What do you mean?'

'He came to ask me to give you to him. He and his wife wanted a child but she couldn't conceive. They were trying to adopt but there were problems. He saw this chance to keep his own child, he thought we could do it in secret. He knew someone who could fabricate a birth certificate, with just my name and the father's name as 'unknown'. So he had told his wife that there was a chance that someone he knew could arrange a private adoption, bypassing the authorities. It wasn't so unusual in those days – lots of single and desperate pregnant women, lots of couples equally desperate for a child. He had convinced her that it would be safe, and she agreed they should try, but she wanted a signed statement from the mother waiving her rights to the child. Not an unreasonable request of course. It was an agonising decision, Patrick, harder even than letting you go to strangers; someone else – another woman – would have both him and you. And yet it seemed the right thing to do. I trusted him to care for you, something I knew I couldn't do alone.' She stops abruptly; her throat is dry and tight and she feels she is shaking from within.

'Patrick, I knew that man as George Kelly, the son of a Polish mother and an Irish father, but you knew him as Jerzey, the name used by his wife and her sister who so badly wanted him to claim his Polish roots.'

The garden is entirely still and Dot sighs and shifts in her seat. 'So now you know the deception at the heart of your family. The man who adopted you was your real father, and the woman who raised you as her own was deceived about your relationship to him. I wonder if you can believe that at the time both your father and I thought we were doing the right thing? I abandoned you, Patrick, but your father didn't. I hope that you can, at least, find some comfort in that.'

Patrick is silent, leaning forward, arms resting on his thighs, hands clasped between his knees, looking down at the ground. Dot gets to her feet, swaying with exhaustion, aching to touch him, to tell him not just what happened in the past, but how it has haunted her all her life. She wants to tell him how many times she has resolved to find him and then held back; to tell him how she feels now after all these years and how, in this moment, as she anticipates his contempt, she feels her heart is being torn out.

'I'll leave you in peace now,' she says quietly. 'You need time to think.' And resisting the urge to put a hand on his shoulder, she begins to walk away.

'Dot,' Patrick says suddenly. 'Don't go.'

He too is on his feet now, walking towards her. He is holding out his hands, and she pauses, then steps back towards him and he takes her hands in his. In the shaft of light from the house she can see that there are tears in his eyes.

'He was a wonderful father,' he says. 'I loved him dearly and miss him so much. And my mother, Beate, she loved us both; her family was everything to her. I wish I had known this while he was alive. This makes sense to me in ways that I can't explain even to you. But it's not too late for us, Dot, for you and me. We know each other now but there is so much more to know. Please don't walk away from me again.'

~~~

There are just four of them left at the table now that everyone else has gone home, or five counting Rosie, who has slept through all the clearing up and the farewells. The rubbish is packed into the bins, a box of empty bottles stands by the door, and from the kitchen the sound of the dishwasher is all that disturbs the silence.

'I'm glad Lexie and Patrick took Dot home with them,' Phyllida says. 'It seems the right way to end the day.'

Margot leans back in her chair with a cup of tea, watching Emma, who is watching Rosie. Watching is what she's been doing these last few months: watching rather than trying to intervene, suggest, counsel. Watching rather than fixing or sending out waves of worry and frustration. And now, as she sits here watching her daughter, a catalogue of several years of her own useless attempts to fix Emma runs through her head, alongside the more torturous list of Emma's own attempts to fix herself. Long after Margot had caught on to the fact that her efforts to reach her daughter weren't working, she had still burned with the maternal longing to take on the burden of Emma's distress.

Emma shifts in her chair. 'I don't understand how she didn't work it all out herself before now,' she says. 'All the clues were there: the Polish wife, the surname. It's weird.'

'She *did* know the surname,' Laurence says, 'but Kelly is a very common name.'

'And she didn't know his wife was Polish,' Margot adds, 'nor even that Patrick was adopted.'

'It's an incredible thing to face, your past life unravelling like that, especially at our age,' Phyllida says.

Emma finishes her tea and pushes the cup away. 'It's all so weird,' she says. 'Like being a minor character in a soap opera or a saga – one of those books about families and friends that stretches out over years and weird things keep getting revealed. Only in this case they're all crammed into just over a year.'

'Not such a *minor* character, Em,' Margot says.

'Yes, but *your* lives are so complicated. Families are complicated, I suppose, and we just take it all for granted, until something happens to make us start asking questions.'

'Or until you read the novel,' Laurence says, glancing across at Margot with a grin, 'in which family history masquerades as fiction, and characters act out the roles of parents, children, aunts, uncles, old friends and new lovers.'

'You haven't, Margot!' Phyllida says. 'You haven't written about us?'

Rosie stirs in her chair, rubs her eyes and looks around her, blinking at the light.

'Oh, Mum, no!' Emma says. 'Please say it's not about us. Tell me I'm not in it.'

Laurence throws back his head and laughs. 'Who knows what Margot's written? She's being very cagey about it. Does it include a gay husband or the dark secrets of a dead brother-in-law?'

'Mum,' Rosie says, grabbing Emma's arm, 'I want to sit with you. Mum, pleeeease.'

Emma gets up and slides down into the big chair with Rosie, pulling her across her lap, putting her arms around her. Rosie snuggles up, bleary eyed.

'Is there any juice?' she asks, and Phyllida pours some into a glass and hands it to her.

'Shall I take you up to bed, darling?'

Rosie gulps the juice and shakes her head. 'I want to stay with Mum,' she says, shifting around to find a comfortable position.

'Come on then, Margot,' Laurence says. 'Own up.'

Margot shakes her head. 'You all amaze me,' she says. 'Do you think I have nothing to write about, nothing to say, that doesn't need you lot as its focus? Haven't you heard of fiction, or imagination?'

'But does it have a happy ending?' Emma asks.

Margot hesitates. 'I think . . . I hope it has a satisfying resolution,' she says.

⚭

The early morning sun is kinder than the scorching heat of the last week, but even so, as she sits in her little garden with coffee and a croissant, Vinka wishes it would rain. Her plants are barely holding out against the endless summer heat. Still, this morning she feels pleasure in the very ordinary things, the brush of a leaf against her arm, the sound of a neighbour talking to her cat, the comforting knowledge of her proximity to the city. A weight has lifted and although it has left her with some sadness, there is also satisfaction.

Vinka has long had questions about Patrick's biological father, questions she has never been able to ask. Only once had she come close to voicing them and then it was to Beate in a gentle attempt to nudge the subject open, to see if Beate saw what she saw. Patrick was eighteen at the time, nineteen perhaps, studying at university. He was in the garden, helping Jerzey to build a chicken coop, while Vinka was inside the house with her sister. As she watched them from the window, the similarities she had noticed in the past seemed more marked than ever.

'Do you think,' Vinka had asked, taking Beate's arm and drawing her over to the window, 'that it is possible for a child who is adopted to be so close to his father that he grows to look like him? Is that scientifically possible?'

'Children copy things,' Beate had said. 'Sometimes I see that Patrick has the same gestures as Jerzey, sometimes he sounds a little the same. But he cannot grow to resemble him physically.'

'But look,' Vinka had persisted. 'The two of them together. They're so alike they *could* almost be father and son.' She was so sure she was right that she had almost convinced herself that Beate knew something that she did not. Had she and Jerzey arranged for him to father a child with someone else so that they could adopt it? These things happened, people found all sorts of ways to get what they wanted.

'You think so?' Beate had asked, tilting her head to one side, screwing up her eyes as she watched them. 'I can't see it. The height is the same, yes, but they are not much alike in other ways.'

Now Vinka wonders if Beate lied to her. Had she known the truth and pretended that she couldn't see it because she wanted it hidden? When Dot's name and photograph started to appear in the papers, had she gone back to that waiver, looked again at the signature? Had she started asking questions? Had Jerzey told her? If he had it would further explain Beate's interest in Dot and her unfolding career. Was that her way of coming to terms with Jerzey's past? By getting to know Dot through her writing was Beate defusing her own fear of the woman who had loved her husband and whose child she had adopted? Vinka favours this explanation. She favours it over the one which says that Beate was deceived all her life. She prefers it for the reasons Dot gave her in the hospital.

'Take the risk,' she had said, 'bet on the love, on the happiness, at our age we have no time left for caution.'

And so Vinka chooses her truth, she *makes* it *her* truth, her bet on love, a truth which is life-enhancing and with which she can be a part of Patrick's future with the people both he and she have come to love.

THIRTY-TWO

It's April and still it feels as though the summer will never end. They walk together along the paved pathways between banks of scorched grass that have fallen short of the reticulation, and alongside the greener surrounds of graves where even the freshest of flowers are wilting in the heat.

'It's this way, I think,' Phyllida says, taking off her sunglasses. 'This place is enormous and the signs aren't very good, are they?'

'There's a seat there in the shade,' May says. 'We could sit down for a minute and try to locate ourselves on the map.'

Phyllida pulls a water bottle from her bag and gulps some. 'Excellent idea. This heat is awful – will we ever get some rain? I should have suggested early morning or late in the afternoon.'

'Well we're here,' May says, 'that's what matters. I've been in here before to a funeral but not from this direction.'

'Same here. I've always parked over on the other side because it's nearer the chapel.' Phyllida holds out the water bottle. 'Want some?'

'I've got some here, thanks,' May says, rummaging in her bag. 'When are you moving house?'

'Two weeks,' Phyllida says, patting her forehead with a tissue. 'I can't believe how much there is to do, but at least I've found a place. It's much smaller of course, but rather sweet, with a really lovely garden, not far from the golf club, and on the bus route.'

'Bus?' May raises her eyebrows. 'I didn't know you were a bus person, Phyllida.'

'I'm not, or at least I haven't been. I'm wedded to my car, but I'm trying to think ahead. An old friend of Margot's, now a friend of mine, stayed with me over Christmas because she'd had a fall. It made me think that I'm approaching a time when, unlikely as it seems right now, I may not be able to drive.'

'It certainly does seem unlikely,' May says. 'Will your niece go with you?'

'Initially,' Phyllida says. 'I've asked her to – I've loved having her with me and I do rather dread moving in somewhere strange on my own. So Emma said she'd stay for a month or so and then look around for a place of her own.'

'Donald talked about her a lot,' May says.

And Phyllida can't help noticing that May refers to him far more frequently than she herself does.

'He was very fond of her – well, both the girls, but particularly Emma,' she says. 'We had both very much wanted a child of our own.'

'I have a daughter,' May says, taking off her sunglasses and polishing them on the tail of her white shirt. 'She'll be thirty-two next month.'

Phyllida swings around to face her. 'Really? You never mentioned her before.'

May shrugs. 'We haven't talked much, except about Donald and this situation.'

Phyllida hesitates. 'Did Donald ever meet her?'

'No. Alice lives in Hong Kong and when she did visit here she always refused to meet him. She disapproved of us,' May says with a wry smile. 'She lectured me at length about the relationship.'

'How sad for you. So you had no one to confide in?'

'No one at all,' May says. 'You're right, it wasn't easy. Shall I have a look at the map?'

Together they pore over the crumpled photocopy, finally locating themselves and the place they are heading.

'We should have saved some water for the flowers,' Phyllida says, dropping her own empty bottle into a nearby bin. And they walk on, and fortunately there is a path they can take through shade, to a far corner of the cemetery and a line of small bare graves close to an old peppermint tree.

'It's one of those, it must be,' Phyllida says. And side-by-side they move slowly along, stopping eventually at a narrow plot with a modest, white headstone.

'There,' May says, 'there it is. Look . . . *Tony Stiles died 3 August 2002, age unknown*.'

The tapering leaves of the peppermint, moved by a sudden breeze, brush Phyllida's hair but she stays as though fixed to the spot, swamped by a surge of sadness and anger.

'The Salvation Army looked after the funeral and put up the headstone,' she says eventually. 'After he died, when the police were trying to trace relatives, someone from the Salvos' hostel recognised the photograph. He'd stayed there on a couple of occasions, but no one seems to have known anything about him. He'd been living on the streets for years. He was so young, the file said sixteen or seventeen years. He was just a kid who fell through the cracks.'

May bends down to pick up an empty glass jar that has been left on the grass between the graves. She takes it to the nearby tap and fills it with water, unwraps the flowers they have brought with them and sets the jar close to the headstone.

'Next time we should bring a vase,' she says, stepping back.

'Next time?'

'We will come again, won't we?'

Phyllida pauses, looking at her. 'I was intending to come again, yes.'

'So perhaps . . . I mean, if you would like to we could come . . .'

'Together? Yes, I'd like that. You know, May, someone somewhere must have known this boy. A parent, a friend, a social worker. No one seems to have searched for long – too many other priorities, I suppose – but I want to try. It's a long time ago but somewhere someone might be waiting for him . . .'

'Yes, hoping he'll come back, or even just waiting to know why he doesn't.'

'I think so,' Phyllida says. 'And I'd like to find them, to tell them. It seems like a very small way of paying him some respect. Would you . . . could we . . . ?'

'Yes,' May says. 'I would like to do that.'

'Then we'll do it together,' Phyllida says. 'It seems the right thing to do.'

ᴖᴖᴖ

Lexie rings the bell and stands on the step holding a large cardboard box, waiting for Patrick to open the door.

'Oh! It's you,' he says, opening it and taking the box from her. 'Where's your key?'

'Forgot it,' she says.

'Okay, what's in the box? Oops, it rattles.'

'Yes, careful, it's crockery.'

'What for?'

'It's the first box. There are more in the car.'

'But what . . . ?'

'I'm moving in,' she says.

Patrick puts the box on the kitchen table. 'But I haven't asked you yet.'

'You asked me in November and then again at Christmas.'

'Yes, and you said ask again at Easter. It's not Easter yet.'

'It's only another week, so I decided not to wait,' Lexie says.

'What if I've changed my mind?' he says.

'Too late, I'm here, and so is my best tableware, and in the car there's more and some bed linen and a couple of suitcases of clothes.' She drops her bag on the table and puts her arms around his neck. 'Just try changing your mind now and see what happens.'

'I actually think I'm onto a really good thing,' he says. 'Your tableware is much nicer than mine. But why? Why so suddenly? Why not wait until Easter so that you could torture me a bit longer?'

Lexie lets go of him and looks around her, around the neat, well-organised kitchen, and beyond it through to the garden. 'I like it here,' she says. 'It's a lovely house and best of all it's got you in it. And besides, everything you said is true. Impecunious student, needs help with assignments, needs someone to cook dinner and pour me glasses of wine while I struggle with essays. And I've got an exhibition to organise, and a campaign to run.'

'So you're here because you're overworked and financially needy?'

'Guess so,' she says. 'Oh yes, and there's the other bit.'

'What bit?'

'The bit about how I love you and miss you, and how I finally feel safe enough to take the plunge.'

'Well I'm glad you managed to squeeze that bit in. This wouldn't have anything to do with Dot, would it?' he asks, turning to switch on the kettle and pull two mugs from the cupboard.

Lexie sits at the table watching as he makes the tea. 'Only in a roundabout sort of way,' she says. And sitting there she knows it is right, the right time, the right place and definitely the right person.

'I think I was convinced already but the night you found out – and that business about Dad – well that night I realised how easily I might have lost you. And it mattered that you understood how it would have been for Dot and why she and your father kept the secret – you were able to see beyond yourself. So I thought I'd better grab you while I've got the chance.'

Patrick pours water on the tea bags and carries the cups to the table.

'I may have got you under false pretences then,' he says, 'because it wasn't that hard. I knew I was adopted but I grew up feeling loved, really quite unconditionally. And then finding out Dot was my mother *was* pretty weird, but it was also totally brilliant.'

Lexie gives him a long hard look. 'Are you really saying that you never had a moment of feeling hurt or angry that she gave you up?'

'Of course I did, but I kept trying to remember the circumstances, although I did feel somewhat less than generous during those few days when she wouldn't talk to me. Anyway,' he laughs, 'as I told her the other day, it's a relief, really – she wouldn't have had a fraction of the patience Mum had, she's a lousy cook and I would have had to do my own ironing. But I wish I'd known while Mum and Dad were alive. Aunty Win thinks Mum may have known, that either she guessed or he told her. But we're never going to know the answer to that one.'

'Mmm,' Lexie says, pouring milk into her tea. 'Well thank goodness Vinka's okay with it all.'

Patrick laughs. 'She is but I suspect that she's also feeling a bit possessive.'

'Dot moving in on her favourite nephew?'

'Her *only* nephew. Anyway, what have you decided to do about your place?'

'All settled,' Lexie says. 'Phyl and Emma are moving to

the new house in two weeks and Em's promised to stay until Phyl's comfortable and after that she's going to rent my place, and I'll be able to pay my way here. I'll look for some part-time work when I've survived the first semester.'

'You can be a kept woman,' Patrick says. 'I mean it.'

'I know, and it's lovely of you. But I need my independence. Besides, you have the most terrifying mother and aunt in the world, and they might think I was taking advantage of you. Not sure I can cope if *they* start to gang up on me.'

∽

'Nobody told me I'd have to take my clothes off,' Dot says, clutching her arms around her. 'If they had I wouldn't have agreed. I don't mind being in this exhibition but I'm not doing it if it's like that Calendar Girls thing. I'm no Helen Mirren, you know . . .'

'It's not like that,' Emma says. 'We just want your head, neck and the top of your bare shoulders. You'll look lovely, Dot. Look – here's Mum's picture. Doesn't she look terrific?'

'Mmm, she does actually,' Dot says, relaxing a little as she studies the picture of Margot, neck and shoulders bare above the soft cream wrap.

'Yes, and this is Phyl's and here's Alyssa's Nan – all the same you see. We've done a couple of each – can't decide yet whether to use the black and white or the sepia. With yours we'll have thirty portraits of women between sixty-five and ninety. Don't you think that wrap, draped just below the shoulders, is very flattering?'

'Well, yes, it is rather, I suppose,' Dot says, somewhat mollified. 'Although my shoulders haven't seen the light of day for a very long time.'

'So, if you just slip your t-shirt off and slide your bra straps down . . .'

'Bra straps?' Dot says, laughing loudly. 'I haven't worn a bra for decades, Emma, never had much to put in one and what there *was* is long gone.'

'So that's easy, isn't it then?' Emma says. 'I'll leave you to it and when you're ready come on through and Andrea will take the pictures.'

Dot peers out of the window to where Margot is inspecting those of her plants that have survived the still unbroken weeks of drought. Sighing with resignation she closes the blind and takes off her t-shirt and stands naked to the waist in front of the mirror. Hideous, she thinks, a scrawny old chook. She turns her head to the left and right and leans closer in to the mirror. Neck like a turkey, shoulders like a coathanger. Dot has always hated the way she looks; despite the things she has spoken out about all her life and most recently a few weeks ago, about not judging women on the way they look, she has always judged herself very harshly. She has managed to convey the impression that she doesn't care how she looks, but in truth her appearance has always been an artful construction: the dyed hair, the basic black always worn with something else of a vibrant colour, a skirt, trousers, a vivid scarf or shawl, bright beads or bangles.

'You need a signature look, Dorothy,' a fashion writer had told her early in her career. 'You're not beautiful and you're rather small and skinny. You don't want to look insignificant. We need to do something with you, something that will help you stand out, make an impression. Black, I think, and we need to do something about that mousy hair. It's so terribly dull.'

A week later Dot's hair was cut into a sleek bob and dyed a rich burgundy, and her wardrobe contained a selection of black clothes and various contrasting scarves, wraps, bangles and beads. And while lengths and styles have changed with the mood of fashion, the look remains the same. But now, in the mirror, she looks weird: pale, vulnerable and old – older than she is. Thinness does that to you, she thinks, how unfair.

She picks up the cream wrap and drapes it around herself like the stoles she wore in the fifties and sixties, loose and falling into soft folds. It's a remarkable improvement, and she twists around, looking at herself with some satisfaction; she is not going to look quite so awful in the photograph after all. There is a tap at the door.

'Nearly ready?' Margot asks, coming in. 'You're the last, you know, everyone else has been done. It's taken them four weeks. You look great, Dot. I, on the other hand, look like a suet pudding.'

'Don't be ridiculous, yours is lovely,' Dot says. 'Emma showed me. It's made me feel more confident about my own.'

'Ah well,' Margot says, and she drops down onto the edge of the bed and kicks off her shoes. 'That's us, isn't it – women! We're never satisfied with the way we look.'

Dot hitches the wrap a little higher and joins her on the bed. 'I've always envied you being so voluptuous, Margot; you don't know how lucky you are.'

'Huh? You're joking. Voluptuous means gorgeous sexy curves; I've always been a shapeless sort of blur. There have been many times, Dot, when your slim and willowy frame has been a severe test of our friendship.'

'I don't think it's possible to be willowy if you're as short as me,' Dot says. 'But *listen* to us, still so self-critical, still worried about our bodies, about how we look.'

'Will you be much longer?' Emma asks from the other side of the door. 'Andrea has a five-thirty appointment on the other side of town.'

'She's very nice,' Margot says, dropping her voice. 'Andrea, I mean. She made me feel fine about being photographed.'

'Just coming!' Dot calls out. 'Is my hair okay, Margot?'

Margot picks up a brush from the dressing table. 'There's a bit sticking up at the back,' she says, tidying it. 'Go on then, off you go. We can sit and have a drink when the girls have gone.'

~∾~

Margot stands at the back of the room watching as the photographer positions Dot, talking to her reassuringly, and Emma twitches the wrap to achieve more flattering folds.

'And try to stay still, please, Dot,' Emma says, stepping back. 'Just move when Andrea tells you, or I may have to chain you to the chair. After all, that's sort of your comfort zone, isn't it – chains?'

And Dot lifts her head and laughs and the camera flashes, again and again, and as Dot turns her head, moves side on, looks up or down as instructed, Margot watches her many faces, all the faces she has come to know throughout the decades of their strange, sometimes fractured, often close and lasting friendship. Andrea stops for a minute and murmurs something to Emma, who moves over to Dot and crouches by the chair to adjust the wrap again, and encourages Dot to rest her elbow on the arm of the chair and her chin on her hand. As she does so, Dot reaches out and takes Emma's hand and Margot sees that she squeezes it and Emma responds, smiling down at her with apparent affection before she ducks out of view.

'It's been an odd time, hasn't it?' Margot says sometime later when Emma and the photographer have left. She tips a packet of pistachios into a dish and puts rice crackers alongside some avocado dip.

'Mmm . . . nice!' Dot says, taking a couple of pistachios and flipping them out of their shells. 'What sort of odd, d'you mean?'

'Well, a lot's happened since you got back from India, since your shopping centre stunt.'

'I suppose so. Not that I think that had much to do with any of it.'

'But it all began that weekend, everything else rolled on from there. It was the start of something, lots of things, that weekend.'

'I guess it was,' Dot says. 'I never really thought about it, but you obviously have and I can see what you're doing.'

'What am I doing?'

'You're building a narrative from it, Margot, wondering what you can do with it, wondering which tiny fraction of one of the many things that have happened in the last year or so might be the start or the middle or the end of a story.'

Margot laughs and opens the fridge. 'Perhaps I am,' she says, taking out a bottle. 'You're a wily old thing, Dot.'

'Yes,' Dot says proudly, 'I am, aren't I! Oooh good! Champagne . . . Moët no less! Are we . . . could we be . . . ?'

'Celebrating? Yes,' Margot says, 'we're celebrating . . .'

'What? What is it – have your heard something? Is it the book?'

'It is,' Margot says, a huge grin spreading across her face. 'I signed a contract for the book this morning. It'll come out next March.' She strips the gold foil from the bottle, pops the cork and pours the champagne into flutes as Dot bombards her with questions.

'Bring the bottle and let's go outside,' Margot says. 'I'll bring the tray.'

'We should be having a party,' Dot says.

'We are, just you and I.'

'But it should be everyone. Do they know?'

'Not yet,' Margot says, setting the tray on the verandah table. 'I wanted you to be the first to know. I wanted to celebrate this with you because apart from Laurence you're my oldest friend. And because I want to celebrate Patrick with you, to tell you I'm sorry I wasn't there for you all those years ago when you needed me, but I'm glad I'm here now to enjoy this time with you.'

She hands Dot a glass and sits down, gazing out over the garden, hoping again for the promised rain, not looking at Dot but feeling her presence; not the strange, tangled, restless presence of the past, but a new grounded presence – something entirely and uncharacteristically peaceful. She feels it in herself too, has felt it coming since she began writing, and now today it is complete. People who know what they are doing have read what she has written; they have called it haunting, eloquent and sensual, said it moved them and made them think. What more could she hope for?

Dot raises her glass. 'Congratulations, Margot. I'm thrilled for you, but not in the least surprised, and this is just the beginning. By the time it's published you'll be the same age as Mary Wesley was – a first novel at seventy – what an achievement.'

Margot smiles and raises her glass. 'And here's to you, Dot. Now that you're a mother and have serious maternal responsibilities, I hope it means there won't be any more sudden disappearances, when no one knows where you are or when you're coming back.'

Dot laughs. 'Okay, I get the message. Isn't it strange – my son, your daughter? Who could have imagined it?'

'I think it's worked out rather well,' Margot says, sipping her champagne.

'Do you think . . . well do you think they might get married?'

Margot turns to her, laughing. 'Well between them they have two three-piece suites, and Patrick measures up for the handsome prince, but since when have you been so interested in anyone getting married?'

'Oh well!' Dot says. 'Maybe I'm getting romantic in my old age. So, do you think they might?'

'Good lord, I hope *not*,' Margot says, laughing so much she splashes champagne on her skirt. 'I wouldn't wish you as a mother-in-law on anyone, certainly not my own daughter.'

And they sit there, laughing, the two of them, talking and laughing until they cry, until their sides ache, and their faces ache, and until the sun sets and the first few warm, fat drops of rain splash noisily down onto the roof.